Frank Janek has just been assigned the case that will make – or break – his career . . .

'Got something for you, Frank. You have to take it over right away. Your kind of case. Psychological.' Hart winked as if he'd made some kind of private little joke. 'Two homicides over the weekend. One in the One-nine, the other in the Twentieth. Monday morning they find this schoolteacher. You probably read about it in the papers. The second one was on the West Side. Tenement building. All-night call-girl type. They found her Monday, too, but we didn't say much about it then even though there was something peculiar that connected the two cases which we weren't actually aware of until yesterday afternoon.' Hart grinned. 'Tell you one thing, Frank. You never had a case like this.'

'Like what?'

'Hold on. I'm getting to it. Understand that what I'm telling you isn't going to the papers.' He turned in his seat so he was facing Janek. His voice turned serious. His tiny eyes were boring in. 'The heads were switched . . .'

Switch

WILLIAM BAYER

SPHERE BOOKS LIMITED
London and Sydney

First published in Great Britain by
Michael Joseph Ltd 1985
Copyright © 1984 by William Bayer
Published by Sphere Books Ltd 1985
30–32 Gray's Inn Road, London WC1X 8JL
Reprinted 1986

Grateful acknowledgement is made to Alfred A. Knopf, Inc.,
for permission to quote copyrighted material from *The Chill*,
by Ross Macdonald, Copyright © 1963 by Ross Macdonald.

TRADE
MARK

Set in Plantin

Printed and bound in Great Britain by
Collins, Glasgow

For L.G.B., storyteller

I had handled cases which opened up gradually
like fissures in the firm ground of the present,
cleaving far down through the strata of the past.

Ross Macdonald, *The Chill*

A Burial in Queens

The air was bad the day of Al DiMona's burial – hot, close, sulphurous. The sky was pewter undercast in yellow and there was a noxious smell, an oil-refinery smell, as if the cemetery were in New Jersey instead of Queens. It was one of those August mornings when the streetlights still burned away; perhaps the person who was supposed to turn them off had forgotten or overslept.

Janek looked closely at the others gathered around the grave, recognized a few familiar faces, old detectives, retired cops with sagging jaws. Lou, of course, the widow – she already had the frantic look that said, Now I have to worry about the mortgage and growing old alone and getting the oil changed. And Dolly, the daugher – her letter had been there on the card table along with the half-finished crossword puzzle and the woodworking tools and that pathetic half-carved wooden flute. She'd written she'd decided to relocate to Houston and could she park the kids for a while and a lot of selfish crap like that. Maybe Dolly's letter had done it, Janek thought, or maybe it was something else. It didn't matter. The trigger had been ready. Whatever made Al pull it was meaningless beside the fact that it had been ready waiting to be pulled.

He had imagined the scene: Al sitting at the card table staring into space, the sound of Lou moving around upstairs, sorting out the linens, then scouring the bathroom sink. It was a hot humid Sunday morning and the front closet smelled like a dry-cleaning shop and the neighborhood was quiet and there was a shiny thirty-eight in the front-hall-table drawer and it took just a couple of seconds to step over there and get it out and stick it in his mouth and pull one off.

Upstairs Lou froze, her sponge poised, the roar of the shot fading slowly, sinking deep, deep into her brain. She knew right away, didn't even have to think. She'd been to the funerals, had

1

heard about these things, knew all about these Sunday-morning things. A year into retirement, the worst time, the time you have to worry most about. *She knew*, and Janek could see her frozen there in the bathroom, not even shaking, standing still as a mannequin until the sound was finally gone. She might have looked half quizzically at her sponge, dropped it into the bowl, then moved to the head of the stairs and peeked down until she could see Al's feet sticking out into the hall.

It would be then, when she saw the worn soles of his shoes, that the bitterness would have come, feelings of despair and betrayal and unfairness too, of how horribly unfair this was. She had worried, prayed, somehow gotten them through the violent risky years only now to have to face the insidious Sunday-morning violence inside. She had known this was coming, had seen it coming for months, was afraid to mention it, afraid he'd blow up if she urged him to see somebody, talk it through and get some help. She tiptoed down, stared at him, made sure he was really dead, then turned into the kitchen and picked up the wall phone and called Frank Janek, because Frank was loyal and Frank would know what to do and Frank would take charge of everything – good old trusty Frank.

A melodrama, Janek thought, a drab lousy middle-class melodrama. Not even a tragedy, because a cop's guilt is too petty and his honor too ambiguous and his flaws too minor to give him tragic stature. His torment comes from little things, not grandiose schemes to place himself above the gods. And so his self-inflicted death is a whimpering little end, just another hot-August-Sunday-morning-old-cop suicide.

There had been a time, Janek remembered, when he might have taken that way out, just after he'd killed Terry Flynn and men turned their back on him and squad rooms turned still when he walked in. It was not remorse over defending himself but for dealing death instead of injury, and the loneliness he'd felt afterward, and the nightmares and the rejection and the endless questions he'd asked himself and the answers he'd never found. Now he wondered how many of the others had thought about suicide, as he looked at the dozen old detectives squeezed together beside Al's grave. They had the heavy-lidded eyes of men who lived by private codes. They stood there thinking about Al and what he'd done on Sunday and whether there wasn't something inside themselves they didn't know about that would come out when there were no more cases left to work, turn upon them and devour.

The priest was muttering. Janek could barely hear him. The yellow-pewter sky was cleaved by jets and there was a tree in the cemetery choked with blackbirds shrieking out complaint against the heat. Hart was there, Chief of Detectives, his tight little eyes sparkling in his squat and sweaty detective's face. Hart would never shoot himself – no way, thought Janek, not Hart. If Hart went mad he'd kill someone else. You did either one thing or the other – that's what the police shrinks said. You turned it all against yourself or else you turned it on the world.

There was someone else at the burial and she didn't fit in with the widow and the daughter and the Chief and the old detectives who had come to pay respects to Al. She was a tall lean young woman in her early thirties, with very good legs and an expensive camera hanging from her shoulder. Her light-brown hair was layer-cut, she was dressed very well, her face beautiful and she stood still and very straight.

Janek studied her, then he squinted as he recalled Lou's words on Sunday after they had taken Al away:

'... he was working on something, Frank. That's why none of this makes sense. He said it was an old case, one of those old ones that gnawed away at him, and he had some new ideas about it now that he had so much time to think. He said he was going to go back over things, check some things he'd forgotten at the time. He went out afternoons. Sometimes he'd stay out till nine or ten. He was working. I could tell. I hadn't seen him like that in years. He came alive, you know, the way he used to be in the old days when he was onto something and closing in. Maybe – I don't know. Maybe it was important. Maybe if he found something, Frank – you see, that might explain ...'

Janek had nodded, though he hadn't thought Al's actions needed explanation; the scene in the house that morning, he thought, had just about said it all. But Lou was convinced Al had been working and there was always the possibility that he had, so Janek had said he'd check it out when he had the time and Lou should save everything, any papers Al might have left around the

3

house or in his clothes, and even then it had occurred to him that maybe Al had had something going on the side. But not a girl with legs like this, a Leica on her shoulder, expensive shoes, clutching an expensive purse. She looked like a model; she wouldn't have noticed Al, wouldn't have bothered with him if she had. Who was she? Why was she here? Why was she standing as if she wanted to be here and, also, apart? Janek decided to talk to her after the burial. If she left too fast he could catch up with her at the gate or by the cars.

The priest was finished. They were lowering the coffin. The blackbirds were shrieking even more. Lou still had that frozen frantic widow's look and Dolly was sniffling and Hart was looking straight at Janek while he whispered to a uniformed sergeant at his side. The sergeant stepped back to detach himself from the group. Janek did the same; he wanted to edge closer to the girl. A second later the sergeant was at his side. He laid his hand on Janek's arm.

'Chief asks if you'll ride back with him.' It was Sweeney, guardian of the portals, who sat at the desk outside Hart's office directing traffic – detectives, journalists, politicians, supplicants.

'Can't,' Janek whispered. 'I got my car.'

'Give me the keys.'

'*What?*'

'I'll drive it in for you. Give it back to you downtown.'

'I wasn't going downtown.'

'You are now, Lieutenant.' Sweeney shook his head and smiled. How funny, his smile seemed to say – Janek didn't understand; years in the department and still he didn't know an invitation to ride with the CD was nothing less than a command.

The gathering was breaking up. Janek hurried toward the girl. She smiled softly when he introduced himself. Her forehead was damp and her eyes were brown and moist. 'Al mentioned you,' she said. 'He trusted you a lot.'

'I'd like to talk to you about that.' She stared at him curiously. 'Could I have your number?'

She studied him a moment. 'Sure.' She reached into her purse and handed him a card.

4

Hart

'Air's bad,' said Hart. 'Like breathing fumes.' He rubbed the back of his neck and peered out the window with disgust. They were on the Triborough Bridge; girders were whipping by. Hart's ears stuck out and his gray hair was shaven practically to his scalp. The big black car was air-conditioned. They sat in the back; the driver was a cop.

Janek turned, saw his own car driven by Sweeney trailing them at fifty feet. 'Didn't know you knew Al.'

Hart turned to him slowly. His small cold blue eyes twinkled like freezing little stars. 'I try to get to these things even if I didn't know the guy. DiMona was a detective after all.'

'He was a close friend.'

'Your rabbi – yeah, I heard. Well, it's a lousy thing, Frank. Ought to take away their guns. Never bought this idea they should keep them. Look what they do with them. Eat them for Sunday brunch.' The Chief shook his head, tightened his lips, about as sensitive an expression, Janek knew, as Hart could bring himself to make. It was a major effort for Hart to pretend to be a human being. Still Janek wondered why he had bothered to attend the burial.

'... Not working on anything important you couldn't dump now if you wanted to?'

So that was it. Hart hadn't come to pay respects to Al but to talk to Janek on the way back into town.

'Got something for you, Frank. You have to take it over right away. Your kind of case. Psychological.' Hart winked as if he'd made some kind of private little joke.

'Everything's psychological.'

'This is *psycho*-logical.' He grinned, pleased with himself; master of wordplay, he wouldn't need a ghostwriter when he retired and wrote his book.

Janek waited to hear about it, but now Hart was onto something

5

else. '... couple asshole detectives acting like goddamn four-year-olds. Embarrassing scene, personally embarrassing to me, at the Medical Examiner's yesterday afternoon.' He glanced at Janek. 'You want to hear?'

'Sure. What happened?'

'Couldn't believe it. Couple of goddamn four-year-olds.' Hart wiped his forehead. There was still a strip of sweat above his lip. 'Two homicides over the weekend. One in the One-nine, the other in the Twentieth. Monday morning they find this schoolteacher. You probably read about it in the papers.' Janek had read about it: a female teacher at a private girls' school found murdered in an East Side brownstone; the afternoon papers had made a big deal about it because the school was classy and the woman lived at a good address. 'The second one was on the West Side. Tenement building. All-night call-girl type. They found her Monday, too, but we didn't say much about it then even though there was something peculiar that connected the two cases which we weren't actually aware of until yesterday afternoon.' Hart grinned. 'Tell you one thing, Frank. You never had a case like this.'

'Like what?'

'Hold on. I'm getting to it. Understand that what I'm telling you isn't going to the papers.' He turned in his seat so he was facing Janek. His voice turned serious. His tiny eyes were boring in. 'The heads were switched. Get what I'm saying? The head of the teacher was with the body of the hooker and the other way around. Now, you see what that means. Someone took an awful risk. Ever hear of anything like that? Like a terror movie or a book.'

Janek looked down at the floor of the car. Hart's shoes were elevated – he hadn't noticed that before. He didn't know if it was the smell in the air, or Al's suicide, or the thought of heads being switched, but whatever it was, it was starting to make him sick.

'... The killer decapitates victim A, then goes crosstown and decapitates B, then takes B's head back to A's apartment and places it with her corpse, then goes back crosstown with A's head and places it so it looks like it goes with B.'

Maybe much simpler than that, Janek thought, but Hart was probably right – you usually don't carry around a victim's head when you go out to kill someone else. Hart was right about the risk, too, and that the case was psychological. Some sort of crazy

6

statement by a psychopath. But it was not the kind of case he liked.

' . . . There has to be a reason, right? That's where you come in. Figure it out. I'm handing it to you. Two heads on a silver platter. Interested?'

'What happened at the Medical Examiner's?'

Hart groaned. They were speeding down the FDR; the UN Building was just ahead. 'Couple of jerkoffs got the calls. Stanger in the One-nine. Howell in the Twentieth. Know them?'

'Stanger – vaguely.'

'Then you gotta know he's a jerk. Take it from me, Howell's just as bad. Okay, Stanger gets a lousy ID on the teacher from her building super. They cart her downtown and then there's some trouble getting someone from the school to look at her, and her parents live in Buffalo, so they can't get down here right away. Meantime Howell gets the hooker, they cart her down, and at noon yesterday the ME starts to scream. There's a mixup. The heads are switched. Like someone fucked the bodies up.'

'They're not perfect down there. They get sloppy, too.'

'I know, but not this time. We got photographs. That's the way the bodies were found. Anyway, Stanger and Howell rushed down there and they get into a fight. "Whose case is this anyway?" "You got my head. I got yours." "Let's switch them back and do our own investigations." "No sweat – we'll go our separate ways." They tried to make some kind of bullshit deal, with the photos staring them in the face.' Hart shook his head. 'Can't believe it. Next thing they started swinging. A fistfight down there between the bodies with the whole staff of pathologists looking on. Why? Because they're morons. They're both detectives, they each got a homicide, each guy wants to work his own case, and if they have to share – I mean God forbid the two killings should be connected! – then they both know one of them's going to end up getting screwed.'

'So now you need a lieutenant from outside.'

They were passing under the Brooklyn Bridge. 'I need a real detective, for Christ's sake, Frank. That's why I'm giving this to you.'

Two men were waiting in Hart's outer office. Janek recognized Stanger; the beefy one, he guessed, was Howell. They were sitting at opposite sides of the room studying the carpet. Stanger had a black eye. Hart didn't acknowledge them. Janek followed him in.

'Set yourself up in that special squad office on the second floor of the Sixth. I'll call Taylor and tell him you're coming. You'll want some of your regular people, I guess.'

'Sal Marchetti and Aaron Rosenthal.'

'Don't know Marchetti. Aaron's good. Now what am I going to do about those repentant jerks out there?' Hart motioned toward the waiting room.

'They drew the calls.'

'Yeah. And disgraced the division. Still, if you can stand them you can have them. Just sit here and nod while I tell them what kind of creeps they are.'

Stanger and Howell were called in, and Hart went at them mercilessly. They were assholes. Jerkoffs. Four-year-olds. He ought to discipline them. He ought to take away their shields. But this time he was going to be generous. He was going to give them a chance to redeem themselves. It was one case now, Janek's case. They were both going to work for Janek, and they were going to work their butts off, too. Any questions? No questions – good. Then get the hell out of here. And one other thing – not a word about the switch. Any leaks on that and the axe will fall, and then there'll be four goddamn heads rolling around the morgue.

When Janek left, Sweeney handed him the keys. 'Nice car, Lieutenant, but something funny about your engine. I happen to know an honest garage. They give a good discount to NYPD.'

Hallowed Ground

Stanger made the presentation from the middle of the room, a studio apartment on the top floor of a brownstone on East Eighty-first. Howell stood back against the door. Sal Marchetti stayed close to Janek. Aaron was busy and would join them the following day.

Stanger and Howell had made up. They were serious and tried to act competent and Janek was glad of that. But he had trouble concentrating. His mind kept drifting back to Al. He knew he had to bear down, give shape to this investigation. More than forty-eight hours since the discovery of the first body, a crucial period, usually the most crucial in a murder case, and this time there were two homicides and the time had been squandered away.

'Amanda Ireland,' Stanger said. 'Taught French at the Weston School. When she didn't show up Monday – they're running some kind of summer makeup session now – someone called, and when she didn't answer the phone the art teacher, male, Caucasian, a friend, taxied down here and got the super to open up. Soon as he saw the mess he turned away and vomited. Neither he nor the super looked too closely, which was why they didn't observe the other girl's head.'

Howell guffawed.

There was a quality to the apartment that aroused Janek's compassion. *Hallowed ground*, he thought. Ground that had been made sacred by the terrible act performed upon it, the taking of human life, the spilling of human blood.

Plants hung from the ceiling in front of the windows – he felt like watering them; already they'd begun to wilt. A cloth bedspread in faded rainbow stripes – needed a laundering; now it was stiff with congealed blood. Pile of quiz papers on the desk, half of them graded, half still unread. It was the apartment of a nice person who tried to create a little refuge for herself. A dog dish half full of water stood just outside the kitchenette. A leash and a light-tan belted raincoat hung from an old-fahsioned coatstand beside the door.

The crime-scene crew had been thorough. No physical evidence, tracks, fibers, prints. Neither apartment had been ransacked, and both were double-locked. Stanger, who was balding and cadaverous, was pointing through the bathroom door.

'Stabbed in here. Toothbrush on the floor and toothpaste in her mouth. Seems she was brushing at the time.' He stopped, noticed they were gaping. 'Well, guess that's pretty obvious. Anyway, he must have been waiting for her in the tub. Stabbed her in the back through the shower curtain. Plastic's shredded. Protected him from spatter. Then turned her over, still wrapped in the curtain, and started working on her chest. No defensive wounds on her palms or arms. Looks like he took her by surprise.'

9

'Brilliant,' whispered Sal.

'Excuse me,' said Stanger. 'I'm trying to make a presentation to the lieutenant here if that's okay.'

'It's okay,' said Janek. 'You're doing great. Go on.' He glanced at Sal, a signal to lay off

'After he killed her he wrapped her in the shower curtain and dragged her over to the bed. Undressed her, laid her face down, then cut off her head. Medical Examiner says two different weapons – short pointed knife in the can, something longer with a sharp blade out here. No sexual assault – front, rear or mouth. And nothing missing far as we can tell, except her keys. No one heard anything or saw anyone enter or leave.'

Janek shook his head. 'Nobody heard *anything?*'

'Just the dog. The dog barked, but she did that every night. She barked whenever anybody crossed the hall. People have complained a lot about this dog. Someone even wrote a letter to the landlord a couple of months ago.'

'Well, there's your motive,' said Sal.

'What happened to the dog?'

'Injured. Killer kicked her in the head. ASPCA took her away. Put her to sleep, I guess.'

'There goes your witness.'

'Knock it off, Sal.' Stanger was still too beaten down to stand up to razzing. He'd made a fool out of himself at the morgue, been dressed down by the CD, suffered the indignity of a black eye, and now Janek knew he'd be useless if someone didn't puff him up. 'Any idea how he got in?'

'Assuming for now the perpetrator's a he, Amanda could have let him in, though that doesn't fit with hiding in the shower. No sign of forced entry, so I checked out the super. He carries his keys on a huge ring on his belt, and everyone who knows him swears by him up and down. My gut feeling is our guy came in off the fire escape. Now, notice there's an accordion grill. It was closed, but there isn't any lock. Seems strange, maybe, since she's got a high-security lock on the door, but a lot of these girls are afraid to lock their grills. Makes them nervous. They want to get out fast if there's a fire.'

So, Stanger was a self-styled expert on the lifestyles of East Side single girls. Janek didn't agree with Hart, he didn't think Stanger

10

was a jerk. Just a reasonably hard-working mediocre detective. No wonder he wanted to keep the case. A chance for glory: society girl homicide. He could hang out at Second Avenue singles bars for weeks talking to her friends, cadge himself a hundred drinks, get laid a couple of times, maybe even get lucky and pick up something that would help him break the case.

'What about a boyfriend?'

Stanger shook his head. 'She didn't go out. A loner. Lonely sort of girl. No one ever heard anything through the walls. And so far as anyone around here knows she never gave a party or had a guest stay overnight.'

'Little Miss Perfect,' muttered Sal. 'I don't buy that. I don't believe in that.'

'This one comes close. Good teacher. Everybody liked her. Not bad-looking either. Walked her dog on a regular schedule: before she left for work, soon as she came home, and every evening around nine o'clock. Both parents teach school upstate. A married sister in Hawaii. I think the guy came in through the window when she was out with the dog, which suggests he knew her habits. He might have seen her coming out of school one day. There're creeps who linger around up there. The school warns the girls not to talk to them. He could have spotted her there, followed her home and she never even noticed. Once he picked up on her routine he'd know when it was safe to slip inside and wait.'

A perfectly decent second-rate theory, Janek thought, except it didn't take into account the other girl and the switch. Stanger still hadn't come to grips with the fact that Amanda Ireland was not an isolated case.

As they drove over to look at the other apartment Janek instructed Sal. Check the taxi sheets and the drivers of the crosstown buses. Time how long it would take to walk. Talk to patrolmen who were on duty that night and find out if any cars were ticketed or double-parked. Talk to doormen along the route. Did anyone see a man coming back and forth on Saturday carrying some sort of package or bag? The killer crossed town at least twice and possibly three times. He was carrying heads, and also weapons. He returned to one of the crime scenes and possibly to both. He might have had blood on him. He might have acted strange, impatient, nervous, tense. That was Sal's job – run down the mechanics, figure out how the killer had gotten back and forth. And yes, for now, work on the assumption the killer is a male, but don't forget to ask about a woman too.

The call girl's name was Brenda Beard; she'd used the name Brenda Thatcher in her work. She'd lived on West Seventy-third between Broadway and West End, a good/bad block – addict center and a welfare hotel along with expensive apartments carved out of once-elegant private homes. Her studio was on the third floor of a subdivided Victorian mansion, accessible by a small self-service elevator and a set of seedy stairs. No fire escape, no way in except her door, which meant she let the killer in, which meant she knew him, or had taken him for a john.

Howell made his presentation. There wasn't much to tell. She'd been killed in her bed, had been naked when it happened. The killer turned her over, sliced off her head, then turned her back and mounted Amanda's head on her, face up. The bed should have been drenched with blood but wasn't, which suggested something similar to Amanda's shower curtain, a plastic sheet perhaps, though nothing like that had been found.

Late Monday morning a man called the police emergency number. Howell had dug up the tape recording of the call. The man reported a murdered girl, gave the address, then hung up. Police broke down the door, found the body and ID'd it on the basis of documents in her purse. Howell speculated that the person who had called was not her killer but her pimp.

'... the way I see it she was supposed to turn up somewhere and give him her money and when she didn't show up he came looking for her at home. He had a set of keys to the apartment – pimps insist on that. He took one look, saw there was a murder, knew it wasn't her, got spooked, and ran down to a phone booth and called it in. Maybe he even stuck around to see her carried out. Probably still doesn't know what's going on. I don't think the killer would have called. Everyone knows we tape, and there weren't any calls on the East Side case.'

Janek was pleased – Howell, at least, had joined the cases in his mind. 'So who's the pimp?'

Howell smiled. 'Only had this case a couple of hours yesterday. Give me half a day, Lieutenant, and I'll have him for you. And plenty of stuff on this Brenda, too.'

Sure of himself, Janek thought. Probably knows lots of call girls, pimps and other lowlife in the neighborhood. While Stanger was thin and his expression desperate. Howell was heavy and full of bluster, a good-natured bully, a basic street cop who happened to carry a detective's shield.

Janek told them what to do right there in the apartment. He was tired of them, wanted to get rid of them, be alone and look around.

'Each of you has a girl. Go to work on her. Run down everything, then write it up. How did she live? Where did she shop? Where did she hang out? Who did she know? I want their personal address books, too. Tomorrow Aaron can put them together and cross-match. Killing two people is one thing. Switching their heads is something else. Someone, let's say for now a male, knew them, killed them, then he made the switch. Why? Maybe he wanted the whore's head on the goody-goody's body, or the other way around, or both. Maybe he had a goddamn Madonna/whore complex. Maybe he had some sort of obsession about rearranging their personalities and he felt compelled to bring it off. Maybe this is voodoo, hocus-pocus, some crazy terror cult. Whatever it is, the benefits were temporary – he had a few seconds to admire his handiwork, then he left the mess for us. Didn't try to cover up. Knew we'd discover the switch, and didn't care. *Why? What's the connection?* Somewhere, sometime, both girls had contact with our guy. And that's how we're going to find him, by finding out where their lives intersect. Because he had a reason, sick as it was. He went to a lot of trouble and took a lot of risk to arrange things almost faultlessly in a very peculiar way.'

Stanger and Howell listened carefully. Both seemed to respond to his authority. He warned them again about leaking the switch to the press, then dismissed them but signaled Sal to stay. 'What do you think?' he asked, after the other two had left.

'I liked what you said about a Madonna/whore complex.'

'You think they knew what the hell I was talking about?'

'Probably not. But they will when you're through with them.'

'Hart thinks they're jerkoffs.'

'They seem average enough to me.'

'Clods, right?'

Marchetti nodded and grinned.

He was an excellent detective, young, in his late twenties with a

13

good mind and the kind of wilfulness Janek liked. He had thick black hair, sideburns, a mustache, was divorced, played the stock market, followed hockey and prided himself on his marksmanship. He had worked narcotics for three years and had acquired the habits of a narc – toughness, compassion, quick reflexes and stubbornness. Janek knew lots of narcotics detectives and knew all about their faults. What he liked about them was the way they leeched onto a case, then stuck to it, refusing to give up.

'You called Amanda "Little Miss Perfect." Really think she's too good to be true?'

Sal shrugged. 'Don't know, Frank. Taught school. Walked her dog alone. No boyfriend. A little too young and attractive to be such a spinster, don't you think?'

'There are girls like that.'

'Yeah – I guess.'

'Well, we'll see , won't we?'

Marchetti nodded. Janek sent him on his way.

He sat alone then in Brenda Thatcher Beard's apartment, trying to imagine the sort of life she'd led. Phone ringing all day, clients calling, making appointments, lots of no-shows, then strange men coming in to spend the night. The place was decent enough. There was a bamboo bar with three stools, bottles of whiskey and liquers on the shelf behind. The couch was the same dusty chocolate velvet as the drapes, and there were red light bulbs in the lamps, with dimmer switches attached.

He opened the closet. It was stuffed and there was an overpowering aroma of perfume. No cheap whore's perfume, but a scent that was erotic, heavy and dark. He examined some of the clothing, a black silk nightgown, a black leather outfit complete with chrome chain belt, and a red satin dressing gown with padded shoulders and an Oriental monogram, the sort of thing women wore in 1940s films.

It was a working whore's closet filled with the artifacts of her maligned and necessary trade: spiked heels, black underwear, douche bag hanging from a hook. In the bathroom he found an array of antibiotics, a leg razor, a hair dryer, a hair curler, cosmetics, plus assorted dildos stored with the spare rolls of toilet paper and a pair of handcuffs in the cupboard beneath the sink. Traces of an attempt at something better, too. Brenda had tried to

14

be a model once, had had amibitions to be an actress – there were glossy photos and resumés stashed with the spare light bulbs and the sewing kit.

Janek looked around. In both substance and mood the place was completely different from Amanda's. Not a refuge but a shop, a place to practice an ancient craft. In the stills Brenda's hair was curled, while Amanda's hung long and straight. They were completely different people, who lived totally opposite lives. But, somehow, their lives were joined.

Something had gone wrong for both girls, someone had come in and murdered them and switched their heads, and suddenly Janek was terribly tired, weary of the case, even though he had just started out on it and it showed promise of being the kind that could make the papers and win him a commendation if he should manage to bring the killer in. Maybe that was what made him feel tired: the thought of having to hunt a person so deranged. Yes, potentially it was a great case, bizarre, spooky, the sort that give nightmares to single women and middle-aged detectives too. But he was already exhausted at the prospect of those nightmares, of having to go up against a mind so twisted and unfathomable that he knew he would have to reach down to the twisted unfathomable depths within himself if he was ever going to manage to link in. Hart was right – this was *psycho*-logical, and he was not looking forward to becoming obsessed with it, probing himself to discover who and why.

'Please, God, let it end tomorrow,' he whispered. 'Make the bastard come in tomorrow and confess.'

He was careful locking up the apartment, Brenda's lock and the police lock the crime-scene crew had installed. The door should be marked, he thought, with a cross, the way in Europe they marked a spot on a road where a fatal accident had taken place – to inform passersby of hallowed ground.

The Photographer

He lived fifteen blocks north on West Eighty-seventh between Columbus and Amsterdam. He walked uptown on Broadway in the early-evening heat, past old people sitting on benches in the center strip, through the crowds, the West Side ethnic mix, people hurrying home from work stopping at supermarkets, turning into bars. He tried hard to put the case out of his mind. He only wanted to think now of Al DiMona and to grieve.

His apartment was cool, a semi-basement with cage-door entry under the stairs to the house where his landlord's family lived. He hadn't done much to fix it up, had furnished it out of the Salvation Army, and had installed his father's old accordion bench against a wall, where it was littered now with tools and the inner workings of broken accordions. He found a beer in the refrigerator, took off his jacket and dug out the card the girl had handed him at the cemetery. 'Caroline Wallace,' it said, 'Photographer.' He sat down on his bed and dialed.

The phone rang six times and he was about to give up when she answered in a hurried breathless voice.

'This is Frank Janek.'

'*Who?* Oh – right. Hold on.'

He imagined her putting down packages, unslinging her camera, maybe blotting her forehead with her arm.

'Yes, Lieutenant Janek – '

'Frank, please.'

'Right. Ah – how are you?'

'Can I see you this evening?'

'This evening? What about?'

'Like I told you this morning …'

'You said you wanted to talk. You didn't say anything about a meeting.'

'Is there some problem with a meeting?'

'No problem. I'm just curious what you want.'

16

'You know I was close to Al.'

'Yes. Of course ...'

'I wanted to ask you some questions about him.'

'Was there something special?'

'Yeah. A few things I don't understand. Louella DiMona told me he was going out a lot. That he was away from the house most afternoons. And I just wondered...'

'You wondered if I could enlighten you about where he was.'

'Yes. Something like that.'

'Well, I guess I can.' There was a pause. 'I'm in Long Island City. Want to come over here?'

'If tonight's no good – I don't want to trouble you –'

'Tonight's fine. Let's get it over with. Look – I just brought some Chinese food. If you get here quick enough you can help me eat it up.'

He felt a little strange as he drove to Queens. He didn't know anything about her, had no idea how well she'd known Al, and from the look of her it didn't add up that she and Al had been having an affair. But she had picked up very fast on his probe about Al spending a lot of time away from home. She was going to 'enlighten' him. It was as if she'd expected him to ask what had been going on.

Traffic was light on the Queensboro Bridge. He glanced into his rearview mirror back at Manhattan, saw the city strung out with lights. There was still a glow in the sky behind the buildings. He loved this romantic vision of New York, luminous city set powerfully against a fading sky.

Coming off the bridge he thought of Hart eating dinner with his wife (he'd seen her once, at the ceremony when Hart had been sworn in), and Stanger studying women from a lonely bar stool, and Howell shaking down a pimp, and Sal Marchetti slicking down his hair for a date, and Lou DiMona grieving, and his own wife, Sarah, sitting in the Staten Island house where he had left her two years before, perhaps missing him a little, missing his brooding presence, as she stared blankly at the television set watching the horror of the local evening news.

Long Island City was an old industrial area just across the East river, a low-crime area inhabited by serious working-class people, members of unions devoted to their families. Caroline Wallace's

17

building was a prewar industrial structure; she'd described her apartment as a loft. Janek knew there were painters and sculptors and photographers who had moved to this section when the Manhattan artists' area, Greenwich Village and SoHo, had become fashionable and the rents had gone too high.

He parked, entered, found her name. She'd clipped down her business card to fit the slot beside her bell.

'Yes.' Her voice was distorted by the intercom.

'Frank Janek.'

The buzzer throbbed.

The lobby was spacious, befitting a building of its era. There were bicycles chained to a rack bolted to the granite floor. Thick gray walls and iron stairs – she lived up two lengthy flights. There were two lofts to a floor, industrial-steel doors set opposite on the landings. As he climbed he could hear the muffled thump of rock music coming from another loft above.

'Hi.' She inspected him, then stepped back to let him in. She was wearing the same gray skirt she had worn at the cemetery, a different blouse, and sandals now in place of expensive shoes. There was warmth in her smile; she wasn't tense. Again he noticed the perfection of her legs and the dark-brown beauty of her eyes.

There was a galley kitchen along one wall. He could smell Chinese food. She poured him a glass of wine, told him to make himself comfortable while she reheated their dinner and fluffed the rice.

He looked around. The loft was large and nicely done. A vast wooden floor, glossy like the floor of a gym, windows on three sides, a row of structural pillars with modified Doric capitals. He noticed a pair of tennis rackets and cans of balls in a basket near the door. She had set a bottle of soy sauce on the dining table, had laid out chopsticks and napkins, little teacups and a bowl of fruit.

He explored, ran his hand along the headrail of her brass bed, set beneath a slowly revolving ceiling fan. He found his way to a grouping of chairs, chrome legs and sling seats, arranged in an entertaining area with a couch. In one section there was a darkroom – he smelled the faint odor of photographic chemicals. She worked, cooked, ate, bathed and slept in this enormous space.

On the walls between the windows she had hung huge mounted photographs.

18

'This all your stuff?'

She turned from the stove. 'Yeah. My private gallery. Prices on request.'

He took his time examining her work, pausing before each photograph. There were two shots taken in Vietnam: dog-tired soldiers in a trench, their eyes smoldering in faces dark with agony and fatigue; an old Vietnamese woman looking up with terror, the sky behind her filled with fluttering helicopters looking ominously like wasps. There was an action shot of a boxer Janek recognised as a coming middle-weight; she'd caught the moment of impact of a punch, the features distorted, the cartilage crushed against facial bones. There was a shot, too, of a Russian chess champion, intense, studying his position, an interesting combination of concentration and fear in his eyes. She was good. She knew what she was doing, her work was powerful and there was something fearless about her eye.

She was bringing the food over to the table.

'Can I help?'

'No, thanks. I got everything. Sit down.'

'Well,' he said, 'this stuff looks good. Not the usual carry-out.'

'It is good. Eat.' She heaped pork with black-bean sauce on his plate. 'I made you this morning before you came over. I knew it was you from the way Al described you once.'

He was amused to hear police jargon. 'Made you': he smiled at that. 'How did he describe me?' he asked, fumbling with his chopsticks, wondering if he should ask her for a fork.

'Said you moved like Robert Mitchum. And you do, Janek. In a way you really do. Do you mind if I call you Janek? Al always did. He never called you Frank. Janek's a good name. Seems so right for a police lieutenant. Do you mind?'

He said he didn't mind. She smiled at him and he smiled back. He liked her. She was as direct as her photographs. She didn't flinch or blink when he looked her in the eye.

'Sorry about this morning. I didn't mean to be so abrupt.'

'That's okay. I was glad you came over. I didn't know anyone there and I felt kind of outside the thing. But I wanted to be there anyway.'

'You and Al were pretty close, I guess.'

'Is that a question or a fact?'

'Neither. More like a feeble query.'

'We were friends. I liked him. He liked me.'

'Not lovers?'

'No, we weren't. It could have gone that way, at least maybe in Al's mind, but not in mine and I made my feelings clear. We gave each other signals and after that we settled down. He used to come by afternoons. He liked to sit around and talk. I liked listening to him. He talked about his work and I talked about mine. Sometimes when I was working in the darkroom he'd just sit out here reading magazines. It was good to have him around. We enjoyed each other's company. And that's all there was.'

So – they just sat around and talked afternoons; they were friends and nothing more. He believed her, had no reason not to, but still, he thought, it was a curious relationship, the old beat-up depressed retired cop and this very attractive no-nonsense young female photographer.

'You really liked him?'

'He was a great guy. Told terrific stories. Loved talking about his old cases, and he had a lot of good ones to talk about. He was a real person. That's what I liked. And I guess, too, he reminded me a little of my dad. Maybe that's what we had going – a sort of father-daughter thing.' She looked at him. 'I'm the daughter of a cop.'

'NYPD?'

She nodded.

'So we're part of the same family.'

'Guess we are. You, me, Al, and maybe one hundred thousand other people too.'

'You said Al mentioned me.'

She nodded. 'He liked you very much. He was your rabbi, he told me, and I knew what that meant: the guy who watched out for you and gave you advice when you started out. He was proud of you, Janek, that you'd done so well and made lieutenant, even after that business with your partner. He said you took a lot of static over that but that you rebounded from the tragedy and turned into one of the best detectives around. He said you understood people and that's what being a detective was all about. He said you were better than he'd ever been, but maybe not so great as you liked to think.'

'He really said all that?' Janek was surprised at how smoothly she poured it out. And, too, that Al had told her about Terry, and had used the word 'tragedy' – the very word he had denied to him while standing that morning by his grave.

'He said you were very good, but you thought you were better than very good.'

He laughed. 'I'm not sure I ever thought I was all that great.'

She laughed, too. 'Well, maybe Al was wrong.'

A pause. Their eyes met. Then he asked her about her work. She'd done two books, she said, the first when she was starting out, a very emotional collection of stuff she'd shot in Vietnam. She'd gone out there practically as a novice. 'I was very ambitious, I wanted it all. I wanted to win the Pulitzer Prize. I stayed a couple years, made good contacts, got pampered a lot by the press corps and the military because I was a woman. I was lucky. Nothing happened to me. I know now I was reckless, but back then I thought I was blessed. Anyway, the book got good notices and when I came back here I wanted to try something different, so I went into my cruel period. That's what I call it now.'

'I thought I detected a cruel streak.' He gestured at the blowups on the walls.

She shook her head. 'No, not like those. My cruel-period stuff was – well, it's a little hard to explain.' She laid down her chopsticks, got up, fetched an oversized book, brought it back to the table, then watched as he flipped the pages and looked.

It was called *Celebrities*, a book of portraits of film directors, painters, famous writers, other photographers, and she seemed to have caught them all exhibiting a sad and vacant stare. Janek understood what she meant by 'cruel' – there was a sameness about these people, not a physical sameness, since they were men and women, young and old, but something similar in their expressions, repeated in their eyes: meanness, selfishness, vanity, and beyond all that a sense of emptiness and vacancy, even disappointment with their lives.

He nodded. 'Yes, I see. You got them all to pose a certain way. How did you manage that? I imagine some of these people were upset.'

'Some I guess.' She shrugged. 'I really wasn't trying to be mean. Just looking for something, a kind of aftereffect. I'd tell them to pose, they'd puff themselves up, then I'd catch them with a second click just as they were letting out their air. I wasn't trying to say

21

they were phonies, though that's what a lot of people thought. I was working on the premise that even the most handsome, most beautiful, richest, most successful, most secure, glamorous and confident people are vulnerable. Not that they're vain, but that they're human and that time and age will break them, too.'

She had looked right at him, giving him the feeling she was telling him something important about herself. And as he looked at the portraits again he saw exactly what she meant. Her pictures weren't cruel so much as compassionate. 'I guess if you'd taken shots like these of drunks and bums, no one would have accused you of being mean.'

She laughed. 'They would call me pretentious. Mock me for an unearned social conscience. But because my subjects were rich and famous everyone assumed I was putting them down. I wasn't. All I was saying was that their confidence was a mask, that they lived with the same background fear as the drunk and the bum – that even when life is sweet, it's much, much too short.'

He was startled to hear her say such a thing. She was young to have worked from such a vision. But he could tell from the portraits that the vision was deeply felt, not a borrowed sentiment. He looked at her again. He hadn't expected her to be like this. He had taken her for a model when in fact she was an artist. 'I can see why Al liked to come around,' he said. 'He may have told good stories, but you're pretty special yourself.'

She smiled; she liked his compliment. 'We didn't talk like this much, Janek. We really just bulled around. It was fun. That's all it was. An honest friendship. Pleasure in each other's company.'

'How did you meet?' She was loading more food onto his plate.

'That was a funny thing. I play tennis fairly regularly at a club a mile or so away.'

'That thing on the river under the plastic bubbles?'

She nodded. 'That's the place. I generally bicycle over there. I use my bike a lot around the neighborhood. Anyway, one day I was riding home and I hit a pothole and fell down. I got bruised and twisted my ankle, Al just happened to be walking by. He came over, helped me up, and checked my leg to see if I was hurt. He was very nice and he ended up walking my bike and supporting me as I limped back here.'

'I bet he offered to carry you up the stairs.'

22

'He was very sweet. I could tell right away he was a cop. When he got me to the door I thought the least I owed him was a drink. So I asked him in and we just started talking while I soaked my ankle, and that's how it started. And it just went on from there.'

A nice story – it pleased Janek, sounded like the sort of gentle pickup Al would make. A little too slick, maybe, especially the coincidence that Caroline's father had also been a cop, but such things happened and he had no reason to doubt her. He reminded himself he wasn't interrogating a suspect, just checking up on Al and his absences from home.

'Lucky meeting for both of you. When did all this happen?'

'Couple of months ago. Late June, I think.'

'Did he ever talk about a case?'

'That's all he talked about. There were so many. But if you mean did he talk about a particular one, no. He'd just go on from one to the other in a chain.'

So there it was – Al had told Lou he was working on an old case because she wouldn't have understood a friendship with a girl half her age. She wouldn't believe Al just came here to talk and listen, a release from the prison of the house, a chance to laugh with someone young.

'I had no idea he was depressed,' she said. 'I just couldn't believe it when I heard he shot himself. There was no sign of anything like that. He was happy when he was here. Sometimes we'd order in Chinese food like tonight, and he'd stay on until I'd throw him out. "Go home, DiMona," I'd tell him. "Get your butt out of here so I can take a bath." We'd listen to music. Play chess and talk. He seemed a reasonably happy man.'

'He kept it from you, obviously. You were probably the only nice thing he had going the last few months.'

'But *why*, Janek? Why did he do it?'

He shrugged. 'Old detectives, cops – it happens to us a lot. One of the highest suicide rates. No one's sure exactly why. They warn us about it. Preach to us about depression. Something to do with the job. We end up tired, disillusioned, bored. All that stress and tension, that confrontation every day year in, year out, and then suddenly nothing but your thoughts and then you start to brood. Guys take it different ways. I knew Al twenty-five years and I wouldn't have figured him for what he did. Except I've known other guys I didn't figure for that kind of move, and they surprised me, too, so now I'm not all that surprised.'

He helped her carry the dishes to the galley, rolled up his sleeves, rinsed the dishes, then handed them to her so she could place them in the dishwasher.

'This is very domestic. You're a domestic guy.'

'It's been a while,' he said. 'I'm divorced a couple years. I usually eat at a delicatessen, or buy carry-out and eat off paper plates. Not much in the way of appliances where I live. Got a coffee maker and a toaster. That's about it.'

They sat in her chrome-and-leather chairs after everything was stowed away, and she told him about her current book, the one she was working on now. It was called, tentatively, *Aggression*. The blowups on the walls were part of it. She was shooting men at moments of physical stress: prize-fighters, football and hockey players, a truck driver yelling at a pedestrian, a cop collaring a thief, lawyers quarrelling, a fencer about to thrust, a bullfighter facing horns. 'The aesthetic of male aggression,' she told him. 'It's always fascinated me. Maybe that's why I like talking to cops so much. You guys see it all the time. You live with it constantly. Most of us just see people in vapid moments, but you see them at the heights of stress.'

'Interesting. Sort of a curious subject for a woman.'

'Come on, Janek, you don't believe in stereotypes. Anyway, male aggression can be a turn-on. I saw more than my share of it when I was covering the war, and I found myself attracted at times. So, the subject is aggression, but there's a strong erotic theme. What's next? I wonder. Still lifes? Water swirls in the sand?' She shook her head. 'Wish I knew. Not going backwards, that's for sure.'

It was nearly midnight when he left. It had been an exhausting day – the funeral, the switched-heads case – but for all of that he felt refreshed. Caroline Wallace was extraodinary; he couldn't put her out of his mind. As he drove back to Manhattan he found himself starting to envy Al. Friendship with a woman like that – how very lucky Al had been.

The Mystery of Destruction

Chief Medical Examiner Gerald Heyman was not his usual cheerful self. 'I told Hart straight out,' he said, 'don't send any more of your goons down here.'

Dr. Heyman was in his early fifties, with a permanent tan and the look of a man who jogged laps around Central Park at dawn. His iron-gray hair was parted in the middle. His chin was squared off and he sat rigidly in his chair behind his precisely ordered desk.

'We have our temperamental flare-ups. We're human beings, too. But we're also professional men and we observe the normal courtesies. When we have a disagreement we talk it over. Sometimes voices are raised. What we don't do is try and settle things with fists. Another thing we don't do is get pieces of bodies mixed around. When someone's been dismembered, and I don't care whether it's limbs or heads, we tag the pieces and keep them together, and the photos always back us up.'

'There was never any question of a mixup. Hart was very clear to me on that.'

'Fine. I just want to make sure you know where I stand. I don't want this to reach a point where some baby prosecutor or some simpering defense starts claiming we made the switch down here.'

'I don't think that's going to happen.'

'I predict, absolutely, that it will.'

'The photos would certainly dispute such a claim.'

'Exactly.'

Well, then, Janek was tempted to ask, who gives a good goddamn?

He restrained himself. No point in being argumentative. Dr. Heyman, satisfied that he had conveyed his position, turned him over to David Yoshiro, the deputy examiner who had performed the autopsies.

Yoshiro was a short, serious, formal young Japanese-American who wore black-frame glasses and seemed dwarfed in his starched white coat. He spoke neutrally, methodically, in a deep resonant voice.

'Ireland was stabbed through her shower curtain once in the back and an even dozen times in a cluster pattern across her chest. I found pieces of the curtain in the wounds. She was then carried or dragged to her bed, unrolled, turned over and decapitated as if by an executioner – a single powerful blow straight across the back of the neck. Later the killer or executioner made an effort to affix the Beard head to the place where the Ireland head had been. He cut both of them in the same place, so the pieces fitted together fairly well.'

Really, thought Janek, this is an atrocious case. Absolutely nauseating. 'What about Miss Beard?'

'I count eleven wounds, also in the chest. These were deep plunges, grouped closely around the heart. The extra thrusts were not necessary. Clinically speaking both women were killed almost at once. Beard was stabbed through a sheet, decapitated from the back the same as Ireland, then turned over so that Ireland's head could be pushed onto her neck. I have the impression that the heads were transported in plastic bags. Carefully, too, because the hair wasn't bloodied much. No finger marks anywhere. The killer was very careful. I suspect he handled the heads through the plastic, pulling the bags off slowly once he had them mounted the way he liked.'

Plastic bags. It was Wednesday – if the bags had been dropped into a street barrel the evidence had long since been ground in a cartage truck.

'How close in time?'

'Certainly within a couple of hours. I'd say that Ireland was murdered first. I can't swear to that, but there are signs.'

'Weapons?'

'Two. The stabbing weapon, a sharp-pointed hunting or kitchen knife, and the decapitation instrument, a long-bladed knife, very sharp, very heavy, very fine. The work was precise – single blows. The executioner did not hesitate. It is not that easy to decapitate. You can hack and hack. But in this case it was accomplished with a single stroke.' Yoshiro made a gesture as if bringing down from over his head a sword gripped in both his hands.

'Could this have been done with a sword?'

'Conjecture. Even if you brought me such a weapon I might not be able to say for sure. It was a very clean cut. No kind of weapon signature. Of course, if I had a sword with blood and tissue on it, then I could link it to these women. But I already checked on that, and I suspect you are not going to find it uncleaned.'

'What do you mean you checked?' Yoshiro's formality was starting to get on Janek's nerves.

'I thoroughly examined both sets of wounds. No tissue cells or blood from one in the wounds of the other. I would surmise the same instruments were used but cleaned up in between. I understand, by the way, that the drain checks were negative for blood in both apartments.'

Janek looked at him. The man was obviously upset.

'You discovered the switch, didn't you?'

Yoshiro nodded. 'I was working on the Ireland cadaver and right away I realized the two pieces didn't fit.' He shook his head. 'We've had decapitations in here before but never with the heads placed back on. I want to emphasize the oddity of that. The heads were not placed atop the bodies casually. They were literally pressed into the bodies as if an attempt was being made to recombine the heads and bodies in a way the killer preferred.'

'Yes,' said Janek. 'I see. That does seem very odd.'

Yoshiro looked at him. Suddenly he swept off his glasses. 'I am a forensic pathologist, not a psychologist, Lieutenant. But I would say, based on my understanding of human nature, which comes from personal observation, the reading of poetry and literature, and some courses I took at Cornell Medical School...'

'Yes?'

'I would have to say that it seems to me that this man was trying to create people as much as to destroy them. Do you see what I mean?' Dr. Yoshiro snatched up his glasses and put them on again. 'He killed them, certainly. But to use the parts his own way. So in a sense we could say he was a creator. Destroyer and also creator. Both. It's a difficult concept, I know. I've had some difficulty even thinking about it. I can't seem to deal with it, which is strange considering the sort of work I do. Normally I am quite imperturbable. Taking apart bodies, performing autopsies – none of that disturbs me at all. But I am confused by this case. It disturbs me very much. I sense a man here who has presumed to create new

27

human beings, who has presumed to play at being God. And now please excuse me. I have a terrible headache. I must take some aspirins and lie down. You will get a complete report, of course, as soon as we finish up. Excuse me now.' He rose and bowed slightly from the waist.

Janek nodded and withdrew. A strange little man, he thought, with a strange and sensitive reaction. A scientific man, assured and confident, until he begins to ponder the meaning of the crime and then his head aches and he becomes confused. He senses mystery, creation and destruction, vectors he cannot reconcile. And such irreconcilability strikes hard at a man who slits open bodies and weighs organs and deals daily with the gross carnality of human beings.

It was also striking at himself, Janek thought, as he drove over to the precinct house. There was something here that transcended a brutal homicide. Something awful, evil, and fascinating too.

Sixth Precinct headquarters was one of those new police buildings that had grown old very fast. Built a dozen years before to be as indestructible as a public school, it had quickly acquired a patina of grime and the stench of all precinct stations: stale cigarette smoke, stale sweat and the effluvia of human distress.

Aaron Rosenthal had already organized the special squad office on the second floor in back. Desks, telephones, filing cabinets, a map, and a wall-size cork bulletin board to which he'd tacked the crime-scene photographs. The Ireland photos were on the right, the Beard photos on the left. Between them was a diagram showing the various routes between the two apartments. There was plenty of room left for any new documentation that might later come along.

Aaron was a superb detective, a fine tracker, excellent at interrogation and brilliant on the phone. He was a forty-three-year-old detective second grade, equivalent to a sergeant, balding, paunchy, bespectacled, with hideous muttonchop sideburns, a quick smile, a lovely wife, four gorgeous daughters, and a hard-edged New York cynicism which Janek greatly enjoyed. Occasionally he wore a yarmulke to work, a mystery to his colleagues, since there was no correspondence between this action and any known Jewish holidays. There was speculation that Aaron was doing private penance for a misdeed in the past, but like so many mysteries facing the Detective Division the mystery of Rosenthal's yarmulke had been relegated to the 'unsolved' file drawer.

'How do you like the case?' Janek asked. He'd only spoken briefly with Aaron the day before.

'Goddamn horror show. Sorry about Al, Frank. Lou all right?'

'She'll make it,' Janek said. 'You talk to Taylor yet?' Taylor was the precinct commander, a uniformed captain not overly fond of detectives who used his space but were not under his control.

'He's pissed at Hart. Wanted these rooms for a rape crisis center.'

Janek looked around. 'Nice. Sweep it out yourself?'

'Everything but the interrogation rooms. Thought I'd leave them just the way they were.'

Janek checked the pair of cubicles separated by a short corridor which allowed observation through narrow slits of one-way glass. 'Better buy some roach spray,' he said. 'You know . . . yesterday I couldn't stand having to deal with this. I actually prayed aloud the guy would come in this morning and confess.'

Aaron shrugged. 'Yeah. Well, when they're that easy they're no fun.'

They went downstairs, then out to the Taco-Rico on Seventh Avenue South where they ate lunch and talked. Aaron knew all about Stanger and Howell and the fistfight in the morgue. Everyone knew about it. 'It's Sweeney. He blabbed, and how now they're being punished by having to work the case under you.'

'Sweeney's saying that?'

'That's what's going around.'

'That prick. Yesterday I let him drive my car.'

'He told you you needed a ring job, right?'

'Said my engine sounded bad.' Janek glanced at Aaron. 'He's blabbing about that too?'

'Not that I know of. But cars are his sideline. He owns a piece of a garage.' Aaron eyed him carefully. 'You know, Frank, you really ought to be more excited about this case. Got great potential. Kind that can make you famous.'

'Yeah, I know, it's the big bizarre case you wait for all your life. Great if you solve it. The worst kind if you don't.'

'We'll solve it.'

'I'm not so sure. Anyway, I don't like it all that much.'

'Right now you don't. But you will, Frank. When you get into it you will.'

After lunch they returned to the office and stared together at the crime-scene photographs. They each stood before a set, then changed places, then changed again. Then Janek started pacing, back and forth, looking for something which he felt was there that he had missed before. What was it? Something revealing, abnormal, even beyond the abnormality of the switch. Something about the way the crime scenes looked. Something . . . he didn't know exactly what.

'See anything?' he asked Aaron finally.

'Guess you do, the way you're pacing around.'

'Do you?'

'Crime-scene photos.'

'Yeah, of course.'

'Maybe there's something else.'

Janek waited, and when Aaron didn't continue he became impatient, wondering if he hadn't looked too hard seeking an aura which wasn't there.

'Too perfect,' Aaron said after a while.

'Interesting. What do you mean?'

'Not sure.'

'Come on, Aaron.'

'They're contrived, somehow.'

'*Yeah?*'

'Like they were meant to be photographed, whatever the hell that's supposed to mean.'

'The killer didn't take the pictures.'

'Of course he didn't. Still . . .'

'You mean the scenes look like they were arranged to be photographed?'

Aaron was bent over now, peering very close. 'Hmmm. I'm not sure about that either.'

'You said "too perfect." Now, just what does "too perfect" mean?'

'I don't know.'

'Symmetry?'

'Sure there's symmetry when you switch heads around.'

'We know that already. But is there something else?'

'There is something, Frank. Something that hits you until you look too hard and then you don't see it anymore.'

'So what is it, for Christ's sake?'

Aaron stood back, shook his head. 'Beats me.'

'Well, I'll tell you what I think it is. Arrogance. Conceit. "I defy you to solve this crime. I defy you to figure it out and find out who I am. I did it and I'm superkiller and you cops are suckers. You'll never find me and if you do I'll never tell you why."'

Aaron nodded. 'Yeah. There's definitely that, and maybe something else, like our killer set this up to drool over. I think that's what I meant by contrived.'

Something to look for, if and when a suspect came along. The murders were bizarre. Maybe that was it: they were *too* bizarre. As if they were *meant* to be bizarre – crimes that were bizarre were generally not committed that way intentionally.

Janek planted his elbows on his desk, rested his forehead against his fingers. When Sal came in he felt relieved; he could stop thinking about how crazy this case was going to get.

Sal read to them from notes. 'Taxi sheets covered. Notices up in the fleet-company garages. Circulars out to the owner-drivers. So far no one remembers any particular crosstown passengers that night. Bus drivers don't remember, either. "Don't even look at them," they say. Bus driver/passenger relationships tend toward the superficial. I guess that's what they mean.'

'I see this investigation is broadening your sensibilities,' Aaron said.

'I'm getting to be a regular crosstown-transit expert, yeah. Talked to some of the doormen. Nothing yet. They have special weekend shifts. The men rotate. I'll try a few more tonight.'

When Stanger and Howell called, Janek told them to come in. When they arrived the five detectives pulled their chairs into a circle. Janek turned to each of them in turn. Aaron took notes on a legal pad.

Stanger reported that Amanda Ireland's parents were in town, staying at a Tenth Avenue motel. 'Very nervous people. The kind that hate New York. The father ID'd her. Mother wouldn't go. I didn't mention anything about the switch. Thought maybe you'd want to talk to them and bring that up yourself.'

'I do want to talk to them,' Janek said. 'Set it up at the motel. No reason to mention the switch unless, of course, they're not sufficiently outraged.'

'Oh, they're outraged all right.'

'They say anything about boyfriends? She ever mention anyone in her letters.?'

'No one except this art teacher, the one from the Weston School. But he's gay. Very up-front about it. Nice kid. They were close. In fact – '

'Bring him in.'

Stanger looked surprised. 'I spent a couple of hours with him, Lieutenant. He's okay. Remember, he threw up.'

'Something funny there. If he's an art teacher why didn't he notice he was looking at someone else's head?'

'He's very sensitive.'

'A lot of killers are sensitive. If they were close they exchanged confidences. He may be holding something back. Maybe Amanda liked girls. You get to stay the good guy, Stanger. I want a go at him myself.' Janek turned to Howell. 'What about the pimp?'

'There was one. People in the building saw him. And they were seen together on the street.'

'Who is he?'

'An Oriental. Funny name. Bitong. Supposed to be very slick. Soon as I find him I'll haul him in. I got a theory maybe he was trying to teach a lesson. Switching the heads and all as a warning to his other girls. You know, like you get your head cut off if you don't do like you're told.'

'Doesn't sound very slick to me. Why the schoolteacher and why the switch?'

'Who knows? Chinese mumbo-jumbo. Maybe Amanda was doing high-class tricks for him. East Side. You know – discreet.'

'Forget it,' snapped Stanger.

Howell ignored him. 'Or maybe Amanda was just a target of opportunity. I mean I try to put myself in a whore's place.' They all broke up at that. 'I'd be scared shitless by what happened to Brenda. I'd kiss the Chink's behind all night and never think of crossing him again.'

'We're getting too theoretical,' said Janek. 'What have you got on johns?'

'She ran an ad in *Screw*. Every other week. With a telephone number, too. What's odd about that is that when they advertise they usually work in pairs. Two girls. Roommates. That way there's some protection in case they run up against a creep. Running a phone ad's just one notch up from the street, and on the street at least you get a look at the guy. With a phone ad you're working blind. Calls from out-of-town businessmen, kids, crazies too. Anyone. Everyone. There's no protection against weirdos. Working alone like that, Brenda took a chance every time she opened up her door.'

'I like that better than the pimp-punishment idea,' said Sal. 'A blind call. He sounds good on the phone. She lets him in figuring she can handle him. Then he turns on her, so fast she doesn't have time to raise her hands. Whores get nailed like that all the time.'

Howell was getting edgy. Janek could see he'd already thought of that and now was thinking that Sal and the rest of them were treating him like he was dumb.

'A reasonable theory,' said Janek, 'and so is the pimp. We have to talk to the pimp to eliminate him, anyway. Now let's look at Howell's target-of-opportunity idea, look at it and turn it around. Say Brenda's the target of opportunity. She's easy. All you got to do is call her, act smooth and set up a date. But Amanda's not easy. She's not going to let you in. So say you're after Amanda and you want to do a switch, you need another head, right, so you pick up *Screw*, pick out a whore, and make an appointment – the whore's sole function is to provide you with that second head. Then you see Brenda's just a randomly chosen victim, and it's Amanda who's really interesting.' Janek glanced at Stanger. 'We got to know much more about her. And how, for sure, he got in. It makes a big difference if he came in off the fire escape or if she opened up the door. If Amanda let him in it's a whole new ball game, because that means she knew him, she's the focus and Brenda's just auxiliary.'

They all nodded. At least Janek had a theory that Amanda was the prime target, even if there were no grounds to say that yet. Before they broke up he urged them again to look for connections. 'If the girls knew each other, or if their paths crossed, then at least we have a place to start. Until then we're working in the dark. So far we got a lot of notions but no clear idea what we're dealing with. Is this a one-time double homicide with a purpose, or a thrill-kill that could turn into a series? That's something we all better think about, too, because if the guy who did this thinks he's getting away with it, he just might try it again.

Chinatown

When he was finally alone in the office he telephoned Caroline Wallace.

'Hey, Janek, I was hoping I'd hear from you.' She seemed genuinely pleased that he had called.

'That was fun last night. Now it's my turn.' He suggested he drive over, pick her up and take her to dinner in Chinatown.

She brought her camera with her, the same Leica he'd seen at the burial, slung over her shoulder with half a dozen leather containers for film dangling from the strap. No equipment bag; she said she liked to travel light. She never went out without her camera, she said, since she never knew what she might happen to see.

In the car he asked if she'd had it with her the day she'd fallen off her bike and been picked up by Al.

'Always the detective, aren't you?' She was amused. Then she frowned. 'No, I didn't take it to the tennis club. There'd been some pilfering in the locker room.'

'So you don't always carry it with you.'

'I guess I don't. You're a very clever man.' She smiled, raised her camera, leaned back against her side of the car, took a shot of him driving and smiling back.

He took her to a restaurant he liked, upstairs on Mott Street where the food was cheap and good and the waiters didn't speak English very well. She took a couple more shots of him while he ordered. He played up to her by clowning with the waiter. Click. Click. He liked the idea of being photographed. She must like me, he thought, or else she wouldn't bother.

'You Chink out a lot, don't you, Janek?'

'Yeah, but two nights running is maybe pushing it a little bit.'

'In China they Chink out every meal, so I guess we'll both survive.'

34

'Tomorrow,' he told her, 'I may Chink out again. I got to interrogate a Chinese pimp.'

She said she'd like to photograph him conducting an interrogation.

'To catch my agression?'

'Sure. Especially when you bang him around. You do bang them around, I hope. My dad used to tell me how cops know how to hit a guy, work him over real good, without leaving any marks.'

'Yeah. Back in 1902. I knew you were a cop-hater. Cops' kids always are.'

'I think cops are the best, finest, gentlest men around.' She was serious and he was only sorry he didn't agree.

'What attracts you to agression?'

'Just my hang-up, I suppose.'

'Only men, right?'

'Female aggression might be interesting, but in the book I'm sticking to the men.'

'Is this book going to be a put-down?'

'Of your gender?' She laughed. 'No. Not at all. There's an elegance about male agression. The poses. The stance. The eyes. The look. It's the best part of being human. We're social animals. Aggression makes the world work. And so, too, I guess, does gentleness, but that's another book.'

'I can imagine,' he said, looking at her closely, 'that you could do a book on that.'

'Mothers cuddling babies. Lovers kissing tenderly. It's been done to death, and anyway it's too maudlin for me just now.'

The food came steaming and they attacked it greedily. He complimented her on her dexterity with chopsticks. She told him she'd had quite a bit of experience using them during her two years in Saigon. He asked her what it had been like out there, especially at the end during the final siege and the collapse, and as she talked about it, told him her war stories, it occurred to him that she was recounting her adventures the same way as a man. A very engaging trait, he thought, since she was most attractively feminine. He knew that young women were different now, that their lives could be as adventurous as a man's without their turning masculine. He'd seen it occasionally in young female detectives, but this was the first time he'd experienced it socially, a thought that made him

35

feel old, as if the world had passed him by.

She was sympathetic when he expressed this feeling, and also mildly amused. She said she figured him for early fifties, and when he confirmed that he was fifty-one she said she didn't think that was old at all.

'Al was what? Sixty-six or something. He was old, and he'd retired. He lived in the past, in his old cases, but you're engaged with the world now. No, the world hasn't passed you by, Janek. I have the feeling you're right on top of things, and very much in your prime.'

He liked her for saying that, liked her more than he wanted to admit, and now he wanted to examine that liking, growing in him at such an exceptionally rapid rate, because he was feeling something he hadn't felt in years, and it frightened him a little because it had been so long.

He had been conscious for some time that all his relationships were tainted by his work. The searching look he applied to people, his constant quest for motives, strengths and weaknesses, figuring how to play someone, seize psychological advantage, manipulate, interrogate, break a person down – all of that, which was the essence of being a good detective, seemed to work against any possibility of intimacy. He had wondered if normal relationships were possible when everything from buying a newspaper to making love to a woman seemed to be part of some vast investigation that circumscribed his life. It was as if he could never escape his work. Except now, sitting in this restaurant with Caroline, he was feeling something else.

Attraction? She was very attractive, of course, but he felt something more. His liking of her fogged his instincts. She was no longer just a good-looking woman but someone he felt tender toward. And since he knew she could not possibly feel the same way toward him, he warned himself to be careful lest he get banged up.

They lingered over tea, talking casually. It was hard for him to believe they had met only the morning before. The crumbs of their fortune cookies and the litle paper strips lay before them on the table. Finally they got up, Janek paid, and then they walked the teeming streets, looking into the grocery stores, sniffing sharp aromas, gazing up at laundry drying on fire escapes, hearing strange utterances chirped from windows by old Chinese women with straight-cut hair.

When they finally crossed Canal Street they found themselves in another world; they had crossed the demarcation line to Little Italy. He led her past his car to a coffeehouse he liked, across the street from a Sicilian clam bar where Mafia gangsters hung out and, occasionally, were shot.

They had drunk many cups of Chinese tea; now they sipped Italian coffee. But this was more than an ethnic change; there was a different atmosphere between them now. The walk had loosened him. He had intended to be a listener, but now he found himself talking rapidly, telling her about his adventures when he was a young police officer and Al DiMona was watching over him, of chases and gangland slayings and the code of silence on Mulberry Street which the police could never break. And as he poured himself out he saw a look of entrancement on her face.

'Take me there, Janek,' she said.

'Where?' *What had he been talking about?*

'To the shop. I want to see your father's shop.'

He had been talking about his childhood on Lafayette Street, his father's shop and the apartment above where his family had lived.

It was only a few blocks away. No reason not to take her there. He passed the place often, sometimes drove out of his way just to pass it after work, but he had never showed it to anyone, not even to Sarah, and he had been married to her for eighteen years.

'All right. It isn't much, you know.'

She nodded, took his arm. They walked there, stood across the street, looked at the storefront where his father had worked visible to passersby, repairing broken accordions, the trade he'd brought with him from Prague. It was an olive-oil store now, and the apartment above, on the second floor, looked uninhabited. Perhaps it was now a storeroom. Janek pointed to the window on the left.

'I used to stand there Saturday mornings studying the street. My father was the best accordion repairman in the city then, and the old street accordionists would come to him from all the boroughs and New Jersey too. There was an old man with a decrepit instrument that was always falling apart, and every Saturday I'd watch him from that window as he limped across the street with his little monkey on his shoulder to have the old battered thing repaired. When I saw him I'd go downstairs and stand beside my father, waiting for the moment when the old man would set the monkey on the workbench and beckon me to shake its hand. I hated to do it. That paw was gnarled and scabrous. And, of course, I could have stayed upstairs, but something always drew me down. Perhaps I felt that old man's need. His one accomplishment, you see, was that he had trained the animal to do that simple trick. It made children happy, he thought. It made him happy if I shook the paw and smiled.'

She was photographing him. He hadn't noticed when he was talking, but when he finished and turned to her he saw she had her camera to her eye. It made him feel good, her shooting him. Her clicking shutter gave rhythm to his memories. He turned, started to say something, and then as his eyes met her lens she shot him again. And then she brought her camera down. She told him she'd shot out the roll.

He wondered what she'd seen, what she'd caught. A middle-aged detective reminiscing, or something else? The love he was feeling toward her now – he wondered if she'd caught that too.

'Will the pictures come out?' he asked. 'Not much light here. It's pretty dim.'

'The lens is fast and the film's high-speed. They'll come out, Janek.' There was a nice rhythm to her speaking, as nice as the rhythm of her camera's click-click-click.

They paused at the corner of Baxter and Hester. She stood beside him while he unlocked his car. When he opened her door she just stood there under the streetlamp searching his eyes, and then he kissed her, and felt the warmth of her hand as she reached up and curled it around his neck.

They drove back to Queens in silence. There was just the sound of the city outside, the summer sound of traffic and people, and it all seemed subdued somehow as if set in relief by the murmur of their breathing inside the car. There was a bond between them, he felt, and it heightened the feeling he had as they sat together and he drove, and the city was quiet, a gentler place because of the warmth he felt beside this quiet girl.

Outside her building she turned to him.

'Want to come up?'

'Of course I do. You know I do.' He paused. 'I didn't know,

Caroline, didn't know it was going to be like this.'

'I didn't know, either. How could we know? That's the mystery of it, isn't it? Sweet mystery.'

There was a spell between them and they were both careful not to break it. They moved quietly up the stairs. There was no talk, smiles, jokes, flirtatious looks as they paused and she opened her locks and led him in. The loft was softly lit. She had half a dozen Japanese-style paper lanterns, and they were set in various parts of the huge room. She had left them on when she'd gone out and now they cast a warm glow over everything, making the loft seem more tender than it had the evening before.

She kicked off her sandals, opened a cupboard, pulled out a bottle of wine. He came behind her, stood just a few inches behind, and she turned to him and smiled. She handed him the bottle and a corkscrew, then brought down two glasses from a shelf.

'Music?'

He nodded.

She went to her stereo, chose a record from a rack beneath – Miles Davis playing with Coltrane, subtle and hypnotic, endless too.

They sat side by side in her worn sling chairs, sipping and listening, not speaking at all. Then she stood and brought over a hassock and set it in front of him and sat so her back pressed against his knees.

He reached down into her hair, ran his fingers through it. Then he massaged her neck, kneaded the upper part of her back, running his thumbs gently along her shoulder blades, and it seemed to him that she was purring almost as she moved her head slowly from side to side.

It seemed to him that their lovemaking had been humane when, later, they held each other and stroked each other on her huge brass bed. He had felt consumed by tenderness, had reveled in the slow languorous rapturous way they'd moved at a half-time tempo, never lying still, but without banging or making any motion that was angry or angular, always smooth, always slow and easy. They had been people making love, not animals screwing, and he thought of that just before he fell asleep.

He awoke several times in the night, wondrous at finding himself here sleeping in her loft, with her smooth, young, bare body beside him, listening to her drowsy breathing, feeling the warmth of her back against his palms. It had never been like this for him, at least as far back as he could recall. It had been a long time since he had made gentle love, felt this way toward a woman, held a woman so young and strong and beautiful, held her through the night. And he was amazed that it had happened. It seemed like an impossible dream, something he had longed for, that marked a turning point. It was all so strange, the way they'd met and then fallen in love, without any sort of courtship except her photographing him and taking his arm out on the street. All his detectiveness had melted away, and now he was a man again, reborn, and this seemed a momentous thing, as if his life would be different now.

Suddenly he was scared – he, Janek, who normally was not afraid of anything. Maybe she did this all the time, he thought. Maybe she'd put him on about Al. Maybe she liked old guys, dried-up old detectives. Maybe she had a thing for them, was into handcuffs, authority and thirty-eights. Or maybe, since she was the new kind of woman who lived like a man, could screw around like a man, maybe this was just another night in the sack which didn't mean anything to her. If that was true he knew he would feel awful, more alone than he had felt when he was alone before.

He fell back to sleep. In the morning, when he awoke, he groped for her but she wasn't there. He almost panicked until he heard her moving at the galley and then he smelled the aroma of coffee, and heard her steps as she came back to the bed, sat beside him, set down a tray.

'Hey, Janek.' She was sipping from a mug. She said his name softly, sensuously, as if she loved the sound of it, not the harsh way people called it out at precinct stations or on the street. He pulled himself up so he could sit beside her, his legs still beneath her sheets. She stroked his cheeks, whiskery now, kissed him lightly, then motioned toward the tray. He reached for the second mug, raised it. They toasted each other with coffee. It was six-thirty in the morning, and he still couldn't believe all this had happened, was still happening even then.

Interviews

Ten am at the Market Motel: Amanda Ireland's father came down to meet Janek and Stanger in the lobby. Mid-fifties, clear blue eyes, a weatherbeaten face. He had a shock of gray hair that fell across his forehead and the look of a man from whom something very valuable had been stolen away.

Mrs. Ireland, he told them, was too upset to talk but would be available if Janek needed her. There were three chairs and a glass-topped coffee table in the corner of the lobby. They sat down. Ireland chain-smoked. His teeth were yellow and there were brown stains on the thumb and first finger of his hand.

'My wife always worried about her living here. She'd read an item in the paper about a murder or a mugging or a rape, and she'd say to me, "Let's call Mandy tonight. She's scared to admit she's scared. We have to let her know that anytime she feels like it she can give up the city and come home and live with us." So we'd call her and she wouldn't know what we were talking about, wouldn't even know about the crime. She didn't pay attention to any of that. She loved the city and didn't feel threatened here. She loved her job at Weston too, and going to plays and chamber-music concerts, and the excitement – she kept mentioning that. She said she thrived on the energy of New York.'

'What did she mean by "excitement"?' Janek asked.

'All the people, I guess. The crowds. All the different things going on at once. The pace. The way people walk and talk. She certainly didn't mean bars and discos. She was home most nights unless she went out to a concert or to dinner at a friend's.'

'People we've talked to say she didn't date.'

'Yes, that's true, I guess. She lived a quiet life. She had some boyfriends when she was in college, and when she went to France to study she met a boy in Grenoble and they were engaged for a while, but then it got broken off. We never knew whose decision – his or hers. She didn't want to talk about it, but we had the feeling

41

she'd been hurt. She didn't seem interested in getting married or having a family or anything like that. We have another daughter who lives in Hawaii, and Margaret has four kids. Mandy didn't want that kind of life. She liked being by herself.'

'Excuse me for saying this, Mr. Ireland, but it seems a little implausible that your daughter never went out with anyone at all.'

'I don't know whether it's implausible. I think that's the way it was. Maybe it was just a stage she was going through. She was an adult. She chose her own life. She didn't care what anybody thought.'

'Did she ever speak about her friends?'

He shook his head. 'Not very often. Occasionally about colleagues at the school. She thought we'd be interested, I guess, since her mother and I are both schoolteachers, too. Actually I think she was very content living the way she did. We didn't pry, because there were areas she didn't seem to want to talk about.'

'Such as?'

'Her love life. Her social life. Things like that.'

'But you just told us you didn't think she had any kind of love life.'

'That's what we thought, but how do we know for sure? We took what she said at face value. She never tried to deceive us, but if either my wife or I pressed too hard she'd just shake her head and laugh. "Come on, Mom. Come off it, Daddy," she'd say, and then we'd let it go because clearly she didn't want to talk about it. That was her privilege and we respected her feelings, of course.'

'What about this art teacher?'

'Gary Pierson. She mentioned him. They went out a few times, and then became close friends. She told us he was gay.'

'Did you meet him?'

'Yesterday. That was the only time. Up at Weston, in the headmistress's office. They told us he found her and he wanted to meet us if we came. He is a very nice young man. I felt he was pretty broken up. He took my wife in his arms and sobbed. I'm happy Mandy had a friend like that. He seemed like a person who really cared.'

'What about the other people at Weston?'

'They were very nice to us, but frankly I thought they were more concerned about the reputation of the school, and finding a new

42

French teacher in time for their opening next week. They're going to hold a memorial for Mandy and they asked us to stay for it, or else come down again. I doubt we will. My wife wants to go back to Buffalo this afternoon, so that's what we're going to do. Gary's going to clean out the apartment when you people say he can. The body will be shipped to us and we'll bury her at home.'

He paused, smiled, then his mouth turned bitter. 'Mandy was an old-fashioned kind of girl and I guess what happened to her is what happens to an old-fashioned girl these days. The papers call her "socialite" and "debutante". She wasn't either one. She happened to teach at a school where some socialites send their children and where some of the students become debutantes, so when she was killed all of a sudden it was "East Side Society Girl Murdered in Her Bed," and then, when nothing happened, and there weren't any sensational revelations, the powers that be decided she was boring and dropped the story and that's the end of it as far as New York City is concerned. In a month the landlord will paint up the apartment, double the rent, and there won't be a trace that she was here. The city will absorb her death as it absorbs so many things and we'll be left upstate with all our grief and pain.'

Janek met his eyes. Ireland was angry, and he was showing his anger the only way he could. He wasn't the kind of man who spoke bitterly very often, but now, Janek saw, he would begin to speak bitterly more and more. His friends would notice and say his daughter's death had marked him. They'd point to Ireland's bitterness and his wife's lament and whisper cautiously of tragedy.

'We take this case very seriously, Mr. Ireland. We're not going to forget about it even if the papers do. There are five of us, detectives, and we're working on it very hard. We'll continue to work until we find who did it and bring him in with proof.'

'And then what? He plea-bargains, goes to a mental hospital or makes a deal with the prosecutors and gets six to eight in Attica? We know what goes on and I tell you now it won't make one iota of difference to me. I have personally resolved never to inquire into your investigation. I don't want to know about it, because however it comes out it's not going to satisfy me at all. Now I don't want to be rude, but I don't think there's anything else I have to say. She came down here of her own free choice and lived her life and ended up getting killed. Some succeed down here and some fail and some

43

find love and happiness and some get killed. Mandy was unlucky, her life is over and now we have to cope with that. I appreciate your efforts, certainly, but I can't relate to them. All I'm thinking about is how to keep my wife from going crazy and how to help her heal this awful wound.'

Stanger hadn't said a word during the interview. He remained quiet after they left the motel. Mr. Ireland was out of the case now, but it would be hard to forget what he'd said. However much talk there was of justice and one's duty to uphold the law, policemen were motivated by a need to make things even, redress the wrongs inflicted on a victim, and now Ireland had canceled out that need.

Out on the street Janek was thinking about the various ways human beings express their grief: anger, cynicism, bitterness, tears, mental breakdown, or just feeling a hard sore knot inside, the way he'd felt on Sunday when he'd seen what Al had done.

'You're walking by the car, Lieutenant.'

Janek turned. Stanger was waiting. Janek nodded, and walked back and got inside.

'Better check out that super again.'

'I did. He's clean. No wife or son or anyone else with access to his keys. Very careful. Hangs the ring on a hook in his closet when he isn't wearing it on his belt. Worked that row of buildings for fifteen years. Everyone swears by him. Even has an uncle on the force. I still say our guy came in through the window. Makes sense, since her keys are gone.'

'Okay, then tell me why the guy would bother. Climb up a fire escape, open the window, wait in the shower, stab her and cut off her head. Just tell me, please, for Christ's sake, Stanger, why the hell anyone would do something like that, and not take anything, or rape her, or use her in any way. Tell me – what's the goddamn point?'

Stanger had the ignition on. He was revving the engine. 'He did take something, Lieutenant. He took her head. He used her head. That's a major robbery. A lot bigger deal than a rape.'

Janek looked at him, felt ashamed at his outburst, and now it occurred to him that maybe Stanger wasn't as mediocre as he'd thought. 'All right – let's get into that. Say he stalked her like you said. Say he saw her as a certain type, the schoolmarm type, the virgin type, a nice clean lonely girl with a nice clean dog and he decided he wanted her head. Did he just pick her out at random, notice her on the street, or did he know her some other way before?'

'You want to talk to Pierson today?'

'Damn right I do.'

'He's nice. A very mild guy.'

'You told me that yesterday.'

'I don't see him doing a thing like this. You going to get rough with him?'

'No, not rough, Stanger, but I'm going to apply a little stress.' Stanger nodded. 'Something else. If Amanda knew this guy and let him in, it doesn't make sense that he'd hide in her shower.'

'Like I keep telling you, Lieutenant – he came in off the fire escape.'

Janek called Caroline from a booth outside the precinct house. She wasn't in; he got her machine: 'This is Caroline Wallace. I'm out. Please leave your name and number and I'll get back.' Her recorded voice was clear and crisp. 'This is Janek,' he said when he heard the tone, 'thinking about you. Call you later. Hope you're free tonight.'

After he put down the phone he felt dissatisfied. Why hadn't he said he was mad for her, that she was the best thing to happen to him in years? He put in another dime, and told that to her machine. He felt better. Maybe, he thought, she was going to be his guardian against the demons that ruled the night.

Aaron referred to interrogation rooms as shithouses. 'Let's take him to the shithouse,' he'd say when he thought a stressful talk would be appropriate. The two cubicles off the special squad room on the second floor of the Sixth were small and grubby and faced with acoustic tiles. Furniture was sparse – two hard chairs and a small wooden table. The aroma was precinct intensified to double strength. Caged hundred-watt bulbs burned from the ceilings. From inside, the one-way viewing slits looked like clouded mirrors.

Janek and Aaron spent a good part of an hour cramped together in the listening corridor watching Howell pump Brenda's pimp. His name was Prudencio Bitong and he was not, as it happened, Chinese, but a dark-skinned Filipino with a vaguely Oriental face, black eyes, and black hair greased and slicked straight back. Together he and Howell played a nice duet, Howell the brute

45

inquisitor, Bitong the slippery detainee. Howell wanted information. Bitong wanted to save his ass. The dialogue was crude and unpredictable. Janek smiled as he listened. Aaron rolled his eyes and shook his head.

'You got keys to Brenda's place?'

'Don't have keys.' Bitong pulled out his key ring. 'Go ahead, Mister. Check.'

Howell ignored the key ring. 'You ditched her keys after you came out of there. You got scared and called 911 and then you ditched them, right?'

Bitong shook his head.

'Want to hear a tape of yourself? You know what a voice print is?'

Pause. 'Okay. So I knew her.'

'You called 911, didn't you?'

'So, I called 911. Big deal.'

'After you killed her? *Right?*'

Bitong shook his head furiously. 'I loved that kid. I'd do anything for her. How could I harm that kid?'

'She was holding out on you.'

'She wasn't.'

'You wanted to teach her a lesson.'

'She didn't need a lesson.'

'You bounced her around a little and then she got hurt and you got scared. You checked, saw she was dead, then you ran out. Isn't that how it went?'

'No. I came in and found her. I saw the blood. I didn't even go close and look.'

'*You didn't look?*'

Bitong shook his head. Some of his slicked hair fell loose.

'You saw something funny. What?'

Aaron elbowed Janek. When Janek glanced at him he gestured downward with his thumb.

'It didn't look like her.'

'Who the hell did it look like? You trying to tell me that was someone else?'

'It didn't look like her. Just a dead broad in Brenda's bed.'

'So you *did* look close?'

'I looked to see if it was her.'

46

Janek elbowed Aaron, gestured thumbs-up. Aaron made a fifty-fifty gesture with his hands.

'*Was it?*'

'Didn't look like her.'

'Shit, Prudencio, we got an ID. We took her fingerprints. We know who the hell we got. You trying to tell us she was someone else?'

Bitong appeared confused. 'It didn't look like her. That's all. It wasn't her face.'

'So who was dead in the fucking bed?'

'I don't know what the hell is going on.'

Bitong smiled crookedly. Janek shook his head.

'Let me at him, Frank,' Aaron whispered. 'Howell's not bad, but he isn't taking him anywhere.'

Janek nodded. Aaron smiled. He strode into the cubicle, took Howell's chair, turned it around, sat in it, then rested his arms across the wooden back.

Watching Aaron after Howell was like watching a master take over from a novice. Destination was everything – the best interrogators knew where they wanted to end up. Aaron knew that and also how to find a cavity, tickle it, wiggle around in it, make it start to hurt. After his first question Bitong was looking scared.

'You got a lawyer, Prudencio?'

'What I need a lawyer for?'

'You got a lawyer?'

'No.'

'Maybe we can find you one. I think maybe you're going to need one later on.'

'Why the hell I need a lawyer?'

'You're in a lot of trouble. This is homicide.'

'She was my girl.'

'You think a john did it?'

'I think so – yeah. But she was careful. I taught her. She didn't let everybody in.'

'How did she handle it?'

'She'd tell them to call her from the corner. She could see the booth from her window. If she didn't like the look of the guy she'd tell him she was sick. She wouldn't give him the address.'

'And if she *did* like the look of him?'

47

'Then she'd go down and meet him. Sometimes she'd take him on a walk around the block. She was very careful. I told her to be careful, because she was up there all by herself.'

'What about if she knew the guy?'

'If he'd been there before she'd tell him to come right up.'

'How'd she keep them straight?'

'I don't get what you mean.'

'How'd she know if she'd been with him before?'

'When he'd call from the corner she'd look out the window. If he'd been with her before she'd recognize his face. If she didn't, like he was a businessman from out of town and it had been a year or so and she'd forgot, she'd go downstairs and look at him up close. Those were the rules. She always followed them.'

'She never deviated? *Never?*'

Bitong shook his head.

'You the only one with the keys?'

'Just the two of us.'

'You just blundered in there when you felt like it?'

'She had a signal. She'd leave the shade half up.'

'Was the shade up Monday morning?'

'No.'

'So why did you go up?'

'I hadn't heard from her. She wasn't answering the phone. I wanted to see what was going on.'

'Then what?'

'I rang. No answer. So I let myself in. I took one look and then I ran.'

'And locked the door after you?'

'Yeah.'

'Why?'

'I just locked it – don't know why.'

'Then you called 911?'

'Yeah.'

'From the booth on the corner?'

'Yeah.'

'Why didn't you use her phone?'

'I wanted to get out of there.'

'You didn't take anything?'

'No.'

'You just looked and then you ran out and locked the door?'

'That's it.'

'You took the elevator?'

'No. The stairs.'

'And then you called 911 from the corner?'

'I told you that.'

'They cut off people's heads in the Philippines, don't they, Prudencio?'

'What the hell you talking about, man?'

'If, say, a girl's been bad and her man's upset, real pissed off, he just goes to her and cuts off her head. That's the tradition, right?'

'I never heard of that.'

'You're a Filipino pimp and you never heard of that? You must think I'm stupid, Prudencio. If I heard of it you *got* to have heard of it. You'd do it, too, wouldn't you, if you were mad enough?'

'I wasn't mad. What happened to her head?'

'You tell me.'

'I don't know. It looked like someone else. You're telling me that wasn't her head?'

'Was it?'

'I didn't think so then.'

'Because it looked different?'

'I thought I was freaking out.'

'You do drugs?'

'Sometimes.'

'But you weren't so freaked out you didn't clean out her stash?'

'I never touched her stash.'

'Then where's the money?'

'I don't know.'

'You took it. You saw she was dead, you cleaned her out, then locked the door and went downstairs and called 911, very very cool.'

'I didn't take anything.'

'Where'd she keep it?'

'In the closet. In a pocket of her coat.'

'What coat?'

'A long gray overcoat she's got in there. There's a zippered pocket in the lining. She kept the money in there.'

'And you think it's still there?'

'I don't know.'

'It better be there, Prudencio. Detective Howell is taking you over there now, and he'd better find that money just where it's supposed to be, because if it's not there we're going to fry you. You understand, Prudencio? You're going to need a lawyer real bad if that money isn't there.'

The pimp nodded. Janek shrugged and left the viewing corridor. He thought Bitong was telling the truth. He was a small-time amateur, venal, slippery, slimy, not the sort to cut off a pair of heads, switch them around, then try to make them fit.

Stanger brought in Gary Pierson at four o'clock. He was medium-tall and slim, about twenty-six or twenty-seven years old. Friendly face, pleasant smile, soft wavy brownish hair. He wore expensive resort-style clothing, his shoes shone like mirrors and his trousers were perfectly creased. Neat as a pin, compulsive, a little rigid in his posture. Janek watched and listened while Stanger doodled him around: hometown, position at Weston, how he'd spent the first half of the summer painting watercolor beachscapes on Nantucket, where he'd rented a little cottage from his aunt.

How had he met Amanda Ireland? They'd both started at Weston three years ago this fall and had struck up a friendship at once. She'd spent a week with him on Nantucket in July – idyllic days reading and painting on the beach, stargazing and intimate conversation at night. During school terms they ate lunch together nearly every day, often spent weekend evenings attending movies or chamber-music concerts at the YMHA and the Metropolitan Museum.

When Janek had a sense of him he stepped in, was introduced, then motioned Stanger to leave. He looked at Gary hard. The young man evaded his stare. He was nervous, but then he wasn't accustomed to being in a windowless interrogation room where the air didn't smell very good with a gray-faced detective glaring into his eyes.

'How would you describe your relationship?'

'With Mandy? We were very close.'

'Lovers?'

Gary smiled. 'I'm gay, Lieutenant. I told Detective Stanger that.'

'We certainly appreciate your honesty.'

'I don't hide it.'

'That's very nice. Now what about your relationship? Did you ever sleep with her or not?'

He shook his head. 'We necked sometimes. We were more like confidants.'

'You exchanged confidences?'

'Yes. She knew everything there was to know about me and I knew everything about her.'

'Like what?'

'What do you mean?'

'What did you know about her?'

'I told you – everything.' He paused. 'Maybe a lot of the time I talked about myself. I guess I liked to talk about my problems and she just liked to listen.'

'So it was one of those one-way confidential relationships?' It pained Janek to be sarcastic, but he didn't know any other way.

'She knew all about my affairs. My lovers. My problems. Everything.'

'And what did you know about her?'

'I knew who she was.'

'What's that supposed to mean?'

'Her values, feelings. She was a wonderful girl. Decent and sensitive. Thoughtful. Intelligent. I think Mandy Ireland was the most compassionate person I've ever known.'

'Was she gay, Gary?'

'Absolutely not!'

'No need to get jumpy about it. If she was I need to know.'

'She wasn't gay.'

'And she didn't date?'

'No.'

'Then what kind of sex life did she have?'

'That's a lousy question.'

'I don't think so. We're investigating a homicide.'

'I mean what the hell? What difference does it make? She's dead now. She didn't talk about that at all.'

'Maybe she didn't trust you.'

'I think she did. I just don't think there was much to tell.'

'What's not much?'

'I think she was more or less celibate.'

'She was good-looking.'

'Very.'

'And young and single. I don't get it. It doesn't add up. She lived in Manhattan, met people at work, people who must have been attracted to her, at least enough to ask her out. You're telling me she didn't have any kind of sex life. I say that's unlikely. Someone came into her apartment and stabbed her all over her chest. Like sticking his big cock right in her. Like a very sick kind of rape. Now, that's a sex life, or a sex death, whatever you want to call it. In my experience that's some kind of sex.'

Pierson was beginning to perspire.

'Shakes you up, doesn't it?'

'Who did it, Gary? Any ideas on that?'

'I've thought about it, naturally. I told Detective Stanger. She didn't go out. Hardly ever. And she wouldn't let people in unless she was expecting them. She had a chain lock and she used it. She didn't have a boyfriend. I just can't imagine who would want to harm her. She didn't have an enemy in the world.'

'Funny the way you reacted when you found her.'

'I got sick. It was a sickening sight.'

'You never saw anything sickening before?'

'Not sickening like that.'

'You live in the Village. You go to bars. Ever go to a leather bar?'

'That's not my scene.'

'Been to them, haven't you?'

'Maybe a couple of times.'

'Right, and they didn't make you sick? Come on, Gary, all that sado stuff right out there for everyone to see ...'

'Yes, it made me sick. That's why I never went back.'

'You turned away when you saw her.'

'Anyone would have turned away.'

'You notice something funny, Gary?'

'What?'

'Something funny?'

'What was funny?'

'Strange. Funny-strange. Maybe something about the way she looked.'

'There was blood.'

'What else?'

'It was awful. Horrible. I felt sick right away.'

'You wear glasses?'

He shook his head.

'You're an artist. An art teacher. You're a visual man. You didn't see anything funny when you looked in there, maybe something that *made* you feel sick?'

'I don't know what you're talking about!'

'Then let me spell it out for you. Did you notice, perhaps, that she'd been decapitated? That someone had cut off her head?'

Gary Pierson looked straight into Janek's eyes, peered into them to see if he was telling the truth, and when he saw that he was he began to choke. He turned his head to the side and Janek could see the tendons in his neck quiver and his throat contract and then something like drool appear on his lips. Watching Gary Pierson try to control himself and swallow, Janek was not proud of the way he had delivered the gruesome news. It was an old interrogator's trick and it generally worked. He stood up, moved behind the boy and placed his hands on his shoulders to calm him down.

'Take it easy, son. It was a very bad scene. She was attacked through her shower curtain. The killer was waiting in there when she came in to brush her teeth. We think she had just come back from walking her dog. And just as she started to brush, this guy started stabbing away. He killed her instantly, but he kept stabbing and then later he took something else, a sword maybe, and he cut off her head.'

Gary started to choke again, and Janek was just about convinced. He knew there were killers who were excellent actors, and there were coldhearted people who pretended to be squeamish, sociopaths who didn't feel anything but could fake it, thinking that's what everybody did – since they couldn't feel anything they assumed nobody else did, either. But Gary Pierson didn't seem like one of them, and there wasn't anything fake about his convulsions and his sweat. Janek could feel his shivers right through his shoulder bones. He believed the kid. He'd never really thought he'd done it, but he had needed to be sure.

He ruffled the boy's hair and left the room. Aaron was waiting just outside. 'Great performance in there. You took him to the shithouse, Frank.'

'Yeah, and I feel really good about it, too.'

'Take it easy. You had to. There wasn't any other way.'

When Janek came back in with Stanger, Gary was still shaking in his chair.

'Look, Gary, we got to find this guy. It isn't enough to say she just stayed home. You have to think back and remember everything she ever said. If someone was following her, for instance, or if she got strange phone calls, heavy breathers or hang-ups in the night. If she was scared about something, or acted peculiar on a certain day, or suddenly nervous for no reason you could see. You have to think back and tell Detective Stanger everything you know, and then afterwards, if you suddenly remember something, you have to call him and tell him that too. Understand?'

Gary nodded. He said he'd do his best. Janek told Stanger to spend another hour with him, going over the past four weeks. Names. Dates. Habits. Hobbies. Doctor. Dentist. Veterinarian. If she really lived by the clock, took the same bus every day, walked her dog at the same time, then she would not have been difficult to stalk. Janek wanted her schedule, hour by hour, minute by minute if they could work it out. He wanted to know everything there was to know about Amanda Ireland. Gary Pierson would be Stanger's collaborator. Together they would write a book, the story of her life.

Howell was waiting in the squad room. He had Prudencio Bitong and also Brenda's stash. A roll of soiled bills, sixteen hundred dollars, half a bag of medium-quality pot, and a glassine envelope of cocaine, maybe five hundred dollars' worth. And there was a key too, a safe-deposit-box key, and Howell was going over to the bank in the morning and get that box opened up. Maybe Mr. Bitong would find to his surprise that Brenda Thatcher had been holding back.

Blackmail

It seemed to Janek that they melted into each other when he arrived that evening at the loft. Caroline took him in her arms, they moved to her bed without a sound and there made love magically, he thought, as if they were made for each other and had known each other for months.

As a lover she employed no tricks, no actressy little touches she had learned from someone else. She was merely herself without pretense or illusion, more than enough, he thought, far more than he had hoped. Her lean young body was taut with craving. Her breasts pressed firmly against his chest. Her back was beautiful and proud. Her mouth was hungry. She played her fingers upon his shoulder blades, then thrust them deep into his hair.

He kissed her throat and then her eyes, ran his hands along her perspiring flanks and marveled at the sleekness of her legs. She used her toes to stroke his calves. He was awed by her shudders of desire.

He felt she was a sorceress, that in her embraces he was bewitched. They glided, joined, pulled back, then joined again, their bodies beating out a sweet slow rhythm, a long slow intoxicating dance. No frantic whisperings. No. 'What do you like?' and 'Does this turn you on?' No need to ask, because they knew. There was a faultless surety to their every move, a deep instinctive knowledge that told them how to satisfy.

Afterward, lying back, they looked at one another and broke into smiles.

She served him a simple dinner – salad, steak, Italian cheesecake – and as they ate they regarded each other with delight. Talking casually, he became aware he knew practically nothing about her. Family background, education, the men she had known and loved – such things were normally necessary knowledge if he was to fathom another human being. But now they seemed meaningless in the face of the things he had discovered: her vision of the world imparted through her photographs, and the smell and taste of her body, carnal knowledge he now possessed. It was such a relief not to have to care about the other things, to rely upon his feelings, to leave his detective's processes behind. He wondered why he hadn't learned to do this before, separate his life from his work. Until now repairing old accordions and playing them had been his only escape. How wonderful to have found this passionate woman who made him forget the awful sully of his job.

'Have you talked to Mrs. DiMona?'

He looked up at her, a little startled to hear her speak. 'Lou? Not yet. I was thinking about going over there Sunday,' he said.

'What are you going to tell her?'

'Don't know. Haven't decided yet. I'm not going to tell her how Al met you and how he used to drop around. He told her he was working on an old case. That's what she wants to think.'

'You could go along with that.'

'I could. Though I hate to lie.'

'You could maybe smooth it out a little. Sort of turn it another way.'

He understood what Caroline meant: Tell Lou that Al had been looking into something, but it hadn't meant anything, he'd just been puttering around.

'Trouble is I don't know what he told her. When she talked to me she seemed convinced. An idea like that, that he was onto something, had found something dreadful, unbearable – it gives her an explanation and she wants to hold on to that. It's acceptable to her that she lived with him all those years and then on Sunday he shot himself and didn't even leave a note. It means she didn't mean anything to him, that he didn't care enough to explain. That's pretty hard to take, but if there was this old case, you see ...'

'Sure. She could pin it on that.'

'And be absolved.'

'Absolution – God!'

'Yes, absolution. Cops are into absolution. And redemption too. And crime and punishment.'

'For themselves, right? The punishment. Not for the criminals.'

'You understand,' he said. 'Yes. For themselves.'

She shook her head, almost furiously it seemed to him, as if she were trying to clear that thought away. He mustn't forget, he reminded himself, that she was the daughter of a cop. She knew all the strange torments that rotted out cops' minds.

'What about you?' he asked. 'What did you do today?'

'Thought about you,' she said, 'and about what you said to me on my machine.'

He had forgotten about that. So much had happened in the afternoon. 'Was it okay? Didn't embarrass you?'

'No.' She looked at him. 'I loved it.' She grinned.

As he helped her with the dishes she told him about her afternoon. She'd gone to Yankee Stadium, sat in the bleachers, then prowled the aisles taking photographs.

'You weren't shooting the players.'

'I've already shot a lot of them. Today I was after the fans. The wild ones, you know, all curled with tension, ready to pounce out of their seats when they think they've seen a bad call and a favourite player's getting robbed.'

'Aggression.'

She nodded. 'Coming home I had a new idea for a book. The title would be *Janek's World*. I figured it all out. I'd follow you around for months, maybe a year, shooting the world you deal with and your reactions to it – the sordid side of the city through your eyes.'

'That,' he said, scrubbing her sauté pan, 'would not be a very pretty book.'

He was tempted then to tell her about Switched Heads, how the girls had been used, the awful merciless maniacal mind that had used them, but he hesitated because he didn't want to taint their relationship with the sordid passions of that tale. Anyway, he knew he couldn't tell it coherently. He hadn't sorted it out well enough himself. Perhaps when he knew more it would be all right to tell her; she would want to hear it because she would care about the things which anguished him, and he would want to tell it because speaking the words would help him to understand it better himself. Not now. He would wait and, hopefully, would have the full story for her soon. Hopefully because if he had the full story he would be done with it, which would mean, of course, that he was onto something else, another case as ugly or even uglier.

They listened to some Coltrane and necked on the bed, then they made love again, and afterward, their bodies slick, they lay back upon the pillows to rest. And then – he didn't know why – he felt swept by a wave of gloom.

'Hey, Caroline.' He didn't dare look into her face. 'Why me? This old detective with the pouches under his eyes? Wouldn't you do better with a younger guy, your age or thereabouts? One of those glossy types with thick black hair, and a tan, dark glasses, driving a Porshe, in a thousand dollar leather windbreaker with a gold watch flashing at his cuff. You know what I mean. Jesus – why am I asking that?'

'Janek, Janek . . .' She placed her hand on his chest, just above his heart, and he could feel it thumping inside, beating against her palm. She ran her fingers through his gray chest hair matted by the mixture of their sweat. 'Janek ... Janek ...' She spoke his name as if she loved its sound.

He looked down at her. Her head was resting against him, her cheek against his stomach, and she was looking up at him, her hand still above his heart, her eyes large and serious.

'Why? Why me? Of all the guys – why me?' He had tried to pose the question first with humor, but now he could hear a strain of self-pity that made him feel ashamed.

'You're such a cop, you big lunk. So smart about everybody else, so smart and sharp and wise. But you don't know anything about yourself, do you? Or women either. You can figure them at a distance, but you lose sight when they get too close.'

'Maybe.'

'Sure. And now you're feeling sorry for yourself. You just can't believe it, right? This gorgeous doll – I mean what the hell could she ever see in you? You – Jesus! Mr. Middle-age himself. Mr. The-World-Has-Passed-Me-By. She's a broad, right? And everyone knows what broads are interested in. Beefy jocks in sports cars. Muscles, money, clothes and fun. Let's not forget fun, Janek. I mean that's what it's really all about. And, of course, you're just no fun at all. I mean you're so clumsy in the sack. Can't hack it. Make love like an aging ape.'

He was laughing then, and she started laughing, too. During her tirade she'd reached up once and lightly pinched his cheek. Now she straightened out, lowered herself, went down on him, stroking him with her fingers and teasing him with her mouth. And when he was hard she jumped up laughing, grasped up her Leica, switched on some lights, pointed them toward the bed and started taking photographs of him as he lay watching, hands clasped behind his head, his body naked and sprawled out.

'What the hell are you doing?'

'Getting the evidence.'

'Going to blackmail me?'

'Sure. With proof that the old beaten-up cop can still get it up, gets it up real good, in fact. Because that would ruin you, wouldn't it? I mean, your image of yourself, so sad and world-weary and, just to make the caricature complete, impotent besides.'

She took another shot, then set down her camera and sat beside him and took his hand. Then she flung herself against him, grasped

58

him, held him tightly, and at that moment he felt as though no one had ever loved him as much.

Intersection

Janek was waiting for the beat. Sooner or later it would come, he knew – the beat that would establish the tempo of the investigation, tell him how long it would last and how hard the work would be. There were wonderful cases, quick cases where the information streamed in and a detective could become heady on the rush. Switched Heads (officially the case was Ireland/Beard) was not showing signs of being one of those.

The phone rang on Saturday morning. Janek glanced at his watch – 9 am Sal answered. 'It's Aaron,' he said. Janek punched his button and picked up. He had the feeling Aaron wasn't coming in and was calling now with an excuse.

'You know those address books, Frank?'

'The girls' address books?'

'Yeah. Took them home last night. Got a match.'

'Great! Where the hell are you, anyway?' He could hear a strange sound in the background, a blend of music and verbal commands.

'I'm at the point of intersection, Frank. We may be onto something here.'

Sal was gazing at his face, excited, alert. Three and a half days and nothing but theories. Maybe the case was finally going to jell.

'Going to tell me about it?'

'Give me a chance, for Christ's sake. I'm surrounded by distractions. This is a very peculiar place.'

He'd found the same number in both women's address books, but listed under different names. Under 'Hazel Carter' in Amanda's book; under 'X' in Brenda Beard's.

'X? What the hell is X?'

'I got excited about that myself. You know – like "Mr. X" or "extra" or "extraordinary" or something, except it's none of those

59

things. It's "X" for "exercise". Hazel Carter is the name of this woman who runs a place where girls go to stay in shape. That's where I am now. I think you ought to join me. This is a very distinguished situation here. Lots of attractive broads, everyone suited up, faint tang of sweat in the air but nothing offensive. Better leave Sal behind. He could get excited, his being so young and all.'

Janek drove up alone. The gym was near Second Avenue on Eighty-sixth, a short walk from Amanda's place. There was an Indian restaurant at street level, and huge white-brick apartment houses on either side. Doormen in red tailcoats. Matching buildings named 'Versailles' and 'Fountainebleau.' Marble and grandeur in the lobbies, low ceilinged apartments upstairs. Pretentious and high-rent, Janek thought. Studios that cost a grand a month.

The small commercial building which housed the Hazel Carter Fitness Salon was squeezed between these monoliths. It looked like a situation where the landlord had tried to hold up the developers, the developers had said 'Screw' and erected their towers on either side. Now the tenants could gaze at one another across twenty-five feet of chasm, and the air rights to the little building were worthless, the plot too small to justify a tower.

Aaron was waiting at the head of the stairs. Janek could hear band music as he mounted. Aaron was leering and nodding his head to the rhythm. There was a WOMEN ONLY sign posted on the door.

'This is not your typical unisex gym, Frank. But seeing as how we're NYPD they're making an exception and letting us in.'

He held the door. Janek walked into the reception space. Maybe Aaron had been right about leaving Sal behind. That 'faint tang of sweat' reminded him of Caroline, clean, sweet and potent, heady stuff so early in the day.

The girl behind the desk was red-haired, freckled and very young. She wore a tailored ivory warm-up with a black T-shirt showing underneath.

Aaron made the introductions. The receptionist's name was Cynthia Tuttle.

'I told Miss Carter you were coming over,' she said. 'She's still in class.'

'No big deal,' Aaron said. 'You keep records of all the women who work out?'

'Sure. We operate by appointment. We don't take people off the street. Miss Carter's classes are in great demand. We train some of the top models in New York.' She mentioned a few names, Candy something, Cheryl this and Bunny that. The names didn't mean anything to Janek, but he nodded anyway. The place couldn't be all that exclusive, he thought, if they took a hooker like Brenda Beard.

Aaron guided him toward the exercise room. They stopped a few feet from the open door. The room was large, the width of the building. Light poured in through the windows facing Eighty-sixth. White walls glittered. Mirrors and a ballet bar were built in along the back. Music blared from a stereo as a dozen girls dressed in leotards moved in perfect cadence to the commands of their instructress, who wore white bloomers and a sleeveless black T-shirt with the words 'Hazel Carter' emblazoned across the chest.

Watching these women bend and sway, perform jumping jacks, then reach and stretch, Janek found himself transfixed. Young bodies straining for perfection in a huge white dazzling light-filled room – he didn't want to turn away. He could see this was a tough class. One would have to be young and limber to keep up. And the girls were working. Their leotards were soaked. An hour of this three times a week and their conditioning would be superb.

Aaron was chatting up Miss Tuttle. 'You have to be a model to get in?'

'If you're willing to work, then Miss Carter is pleased to have you. She doesn't care who you are as long as you don't slack off. Everyone's treated the same. Model, socialite or secretary. Everyone wears the same uniform, too – we supply everything except shoes.'

The music stopped. The class was breaking up. Some of the girls flung themselves down on mats. Hazel Carter strode out. She walked proudly, a lean, handsome, perspiring woman about forty-five years old with short-cut graying hair.

Cynthia introduced them.

'Just how can I help you, Lieutenant?'

Aaron pulled out his victim photographs, not the crime-scene shots but stills found in the apartments of the murdered girls. He showed Amanda first.

61

'That's Mandy Ireland,' Cynthia said. She gulped. 'At least I think.'

Hazel Carter struck her hand against her throat. 'That poor dear who was killed. Oh my God!'

'She came here regularly?'

'At least once a week.' Cynthia was already flipping the pages of her appointment book. 'Terrible. Such a ghastly thing. And only a few blocks away.' Hazel shook her head.

'Friday afternoon,' said Cynthia. 'She had a standing appointment for our class at four pm. Let's see, she goes back to April, March, February, but not January. I think she started this past winter, but I can check last year's book and make sure.'

'Do you remember her?' Janek asked.

Hazel Carter nodded. 'To me there are only two kinds, serious and frivolous. I tell the frivolous ones not to bother to come back. Mandy was serious. She didn't just go through the motions. She wasn't in a holding pattern trying to keep her figure trim. She was willing to reach deep into herself for that extra effort. That's what I look for and that's what I expect. I'm a demanding task mistress, Lieutenant. I ask a lot, everything a girl has. Anything less is not satisfactory, and when I'm dissatisfied I make my feelings clear.'

Some of the women who'd been in the last class were starting to drift out. Janek noticed one carrying a huge black leather portfolio, the sort that models haul around midtown. The girls that passed glowed with good health. Miss Carter paused to compliment them and she patted the model on her cheek. Janek had a sudden insight into Hazel Carter. He whispered to Aaron, 'Show her Brenda soon as she turns back.'

'What about her?' Aaron asked, offering the second photograph.

Hazel Carter stared. Janek watched her carefully, but her hand stayed at her side. 'Don't know. Familiar. But not a regular, for sure. I may have seen her. Can't be certain. Cynthia?'

Cynthia Tuttle nodded. 'Yes, she's been in, but not as a regular. I don't recall her name.'

'Maybe Beard. Maybe Thatcher. First name's Brenda,' Aaron said.

Cynthia looked through her book. 'Okay, we've had a Brenda Beard. Scattered classes, which means she took cancellations. Noon on July third. Two pm May fourteenth.' She found a few more listings, a total of six. Brenda had always paid in cash. None of her classes was also attended by Amanda, but the girls' lives had intersected, more or less.

A true intersection or a coincidence? People's lives crossed in Manhattan all the time. Outside the fitness center Janek paused, then led Aaron across the street. They stood there for a while watching the entrance. The last girls in the previous class drifted out, and new ones, for the next class, started coming in.

'That doorman on the left,' said Aaron. 'He's interested. He's enjoying the parade.'

'Looks out of place in that stupid coat.'

'For a guy who likes girls he's got himself a terrific job. Gets to look at what comes in and out next door, all day long, six days a week.'

Yes, it could have been the doorman, or someone else who lived near the gym, who'd seen Amanda and Brenda enter or leave and decided to trail them separately.

'Kind of weird setup, Frank. This Hazel Carter place squeezed between those towers. Models coming and going all the time visible to hundreds of up-scale residents and who knows how many assorted domestic help. Then you got Hindus downstairs working in that restaurant, and people like us lingering around, and ones who live behind here, too. I wonder why the hell they put French names on those apartment houses, then dress up the doormen like Englishmen.'

Janek smiled. Only a detective would ask a question like that. 'You get any feelings about that Carter woman?'

They walked to his car, then drove back to the precinct; Aaron had come to the gym by subway from his home.

'I saw that move to the throat, if that's what you mean. She didn't make it the second time.'

'Lot of people react like that. It's a fairly ordinary gesture of shock. By itself it doesn't mean too much, but I picked up on several other things.'

'Like that Hazel's probably gay.'

'That's part of it. I'm sure she is. But more interesting – a strong disciplinary streak. She went on too long about how stern she is. She called herself a "task mistress" and ran that class like a military drill. Women-only place, a perfect setup for someone who likes

63

beautiful girls. Then the whole relationship with Cynthia, sort of mistress/slave it seemed to me.'

'Yeah. I picked up on that.'

'So put it all together.'

'It's the one place we know where the victims' paths crossed.'

'And gay fits in with no semen in their bodies.' Janek glanced at Aaron. 'Say the girls didn't know each other, but they went to the same gym. So we look to the gym to see who knew them. Who do we find? A tough lesbian disciplinarian. Question: Is Hazel Carter capable of having perpetrated Switched Heads? She certainly got the physical strength for it, but does she have that kind of mind?'

'Want me to check her out?'

Janek nodded. 'And talk to Cynthia Tuttle again. Maybe you better try and catch her one evening at home. She didn't stall on Brenda, went right to it, found her name pretty fast in that book. As for Hazel, I can see one thing in her favor. She didn't move her hand to her throat when you showed her Brenda, which suggests she didn't know that Brenda was murdered, since we didn't tell her and there wasn't anything in the papers. On the other hand, she could be a very cool lady. You may want to ask her point-blank just where she was last Saturday night.'

He had called a meeting for noon at the precinct, before they broke for the weekend. Everyone was exhausted. Sal hadn't come up with anything. Taxi drivers, bus drivers, doormen, patrolmen on the beat – the killer hadn't attracted any noticed on his shuttles back and forth. Stanger and Howell's 'books' on the victims were getting thicker, but Amanda still looked like Little Miss Perfect and Brenda like a skilful professional whore. Friends had turned up with the details which fit these acknowledged patterns. There was more work to be done, many more interviews to be conducted, but nothing new was coming in.

Janek analyzed the Hazel Carter connection, and then the possibility the girls had been trailed. 'We got two very attractive young women who took gym class at the same place. Suppose our killer was hanging around. He sees Brenda and trails her. He sees Amanda and trails her. Why these two out of all the rest? Maybe he trailed others before he settled on them. Okay, say he picks them up there and finds out where they live and he follows them around and gets a certain impression of their lives. Then he gets this obsessive idea that their heads should be switched around. He doesn't want to kill them to have sex. He just wants to correct this problem with their heads. He *has* to make the switch, can't rest until this problem of two women walking around with the wrong heads is straightened out. His obsession builds and builds. He *has* to set it right. He plans it carefully, figures out when to do it, then takes the plunge and brings it off. It has to be a desperate act. He has to feel totally compelled. He gets the heads the way he wants them, and then he's exhilarated – the thing that was bothering him is now set right. He watches the papers. Nothing. His brilliant deed is not proclaimed. So, what's he thinking? Maybe that we're covering up. Maybe he's frustrated by that, or maybe he doesn't give a damn. The point I'm making has to do with motive. There's no motive to kill these women *except* to switch their heads. They weren't his enemies. He wasn't after them for money or sex. He had no particular relationship with either of them, and there was no old score he had to settle. He just had this thing about their heads. Now, what good does that line do us, supposing that I'm right? Not much good, because about all it tells us is that the motive is inside the killer's mind. There are no extrinsic facts that can lead us to him. It's one hundred percent psycho crime. Aaron has checked to see if there was ever another crime like it, anytime, anywhere, and apparently there's never been. Lots of dismemberments. Plenty of decapitations. But this is the first switch we know about, and now it's been a week.'

They all knew the odds; there were cops who taught them at the Police Academy. Seventy-two hours after a homicide with a cold trail you were talking one in ten. A week and still cold and you were probably talking less.

'Maybe he'll do it again,' said Sal. 'That would give us another trail.'

'We could stake out the gym. See if anyone hangs around,' said Stanger.

'That's a possibility. I'd have to go to Hart for extra men.'

'Maybe he'll come in on his own,' said Howell.

'I've been praying for that since I got this case.'

'Any way to bait him?' asked Aaron.

'I've been thinking about that. I can't see any way.'

'You could plant a story. Put some pressure on his pride.'

'Yeah, go public with the switch, get publicity, which could push him to write a letter. Then we'd have handwriting and spittle to work with, but of course we could get a thousand letters, too. And maybe if the papers built it up big enough we'd start getting imitations, other switches perpetrated by other weirdos in other boroughs – this is the sort of thing that could feed upon itelf.'

He shook his head. 'No weapon signature. No eyewitnesses. No connection except the gym. The only thing we got is a very peculiar message. What I want to know is: What was the killer trying to say? I've been over it and over it and I can't come up with anything except this notion that he wants the whore's head on the Madonna schoolteacher, and the other way around. Slut and nun. Switch them. Okay, that's a concept, but then the circle's closed. It doesn't take us outside his mind, doesn't lead us to a person. It doesn't lead us anywhere, in fact, except round and round and round.' He looked at them. 'The only thing I can see to do is keep talking, keep widening the circle. You stalk somebody, maybe the person notices, feels it, or feels uneasy, or is scared in a generalized sort of way. Maybe Amanda and Brenda told someone she was scared. So far the primary contacts say no. Maybe she mentioned it casually to someone else. We got to keep looking. Now, maybe I'm missing something. If anyone's got ideas, this is the time to speak.'

Stanger suggested they follow up on Amanda's dog. She walked her regularly, took a regular route. People might have noticed her and maybe noticed someone trailing behind.

Sure. A possibility. Go ahead, Stanger – check it out.

Howell wanted to round up whores. They liked to gossip about johns, he said. Maybe one of them had a head freak, a guy who mentioned casually or otherwise that so-and-so's body would look terrific with so-and-so's head attached.

Sure. Try it. You like the whores. Go ahead, Howell – round them up.

When the meeting broke up, Janek called Sal aside, asked him if he had a date. Sal said yes, but he was willing to cancel. They made arrangements to meet at an uptown coffee shop that evening at eight o'clock.

Rainstorm

Hard light, hard hot afternoon light, broke through the slats of the venetian blinds and fell upon the loft in bars. It striped them as they made love, turned the perspiration on their bodies into pearls.

Caroline's ceiling fan revolved, wobbling slightly in its socket. Her walls, high and white, were a glittering background for her photographs. The railings of her brass bed glowed, felt warm to Janek's touch. Caroline had tilted the big mirror above her dressing table so they could watch themselves in profile. Every so often as they stroked and kissed Janek looked at their reflection. The play of light, the stripes cast by the blinds, seemed to bind them to each other like bonds or straps.

A clatter somewhere in the building, as if the artist next door had dropped a pail of paint. A cat shrieked out on the stairs. In another loft a stereo was blasting; the vibrations reached them through the pillars. Sweat ran down their bodies. The beads merged into rivulets. Janek glanced at the mirror. Caroline's brown hair swung back and forth as she swayed upon him. Her eyes were shut; her mouth was half open as she gulped the humid air. She must have sensed his examination, because she opened her eyes – he could see her inspecting his thighs and legs clasped about her, his thumbs resting beneath her breasts and his fingers pressing lightly against her sides.

Outside a motorcycle coughed. The air hung steamy, almost tropical. Drops ran down between her breasts, fell upon his stomach. She twisted her fingers in the damp hair beneath her arms, raised and lowered herself seeking slow exquisite bliss.

The stripes upon them faded suddenly. Brilliant a moment before, they disappeared as the sky turned dark. Now they were barely visible in the mirror, and the loft seemed filled with dusk. Janek couldn't understand it. Was there a solar eclipse he hadn't read about? A lightning bolt. He arched up, thrust at her while it flashed to them through the slats. A crack of thunder – she moaned and shook. As the summer storm cloud burst she lowered herself upon him. They held each other, wrapped each other as they listened to the slashing rain and laughed.

Water beat against the windows of the loft. Janek could hear a hollow sound as rain battered the tops of cars out on the street. A hornet buzzed across the room. A faint smell of wet leaves and sex. Kissing and laughing, they pulled apart, carefully breaking the seal between their bodies. They lay on their backs, moist chests exposed to the fan. He put his arm around her, held her to him. After a while the sun turned bright and bars leaped again across the loft, striping them light-dark light-dark light-dark.

'What made you decide to become a cop?'

He looked at her. She was gazing up at the fan. 'You mean what's a nice guy like me doing in a lousy racket like this?'

'Oh, Janek.' She turned to him and smiled.

'You ask a tough question.' She waited for his answer. 'Well, whatever it was, it had nothing to do with why I stayed. Ask an old priest why he went into the priest business, or a whore why she started peddling her ass. They can hardly remember. They just fell into it. They were different people then. I was different. I thought a cop was something I'd like to be because it was exciting, paid a decent wage and there was a certain honor to the work. You know – a cop defended the Right against the Wrong. He Protected and he Upheld. If you were a cop you were maybe a little better than other people. You could be counted on. You were the guy they called when trouble hit.'

'You don't believe that anymore.'

He shook his head. 'I've been around too long. Anyway, it doesn't relate to what I do. I became a detective, and a detective is different from a cop. We investigate. We prowl around in people's lives. When we're good we make cases. I like that: get a case, get to the bottom of it, close it out, go on to the next. I like confessions too, like to watch and listen while a person unburdens himself, tells me what he's done. I can feel his need for me, feel I'm of use. And then there's the endless fascination of that thing I'm always looking for.'

'What's that?'

'The shadow. The side that's dark. The place where all the hurt and evil is. The shadow's there, in all of us, sometimes gray and faint, other times very deep and black. I'm attracted to it, and filled with pity on account of it, for all of us for having it within us, for myself too, perhaps, most of all. My wife used to mock me for saying that. "Isn't it just too heavy to bear, Frank, that gloomy load of pity you carry around?" But she was wrong. It's not too heavy. I like the feeling. I think it's the thing I like most about my life.'

He stopped talking and after a while, when he'd almost forgotten what he'd said, he heard her say, 'It's the thing I love most about you, too.'

Reconstruction

He met Sal at a coffee shop called Aspen. Darkness was settling upon the city, and the streets were still slick from the rainstorm that afternoon. Aspen smelled like a McDonald's, but there were copper pots hanging from the walls, the waitresses all spoke as if they'd gone to Finch, and the six-dollar burgers were accompanied by bean sprouts instead of fries.

They didn't talk much. Janek was Sal Marchetti's rabbi, and looking at the younger man he vowed Sal would never be awakened by a Sunday-morning call telling him his old mentor had eaten his thirty-eight.

Sal checked his watch. 'In about ten minutes she starts to walk her dog.'

'Okay, let's get over there.'

Janek left money on the table and they walked out to Madison, deserted this starry weekend night. In other neighborhoods, poorer ones, the heat of summer lured people into the streets, but on the Upper East Side over Labor Day weekend the streets were almost empty, everyone was at the Hamptons and the old apartment houses were locked up tight like silent brooding banks.

They got into Janek's car, drove down to Lexington, found a parking space between Eightieth and Eighty-first. There were five or six other spaces open on the block. No need to use the meter – it was night.

'Let's say he parks around here, waits till he sees her coming down Eightieth with the dog. He waits till she passes the car, then he knows he's got maybe twenty minutes to get inside.'

They got out, walked up toward the brownstone. They passed only one large apartment house. The doorman didn't turn.

'Was on last weekend,' Sal said. 'Didn't see a thing. Doesn't even recognize me now. Quiet around here, Frank.'

'Saturday night was a good night to do it.'

Sal glanced at him; they walked on.

There was a short narrow passageway beside Amanda's building, with a spring-locked grill-cage door. Behind the grill a row of trashcans. It took Janek eleven seconds to slip the catch. A minute later they had scaled a low wall and were in the garden behind the brownstone, beside the bottom of the fire escape.

'Don't like it, Sal. Too many windows in that big building on the corner. All it takes is one person looking out. And on his way up the ladder he's got to pass three apartments very close. Too risky. He didn't do it this way. Let's see if he came down from the roof.'

They went back out through the passageway, then around to the front of the brownstone. Six seconds to open up that door. They crept up the carpeted stairs. Two apartments to a floor, eight doors to pass. At the top Sal unbolted the fire door and they stepped onto the roof.

It was a typical flat asphalt roof sprouting chimneys and ventilator exhausts. The asphalt was still wet. There was a breeze. Janek was breathing hard from the climb; his shirt felt wet against his back.

Sal found the ladder, the built-in kind, rods sunk into the concrete. It led over the back wall of the roof and down the rear of the building to the fire-escape balcony just outside the windows of Amanda's studio. So it was easy, incredibly easy: slip the front-door lock with a plastic credit card, climb up to the roof, then lower yourself and climb on in.

'That fucking Stanger,' whispered Sal.

Janek had to agree. It was basic work on a robbery to figure out how an intruder had gotten in. This was a double homicide. It was inexcusable that Stanger hadn't checked the roof. Now they began to check it themselves, using flashlights they'd brought along. They didn't find anything except some old cigarette butts disintegrating in a puddle of rain.

'If this was a police procedural,' Sal said, 'we'd find a half-eaten eggroll tossed into the corner. We'd trace it back to a carry-out joint on Third Avenue on account of how they always cut their bean curd at an angle of thirty-two degrees. We'd question the help. No one would remember anything – they sell so much eggroll, you know. But then this old mamasan would come out. She'd remember. When the guy paid for his eggrolls she saw this Jap sword strapped on beneath his coat...'

They had climbed down the ladder, were perched now on the grilled balcony of the fire escape.

'... and that was weird because who wears a coat in New York in August?' Sal gently pried the window up. 'The mamasan remembered that and that the coat had these unusual epaulettes. We took her downtown and showed her our epaulette book. She pored over it. We were sweating buckets. Finally she paused. "That's the one," she said...'

They climbed into Amanda's apartment. Janek pulled the window shut and they peered around the dark room. Sal cut his saga short. Exactly a week before, a killer had come in, had stood where they were standing now.

They didn't speak as Sal hung the shower curtain which Janek had purchased on his way to Long Island City that afternoon. When Sal came out of the bathroom, Janek went in, stepped into the tub and carefully pulled the curtain closed.

He could hear Sal open the apartment door, then go out into the hall. Standing alone in the tub, he felt very strange. He didn't know how long he could bear to stand there, but when he heard the bolt snap open again he froze behind the curtain, spread his legs another half a foot, then planted his feet upon the porcelain. When the lights came on in the studio he raised his fist beside his shoulder and tried to control his breathing sounds.

'What about the dog?' Sal asked.

'She releases her as soon as she comes in.' Janek hated having to talk. His voice echoed against the tiles.

'Why doesn't she run into the bathroom and sniff you out?'

'She's thirsty from her walk. She goes straight to the water bowl beside the kitchenette.'

A pause. 'You don't own a dog, do you, Frank?'

Sal was right. He'd made a mistake. The plastic smell of the new shower curtain penetrated his nostrils; he wanted to cough.

Silence. Then the sound of music. Sal had turned the radio on. He walked into the bathroom, strode in like a man. Amanda would have slipped in quieter. Sal flicked on the light. 'Can't see you at all.'

Janek was silent. He could see Sal clearly in silhouette, and for a few seconds, when he tried to imagine Amanda there, he felt his heart speed up and a dry throbbing in his throat. Sal moved to the sink, turned on the faucet, bent slightly as if to brush his teeth. He was just inches away, his image sharp against the curtain.

'You know, it's strange to come in and find the curtain closed. After a shower you usually leave it open to dry the tub.'

'Or leave it closed to dry the curtain. That was her habit. He saw it was and took advantage of it.'

Janek sucked in his breath, then plunged. His fist landed firmly, the curtain pressed against Sal Marchetti's back.

They didn't bother to act out the rest of it, down on the floor with the curtain between them, though Janek imagined the chest-stabbing part, then the dog yelping, and his going into the studio to kick her unconscious, then coming back and dragging the girl over to the bed. Easy to slice off her head, take her keys from her purse, latch the window, turn off the radio and the lights, then let himself out. No sound in the hall. No traffic on the stairs. They walked straight out of the building and back down Eighty-first. When they reached the car they both were breathing hard.

'Madness, of course,' Janek said, 'but simple too. I think he took her head with him. The elegant way to do this is to cross town only twice.'

'What about the dog? I'm not happy about the dog.'

'Neither am I. Should have run an autopsy. By now she's cremated, of course. What about a chemical analysis of the water dish? He could have drugged the water, knocked the dog out that way. But I don't think so. I think he just took a chance and everything broke his way.'

'Could have run into someone on the stairs.'

'We didn't. Anyway, they're pretty badly lit.'

They drove to Seventy-ninth, took the transverse through Central Park, turned left on Central Park West, drove down to Seventy-first and turned right.

'Funny,' said Sal, 'I never figured a private car. Thought the parking would be too tough. But there're places around here too.'

Janek spotted a Buick pulling out, fought a short duel with a Mazda, slipped into the space. They were half a block from Brenda Beard's.

'He leaves Amanda's head in the trunk, goes to the regular phone booth over there. She sticks her head out the window. He waves to her and she beckons him up. She knew him. She wouldn't have let him in this late if she didn't.'

They walked to her building from the booth. 'He rings. She buzzes him in. Takes the elevator. Doesn't care if he's seen. People coming and going here all the time. She has a parade of guys. No one gives a fuck.'

After they went through the motions in the apartment, Janek looked down at the bed. 'He must have used some kind of plastic sheet. Then he took it with him. Now it starts getting cute. He takes Brenda's head down to the car, stashes it in the trunk, brings up Amanda's head and tries to screw it on real tight. When he has everything just the way he wants he goes back downstairs and drives to Lexington and Eighty-first. He carries the head bag up to Amanda's and lets himself back in with her keys. He arranges things there and goes back to his car. A good night's work. He's done.'

They went through it all without talking. No need to enact it, but Janek wanted to in case something happened that would spark off a new idea. Nothing happened. They did it just the way he said. Half an hour later they were finished. The run-through from start to end had taken them an hour and a half.

'Fucking impossible,' said Sal. They were sitting in the car again.

'So possible it kills you, right?'

'This guy had some kind of balls, Frank. Had to be the coolest guy in town.'

Janek nodded. 'Let's look at what we got. First there's a slight problem with the dog. Second, I can't prove Brenda knew him, but I'd bet my shield that she did. Third, two crosstown trips instead of three. And now that we know the parking's easy I think we can count on a private car. Now that leaves one other thing.'

'What?'

'Hiding in the shower.'

'What's wrong with that? You said she kept the curtain closed.'

Janek nodded. 'But I still don't like it. Not the curtain, but the shower. I felt funny in there. Too stylized. Too much like *Psycho*.'

'Like I keep telling you, Frank, this whole thing's like a fucking movie script. Anyway, in *Psycho* the girl was in the shower and the killer surprised her there.'

'Yeah, but it's the same idea. Maybe that's what's interesting. It's like some kind of reverse. Deliberate. Contrived. I didn't feel right in there. The whole thing's much too slick.'

'So where else would you hide?'

'Not behind the door. I have to make sure she's in and can't get out before I make my move.'

'So the bathroom's the best place, Frank. Unless you want to hide in the closet.'

'I guess it is.' Janek paused. 'Okay – let's go home.'

After he dropped Sal off he drove the streets aimlessly. He hadn't planned to go back to Caroline's but to spend the night at his own place and drop in on her Sunday afternoon. When he finally did get home he felt tired but had trouble falling asleep. It had been a tough evening. There was always a certain exhilaration after a run-through; he was never sure whether it came as a result of working hard or on account of something deeper, the vicarious pleasure of pretending to be a killer, trying to imagine the emotions of the ritual, feeling the surge of power a killer had to feel as he played out the drama of his crime. He had felt that on run-throughs before. It scared him. It was like entering a realm of madness. There had been an awful thrill to it this evening, too, something he had loathed and also had enjoyed.

Al's Clothes

Ten o'clock Sunday morning: Janek woke up with a start. The first anniversary, exactly a week since Al had pulled the trigger. Louella had phoned him that Sunday at 10:05. She'd awakened him and when he figured out what she was saying he had clenched his fists and beaten them against his bed.

He shaved, showered, got dressed and went out to a coffee shop on Broadway. He slipped into a seat behind the counter, ordered a mug of coffee and a bagel, and wondered how he was going to handle things today with Lou.

He was still wondering as he drove to Queens. He was going to lie to her and he wasn't going to enjoy that very much. She would look at him with her big sorrowful eyes and believe him because there wasn't any reason why she shouldn't. Already he was feeling uneasy, beginning to dislike himself, and starting to dislike Al too, for pulling that trigger and creating this situation he didn't want to face.

Stupid. How could he dislike Al? If it weren't for Al he'd never have met Caroline. Al was gone now and he was alive. He would just have to deal with Lou the best he could.

The DiMona house was on a side street in Corona that made him sad whenever he drove onto it, a residential street of 'starter homes' inhabited by middle-aged people who knew when they were starting out that they would probably end up there, too.

The house was wood-frame and narrow like its neighbors, with a brick porch added to the back. A big TV antenna, a meager barbecue pit and some redwood outdoor furniture. The clapboard on the outside was starting to peel. Al had said he was going to paint it himself in the fall when the days were cooler and he wouldn't feel dizzy on the ladder.

The card table where he'd been whittling just before he'd fired had been folded up and stored away. Lou led him into the living room. Al had hated it. Gold carpeting. Gold velour upholstered sofa. Gold tassels on the cushions. Coffee table made out of a lacquered antique trunk. They sat on the sofa with an empty space between them, facing each other but with their legs sticking straight out.

'Dolly still here?' Janek asked.

'She went back to Pontiac.'

'What about the move to Houston?'

'She's putting that off awhile.'

'Look, Lou, this is a stupid question. It's only been a week. But I wondered if things were better now.'

She nodded. 'They have counseling people down at Police Plaza. They helped me take care of the paperwork, and there's a therapy group I can join if I want.'

'Think you will?'

'Don't know. They have groups for divorced wives too. Sarah was thinking about getting involved in one right after you walked out. They know about all the problems and they have the support systems to help. For leftover people like Sarah and me. God, I'm sorry, Frank. I didn't mean that the way it came out.'

He didn't answer. She turned away. 'Sarah called me when she heard,' she said. 'She asked about you, too. I didn't tell her much. I think she'd still like you to come back. You ever think about that, Frank? It might help, you know. I hate to think you'd do what Al did. They say being alone just makes things worse.'

He cut her off. 'I know you mean well, but I want you to stop that stuff right away. I don't want to go back to Sarah. If I did I'd shoot myself for sure.'

'She says you never call her anymore.'

'That's right. I don't. When I used to call all she'd do was complain about the appliances. The dishwasher was out. What should she do? The disposal's stuck up. Who should she call to get it fixed? The car won't start. The furnace runs too cold. The water's brown. The roof's sprung a leak. I told her, "It's your house now. It's up to you. You get a good hunk of my salary and you have a bookkeeping job and a nice house and I'm living in a semi-basement and driving a Volvo that ought to be sold for scrap. So worry about your own goddamn appliances." I told her that, and she didn't call me anymore.' He shook his head. 'It's been almost two years.'

Lou nodded. She'd tried, said whatever she'd promised Sarah she would say, and now he knew it was his turn to keep his promise, his turn now to lie.

'I checked around a little about what you told me.'

'He was working on something, Frank. Did you find out what it was?'

Janek paused. 'I don't think he was exactly working on something, Lou, in the sense that he was doing anything more than walking around thinking about things, maybe visiting a few old crime scenes, stuff like that. He wasn't entitled to carry on an investigation, you know. He had a lot of experience and he was like an old racehorse. He liked to get out and trot a little, work up a little sweat. It's hard to stop cold. So he spun his wheels. But there wasn't any particular case he was working on. Unless he mentioned something to you.'

'He said there was a case.' She spoke abruptly to signal he was going to have to work harder if he wanted to change her mind.

'There're always cases, Lou. You know that. Ones you never solve. Al had this expression. He'd say, "Such-and-such case was like that broad in high school you wanted but could never make. You'd make the other girls and then forget them, but the one you couldn't have, you'd think about her all your life".'

She smiled. 'Sounds like Al. Still, he was out so late those times.'

'He'd meet some of the guys after work. They'd have a few drinks and talk. He liked that. He didn't want to stay home all day. You knew him. He was an active guy. I just wish he'd found himself a better hobby than trying to put together boat models and whittle flutes.'

'He didn't like that. He hated that.'

'Why the hell did he do it, then? And make that huge investment in woodworking tools? There must be a couple grand worth of stuff downstairs.'

'God, I wish I knew. It was like he thought, All right, now I'm retired, so the thing to do is have a hobby. So then he went out and bought himself a hobby without even trying it out to see if he liked it first.'

'Okay, Lou, let's suppose he was working on a case. Let's even say he was working seriously, unauthorized, you understand. Now, does it make sense, then, that he would have shot himself? You know it doesn't. He hated to leave anything undone. That's why I say he was spinning wheels.'

She studied the carpet for a while, then looked up and nodded. She believed him, as he knew she would. It wasn't a bad lie, nothing wicked, nothing that would do her any harm, but it made him feel uneasy, and then, as if she could read his mind, she suddenly asked him a question that made him turn away.

'How about you, Frank? Someone in your life?'

'Did Sarah ask you to ask me that?'

'Of course not. Oh – Frank . . .'

He studied her, could see that she was lying, and he was glad because that made him feel better about having lied to her.

'There wasn't for a long time,' he said. 'I'm not a woman chaser –

you know that. But recently I met someone, and, well, it's someone I like a lot. She makes me happy. I'd be even happier if I wasn't boxed in with a stinking case.'

She asked if he wanted another cup of coffee. He looked at his watch and shook his head. She led him down to the basement to Al's den where he'd kept his woodworking tools, his unconstructed model kits, his little refrigerator stocked with beer and his supplementary TV. She had gathered all his clothing together, everything she could find in all the drawers and closets of the house, and she had it all arranged neatly in piles on the couch and the chairs and on the workbench too.

'I called the Salvation Army. They're coming tomorrow. Anything you want, better take it now.'

Janek looked at the clothes. He didn't want anything. He shook his head. 'Wrong size,' he said.

She hugged him suddenly and he hugged her back and patted her hair and cuffed her on the shoulder and told her she should call on him, that he was always available, that he'd always come if she needed anything.

'I know that, Frank. We both loved you very much. I hope you're happy with this new gal of yours.' She walked him to his car.

Janek in Love

There was a note tucked into Caroline's door telling him she was at the tennis club. He decided that rather than wait he would go there and watch her play. He drove the short distance slowly, examining the neighborhood – industrial buildings, warehouses, auto-body shops, a delicatessen, a discount rug outlet store and a Laundromat.

He parked in front of the club, wandered in, finally found her playing mixed doubles on one of the outdoor courts. She waved when she saw him. The Sunday sun was hot. He found an old aluminum-frame chair, dragged it over to one of the net posts and sat down.

She was wearing a skimpy tennis dress that exposed her glistening back. She didn't play girlish tennis, but stepped powerfully into her strokes. He liked the way she moved, economical, direct. She played without tricks, the same way she made love; there were solid thunks when her racket met the ball.

Her partner was a lean young man with muscular arms and an athlete's vacant stare. The opponents were an exuberant bearded man with a strong squat torso and a willowy girl who uncoiled a ferocious serve. Janek was no tennis expert, but he could see that the women were the superior players. It was a serious match – rushes to the net, leaps to smash, hard backhands fired crosscourt. Tough competitive play, not social Sunday tennis. He felt a little envious, wishing he were part of it.

After the match the players met at the net, then Caroline brought them over to be introduced. They all moved to the club terrace, took a table and ordered. Cokes and beers. There was talk of an upcoming autumn tournament, rackets and string jobs, an assistant pro trying to make out with someone's daughter. Listening, he felt separate, dressed differently and cool, while they sat warm and pungent, bounded by their play.

Caroline must have sensed his awkwardness. She turned to him often and smiled. When she mentioned that he was a detective there was a small stirring around the table. The bearded man, a cardiologist, announced that Janek was the first detective he had ever met.

'I met one once,' the floppy girl said. 'Real nice guy. Interviewed me after I was mugged.'

'They get the mugger?' Caroline's partner asked.

When the girl shook her head, Janek added, 'We rarely do.'

Later he wondered why he'd said it; he'd sounded defensive in a way he hadn't meant. After that exchange the conversation wound down. One by one the players left for the locker rooms until finally he was left alone.

When Caroline returned he had finished a second beer. Her hair was still wet from her shower.

'Sorry about those people. They're not important. Just tennis friends.' She smiled.

'Nice people. Don't apologise for them.'

'Boring people. And you're right – I won't.' She studied him.

'Something the matter? Bad this morning with Mrs. D?'

He shook his head. 'That went pretty much the way I thought.'

'But something's bothering you. I can tell.'

He nodded.

'Want to talk about it?'

'It wouldn't be the nicest story you ever heard.'

'Why don't you tell me anyway.'

He saw she was serious, waiting for him to speak. For a moment he hesitated. He'd resolved not to burden her with his case. But it was part of his life, it was gnawing at him, and now she was asking him to share. 'Okay,' he said, 'but stop me when you've heard enough.' Then he told her the saga of Switched Heads.

She listened well. He could not imagine Sarah ever listening to him so well, or Lou DiMona, or any other detective's wife. Such women cut off or turned brittle when the conversation turned to work, as if the substance of a detective's life was so awful it was best ignored. But Caroline was different, had photographed a war, had been intimate with violence, cruelty and death.

'... still got to look at that gym teacher,' he said, 'but I doubt there's anything there. Last night, standing behind the shower curtain, I had this feeling there were things I'd seen that hadn't registered on me yet. Things I knew but didn't understand, that kept backing out of reach. Thought about it again this morning and just now when you were changing. I keep coming back to those photographs.' He glanced at her. 'Ugly. Really ugly stuff.'

'I've seen a lot of ugly stuff. You want me to look at them?'

'Would you?' She was marvelous; by some miraculous process she could read his mind.

'Of course. But I'm no detective.'

'I wouldn't want you to be. I'd just like you to look at them as a professional photographer and tell me what you see.'

She stood up. 'Okay. Let's go.'

'Drive into the city now?'

'Why stall around? You want me to look. Take me in, Janek. I'm ready to go to work.'

As they drove into Manhattan he told her more. 'I knew, soon as I got this, it wasn't going to be my kind of case. I'm good when I can see things through someone else's eyes, but this is so far from anything I can understand that I knew up-front I wasn't going to link in without pushing myself to a place I'd never been.'

Her eyes glowed outside the precinct house. She sniffed the air expectantly as they walked through and then up the stairs in back. 'Perfect,' she said, 'that crummy smell.' She smiled. 'Criminals and cops.'

When they reached the squad room he exposed the wall where Aaron had mounted the crime-scene photographs. Then he withdrew to his swivel chair, waiting to hear what she would say.

She stood before each shot, stared at it, then moved on to the next. The room was still. He could feel her concentration, the intensity of her gaze, although he could not see her eyes. Watching her from behind, he felt moved by her posture, the proud way she stood before each awful photograph.

It was ten minutes before she spoke, a long time, time enough for a large amount of tension to build up. When she did speak finally, she didn't turn, but continued to stand with her back to him, facing the wall.

'Photography's primitive, but these are powerful pictures. Tabloid style. It's all the rage today. Some of the serious young photographers are trying to imitate it. You know – shoot like street paparazzi, pop off flashbulbs and capture the hard surface of events. Stick these shots on the wall of a trendy gallery and some critic will come along and call them art. "As sensational, powerful and pure as a blundering crime-scene photographer's work". But this isn't a gallery. These were taken by a real police photographer. Still, there's something self-conscious in them. A special artistry. And power.'

She paused, peered at the wall again as if trying to discover what she meant. 'No attempt to pretty up. This isn't the German School of Artistic Cruelty. No models posing like they're dead. These women *are* dead. But there's something going on.'

She paused again: 'Maybe it's the tension. Between the artlessness of the camera work and the artistic way that everything's arranged. I don't know. Looks to me like the subject matter, the girls, their heads, the bedding, the blood – like all that's been arranged for maximum effect.' She turned to him with a querying expression. 'Guess that doesn't make much sense.'

'We'll see if it does,' he said. 'What do you mean by "arranged"?'

'Like it's been set up.'

'You mean whoever did this set things up so what he'd done would get photographed in this powerful way?'

'I know that sounds crazy...'

'Why don't you show me what you mean.'

She turned back to the wall. 'The heads, of course. The faces and all that. But I'd go further. I'd say the wrinkles on the sheets. They're not random. Too perfect, too precise. You could spend an hour setting up shots like these, altering the bedding, creating shadows on the pillows, stringing out the hair, fluffing it out the way it's fluffed out here. It's as if killing them and switching them wasn't enough. As if he had to fuss with them afterward. Arrange things for his pleasure. You know – to please his eye.'

She paused again, but he didn't cut in; he could sense she had more to say. 'There's another thing. Don't quite know how to explain it. But...' She paused. 'It seems to me there's something almost loving in these shots. Not loving towards the victims. I don't mean that. But I feel somehow that afterward, after he did this cruel thing, they were handled... lovingly.' She turned back to Janek, perplexed.

They drove uptown in silence. He found a parking space near his building, then guided her on foot into Central Park. The sun, low in the sky, about to sink behind the apartment houses on Central Park West, cast a soft glow over the meadows and lengthened the shadows of the elms.

He placed his arm about her waist as they strolled along a bridle path. There was a scent of foliage about to decay, the sweet smell of late-summer grass. To Janek the park, so roughly trod upon through July and August, became suddenly transformed. This living room of the city, so badly used for months, became a garden of delights. Each tree seemed etched from every other. Each leaf and bush asserted itself as unique. Even the vandalized streetlamps and ruined benches looked graceful despite abuse. He was suffused by a sense of beauty, the perfect symmetry of nature, of his and Caroline's place in the scheme, and was filled with a mellow happiness.

He looked at her, could see that her thoughts were someplace else. Feeling her restlessness, he asked her gently what was wrong.

'Just wondering – am I going to end up like that?' She glanced quickly at him, then stared ahead.

'Like what?'

'Those girls. The ones in your case.'

He tightened his arm around her. 'How can you think a thing like that?'

She shook her head. 'Just seeing those pictures, the way the girls looked. Aggression, violence – my subjects maybe because they scare me so much and I'm working with them now to try and confront my fear. I've wondered why aggression intrigues me. I think I've always had this idea I was going to end up a victim of it, bloody, broken, maybe cut up. I have a recurring fantasy of myself trapped in a smashed-up car, with frightened people peering in through the windows and others trying to drag me out of the wreckage and my life just seeping away in a steady stream of blood. I look around and notice almost casually that one of my legs is gone. "My goodness," I say to myself, "I seem to have lost my leg." And then I close my eyes and die.'

She grasped him, placed her hand upon his chest so he could feel his heart beating against her palm. He wrapped her in his arms, stroked her hair and told her he would protect her from everything she feared. We all live under the threat of violence, he told her; that's what it means to live in a city – to have fear constantly in the background of our lives. So we protect ourselves by imagining the worst things happen that can happen, a kind of magical thinking, he explained, a sort of talisman against our fright.

It was her first visit to his apartment. Her face was rapt as he unlocked the caged outer door, led her through the short tunnel beneath the steps, unlocked the solid door and showed her in. She looked around slowly, curiously, taking in each piece of furniture. He watched as she moved about lightly touching his refrigerator, his reading chair, his bureau, his bed, and then the inherited workbench covered with the entrails of accordions and all of his father's special tools.

She picked up a small accordion, opened it, touched several of the keys. The sound was blunt and awful. They laughed.

'Play for me, Janek,' she said. 'Please play for me.'

He hesitated. He rarely had time to play; lately, when he touched the instruments it was only to be certain that they worked. His father's old accordions from Hungary and Austria were sentimental artifacts. But when she asked him to play for her he knew he could not refuse.

83

He went to a closet, hauled out his best accordion, a depression-era model made at the Damian shop. She withdrew to his bed, sat there elbows on her knees while he strapped on the harness and turned his workbench chair so it faced the room.

He played some scales, warming up his fingers, then little melodies that whimpered through the pipes. He went on to melancholy carnival tunes, and when he felt limber and glanced at her and saw she was watching carefully he played Scarlatti for her, then shifted to Rimsky-Korsakov, then on to Khachaturian, playing louder and louder, fuller and fuller, playing on until the light faded from the windows and the room finally turned dark. She switched on the lamp beside his bed and he continued playing, all the music he had ever known. He played out of his love for her, played like a troubadour courting his lady, while she sat enraptured, her eyes never leaving his face, the two of them immersed in each other, enveloped by the sound.

Limitless Depths

They overslept Monday morning, woke languorously like lovers on a holiday, and then, as they were sipping coffee, Janek suddenly remembered that he had a case. He moved too fast then, shaved too quickly, and cut the underside of his jaw. He held a tissue to the wound but could not stanch the flow. Caroline inspected it, cleaned it for him, then pressed on it like a sorceress until, miraculously, it closed.

When he dressed she handed him his thirty-eight and watched keenly as he strapped it on. 'They say you can tell a lot about a cop by the way he handles his weapon,' she said. 'But I think it's the putting on and taking off that really says the most. I like watching you do it. In the morning when you arm yourself you show me your competence and power. At night when you put it down gently on the bedside table you show me that you're vulnerable and that you don't have to prove you aren't.'

Driving her to Long Island City, he thought about what she'd said. It was fantastic the way she observed him, read the details of his life.

On his way back to Manhattan, coming off the Queensboro Bridge, he got stuck in traffic – people fuming, honking, while a rookie cop on the ramp tried helplessly to undo the snarl. He looked at two men in the next car and tried to imagine that their heads were switched. There were two women in the car on the other side and he played the same game with them. He looked rapidly from one to the other, switching their heads in his mind. He put the traffic rookie's head on one of the women and then switched the heads in the car stalled in front. The more times he tried it, the easier it became. Back and forth, on and off, try him on her and hers on him – a strange disquieting exercise. He wondered what it would be like to go around the city for weeks working himself into that. Could get to you, catch you up, make you crazy, he thought. Start thinking like that, he thought, and it could lead to something very bad.

It was nearly ten when he reached the precinct house, late for a special squad commander starting his second week on a priority double homicide. He took the steps two at a time, hearing trouble even before he reached the door.

Sal and Stanger were standing at opposite ends of the squad room gesturing angrily while containers of coffee grew tepid on their desks. A full-scale shoot-out: Sal was giving it to Stanger for not checking Amanda's roof, and Stanger was lashing back as best he could.

'What the fuck kind of detective are you? What kind of asshole investigation's that?'

'Fuck you, Marchetti – you've been bugging me from the start. You're such a hotshot, what have you come up with? A big fat zero. Shit.'

Janek told them to shut up. Silence. Scowling. Then some cautious circling around. 'This coffee's crap,' snorted Sal. Stanger laughed. He announced that he was going to start checking on Amanda's dog-walk routine if that was okay with the lieutenant, and that his victim profile book on Amanda was waiting on the lieutenant's desk.

Janek leafed through the looseleaf notebook. 'Looks like you got her down fairly well,' he said. After Stanger left he spoke without looking up. 'Really think it helps to crush his ego, Sal?'

Sal apologized. 'But just thinking about it yesterday pissed me off. Suppose there'd been something up there. Gone now, swept away, or washed away by the rain. He says he checked out the super, but how do we know? Can we trust him or do we have to double-check everything he does?'

Sal left for an interview with an assistant DA about disputed evidence in another case. When Janek was alone he went to the wall and stood again before the photographs. Caroline had said the victim shots looked arranged. Now, when he studied them fresh, he saw what she meant.

The phone rang. It was Sweeney. Hart wanted to see Janek at two o'clock. Back to the wall. 'Arrange things for his pleasure, to please his eye,' Caroline had said. Dr. Yosiro had spoken of a man who had presumed to create new human beings. So, someone artistic, creative, a creative killer. Someone who could turn a double murder into a puzzle, a design.

Aaron came in. 'Scratch Hazel Carter, Frank. But you were right about her social life. She and little Miss Tuttle make whoopie-do together in a hi-rise off Gracie Square. Unfortunately it happens they spent that weekend at a friend's place in Dutchess County, which still leaves the gym as a possible starting point.'

'Well, I'm not scratching her yet, not before you check out the alibi. Talk to the "friend". Look at her hard. Be sure she's telling the truth.'

He told Aaron then about Caroline's analysis of the photographs and about his Saturday night walk-through with Sal.

'Sounds like you walked through a little fast,' Aaron said. 'You did the whole thing in an hour and a half, but she says it could have taken an hour at each end to fix things up. You know, there's something very relaxed about that. Certain and very confident.'

'Superbly planned.'

'Maybe perfectly planned.'

'He knew what he was going to do before he started. But do you think all that multiple stabbing was relaxed?'

'That's what doesn't fit, that violent stabbing and then the precise and careful work afterward with the heads.'

'Two signatures. Two weapons. What about two people? Or one person with two personalities? My photographer friend said she felt he handled the victims "lovingly."'

'Sure, kill them violently, then gently love them up. Once they stop moving you can do what you want with them. Mold them to your will.'

'But they're still warm and bleeding. You'd have to be a freak to be able to play with them and stay detached.'

'For Christ's sake, Frank, we know we're dealing with a freak.'

'An artistic freak.'

'Sure. A very artistic kind of freak.'

In the subway on his way downtown Janek played switched-heads with the other passengers. Crushed together on the seat, their heads at nearly the same level, it was even easier than in the car. Two high-school girls side by side. Bang! Switch them. Then switch them back. If he shifted his eyes fast enough he could do it almost instantaneously. The process reminded him of police artists calling up features onto computer screens. A way to design people, or to redesign them. Police artists. Someone artisic. A painter, sculptor or photographer. After his frenzy the killer was relaxed ... But there was still something gnawing away at the back of Janek's brain. Forget it. Let it simmer. The thing now, he knew, was to improvise a theory he could use to dazzle Hart.

He switched more heads as he crossed Police Plaza, and some more in the elevator on his way to Hart's floor. He switched a pair of secretaries walking toward him down the hall, but knew that the difference between imagining it and doing it was as great as the difference between fantasizing making love to them and raping them in a parking lot.

'Anyone look at that engine yet, Lieutenant?' Sergeant Sweeney grinned at him from behind his well-ordered desk.

'What?'

'Your car. Remember – *I drove your car*.'

'Yeah.' Janek nodded. 'Didn't you mention a garage?'

Sweeney snatched a card out of a drawer, scribbled '20% Discount' on it, stamped it with an NYPD seal, then initialed the back. Janek didn't like Sweeney and for a moment he thought about tearing the card in two and dropping the pieces on the desk. But then there was a buzz, Sweeney picked up his phone, listened, nodded and, in the special tone of an usher on intimate terms with power, whispered, 'CD will see you now, Lieutenant,' while he drew a neat line through Janek's name on his appointment list.

Hart was pale. Like most of the chiefs he spent too much time indoors. Janek recognized the pallor, flesh cooked sallow by fluorescent lamps. And, as always, he was struck by Hart's eyes, cold lifeless glowing little stars.

'So, how's it going, Frank? Things okay? That DiMona woman settling down?'

'Looked in on her yesterday. She's doing about as well as you'd expect.'

'Good.' Hart sounded pleased. 'Better keep an eye on her anyway. I thought she looked pretty raw. Any clue yet what was going on with DiMona the last few weeks?'

Janek shook his head.

'Burn-out, I guess. Postretirement kind. Department commissioned a study some years back. We wanted to know the danger signs so we could put the wives on alert. If that wife of his had gotten the word she might have saved herself a lot of grief. So...' Suddenly Hart beamed. 'How goes Ireland/Beard?'

Janek shrugged. 'Still not coming clear.'

'It will. It will. You must have some kind of theory. I know you're not sitting on your can.'

'Got some theories, sure.'

'Like what?'

'Walked through it Saturday night. Was struck by how thrilling it must have been.'

'A real thriller. Yeah. Looked into voodoo? I was thinking about voodoo the other day.'

'Doesn't check out.'

'Try some of our black detectives. Lots of experience there. Great resource waiting to be tapped. Sex?'

'No semen.'

'So he wore a rubber. I never heard of a whore who didn't have semen in her ears.'

'Doesn't smell like sex to me.'

'Then what *does* it smell like?' Hart was getting irritable.

Janek spoke softly. 'I'd say some very special kind of thrill.'

'You keep talking about thrills. You mean the switch?'

'The whole ritual. The switch would have been part of it,' Janek agreed.

Hart scratched the side of his face. Janek could hear his nails scrape his cheek. 'Sorry, Frank, you're losing me. Just what are you trying to say?'

Janek stood up, picked a speck out of his eye, walked over to the window, peered down at Police Plaza, at the hundreds of people crossing the square, so rapidly, like ants. He turned. 'There's only one connection we can find between the victims, and that looks like a typical New York coincidence.'

'There's got to be a connection.'

'Sure. But it's not like the whore taking French lessons in the morning and the French teacher was whoring after work. The connection's in the killer's mind. It's like you told me in the car. A psychological crime. The killer's fantasy. His stunt. His private little treat.'

Hart held his face as if struck by a migraine. His cold little eyes were sparkling now with pain. 'You're still being enigmatic, Frank.'

Janek turned back to the window, looked down again at the figures scurrying below and practiced switching a couple of their heads. 'When someone's dead,' he said, 'and you do something to his body, you're not doing anything to him ... you're making a display. Like in war when the enemy kills one of your guys and they strip him and set him up in the forest with his genitals cut off and stuck into his mouth. They haven't done anything sadistic to him, because he was already dead before the mutilation was carried out. They've done it for your benefit, the guy who finds him later, and, on a deeper level, they've done it for themselves. The ostensible purpose is to demoralize you. A display like that fills the viewer with anger and despair. It works subconsciously ... breaks down the spirit, replacing the cool skill it takes to fight with a hot and clumsy debilitating rage.' He turned back to Hart. Not a bad improvisation; he wondered if the Chief was dazzled.

'So if that's the ostensible purpose, what's the real one?'

'The underlying benefit is for the displayers themselves, a way of acting out their anger coolly without having to worry about the person fighting back. Or squirming, or screaming, arousing their pity or making them afraid. A dead guy's just so much meat, so you can treat him like meat. Maybe you kill him in anger so you can cut him up afterward with an almost kindly feeling in your heart.'

Hart was slowly nodding his head. 'I think I see what you mean.'

Janek didn't understand how that was possible, since he couldn't see it himself. 'Anyway,' he said, 'here's the bottom line. Whoever did this gave himself a lot of satisfaction, a good part of which could have been the effect it would have on us. The business with the heads is so implausible it makes me wonder if that may have been his point. To add a complication which would be even more disturbing than the homicides. A way to almost beautify his crime, turn his maniacal rage into a twisted kind of art.'

Hart sucked in his lips. 'That's one weird theory, Frank.'

'This is one weird case.'

'What you're telling me sounds very strange.'

'I know. Deep waters. Limitless depths.'

'More like you're setting up to dump this one in the files. Because if you're saying what I think you're saying, you're telling me you may never run it down.'

Janek shook his head. 'All I'm telling you is I don't think I'm going to solve it by turning up some overlooked piece of physical evidence, or, excuse the expression, by good old-fashioned detective work.'

Hart leaned back disgusted. He didn't like the reference to his own frequent exhortations to 'wear down shoe leather' and 'in my experience it's the tedious routine work that breaks the case.' He examined Janek skeptically. 'So how *are* you going to solve it?'

'Maybe by inspiration,' Janek said.

Hart snorted with amusement. His little eyes glinted now with mirth. 'Grand. That's grand, Frank. Well, you just go uptown and get yourself inspired. And if anything hits you and it happens to work out, please be sure and let me know.'

At the precinct house that afternoon, a carnival atmosphere: Howell and his promised roundup of Upper West Side whores. Other detectives assigned to the Sixth came in to help keep order and watch the fun: an endless stream of squealing, chattering, hooting ladies of the night.

Formal interviews: 'Now, in regard to your clients, Ms. Fernandez...' Snappy retorts: '*Head* freaks? Johns into *heads*? Honey, they're *all* into heads. I mean *head* is where it's at...'

Janek enjoyed the parade, a respite from the frustrations of the case, and he could see that Howell reveled in it. Howell would make a great Vice Squad detective, he thought; he took the proper corrupting pleasure in depravity.

While Janek watched he practiced switching heads. He tried out a bleached blonde's on a black girl, and then the reverse. But by seven o'clock things started growing tense. Howell was cutting into working hours, the humor was wearing thin, and none of the women had even heard of Brenda Beard. Janek finally shooed them out; Howell could finish with them downstairs. When, finally, the squad room was cleared, he and Aaron were left alone. Aaron studied the victim profile books. Janek, sensing a glimmer of a notion, went again to the wall and stood before the crimescene photographs.

He looked, stared, peered, walked away, strode back and squinted again, bringing his face up close. Yes, there was something. He tried it again. *Yes.* Feeling a small rush of triumph, he called Aaron to the wall.

'Remember how we stood here the first day? The way we paced back and forth studying the shots?'

'Sure. Something bugged us.'

'Remember what you said?'

'I said "too perfect."' Aaron paused. 'Didn't I?'

'You also said "contrived."'

'Yeah. I remember now. That's sort of like your lady friend's "arranged."'

'You said, "Something that hits you until you look too hard and then you don't see it anymore."'

Aaron agreed that that was what he'd said.

'Okay. I want you to try something.'

Janek unpinned two of the photographs, one from each side, shots taken of each victim from approximately the same angle directly above their beds. He pinned them back onto the cork beside each other in an empty space.

'Now what I want you to do is shift your eyes back and forth and try and switch the heads in your mind. What happens is you hold the image of one and superimpose it for a split second on the other. You may have to practice. I've been doing it all day. Took me a while to get the knack.'

Aaron tried it. Then he stood back and blinked. 'They keep slipping back to where they belong.'

'The idea is to carry a face a little to the side. Try moving one. Move Amanda right to left. Leave Brenda where she is.'

'Okay.'

'Now move Brenda.'

'This is tough work, Frank. All I'm getting is a kind of flash.'

'A flash is good. A flash is all you need.'

'Strange – I mean what I'm doing here is putting them back together the way they were.'

'Right. You're putting them back together. So keep on doing it awhile.'

'It's coming now. You're right. It does get easier.'

'Keep going.'

'What am I looking for?'

Janek was silent.

'Wow. This could get to be a nasty habit.'

Janek stood back; he didn't want to lead Aaron on.

'Hmmm. "Something that hits you until you look too hard and then you don't see it anymore."'

Silence.

'Now I'm getting confused.'

'How?'

'Getting them mixed up.'

'Go on.'

'They seem almost . . .'

'*What?*'

'I don't know – interchangeable?'

Janek exhaled. 'That's it.'

Aaron shut his eyes tight to clear away the images. He turned from the wall. 'You mean that they fit each other so well?'

'You got it. I think that's what we saw before. And it goes with something else that's strange about this case, something we've never talked about. Remember how the people who first found the bodies weren't sure what they'd seen. Pierson didn't notice that it wasn't Amanda. He took one quick look, then turned away. It didn't register on the super either. And Bitong said he thought something was wrong but he didn't know exactly what. When you think about it, that was pretty strange, and that it took the Medical Examiner to discover there'd been a switch. Look at their faces again. They're similar, not identical, not like twins or even sisters, but close enough so you could get confused. Same features, roughly the same-shaped eyes and chins, same hair color, similar haircut, same age and size. If you squint – well, on a quick-glance basis they look more or less the same.'

Aaron studied the photographs. 'I think that's true. Funny it didn't register.'

'You explained it yourself. If you look hard enough you don't see it anymore. The resemblance is superficial. When you look for it it disappears. I think, too, if we'd seen the bodies it would have been clearer than it is in photographs.'

Aaron grinned. 'That's fantastic, Frank. You're good. I'm sure you're right. But -' he looked at Janek evenly - 'okay, you got something. So now tell me what it means.'

Janek smiled, walked back to his swivel chair, sat down and stretched his legs. He waited while Aaron poised himself on the rear ledge of his desk.

'Suppose the resemblance is the connection we've been looking for. Quite a different thing than mounting a blonde's head on a brunette. Seems to me if you wanted to make these women look different you wouldn't choose this particular pair.'

'So?'

'So, suppose you don't want them to look different. Suppose you want to keep them looking pretty much the same.'

'Why?'

'To change them in a certain way, but keep the illusion going that you haven't. Take Amanda: so distant, self-contained, inaccessible. Stick the head of a whore who sort of looks like her on her and you give her a whore's personality. Better still, stick her head on the body of a whore and you get an Amanda who's basically a slut.'

'What about the other way around? Stick Brenda's head on Amanda's body and that way clean up her act.'

'Sure. But why bother? I'm betting on Amanda. She's the one you can't get to, the one you'd want to change. She's so good, you know, so clean, the kind you'd want to dirty up. It seems to me that, once you decide on that, it's a relatively simple matter to shop around for a whore who looks the same and, when you find her, start to plan your switch.'

'A head-hunting expedition. I don't know, Frank. You're in the stratosphere. I mean, if that's what you want to do, why not just mount Amanda's head on the whore and leave it at that?'

'Then what do you do with Brenda's head?'

'What difference does it make? Stash it in the closet. Roll it under the bed.'

Janek shook his head. He felt sure Aaron was wrong. 'You're neat and orderly. You're an artist constructing a puzzle. You're into symmetry and design. You don't like loose ends, so you've got to replace the head you took.'

Aaron gazed at him, then announced that he was going home. He'd participated in some pretty weired brain-storming sessions since he'd been in the division, he said, but tonight's was the weirdest yet. He turned when he reached the door. 'This kind of stuff can make you crazy, Frank. I'd come down off it if I were you. You got a theory, sure, and for all I know you're right. But where does it leave you? How does it help you find the guy?'

Janek wasn't sure where or how, but he felt that it would help, that if he could enter into the madness of this crime the madman would stand revealed. There was always a reason. Killings for gain or revenge were easy, the motives obvious and stark. This was a crime conceived in the shadows and carried out purposefully in the night. There was precision in it and passion. Concentrated rage and a love of order. A need to beautify. Even some strange, unfathomable, as yet uncatalogued species of love.

He sat alone in the squad room after Aaron left. Yes, he was betting on Amanda. He thought of calling Caroline, telling her what he'd discovered, then suggesting he come over and spend the night. He stared at the phone, thinking about that. But in the end he didn't pick it up.

When he left the precinct house he drove downtown, ate dinner at a Greek restaurant on Howard Street, then lingered over his coffee staring into space. When he came out it was nearly ten. He got back into his car, crossed to Brooklyn, followed the expressway to Queens, exited on Greenpoint Avenue, then worked his way to Corona, knowing that though he was pretending to wander the outer boroughs he was heading straight where Al and Lou had built their wood-frame house.

He parked a few doors down and across the street, turned off his ignition and extinguished his lights. Most of the houses were still lit. He could glimpse the glow of TV screens in living rooms, hear the occasional sound of raised voices, of children laughing, a door being slammed, a dog barking from someone's porch.

What was he doing here?

He had no desire now to visit Lou, confront again her confusion and hurt. He had not come to spy on her house, or to imagine Al still alive inside. He felt no particular remorse, did not believe he had let Al down, should have been there, could have been there, might have saved Al if he had. It was something else, something troubling, something he felt but could not confront. He was resisting it just as for days he had resisted seeing the resemblance between Amanda Ireland and Brenda Beard. It eluded him, but, sitting in his car demanding an explanation, he knew finally the reason he was there: he had come to take a measurement.

He drove slowly, fifteen miles an hour, which he guessed was roughly four times the speed of a person moving normally on foot, and made his way by the most direct route he could to the vicinity of Caroline's tennis club. When he was near, roughly halfway between it and her building, he stopped, checked his watch and speedometer and began to calculate. No matter how he figured it, and he tried it several different ways, it did not seem possible that a sixty-six-year-old man could have walked that distance in less than an hour.

And that was just too long for a man who never walked anywhere, who so hated to walk that he'd take his car out on a sparkling autumn day just to drive three blocks for a pack of cigarettes. Which still didn't rule out other possibilities. Al could have come by bus, except he'd have had to change buses three times, or he could have driven over, parked in the neighborhood, then taken a brief stroll around though there wasn't anything worth strolling by or to. Which didn't make it impossible – in the solitude of his retirement Al might have taken to making unexpected expeditions to nondescript neighborhoods in Queens. Oh yes, there were possibilities, infinite possibilities, but the most likely one of all, Janek knew, and the one that wrenched his heart, was that the encounter of the fallen bicycle had never taken place.

The Stash

Approaching the Queensboro on his way back to Manhattan, he passed a line of hookers on Northern Boulevard lingering in the doorways of the closed and shuttered shops. This, he knew, was the infamous 'Truckers' Row' about which there were many tales – of a cross-eyed whore whose eyes uncrossed only when she came, and a Park Avenue socialite the teamsters called 'the Countess' who waited here with the hookers because she required the rough embraces of burly tattooed arms.

Driving by them, Janek wondered if the Switched Heads killer had also cruised this strip in his long search for a prostitute whose face resembled the inaccessible impenetrable Amanda of his dreams.

A bad night for Janek, of blocked trails and ideas he could not sustain: Al and Brenda, Amanda and Caroline; heads mounted on bodies upon which they did not belong. He flung himself from side to side seeking sleep to end his agony, found it finally, but in the morning when he awoke he felt a stab of panic followed by an aching loneliness.

Showering, he heard his telephone. He turned off the water, stood naked and still listening to the rings resound like moans. It was Caroline, he knew, and knew that he wasn't ready yet to deal with her. The thought that when he did he must show her a concealing face caused him to shiver on the tiles.

When he was dressed he called her back, told her he was about to leave for work.

'You sound, I don't know, like you're under strain,' she said.

'Guess I am. It's the case. The pressure's on me now.'

'Missed you last night. Missed watching you take off your gun.' He didn't answer. 'Something the matter, Frank?' He was stunned; this was the first time he could recall her using his first name.

'I think something is the matter,' he said. 'But I can't talk about it now. I'm running late.'

'Tonight?'

'Sure.'

'I hear something in your voice I haven't heard before.'

'Didn't sleep well. I'll try to call you later on.'

A long pause. He knew she was struggling, deciding whether to ask him to explain what she was hearing in his voice.

'Goodbye till later, then,' he said.

Another pause, and then her own rueful 'Goodbye.'

At the precinct house there was the smell of a case going bad: detectives making busy-work; a lack of firm direction and control.

There was no way he could fake it. He had no theory to define the work. He told his team to keep plugging, then took the victim profile books into one of the windowless interrogation rooms, shut the door, sat down at the tiny table, checked out the crummy atmosphere and settled down to read.

He believed in Brenda. There was enough of her there for him to reconstruct her life. He believed in her slow drift downward from aspiring actress through failed model to trick-a-day girl on the escort-agency list. He believed in her alliance with shabby-slick Prudencio Bitong, her love of late-night soul-food dinners, of revival screenings of romantic movies, Tracy and Hepburn, Bogart and Bacall. Her descent into the degradation of the weekly ad in the sex tabloid was balanced off by halfhearted attempts to pull herself back up. She paid a dentist four thousand dollars to straighten her teeth. She attended classes at the Hazel Carter Fitness Center, where she hoped to meet successful models who would help her resume a modeling career.

Yes, Frank believed in Brenda. When he closed his eyes he could see the way she moved. He imagined her slipping out of bed beside a snoring john, padding to the bathroom, rinsing out her mouth, then examining herself in the mirror above the sink until she met her own eyes, froze suddenly and asked, 'What will my life be like in twenty years?'

He recaptured the rainy sullen New York afternoon she clung to Prudencio, sprawled out on her chocolate-colored couch, the way he stroked her and soothed her as he told her how they would make a fortune in Manila, and the way she smiled even as she knew that he was lying when he said he was saving his money to take her there and set her up in style.

Janek imagined her delight as she aroused a sixteen-year-old boy who came to her terrified, then called her 'candy-ass' as he strutted out. And the Thanksgiving Day trick with the balding Dayton businessman who took her out for a turkey sandwich afterward and pressed an extra fifty into her palm when he said goodbye. Brenda was there for him, alive between the lines. She had heart and a kind of passionate desperation. He even thought he might have liked her if she'd lived and they had met.

But Amanda was different. She wasn't there, this Madonna with the self-drawn halo around her head. She was good, oh-so-very-

97

good. Sal had said it first: 'Little Miss Perfect – I don't buy that. I don't believe in that.'

She paid her bills the day she got them. She ironed her blouses, saved gift-wrap paper, sewed her own dresses from patterns in magazines. She wrote a bland letter home every Sunday, kept photographs of her sister's children on her desk. She ate health foods and subscribed to *Audubon* and headed up the blood drive at the Weston School.

Janek looked for indications that belied the perfect image – her strange choice of friends, for instance, selfish demanding people he wouldn't have expected her to like. A sickly couple in their seventies, a complaining failed feminist writer, and Gary Pierson with his narcissistic tales of destructive transient love affairs. No doubt Amanda was attractive to these people, an attentive listener. She shook her head sympathetically and clucked at all the proper times. But was there the hint of a smirk in her responses, a smugness, a superiority? She chose people who would open up to her but to whom she would never have to show herself.

Then there was the dog. Something peculiar and revealing about that dog, a sense that it had picked up her concealed feelings and turned them into obnoxious traits. Nobody liked the dog, named, maddeningly, Petunia – a nasty, yelping, snarling little creature who dragged Amanda along as if she were the one on the leash. This little darling leaped aggressively at strangers while Amanda smiled weakly as if the matter was beyond control. People in the building reported she muttered to it, 'Oh, Petti, there's that *bad* man from the pharmacy,' or 'There's the *mean* woman who lives downstairs.'

No, Amanda did not ring true. There was more to her than Stanger had uncovered. Janek was not yet prepared to say she was a fake, but he felt the absence of a range of feelings he was sure she must have had. Envy. Rage. Inadequacy. Fear of sexuality. Panic at being so loveless, untouched and alone. A whole dimension of her character was missing and there was something infuriating about that, something that could make a person want to crack her porcelain exterior, something that could even drive a certain type of individual to want to stick her smug little head upon the body of a whore.

Sal was amused that afternoon when Janek told him what he

wanted to do. 'Don't blame you, since Stanger swears he went over the place. We know what that means, don't we? But remember, Frank, Crime Scene spent a day there, too.'

Aaron stared at him curiously. 'What do you expect to find?'

'Maybe a real person.'

Aaron nodded and turned to Sal. 'Frank's specialty. Dig out the secret life. But this time I think there's more.'

Janek nodded. 'I'll be looking for her contempt.'

'You're beginning to dislike her, aren't you?'

'I started out liking her fine.'

'But now you've turned.' Then to Sal: 'Hate the victim so you can identify with the killer. I've seen him do that before.'

Sal offered to return with him to East Eighty-first, but Janek said he wanted to make the search alone. He wanted to do it at night, too – felt that was important. And also he realized, though he didn't mention it, that if he did it then he could put off confronting Caroline.

He called her, told her what he was going to do.

'I understand,' she said. 'But I'll miss you, the way I did last night.'

Last night he'd passed just a few feet from her door. Why hadn't he gone up to her and wrapped her in his arms?

'I'll miss you, too,' he said. 'But this is something I can't put off.'

'You don't have to explain. Anyway, you sound better now. I was worried this morning. You seemed so abrupt, and – I don't know. Maybe a little sad.'

When he hung up he asked himself if he was being stupid; it was so hard to believe that she had lied.

Aaron sat with him as he ate a pizza at the Taco-Rico. 'I was up half the night thinking about the resemblance. Even the names are similar. Brenda, Amanda – they end with the same three letters and they almost rhyme.'

'I don't think that means anything.'

'Neither do I. It just struck me, Frank, that's all. What's interesting here is that at first I thought we were looking for intersecting lives. But last night, when you talked about Brenda being hunted down and mutilated just because someone needed her face – well, that's different, that's intersecting destinies. And that sends shivers down my spine.'

The apartment smelled musty. The windows were closed the way he and Sal had left them. Janek didn't open them. He didn't want to sweeten the air.

He didn't turn on the lights either, but sat in darkness in the reading chair letting his eyes adjust to the gloom. He had done this sort of thing many times before but had never gotten used to the feelings: a mixture of guilt at intruding upon someone's privacy and of pleasure at uncovering a hidden life. He had felt both things at Brenda's a week before as he had handled her things and searched her drawers. This expedition was different. He had come tonight to search out a concealed self, deliberately concealed perhaps even in anticipation of such a search. He knew that people who cloaked themselves worried often about what would happen if they were in an accident, whether their secrets would be found out, and, if they were, what the finders would think.

There was always a stash. Brenda had one, that old coat pocket filled with cash and dope. Everyone had a place where he hid his valuables or his porn, old love letters, sex-ad correspondence, the diary he didn't want anyone to read. Amanda kept a diary, Janek was sure of it, a place to set down the feelings she kept pent up. Where was it? Hidden well, he knew, so that even a detective would not find it easily. The worst possible thing she could conceive would be to stand naked to a stranger. She would not want anyone to read her diary even after she was dead.

He stood up but didn't turn on the lights. He preferred to use his flashlight to focus his search. He began slowly and quietly, trying the obvious places, not expecting to find anything in them but warming up as he toured the terrain. He looked behind her books, which were arranged flush to the bookcase ledge, checked the backs of her pictures, slid photographs out of frames, then examined the undersides of desk and dresser drawers where papers could be taped. He opened the kitchen cabinets, plunged a fork into the flour and sugar canisters, went to the closet and examined the zippered compartments of her luggage. He tried the pockets of all her garments and then her refrigerator too – once, on a larceny case, he'd found a million dollars' worth of stolen bearer bonds stashed in packages of frozen peas.

A classical hiding place for narcotics criminals was the bottom of the laundry hamper, the concept being that the soiled clothes would be so disgusting no sane investigator would want to pull them out. Amanda had no hamper and her laundry was practically immaculate, but his search brought him to her bathroom, into air sharp with the odor of the new plastic shower curtain he and Sal had hung. He could not resist. He pulled it aside, stepped into her tub and pulled it shut. Then he stood still, trying to locate the feeling of waiting coiled, anticipating, psyching himself up to strike.

She'll come soon and then I'll get her. The feeling swirled through him, a hatred of Amanda, an irrational compelling hate. He cooled himself and tried to trace its source. *I have to know her to hate her so much. I have to know her well. But how?*

He went back to the living room, sat down again. Willing up the hatred left him drained. He rested awhile, then resumed his work, asking himself questions as he searched.

What were her evenings like, those many evenings she spent here alone? He tried to imagine them, came up with the dog squatting near the door to the kitchenette, her stupid eyes focused on Amanda, anticipating the strange rituals she alone was permitted to observe. The dog knew the real Mandy, the one no one else was allowed to see, the one who muttered savagely to herself and hissed beneath her breath, the Mandy who moved rigidly and compulsively, who would begin to shake if she found an object out of place. The dog's eyes would never leave her mistress, would absorb her actions for hours. Petunia could not talk, could not reveal; no need for Amanda to hide herself from this silent furry witness to her despair.

Where was the diary?

Janek began to move again, probing with his flashlight. He would not overturn furniture, pull the stuffing out of the mattress, or do the traditional detective's thing – tear the place apart. He wanted Amanda's diary to proclaim itself, cry out, 'Read me: Know me by my pain.'

Come on, Mandy, come on, girl, show me where it is. Show me your anger, your rage, all those feelings that make you so ashamed. I feel for you. I understand. I can help you – maybe. But first, babe, you have to show me who you are.

She would write in it in bed at night, he thought, with only the bedside light on and the radio turned low to a late-night call-in show, a kind of background music of other people's grief. And the dog would stare at her, and she would prop the diary up against her thighs, and afterward she would put down the pen and turn off the radio, and then just before she turned off the light she would slip the diary away...

Show yourself. Come on, Mandy. Where is it? Where?

Not under the mattress. Too obvious – though he looked. Not inside the hassock; too difficult – though he unlaced it from the bottom, stuck his hand inside and felt. It would have to be a place that was easy for her to reach; she would be tired after she wrote in it and would not feel like going through a series of complicated moves. The tissue box? He ran his fingers around inside it. The wastebasket beside the bed, so neatly lined with a plastic bag? That would be clever, like the proverbial laundry hamper: if something happened to her it would most likely be thrown away unexamined.

He turned it over onto the carpet, set his flashlight down beside the pile and spread the contents out. Disgusting – all those smudged-up papers, that discarded typewriter ribbon, those soiled tissues, the crushed-up and restuffed tampon box, that disposable vacuum-cleaner bag.

Oh, Mandy, what an awful mess, all that repellent trash. Stanger wouldn't want to touch it, and the Crime Scene mechanics wouldn't bother to examine it. But it's not like you to leave such slop around. I smell a put-up job –

It was there: an envelope containing two one-hundred-dollar bills, a Krugerrand wrapped in a piece of wrinkled foil, a packet of letters and a spiral bound flip-over stenographer's writing pad.

He looked at the letters first. They were written in French, postmarked Grenoble, dated several years before. These would be the love letters sent by the French boy to whom she'd been engaged, folded and unfolded many times, spotted here and there with tears. Janek did not read French, but he could imagine the story well – a quick rush of love and then its slow withdrawal; passionate outpourings terminated with a cutting 'I truly believe we've made a mistake...'

He settled back to read the diary. It was one o'clock in the morning when he finished. All the feelings were there, the ones he had expected: the anger, the disgust and the contempt.

She disliked her students, called them 'shallow' and 'undisciplined.' Her parents were 'tiresome' and 'insipid,' but in

102

another entry she wrote: 'They are the finest human beings on this earth and I hate myself for having hurt them so.' She had harsh words for Gary Pierson: 'pathetic wretched creature.' On a disliked colleague at Weston: '... would like to twist her head right off her neck.' On the old couple she'd befriended whom she served so dutifully: 'Sometimes when I watch them eat I want to stand right over them and puke.' On her sister in Hawaii: 'Moo-cow. Breeder. Sour-smelling kids.' It was all there, the meanness she never showed, the ridicule, the Janus face.

But the worst of her contempt was reserved for herself. Janek was disturbed by its intensity. She accused herself of mediocrity, contemplated suicide, then gave up the idea because it would 'just be another typical Mandy mess.' She described her life, then annotated her descriptions with one-word judgments: 'Yuk!' 'Barf!' 'Puke!' 'Everything about me is little,' she wrote. 'I hold a little job. I live in a little apartment. I own a little dog. I lead a worthless little life.' '... loathe my body. At class can feel fire, but practicing stretches here at night I look down at my nakedness and feel hideous.' '... can't stand my body or the way my mind works, holding on to nothing, going round and round and round.' 'Men don't move me. Think of being touched by one and then I want to puke.' There were pages like that, cruel and merciless, a self-ridicule Janek could hardly bear. He had willed himself up to hate her so that he could imagine how her killer felt, but now, reading these denigrating self-assessments, he was filled with so much pity he felt tears rising to his eyes. He had come that night to know Amanda Ireland, her sorrow and her misery. Now, at last, she came alive for him, and then he remembered that she was dead.

Near the end of the diary, in an entry dated in early August, Janek was struck by the pathos of a line: 'A kiss goodnight. A stingy little kiss. If only it were real affection. Poor me here with Petti all alone ...'

When he finished reading he turned off the light, sat still in the reading chair again absorbing the gloom. He dozed awhile; when he woke up his watch read three-fifteen. He had spent most of the night, had found what he had come looking for, had discovered Amanda Ireland, and now he wondered if that brought him any closer to discovering why she had been killed.

He went to the bathroom, urinated, then stepped into the tub. He did not draw the curtain this time, simply stood gazing at the sink, trying to empty himself of sympathy, trying to recapture again the killer's hate.

I'm waiting here to stab her so I can take her apart and put her back together the way I've dreamed. My plan is complicated and dangerous. Why do I feel so confident?

When he came back into the main room he nearly choked on the air. He went to the window, pulled it open, stood before it and exhaled. Then he noticed something on the carpet, laid his flashlight on the floor, knelt, and looked closely to see what it was. A slight depression, a rectangle, about two and a half feet by five. He went to the closet, found the green exercise mat he'd noticed before, brought it out, laid it in the space. It fit, of course, perfectly.

So it was here by the open window, the same window through which her killer had crawled, that she had done her exercises nude at night. Those difficult, limb-stretching, muscle-tearing exercises she practiced to win Hazel Carter's compliments in class. On the warm summer nights she would do them here with the lights off so nobody could see. She would turn and stretch until her body burned, a kind of ritual self-punishment, and the light from the bathroom, the light she'd leave on so there would be some ambient illumination in the room, would rim the curves of her straining body and outline her naked form against the dark.

Janek stood there at the window. It was black outside. The warm September air was dank and thick. Suddenly he felt a shiver and backed away. There was something out there, something that made him feel exposed. Then, as he retreated into the room, many disparate thoughts which had been churning inside him for a week arranged themselves into a pattern, like iron filings strewn loose upon a piece of paper suddenly organized within the field of a powerful magnet held beneath.

Snapshot

He stayed in the apartment dozing in the reading chair. Then, at first light, he pulled himself up and stood again before the window looking out. After a while he packed up his flashlight and the contents of Amanda Ireland's stash, left the apartment, carefully locked the door and drove downtown to the precinct house.

They started drifting in a little before eight o'clock, Sal Marchetti first, then Stanger and Howell. They wandered in with their containers of coffee, their newspapers and their jelly rolls, observed Janek, unshaven, leaning back with his hands clasped behind his head, said 'Good morning,' then exchanged glances, trying to assess his mood.

Aaron Rosenthal appeared at eight-fifteen. 'Jesus, Frank, you've been up all night. You really look like shit.'

Janek smiled.

'Want some coffee?'

Janek shook his head.

'Do we have to read him his rights before we drag it out of him?' asked Sal. 'Or is he going to voluntarily confess?'

'Let him have his fun,' said Aaron. 'So far fun has not been the distinctive feature of this case.'

Stanger and Howell, not yet admitted to the circle of intimacy, tried to grin as if they were. Aaron pulled a yarmulke out of his pocket, dusted it off, then set it gently on his head. Sal opened his *Wall Street Journal* and checked the values of his bio-engineering stocks.

'Funny thing . . .' They all turned to Janek instantly. 'Monday, when Hart was putting the screws to me I told him we weren't going to solve this by good old-fashioned detective work. I said it to annoy him and he was plenty annoyed. But now it looks like I was wrong.' He turned to Stanger. 'I know you talked to the people in her building. What about the people across the way?'

Stanger looked frightened. 'Amanda's building?' Janek nodded. 'I did the usual.'

Sal groaned. 'What's that?'

'Canvassed the people in the brownstone just across. Then talked to the supers and doormen in the other buildings that face the back. Asked them to query their residents when they got the chance. Then I made up notices and posted them around.'

'Laundry rooms and lobbies, right?'

'That's where I put them, Lieutenant.'

Janek nodded. 'Up to me to decide if you should have taken it further than that.'

Stanger, relieved, took a long sip of coffee. Janek paused while the others pulled their chairs around his desk.

'Here's how it goes. I want to kill Amanda and do a number with her head. Aside from finding Brenda, which is another story, there're certain things I need to know. First, I need to know her well enough to want to kill her, which means I've picked her out without her knowing it and have a way of observing her unseen. Second, I need to know where she lives, the layout of her apartment, that there's a ladder down from the roof to her balcony, and that she doesn't keep her window locked. Third, I need to know that when she takes her dog out at night she's away long enough for me to get in there and hide, and that when she comes back she releases the dog and goes into the bathroom to brush her teeth. Now, unless I'm her roommate the only way I can know all those things is to live in a building that faces her apartment with a good view into her window and her life.

'This morning I stood at her window and counted all the other windows I could see. I may be off by a few – we're going to have to make a sight-line chart – but my rough count was seventy-four, which includes the ones in the brownstone across, the two houses on either side of it, the back of the building on the corner of Park Avenue, and the upper floors of the tall building that fronts on Eightieth Street. Seventy-four windows may boil down to thirty-five residences. Figuring an average of slightly more than two adults per residence, we're talking outside eighty possible killers, eighty possible voyeurs.'

Aaron shook his head. 'I like it, Frank. Now, of course, we check them all.'

'One by one, methodically the way Hart likes. Two teams: you and Stanger; Sal and Howell. Three lists: people who were home that night; people who say they were out but can't substantiate it; people who were out and can. Don't go in like you're looking for suspects. You're just checking with everyone who could have seen anything. No big deal about alibis. Just let them tumble out. No hint you think it was somebody with a view of her apartment. But be sure and check the view. Slow patient interviews like you've got a lot of time. Names, ages, marital status, professions and rough personal impression should do it the first time around. Spend as much time with the old ladies and children as you do with the big strong male headhunter types. Hang out. Absorb the gossip.

Discover the painters, writers, sculptors and photographers. The spooky voyeur guy in Seven B. The seventeen-year-old who drools in the elevator at the girls. Get used to the folks and make sure that they get used to you. Be helpful. Hold open doors and offer to carry grocery bags. Caricature yourselves so each of you is well defined. Howell the Jolly. Stanger the Hawk. Marchetti the Confessor. Rosenthal the Wise. Above all, be tiresomely methodical. Forget things, go back and double-check, then go back and check again. Sooner or later names will emerge, for our short list, the suspects we're going to look at very hard. If we're lucky they may come quickly, but I wouldn't count on it. I have a feeling this may take quite a while.'

At last a theory, a concept that would confine them, a territory limited by Janek's idea. Never mind that he might be wrong – it was a strategy and it made sense. No more floundering. No more screwy discussions about why someone would want to do a switch. Focus in on one of the homicides. Stick to Amanda. Forget Brenda and the switch for now. Stanger and Howell were beaming; this was the kind of investigation they understood.

Janek stood up. It was time to go home and get some rest.

'Terrific, Frank,' said Sal, patting him on the back.

Aaron ceremoniously removed his yarmulke and escorted him to the door. 'You're good, Frank. But we already knew you were. I'm feeling better about this now.' They paused at the head of the stairs. 'You didn't say whether you found her stash.'

Janek pulled out the hundred-dollar bills and the Krugerrand. He handed them to Aaron to send to her parents in Buffalo.

'That it?'

'Not much else. The voyeur idea hit me when I found out she practiced her exercises nude at night.'

Aaron smiled. 'Wonder how you knew about that. There was more, wasn't there? You went in there looking for contempt.'

'I found it.'

'And you worked with it.'

He nodded. 'I wanted to degrade her, bring her down. Wanted to – very much. And then every time I stood in her tub I felt extremely confident. Full of myself, you know. Very strong and powerful. I know I must have studied her quite a while to feel like that.'

'Think he dry-runned it?'

'Positive. To be so sure he must have been in there before. But you notice he didn't bother to fudge things up. It's as if he wanted us to see how precise and sure he was.' Janek paused. 'There's something else. If I'm right there's a good chance he saw me and Sal crawl in there on Saturday night. And last night he may have seen me, too. I had this feeling. He'd have seen my flashlight stabbing around in the dark and the bathroom light going on and off.'

'Then soon as he hears we're working the buildings he'll know we've figured it out.'

Janek nodded again. 'Something to look for, but I get a feeling, from all that confidence, that he's so sure of himself he won't care that we've figured it out.'

He went home, shaved, showered and tried to sleep, but found that he could not. The exhilaration he had felt as he stood at Amanda's window was supplanted now by conflicting thoughts of Caroline. It was always like that: he would experience a moment of illumination, and then another problem would rise and fog his view. To be a detective, he knew, was to be embroiled in an endless investigation. Cases flowed together. He solved some and stored others in the files. But the Big Case, the sum of all the others, was the mystery of human passion, and that case was never solved.

He missed her – her body, her hair, her eyes, missed holding her and feeling her hands upon him, and her lips. But more than any of those things he missed his belief in her. He had longed for a woman without guile or tricks, thought he had found one, and now he wasn't sure.

He called her, got her answering machine. She was out shooting someplace in the city. He had a key to her loft. He could go over there and wait. But he was afraid that if he did he would not be able to resist searching through her things.

He spent the late morning walking the Upper West Side, observing the faddish shops on Columbus and Amsterdam which presaged, he'd read, a retail renaissance. He saw repulsive vinyl garments proffered by young salespeople who wore punk hairdos and lizard belts with tooled clasps.

Growing weary of modishness, he bought two eggrolls from a vendor and wandered into Central Park. He found a bench, sat down, sprinkled on some soy sauce from a plastic pouch, ate, then sat silent like a middle-aged man out of work.

Two equestrians slowly cantered by, an elegant couple in hacking jackets and boots. They were quarreling over the price of a cooperative apartment. The man kept repeating, 'Six hundred K is tops,' while the woman pouted and shook her head.

A little while later a no-hands bicyclist collided with a jogger. A perfunctory apology. An epithet. Then anger mounting rapidly, ready to explode. People stopped. Janek tensed. Then the ugly moment passed. The bicyclist drove away and the jogger staggered off with bloodied knees.

Feeling he'd had enough for a while of the human race, Janek decided to try the Museum of Natural History. He entered and spent an hour gazing at aggressively postured stuffed animals. The bears especially intrigued him, so cuddly and threatening, and he stared with wonder at the whales. Realizing he was wasting his day, he strode purposefully to the primitive-man exhibits and studied headhunter totems to remind himself he had a case. Head-hunting, he saw, could be an art form, a concrete way to deal with guilt and rage. But even while he was thinking this he was growing increasingly apprehensive about the evening, trying to figure out some way to broach himself to Caroline.

Late in the afternoon he reached her from a phone booth. They agreed that he would bring over carry-out food and she would open one of her better bottles of wine.

The rush hour was on by the time he reached the bridge: little surges forward, then hard applications of the brakes; the traffic did not crawl so much as jerk its way across. A week since their dinner in Chinatown, a week since they'd first made love. When he reached her building he still had no idea what he was going to say.

She kissed him as he came through the door. 'Oh, Janek . . .' she whispered, lovingly. Then she helped him spread out the food. 'Beautiful. And so much more than we can eat.' Which was true: he had spent almost fifty dollars, on imported prosciutto, smoked Scotch salmon, lobster salad and black Russian bread. They stared at the array together, then she placed her arm around his waist. 'Crazy old detective.' She squeezed him close.

He opened the wine, they sipped and nibbled. She told him she'd spent her day photographing sanitation workers aggressively heaving trash into cartage trucks, and he told her what he'd finally seen in the Switched Heads crime-scene photographs.

'Interchangeable – why didn't I see that?'

'Because you looked too deeply. The trick was just to glance at them and squint.'

As they talked he watched her carefully, listening for false notes but finding none. She seemed so real he felt disloyal searching for signs of stress and inauthenticity.

After they'd stuffed themselves, having barely devoured half the food, he decided it was time to make his move. Ever since he'd met her there'd been a subject she'd toyed with but about which she'd never opened up. He would start with that and see where it led them. He waited until her talk wound down, then caught her eye and spoke.

'What kind of guy's your dad?'

She looked at him curiously. 'Why do you ask me that?'

'You've mentioned him a few times. I know it's significant to you to be the daughter of a cop. But you've never told me anything about him. Not even if he's still on the force.'

'He's not,' she said. Suddenly she was tense.

'So, what's he doing now?'

'He's not doing anything. He's dead.'

'I'm sorry, Caroline. You never told me.' Which was strange, he thought. 'When did he die?'

'Beginning of the summer.'

'How did it happen?'

'What difference does it make?' she snapped. She met his eyes, lowered hers, then spoke quietly. 'He was killed.'

'Killed?'

'I think "rubbed out" is the expression they used. Look, I don't know why you started on this, but I'm getting the feeling it's not all that casual. If that's true, okay, but at least admit it. And tell me what you want to know.'

'We're just talking,' Janek said softly. 'It's you I want to know.' He paused. 'If you'd rather not...'

'No, no,' she said. 'I guess I've been avoiding this.' She seemed to relax a little then. 'It's such an awful thing, so miserable. And there really isn't much to tell. Dad was a cop for a few years when I was little. Then he left the force. He went into business, failed at it and about that time left my mother and moved away. He owned a bar for a while and then he lost that too. He was sort of a marginal character in the end. A drinker, gambler, that type of man. He used to come around to see me, not especially often, and I can't remember a time he did that I didn't smell whiskey on his breath. He'd call on Christmas and my birthday. When my Vietnam book came out he asked for copies so he could give them to his friends. In the end he got involved with mobsters – in debt to them, I think. The story I got was what he didn't pay up and that he antagonized important people. So they made an example of him, killed him gangland style. A bullet in the back of the head, then his body stuffed into the trunk of a stolen car.'

'Where did this happen?'

'Jersey. Where else? They said he was probably shot in the Meadowlands. The car was left on a Hoboken street.'

'And that's it.'

'Isn't that enough?' A touch of anger in her now.

Janek spread his hands. He could feel her anguish. He wanted to comfort her, but he was sure that there was more. 'Since I'm a detective and your father was murdered, there's a chance I could find out more about it, if you were interested.'

She turned away.

'What's the matter?'

'I can't stand to talk about it. I really can't.'

'Have you been talking about it to someone else?'

She didn't answer, and then, suddenly, he understood. 'You talked about it with Al, didn't you?'

She turned back. 'You knew that?' He shook his head. 'But –'

'How did you meet him?' Janek asked.

He was watching her closely now. He saw her begin to speak: she was going to repeat the story she'd told. When she stopped he knew she was not a practiced liar. He felt relieved, then loving toward her, and then that the time had come to clear the air.

'You fell off your bike just as Al happened to be walking by. I'm sorry, Caroline. I can't buy that. Al didn't take walks, especially in neighbourhoods he didn't know.' She turned away again as if ashamed she'd been found out. 'Listen – I believed your story at first. I thought it sounded a little pat, but I bought it anyway. I liked you. I didn't have any reason not to believe you, and that day

111

I got assigned a horrible case, so maybe my mind wasn't as sharp as it should have been. But it bothered me. There was something wrong. I didn't think about it again until the other night. Now I feel it's important that we clear this up. Not because how you met Al is so important in itself, but because we have to be straight with each other or we won't have anything at all.'

'I see,' she said. 'Well, of course you're right. That isn't how I met him, though I did fall off my bike and there was a man who helped me up and walked me home. I thanked him at the door and never saw him again. I spliced that story in. Not too well thought out, I guess.'

'Why make up a story at all?'

'Because I didn't want to go through all this.'

'Through what?'

She paused as if deciding whether she should answer. When finally she looked up he knew she was going to tell the truth.

'Al called me blind one day last June. He introduced himself and asked if he could come over here and talk. Sure, I said; why not? So he came and he was up-front about the reason. He told me he was a retired detective and that he and Dad had been good friends years ago. He hadn't seen much of Dad in a long while, but he thought there was more to his death – no, he didn't tell me that till later on. He just said he wanted to find out who killed Dad and why, and he asked me a lot of questions and pretty soon he realized I didn't know anything at all. And then it was just the way I told you. He started stopping by afternoons. We became friends. We liked each other. I liked listening to him and having him around. So the only thing I told you that wasn't true was the way we met, the accident.'

She stopped as if waiting for his next question, then remembered he'd already asked her why she'd lied. 'I didn't know you, Janek. You came up to me in the cemetery, then you called that night and said you wanted to ask some questions. I didn't know what you were after. I assumed it was about Dad and I was sick to death of that. So when you asked me how I met Al I combined the story of the bike accident with a true account of our relationship.'

'I still don't see –'

'I just didn't feel like having another detective coming around talking about that awful case. I felt that if I told you about it you'd

112

want to take it over, and then you'd get obsessive about it the way Al did, and I knew I couldn't deal with that. And there was something else.' She paused. 'I had this strong reaction to you. I didn't want to spoil it or mix it up with Dad. Who cares now what gangsters killed him? He's dead. Al shot himself. I mean – I've had enough.'

'The next night we become lovers. Why didn't you tell me then?'

'What difference would it have made?'

'I can understand why you fibbed at first, but later, when we got so close, didn't you want to clear it up?'

'I just have. It's cleared. I think you knew all this anyway.'

Janek shook his head. 'I didn't know about your father or Al's interest in him. I didn't know any of this until just now.'

'Then you really *are* a terrific detective. You bluffed me out and now I've spilled my guts. There's nothing else untrue between us. I feel good about that. I'm glad we're clear.'

He tried to smile but found he couldn't.

'Still don't believe me?' she asked.

'It's not a question of how you met,' he said. 'I asked you if Al was working on something. You told me he wasn't. And now it turns out you knew he was.'

'It didn't seem all that important at the time. More like something his wife was curious about. He wasn't working officially, so it didn't weigh on my conscience. Anyway, it concerned me and my father, not Al, or Al's wife, or even you.' She left her chair, came over to his side of the table, sat down next to him and took his arm. 'You thought I was perfect and now you're disappointed. I've confessed everything. Can't we leave it alone awhile?'

'Everything?'

'What else could there be?'

'You said Al told you he thought there was more to your father's death than ... Then you broke the sentence off.'

'Shit!'

'What did he say?'

'He had some crazy idea.'

'What?'

'Dammit, I don't know. It's over. Forget it. He never came up with anything. He was an old man playing detective, obsessed and secretive and sly. It got so I just couldn't stand to listen to him go on about it. Not about the case but about how tortured it made him feel. I told him that and we made a pact. He wouldn't mention it anymore. And after that he didn't.'

'You're telling me he never said anything substantive about your father's death?'

'Nothing. Just that he didn't think it happened the way it looked.'

Janek stood up.

'Where are you going?'

'I don't know.'

'You're not going to stay?'

He shook his head.

'Why not? To punish me?'

'I'm all wound up.'

'So am I. I'll put on some music. Let's open another bottle of wine and relax.'

'I played my accordion for you.'

'I loved you for doing that.'

He stood silent, his mind churning, fearing he was getting too close, feeling too much pain. 'Maybe I need time to cool off. Maybe it's just my pride. You told me a story no decent detective would believe. I believed it. So now I feel like a jerk.'

'You're not a jerk. You're a brilliant man.'

'And now you don't want me looking into your father's death.'

'*No.*'

'But I have to.'

'Why?'

'Because now it turns out Al *was* working on a case, and that's a very peculiar thing. Because when a detective like Al works a case that's personal, he's not inclined to shoot himself.'

'I don't –'

'Why *did* he shoot himself?'

She shook her head. 'Depression. Burn-out, like you said.'

'You told me he felt tortured.'

'So maybe that's why he did it. I feel guilty about that. I cut him off. I wouldn't let him talk about it. When I did that, maybe . . . *don't you see?*'

Janek shook his head. He turned to her, took her face in his hands, gently touched her cheeks running now with tears. 'It wasn't you, Caroline. And it wasn't the case either. Or that Al was bottled up. That's the kind of torment that would keep him going, not the kind that would make him feel shitty about himself and eat his thirty-eight.'

'What are you going to do?'

'Look into it.'

'His suicide?'

He nodded. 'Al's investigation too.'

She gazed at him stunned; she finally understood. He saw her expression change from wonderment to recognition, then she snapped back her head from his hands. 'You know, I'm getting a very funny feeling about this conversation. About everything that's happened here tonight. Like the very casual way you started asking about my father. And then the way you shifted the talk over to Al, as if you already knew.'

'I told you, I didn't.'

'Yeah. But that sounds a little pat to me. This was an interrogation, wasn't it?' He shook his head. 'Sure it was. I see it now. You knew everything. So maybe you haven't been that straight yourself. Can't blame you. I lied first. Oh, excuse me, I mean fibbed. So you had every right to try and worm the story out. Except that we're supposed to be – what? Lovers? Or more than that?' He reached for her, but she broke away, stood up fast and began to pace the loft.

'Fuck it anyway. I can't believe you'd come on to me the way you did just to . . .' She kicked the wall; when she turned back Janek saw that her foot had left a mark. 'No, that's impossible. You couldn't be so false. Forget it. I'm sorry. So, okay, you're going to look into it. Al was working on a case and you owe it to him to investigate. You're going to do that whether I want you to or not.' She stopped, turned and stared at him. 'Am I right?'

He nodded.

'Fine. Do it. Get obsessed.' There were tears in her eyes again. 'Maybe you'll end up shooting yourself, too. That would be just great, wouldn't it? Great for me. Two detectives. Plus my dad.'

She turned suddenly and strode into her darkroom, the portion of the loft partitioned off from the rest. She came out a few seconds later and handed him a photograph.

115

'Here! Take it! Torture yourself. Get obsessed – just like Al.' She wiped her eyes. 'He gave this to me the last time he came. That was about four days before he died. I don't know why. To me it's just a picture of three guys. But he gave it to me with some ceremony, pressed it into my hand like it was special. The guy in the middle is my dad. And of course that's Al on the left. I don't know who the other guy is. I'd say this picture was taken by an amateur about twenty-five years ago. That's all I know. You're the detective. You figure it out. And now I'd like it if you'd leave.'

'When we've cooled off –'

'I love you.' She stamped her foot: '*So damn much.*'

'Caroline –'

She turned away. 'Just go now. Please.'

'We'll talk tomorrow.'

'Sure.'

Janek stood there feeling helpless, wanting to move toward her but knowing from her posture she'd rebuff him if he tried. He backed toward the door, then stopped again waiting for her to turn. She didn't. 'Good night,' he said. Then, very quietly, he left.

He sat in his car staring at his hands. They were shaking and he couldn't make them stop. He knew he had opened up some kind of awful wound, and yet he did not see how he could have avoided it. He sat for a while and then, when the shaking stopped, he drove slowly back to New York.

Later, at home, lying on his bed, he examined the snapshot: three men, three cops in uniform, their arms tossed lightly about one another's shoulders, grinning, almost leering at the lens.

He turned the picture over. There was a patch of paper glued to its back, soft porous photo-album paper as if it had been mounted in an album and then torn out.

He turned it again and examined the faces. In the middle, Tommy Wallace: handsome, confident, the face of a bluffer, a salesman's face. Al DiMona on the left, happy, perhaps happier than Janek could remember ever having seen him, but looking wary too, as if he couldn't quite believe in all this leering happiness. And the third man, the one on the right, the one wearing the sergeant's stripes, with the expression that said 'I've got the world by the tail' – that was Hart.

Carmichael

On Friday afternoon the two teams of detectives began conducting interviews. They worked flat out through the weekend. By late Tuesday they had talked to sixty people, with each interview carefully written up and logged. Janek had only to glance at drawings on the squad-room wall where all the overlooking windows had been charted, decide who interested him, then read about him or her in one of four thick black looseleaf books.

But, for all the pressures of Switched Heads, the problem of Al and Tommy Wallace kept intruding. Over and over Janek asked himself if and how Al's suicide was linked up with Tommy's death.

He also brooded over Caroline. They spoke Friday on the phone. ('How are you?' 'Fine. What about you?' 'Good. Cooled down.' 'Well... that's good.') On Saturday he took her to dinner in Little Italy. They drank, laughed, but when he dropped her home she neglected to invite him up. Late Sunday afternoon she called from her tennis club, announced she'd just won a hard-fought match and was in desperate need of sex. He rushed to her loft, where she greeted him in a white terry-cloth robe and nothing underneath. Her lovemaking was greedy; afterward she said 'Thanks,' slipped back into the robe and talked for an hour about her book. 'Want another go?' she asked, suddenly. When he nodded she pulled him back to bed. 'Great,' she said afterward, 'really good to tear one off.' When he gazed at her astonished, she grinned and turned away.

Okay, he thought, driving home (she had not suggested he spend the night), *she's still angry and wants me to know it. By not talking about Tommy or Al we're saying our positions haven't changed. Fine, I'll do what I have to do, wait her out, and eventually we'll recapture what we had.*

But still he was hurt.

On Monday he began to wonder whether her message had been stronger. *Maybe she's telling me I risk losing her if I insist on going on.*

117

But what was his alternative? Forget about Al now that he knew he'd been working a case? Impossible, especially after he'd seen that snapshot which told him that Hart had lied in the car when he said he hadn't known Al and had only come to his burial out of professional respect.

That afternoon he made a series of calls to people in New Jersey law enforcement. At noon on Tuesday he walked west from the Sixth Precinct house, entered beneath the soot-encrusted marquee of the Christopher Street PATH station, descended the narrow windy stairs to the platform and waited for the Trans Hudson train.

It was a fast ride through the tube beneath the river. When he emerged he was in Hoboken, a rough and honest blue-collar town. There were magnificent views of Manhattan from the deteriorating port, and the old flea-bag sailors' hotels were being gentrified.

A two-block walk to the turn-of-the-century Clam Broth House. The restaurant was noisy and jammed. Construction workers sucked up raw clams. Real-estate developers were devouring lobsters. Janek scanned the tables searching for a detective. When he thought he spotted one he approached.

'Carmichael?'

'Janek?'

They shook hands and Janek sat down. Then several seconds of smiling silence as they sized each other up.

Carmichael had the right tough and weary face, flat at the bottom like the base of a paper bag. His thick iron hair was cut short, but there was sensitivity in his features; for a moment he reminded Janek of Al, the same troubled vulnerability, the same all-it-would-take-is-one-more-lousy-thing-to-make-me-throw-in-my-shield-and-retire.

Carmichael signaled he was host by suggesting several dishes. They both ordered the mixed-seafood platter and, when the beers came, simultaneously began to sip.

'Not so often we get one of you New York guys over here,' Carmichael said. 'Usually it's the other way around.'

'Check me out?'

Carmichael nodded. 'Know you're the guy who killed Flynn, if that's what you mean.'

Janek felt his stomach tighten. But then, to his surprise, Carmichael went on:

'It was fifteen years ago. You killed your partner in self-defense. The people who count thought you were justified. Now you're a star lieutenant of detectives. If you'd played your cards a little better you'd probably be a chief. In which case we probably wouldn't be having lunch.' Carmichael's eyes were steady; he didn't come on too strong, nor did he seem particularly impressed. 'Wasn't hard to check you out,' he explained. 'Plenty of guys born here working over in NYPD.'

Janek smiled. He liked Carmichael. 'Figures. The great towers beckoning from across the river.'

'Especially at night.'

'Yeah, New Jersey boys lying in bed with hard-ons for our sordid city.'

Carmichael grinned. 'You're just our backyard,' he said.

The sea-food platters were piled high with clams, shrimps, crab, a lobster tail and french fries. They ate in silence. Then, after the first pause for beer, Janek laid it out.

'Meet a guy named Al DiMona?'

Carmichael nodded as he chewed. 'I surely did.'

'Shot himself couple weeks ago.'

Carmichael stopped chewing. 'Think you've figured a guy...' He shook his head.

Janek leaned forward. 'How *did* you have DiMona figured?'

Carmichael squinted. 'Guy who thought he was onto something. Guarded but nervous too. Sensitive guy with lots of wheels spinning inside. Last guy in the world I'd have thought... How did he do it, Janek?'

'Ate his gun.' Janek paused. 'He was my rabbi. We stayed close, though I didn't see him much after he retired. I got divorced couple years ago, and since my wife and his were friends... Anyway, I want to play this straight. I'm here on my own. There wasn't anything phony about his suicide. Didn't leave a note, but he pulled the trigger and, naturally, his wife's upset. Says he was working on something, probably over here. I promised her I'd look into it. That's why I called.'

'Wallace?'

Janek nodded.

119

'Yeah, DiMona was around to see me about that.'

'Can you talk about it?'

'Don't see why not. He came around, said he'd worked with Wallace, cared about him, wanted to know what happened and wasn't here to bug me or butt in.'

'I'm not, either.'

'Appreciate that. What do you want to know?'

'Let's start with Wallace.'

Carmichael nodded, then slowly exhaled. 'Looked like a gangland killing. Body stashed in the trunk of a stolen car. Shot in the head close range someplace else. I checked around. Wallace was in trouble. He gambled and he couldn't pay. He'd been threatened, too – told people that. Looked like they wanted to make an example of him and called in a professional to do the job.' He shrugged. 'You know, you can bust your ass on a case like that and never get to first base. There wasn't any pressure, so I put it on the shelf.'

'Not even from the DA?'

Carmichael snorted. 'No one gave a shit. Then your friend came over. Took me to lunch. We ate at the table over there.' Carmichael gestured toward a booth. 'Asked me what happened and I told him what I've been telling you. He confirmed that Wallace had been threatened, but then he asked how thoroughly I'd checked that out. I told him the truth, that I didn't have the time, that it was pretty clear what happened, that I could spend the summer on it and waste the summer too. So then he offered to help me out. Not in a pushy way. Just said that he had the time, he cared and would I mind.'

'And you said, "Sure, go ahead."'

Carmichael met Janek's eyes. 'The guy was willing, he seemed on the level, and what the hell difference would it make? I even gave him some names. Low-level mob informants. If I'd had the time I'd have checked with them myself. Now here was an experienced retired detective offering to do my shit work for free.'

'What happened?'

Carmichael grinned. 'That's when it started getting interesting. DiMona went to see these guys and he must have been pretty good with them, because they agreed to check around.' *Al gave them money*, Janek thought, but he didn't say anything, just let Carmichael go on.

'Word came back. There wasn't any contract out on Wallace. The people who order that kind of stuff wanted that clear and also that they were pissed. Wallace was small-time. He was into them for ten grand tops. Sure, he'd been told to pay, and, yeah, there'd been some pressure. But nothing serious, nothing like a bullet in the head. Because Wallace was the kind you just wrote off and forgot.'

'Someone killed him.'

'Right. That's why these guys were mad. Someone had offed Wallace and made it look like a professional job. The mob guys didn't like that. Bad publicity. When they make an example they want the credit, but they don't like getting blamed for stuff they haven't done.'

'So then what happened?'

'Your friend got pretty excited. Took me to lunch again. Said this showed there was more to the Wallace killing than met the eye. I had to agree with him, and I knew what he wanted, too. He started making nice about how it was clear we were overworked over here, and how he had a lot of experience, et cetera, and since the investigation would have to be reopened anyway, how did he think my chief would react if he volunteered to help? I told him forget it. My chief would never accept an overinvolved retired New York City detective nosing around in a New Jersey case. He looked kind of stricken, so I promised I'd work hard on it and call him if anything came up. Frankly, I wasn't all that sincere, because I was getting a funny feeling from DiMona, that he was a little too eager, that he knew more than he was letting on, and that maybe the best move for me was just to leave this thing alone. Sooner or later I figured he'd come around again, and then I'd press him and find out what he knew.'

'So you didn't call him?'

Carmichael shook his head. 'Thought I'd let him simmer awhile.'

'Did he call you?'

'Yeah. Couple of times. And one day in July he actually showed up. It was one of those broiling humid days. He said he was just driving through. Bullshit! I was annoyed. Told him I was busy and couldn't talk. He looked really hurt. I figured he'd be back inside a week.

'But then a weird thing. Something actually happened on the

case. The guy who owned the car where Wallace was stashed came around to get some insurance papers signed. Seemed there'd been some problems with the car he hadn't noticed when he got it back. Seemed it didn't work too well, stalled out, sputtered, leaked, stuff like that, and when he took it into his garage the guy there told him it was filled with crap. Okay, he knew the stereo was missing. But it turned out there were other things. Good parts had been stripped off and replaced with junk. And the tires were cruddy, worn out, not the practically new ones he'd had on before. So suddenly this guy's telling me this I get a flash on the Wallace case. He'd been put in the trunk of this stolen car that turned out was cannibalized, which suggested the car hadn't been stolen just to store his corpse, so maybe he was mixed up in stolen cars.

'I called DiMona. Told him I had something. He was over within the hour. I sat down and watched him carefully because I was wondering if he was mixed up in Wallace's death himself.

'I told him about the car. Laid it out for him. I could see he was getting excited. But then when I asked him what he thought it meant he shook his head and got up to leave. That's when I got pissed. "Look," I said, "you asked me to let you in on this. I just told you a lot. Now you act like you're holding back. What kind of asshole deal's that?"

'He glared at me. Highly indignant. Then *he* started in. He'd been the one, did I forget, who'd picked apart my contract-killer theory that I'd been too lazy to check up on myself. I could see we weren't getting anywhere, so I told him to get out. And that was the last time I saw him. He didn't come around again.'

'Did he call?'

'No.'

'So what happened with the case?'

Carmichael shook his head. 'Nothing. So, okay, it's not a mob thing. So maybe it's a car-ring thing. Sometimes I wonder about it. It's there in the back of my mind. But it's not on my list of most haunting unsolved cases. Except now that you tell me DiMona ate his gun . . .' Carmichael paused. 'Look, first this retired New York detective comes around asking about a nothing case. Now you say you think it may be related to his suicide. Tell you, Janek, I'm getting kind of tired feeling so left out. Is there something going on I ought to know?'

Janek could see the hurt in Carmichael's eyes, and that he was wondering whether he was going to be treated now the same way he'd been treated by Al.

'I don't know what's going on,' Janek said. 'But I think you're right. Al did know something and he didn't play it straight with you at all.'

'So now what happens?'

'What happens is that if and when I find out what he knew I bring it back to you. And that's a promise.'

Suspects

Wednesday morning Aaron ran down his first-round list: 'Got an even ten to look at. Fancy lawyer who was home alone that night – family away on Martha's Vineyard. Old coot who won't be interviewed – Sal got very bad vibes from him. Stockbroker who his doorman says regularly has call girls in for overnights. Two head-related guys: a hairdresser and a cartoonist. One sex-problem counselor. One spatter-film director. One far-out fashion photographer. Thirty-five-year-old retarded man who lives with his parents – yeah, I know, Frank, but everyone says he's spooky and weird. And a live-in Japanese cook who works for a Swede, a high UN official – people in the building say he's into martial arts, so we were thinking about what Yoshiro said, you know, about, maybe, swords.'

'No women?'

Aaron shook his head.

'Okay, see who you can clear up by tomorrow night. Concentrate on the easy ones. I got my doubts about the retarded guy. Whoever did this may have been weird; but one thing he wasn't was retarded.'

He took Caroline to dinner in Chinatown, the same restaurant they'd dined at so magically two weeks before. He hadn't seen her since Sunday; it had been a week since their quarrel. He wanted to show her that he cared and that he was eager now to make peace.

In the car she started talking about her book, picking up from where she'd left off Sunday night. She said she was considering bringing in a writer, and its pros and cons. '... maybe a serious feminist, but then my feelings about male aggression could get lost in the tirade. Also, a text might start to dominate. A collaborator could be dangerous. Whose book would it really be? The other possibility is to go with quotes.'

'Why not just let your pictures speak for themselves?'

She glanced at him, irritated. 'Haven't you been listening, Frank? I'm worried they're not eloquent enough and that the book might look like a jerkoff job.'

'What are you talking about?'

'You know, like I'm one of those women photographers who get turned on photographing aggressive men.'

She talked on, but he tuned her out. He was hurt by her 'Haven't you been listening, Frank?'. He wondered if her concerns were genuine, whether she was really struggling with her book or sending him the same message she'd been sending for a week: that unless he capitulated, agreed to leave her father and Al alone, he could expect nothing but merciless self-involvement instead of the care, concern and sharing she had offered him before.

At the restaurant he told her he'd been over to Hoboken.

'That's fine, but I don't want to hear about it. Okay?'

'You talk about what's on your mind. But I can't talk about what's on mine.'

'You can, of course. Except for that. That's between you and yourself.' She grinned. 'So, what's new on the case?'

She had staked out a piece of forbidden territory; he could go into it if he liked, but he would have to go in alone. He shrugged off her question and switched the subject back to her book, urging her not to worry about what people might think, because her photographs were plenty eloquent enough. She nodded, seemed touched, thanked him, told him she appreciated his help. But then, at the end of the meal, she complained of a stinging headache and insisted on taking a cab home alone.

'Don't know what's the matter,' she said, kissing him on the cheek. 'MSG syndrome or something. Anyway, I want you to come to dinner Saturday night. Good night, Frank,' she said gently as she settled into her cab, the nicest words she'd uttered since he'd picked her up at the loft.

When he got home he unstrapped his revolver, took off and carefuly folded his pants, pulled out an accordion, sprawled out on his bed, his back against the wall, and played.

Not music – certainly not music. Squeaks and moans, wails that filled his basement apartment.

And when he pushed the bellows he felt as if his heart was being crushed.

Late Thursday afternoon Aaron was ready. At six o'clock he placed a sheet on Janek's desk. 'My short list,' he announced.

Janek picked it up. Six names and after each a number designating the apartment keyed to the master chart that now dominated the squad-room wall.

'Who do you like?' Janek asked.

'Maybe I like them all.' Aaron paused. 'Really want to know?'

Janek shook his head.

Aaron made his presentation from memory, standing before the chart. He'd eliminated the retarded man, the lawyer, the stockbroker and the cook. The lawyer, it turned out, had not been home alone – he was with his secretary with whom he was having an affair, which he hadn't mentioned the first time around because he was worried it might get back to his wife. The stockbroker categorically denied he'd ever been with a call girl – he simply dated a number of very good-looking women; the doorman who'd made the accusation retracted it, and Aaron had personally bawled him out. The live-in chef had been eliminated based on information from his employer: he'd worked for the Swedish family for more than thirty years, he was Chinese, not Japanese, and he didn't practice martial arts but a system of nonbelligerent Oriental exercise.

Which left the six men on Aaron's list, who ranged in age from twenty-eight to sixty. All six admitted they'd been home the Saturday night of the killings. At least two were obvious suspects. The other four, for one reason or another, had to be considered.

'First we have this therapist, Raymond Evans, a Ph.D. clinical psychologist. Soon as he learned we were cops he told us he'd once been arrested as an exhibitionist. No attempt to cover up and no fudging around. Came right out with it. Happened eighteen years ago. Was hanging around a girls' camp in the Adirondacks and showed himself couple of times. No prosecution provided he went

125

into therapy. He did, successfully, he says, and now he's a successful practicing sex-problem therapist himself. I liked him and trusted him. But with that arrest he needs a second look.

'Next we have this Michael Hopkins who people in Amanda's building call a peeping Tom. Couple of them report seeing him using binoculars. When I pressed he started wriggling hard. Said he didn't own binoculars. Then admitted that he did. Said he's a bird-watcher, no kind of goddamed voyeur, and who was trying to make him out to be a pervert? My feeling is he's a nasty little freak, that he may have spied on Amanda and that he knows admitting that would not be cool. Now, what's interesting about Hopkins is that he's a hairstylist. Got this small very fashionable second-floor shop on Madison.'

'Hmmm. *Shampoo*.'

'Right. Remember: "I got this head waiting"; "She's another head." Clients are "heads" to these hairdresser guys. Which may mean something or may not.'

The third name was on the list because the man had refused to talk. This was the sixty-year-old, Spalding, regarded in his building as a crank. Slammed the door in Sal Marchetti's face. Later hung up on Aaron. Said they'd have to get a subpoena if they wanted to question him and then he'd bring in his lawyer and sue.

'Mean,' said Aaron. 'Nut-house case. Never has visitors. Always complaining to the building staff. For years the co-op board's been looking for a way to get rid of him, but they're scared because he's litigious and he's rich.'

The last three men were artists, selected because Janek wanted all the artists carefully screened. There was the film director, critically acclaimed though commercially unsuccessful; the very successful fashion photographer who lived and worked on the upper two floors of the house directly across from Amanda's; and a famous syndicated political cartoonist who also worked at home, in his penthouse at the top of the tall building on the corner of Eightieth and Park.

'You might think the cartoonist is interesting. Hatchet-job headhunter type. He draws these animal bodies, then he sticks on a big caricature of the face. The usual objects of derision: mayor, governor, president.'

'What about the photographer?'

'I'm saving him.'

'You like the director.'

'Goddammit, Frank, what do I do that tips you off?'

'Always list your favourite second-last.'

Aaron laughed. 'Jesus! No wonder I'm no good at poker. Okay, I like him, and because of a couple different things. First, his movies. Lots of creepy sex and blood. Then there's the way he acts. Interviewed him myself. Very cool, which you wouldn't expect, and fascinated by the Ireland homicide. Was happy to tell me he'd seen her exercising. Even took me to the appropriate window to show me what a good view he had. Asked a lot of questions and when I asked him why he was so interested came right out with it, said the killing would make a fantastic opening for a film.'

'Sounds like an honest man.'

'Maybe too honest. And there's another thing. He goes with your *Psycho* association to the shower attack.' Janek shrugged. 'You think I'm reaching?'

'No more so than with the others. Tell me about the photographer.'

'He's hot right now. Does these pictures with the models under attack. Dobermans yapping at their legs, that kind of stuff. Also leads what they call "an avant-garde lifestyle." Orgies, pot, cocaine . . .'

Janek nodded. '"When in doubt go for the obvious." A kinky photographer who gives sex parties is obvious, but I like your list; we'll look at them all. Put Howell on the therapist. He'll be relentless on account of that old arrest. Sal gets Mr. Shampoo. Forget the crank for now. Stanger can check out the cartoonist. You like the director, so you get him. What's the photographer's name?'

'Jack Ellis.'

'I'll take him.'

Aaron sighed. '"When in doubt go for the obvious." I don't know, Frank – maybe we've been working together too many years.'

Crosscurrents

Janek gave them leeway; each could pursue his suspect in his own way. And so by their divergent strategies they revealed themselves as detectives and as men.

Howell was confused by Dr. Raymond Evans, perhaps disconcerted by the absence of a hard surface upon which to hammer. Accustomed as he was to brittle whores and sleazy pimps, his tough-guy manner proved ineffective. In the end the therapist refused him nothing except eyes downcast with shame.

Howell brought him in for questioning. Just before the crucial passage of his interview he invited Janek to the one-way window to watch his suspect take the heat:

'So you saw her?'

'Sure.'

'How many times?'

'I'd say around a dozen.'

'Turn you on?'

'Not in the slightest.'

'Why not?'

'It's showing, not watching, that turns me on.'

'What did you feel?'

'Pity. I thought she might need help –'

'*Might?*'

'– couldn't be sure about her motives. Was her exposure accidental? Did she know she could be seen? Did she care? I watched her enough times to be fairly certain she wasn't acting out. Then I stopped. No point after that. Wasn't a case anymore of ... there-but-for-the-grace-of-God.'

Janek knew then that Raymond Evans had not killed Mandy Ireland, let alone switched her head with that of Brenda Beard. Evans was a compassionate man who relieved his suffering by treating others. Howell would eventually see that, too, he thought, although the detective continued the questioning another hour.

*

Sal Marchetti chose to play hard-ass; Michael Hopkins' lie to Aaron about owning binoculars was an insult to be repaid. Sal made the rounds again of residents in Amanda's building. Had the hairstylist across the way been spying into windows or had he just been watching birds?

'Birds!' exclaimed the silver-haired woman who lived in the apartment below Amanda. 'He'd have to climb halfway out his window to see high enough.' Would she be willing to swear out a peeping-Tom complaint? 'I most certainly would! You ought to lock him up.'

Armed with affidavits from five complainants, Sal confronted the voyeur late Friday at his hair salon. Hopkins, about to leave for his weekend home, was extremely irritated by the intrusion.

'I told that other detective –'

'Nice place you got here. How many heads you do a day?'

'I personally see eight or so clients. But I don't see what that has to do –'

'Eight heads, huh?'

'I supervise eighteen or twenty more.'

'That's a lot of heads.'

'What are you trying –'

'You must dream about them.'

'What?'

'All those heads. Ever get them mixed up? Switched? The heads, I mean.'

'Look, young man, I don't know what you're getting at –'

'You're a pervert, Hopkins. Five people in the building across say you are. They want you put away. I'm going to stick you in a line-up so they can pick you out. And then, Hopkins, you're going to be fucked.'

Which, it turned out, was more or less what Hopkins wanted, or so Sal interpreted his confession when he reported it back to Janek later that night.

'Admits he's a peeper, Frank. Admits he gets off on it. Likes to peer out with the old binocs. Sure, he saw Amanda. Lots of times. But the crazy thing is he couldn't stand her. Hated it when she stood there stretching herself, because, get this, *she interfered with his view*. Sounds crazy, I know, but I went home with him and it's true. And here's the kicker. That guy Ellis you're working on who gives the so-called sex parties – stuff that happens at his place gets reflected in the windows of Mandy's building when the lights are off inside. In other words, if you live, like Hopkins, in the building next door to Ellis sometimes you can see what's happening at Ellis' place by looking at the reflections across the way. Because Ellis doesn't close his blinds. And he doesn't turn off his lights. So Hopkins sits at home and watches and sometimes late at night he sees the scenes. When I was there I didn't see much. Just some people sitting around sipping drinks. But I got the point. The windows on her brownstone act like mirrors. So Hopkins is peeping out at fucking orgies, Frank. To him Mandy was a nuisance. She was in his way.'

There was something else too. Sal dropped the word 'head' about forty-nine times before Hopkins finally picked up on it.

'I asked him then wasn't that what hairdressers call their clients. "Not me," he said. "To me they're silly cunts." So, Frank, there you are. Like Aaron said – he *is* a nasty little freak.'

'No way, Lieutenant. This is one gentle guy. There're five kids all under ten crawling around up there, plus two dachshunds and four cats. Not to mention the fact that physically he couldn't have done it. He's got some kind of degenerative muscle-tissue disease.'

Stanger had spent all of Thursday afternoon with the caricaturist, Nicholas Karpewicz, known as 'Karp,' watching him draw, listening to him speak on the phone, observing his relations with his children and his wife. But then, after he eliminated Karp, Stanger got interested in something else.

'The room where he works has this huge picture window. He owns the commanding position on the area. From up there you can see everything. So I start asking him about people. This couple I talked to. That single guy. The old bag in the garden apartment. And he knows who I mean, picks up on them right away. Starts doing little sketches, just a couple of strokes, and he gets them right, the faces, the expressions. That's his thing. Features. Heads. Later he draws in the body to make his comment. Maybe because he's sort of a cripple he's developed this way of letting the air out of people by sticking them on animals, a mule, say, or a goose.

'Anyway, I threw him some of our suspects. First Ellis. Then Lane, the film director. Then I toss him Hopkins, who he's never seen. Then Evans. Then that old crank, Spalding. Ask him what kind of body he'd put under those guys. Right away he puts Spalding on a turtle.'

Stanger laid Karp's sketches on Janek's desk. Spalding's huge head was sticking tentatively out of a tortoiseshell, a good caricature of a mean, frightened, overarmored recluse.

Dr. Evan's face, dominated by deep sad droopy eyes, was mounted on a miniature shaggy Saint Bernard. The watchful eyes of Peter Lane, the moviemaker, were implanted in a silent brooding owl. And Jack Ellis, the orgiastic fashion photographer, was depicted as an opportunistic baboon.

'I asked him finally,' Stanger said, 'to draw me his vision of Amanda. First he didn't want to do it. Then, I don't know why, he picked up his pen and started to draw. She came out kind of different from the rest.'

Stanger pushed the drawing forward.

It was a chilling work Janek saw, a fine careful drawing bearing no relation to the other swiftly sketched cartoons. The background was black, with the girl emerging from it like a phantom, her body rigid, withholding, her face a mask, expressionless, yet yearning too.

Aaron was playing his cards close. When Janek asked how he was coming with Peter Lane he smiled, then lightly bobbed his head from side to side.

'Got to hand it to Stanger,' Janek said. 'Didn't know he had it in him.'

'Sal still thinks he's a fuck-up.'

'He probably is. But maybe not a shallow fuck-up like we thought.'

'It's either your guy or mine,' Aaron said. 'How you doing with Ellis?'

Janek shrugged. 'Maybe it's none of them, Aaron. Maybe my window theory's full of shit.'

Jack Ellis was the most likely perpetrator of Switched Heads:

He lived directly across from Amanda's, with a perfect view into her window.

He indulged conspicuously in drugs and kinky sex.

131

He was a professional fashion photographer accustomed to manipulating models.

Moreover, his work was notoriously cruel.

The moment Janek laid eyes on him he realized he'd seen him before. Recently. But he couldn't remember where.

'Just so we know where we stand,' Janek said, 'you're a suspect in the Ireland case. I'm going to ask you questions. If you want you can call your lawyer first.'

The Great Decadent Photographer was suddenly an innocent little puppy. Rarely had Janek seen a man so quickly abandon a pose. Ellis declined to call his lawyer; he had, he said, nothing to hide. Furthermore, Janek ought to know he fainted regularly at the sight of blood and detested violence of any kind.

As they talked Janek looked closely at his eyes. They were tight, mean, small-time shrewd, like the eyes of a mediocre estate lawyer. And then Janek remembered where he'd seen those eyes before: a fleeting image while leafing through a book.

Caroline had photographed Ellis for *Celebrities* in the same slackening pose she'd been after in all her subjects wherein the famous personality unwittingly revealed 'the incipient decay of his public face.'

'What did you know about the girl?'

'Nothing. I swear.'

'Never looked out and saw her standing there?'

'Don't look out. People look in at me.'

'You've noticed that?'

'God yes! They even call up and complain. "At least buy some shades," they say.' Ellis laughed and shook his head.

'So why don't you buy some shades?'

'Don't like shades.'

'And you don't care what people think?'

'If they don't like what they see they don't have to watch.'

'Enjoy flaunting yourself, don't you, Jack?'

Big grin. 'Sure.' Ellis paused a moment, exhaled. 'Please understand, Lieutenant, it's all PR. That's the business, the way this city works. I pay a press agent a grand a month to preserve a certain image.'

'What's that?'

'The sinister photographer. The guy who shoots his models

under attack by dogs. I don't use cocaine. Can't stand the stuff. The reason I don't buy shades is I'm putting on a show. It adds to the image when the neighbours start to bitch. Say I'm bringing down the neighborhood. Holding orgies. Terrific!' He looked down and then he met Janek's eyes. 'Doesn't hurt, either, that there's been a murder across the way.'

So, Janek thought, a man who wishes to impress. Ellis' public persona fit the crime, but Karp the caricaturist had seen through it. And so had Caroline. Recalling her portrait, Janek realized it was stunningly accurate, much more so than if she'd simply caught Ellis in a candid moment, for it exposed the contrast between his desperate longing for notoriety and the feeble quality of his effort.

Tommy

Saturday night Caroline served him a lavish feast of stuffed Cornish hens, endive salad and Italian cheesecake accompanied by a bottle of vintage Amarone. She seemed relaxed, and the way Janek read the dinner she was telling him she wanted to feel close to him again.

After they ate he went to her bookcase, pulled out a copy of *Celebrities*, opened it to her portrait of Ellis and asked her what the photo session had been like.

'Like most of them,' she said. 'He wanted desperately to be in the book.'

'Think he's capable of cutting off a couple of women's heads?'

'That's a terrible question.' But she thought about it. 'Tell you the truth,' she said finally, 'I'm not sure he's capable of cutting up a steak.'

'Did he come onto you?'

'I suppose he did.' She smiled. 'That's what my portrait sessions were all about. Get them to come onto my lens. Make them show me their best stuff. Then catch them just when they realized it didn't work.'

Janek nodded, amused. 'So that's how you did it.'

'That's the way. Hey, are you here as a detective? My lover? Or what?'

There was something then about the way she acted with him in bed that badly disconcerted him, something harsh and taking that canceled out the good feelings he had gotten from her at dinner. It was the same greediness he'd felt when they'd gone to bed after she'd called him from the tennis club to boldly announce her desire: a hard, disturbing, almost antagonistic style, different from the slow, giving, pleasuring sensuality of their lovemaking before their quarrel.

Afterward, pondering this change as she clung to him, her flesh hot against his back, he decided he couldn't keep his feelings to himself.

'Before we made love,' he said sadly. 'Now it seems we just...'

'What?'

'Fuck.'

She pulled back abruptly, stared at him, her eyes showing bewilderment, then hurt. She got up, found her robe, put it on and tightened the sash.

'Yeah,' she said, speaking carefully, 'you're right.' And then, after a pause: 'What did you expect?'

'Please, Caroline, don't start going hard-boiled.'

'When you use words like "fuck," I'm sorry, I start feeling hard.'

'Last weekend you talked about "tearing one off."'

'Maybe that's the way it felt.'

He stood up and began pulling on his clothes.

'Going home?' she asked.

'Dressing for battle. Want to watch me strap on my gun?'

'Fuck you, Janek!'

He turned to her. 'I like direct anger. Better than having you take it out on me in the sack.'

She gaped at him. 'You weren't satisfied?'

'Come off it. That's not the point.'

'What is the point? I seem to have lost it.'

'Instead of punishing each other, why don't we try and talk.'

'I wish that were possible. But you're so' – she shook her head – 'stubborn.'

'Me?'

'*You*. With your solemn duty to the dead.'

Dressed now, he stood over her, staring down into her sullen eyes. 'What about *your* duty?' he asked. 'Don't you have a duty to yourself?'

'What's that supposed to mean?'

'That you can't let a little matter like the fact your father was murdered because "I'm sick of it, I can't deal with it," and a lot of selfish crap like that. You stand aloof and declare it turns you off, and now you're pissed because I won't go along. Tuesday night I started to tell you something, but you wouldn't let me finish. I went over to Hoboken and talked to a detective, the one working your father's case. Turns out there were loose ends. Turns out Al was onto something real. That's important, to be confronted even if it hurts. I don't see why you don't understand that, considering the sort of work you do.'

'What's my work got to do with it?'

'Every day you go out with your camera hunting for aggression. Okay, here's some real aggression, you see it and you turn away.' He paused. 'Maybe because you don't have the luxury of looking at it through a lens.'

She gazed at him hard. 'That's rough, Janek. Really rough. And suppose you're right. Suppose I *do* distance myself. So what? I told you aggression frightens me. Which is why I'm working on it. *I told you that.*'

Watching her carefully, he saw a tremor in her eye and suddenly had a thought: that there was a connection between her fear and fascination with male aggression and her resistance to dealing with her father's death.

'What was he like?'

'Who?'

He softened his voice. 'Why's it so hard for you to talk about your dad?'

'I thought I did.'

Janek shook his head. 'You said he was a failure and he called you on your birthdays and he drank and you smelled liquor on his breath. That's not enough. The guy was your father. You must have more to say about him than that.'

'What are you now? My therapist?'

He ignored her sarcasm. 'Obviously you have some grievance

against him, but you've got to know that whatever lousy thing he may have done he didn't deserve to be killed.'

She looked at him in wonderment, then tears started pulsing from her eyes. She didn't wipe them away. He put his arm around her, brought out his handkerchief and tenderly dabbed her cheeks.

'Talk about it,' he urged.

'So damn difficult.' She was weeping now.

'You'll feel better.'

'Don't know where to start.'

'Start anywhere. Just let it out.'

Her anguish upset him. He went to the galley to make coffee and give her time to settle down.

'I'm sorry,' she said. 'I know I've been acting like a bitch.'

'You've been hurting. There's nothing wrong with that.'

When he came to her she took the mug of coffee gratefully, then settled back onto the couch. He watched her, feeling she was ready, waiting patiently for her to begin.

'He was real good-looking. A handsome guy.'

'I could tell that from the snapshot.'

'When he was young, I mean; later he wasn't so handsome. But always charming. He was a charmer. He could charm anybody out of anything.' She paused, took another sip, then gulped. 'He was a bastard too. Terrible temper. It came out when he was drunk. All his anger came out and then he was dangerous. He'd make threats: "One of these days I'm going to snap. Going to go into work, pull out the old thirty-eight and kill them, mow them down." Never knew who he meant. The other officers. The bad guys. Or just anyone who rubbed him wrong.' She paused. 'He hit us, Frank. My mother, my older sister and me. I'm not claiming we were battered women. He didn't beat us up, but when he was mad he'd slap us. A single hard stinging smack across the face. So maybe we *were* battered. I remember once he knocked my mother down. Then he got remorseful and promised he wouldn't do it again. But still he'd warn us: "Don't push. Push too hard and I'm not responsible. No telling what I'll do if I'm feeling pushed."

'He could also be gentle.' She smiled. 'I remember some terrific times. Like playing hide-and-seek with him between the sheets hanging on the laundry lines in our backyard, and him walking me to school in his uniform, taking my hand as we crossed the street. There was a time, I remember, when he seemed to have a lot of money. Then, later, he was broke. That period when he was flush he rented us a house for the whole summer down on the Jersey shore. The first day he took me into the water and held me up in front of the waves. I started to cry and he said, "It's all right. trust me. I'm holding you. I'll never let you go." But I couldn't trust him, could never be sure, never know when he'd turn furious. Whenever he started to drink I knew there might be trouble. But then sometimes he'd get drunk and turn sweet, almost maudlin.' She shook her head. 'I never knew.'

'He said, "Trust me," but he wasn't dependable.'

'That's right. That was the whole damn trouble.'

'What's your best memory of him?'

She laughed. 'One time when I was little and it was winter, really cold, I came home from school, my toes so frozen they were numb. He scooped me up and carried me to my room, put me down on the bed, peeled off my socks and slowly massaged my toes till they were warm.'

'And the worst?'

She looked away. 'Seeing him hit my mother, hearing her cry, then the anger on his face as he turned away, the sound of the front door slamming and the car roaring off. Then his curses hours later when he came home from a bar. Being afraid to go to sleep, afraid of what he'd do.'

'A violent man. The worst kind of cop.'

'But he could control it.'

'Sure. That's why he became a cop. A cop carries around a big burden of menace. But he's disciplined. There're all these rules. I've known a lot of men like your dad.'

'I loved him. Even the last years. I was disappointed in him, hated the way he lived, but I loved him anyway. He'd smile and when he did, it just lit up his face. And then it didn't matter that he was a loser and a drunk. He was almost...'

'What?'

'Irresistible.'

'So you cared a lot when he was killed.'

'Yes,' she nodded. 'I cried.'

'And you were relieved too.'

She nodded again. 'Because I didn't have to be disappointed in him anymore.'

Janek sat back and studied her. 'When did you start *Aggression*?'

'Oh, some of those shots go back a long time.' She gestured toward the walls. 'I did that chess player five years ago.'

'When did you decide to do the book?'

'It was just one of maybe four or five ideas.'

Janek smiled. 'You're not answering my question.'

'Okay. It was sometime in July.'

'And you don't think there's a connection?'

'Sure there is. Of course.'

'This idea you have about men and violence, the way it attracts you and also turns you off – you must know that comes from your experience with your father, the way you could never be sure if he'd be loving and warm your toes or turn on you and slap your face.'

She nodded slowly, then looked up at him. 'You're such a different kind of cop.'

'What kind am I?'

She thought awhile before she answered. 'You're the cop I wished he could have been. Hey, come over here.' He went to her on the couch. 'You're confident and competent.' She began to trace her forefinger upon his face. 'Not a blusterer or a hothead. Not like him at all. You know how he strapped on his gun? Angry. And he wore it in the house. He never drew it even when he was drunk, but it was always there, strapped to his waist, a threat. He could have pulled it out anytime and shot us all in his awful rage.'

Janek did his best to soothe her, holding her, rocking her gently back and forth, lightly kissing her hair.

Lou

He parked in front of the house. This was the third of the last four Sunday mornings he'd driven here. Perhaps a reprieve from the puzzle of Switched Heads, but Janek had the feeling he was about to complicate his life.

The air was still as he approached the door. He rang the bell, heard the chimes go off but no footsteps. He walked around to the side. The blue Honda was in the garage. He went to the back door and looked into the kitchen. There was a half-empty bottle of vodka on the counter.

He rang the back-door bell. No chimes this time – just a loud shrill ring. The gracious amenities were confined to the front of the house; the rear was functional and brash.

He was about to leave when she appeared in the kitchen. She was wearing a pastel-pink robe, her hair was disheveled and there was a look of panic on her, the panic of a woman who was tearing herself apart.

'Frank!' He saw her mime his name. She opened the door and forced a smile.

'Sorry, Lou, I should have called –'

'Whyyoucomearoundtheback?'

'Did I wake you?'

'Big surprise you coming by.' This time she spaced her words.

She poured him a cup of coffee, asked if he wanted anything else, and when he said he didn't she led him into the living room, where they sat side by side on the couch.

'Want to show you something.' He pulled out the snapshot of Al, Tommy Wallace and Hart. 'Ever see this before?'

She nodded.

'Torn out of one of Al's old albums, wasn't it?'

She nodded again.

'Mind getting it for me, Lou?' She stared down at the rug. 'What's the matter?'

'Where did you get this, Frank?'

'We'll get to that. Why don't you get me the album first.' He watched her as she moved solemnly up the stairs. When she came back she was holding the album in both her hands. He didn't like the way she was walking, as if she were in some kind of trance. She handed him the album, sat down, then folded her hands neatly in her lap.

She looked at the rug while he turned the pages until he found the one from which the snapshot had been torn. The patch of glue matched the patch on the picture's back.

'Know this was missing?' She began to jiggle her foot. 'Why are you so nervous, Lou?'

'I'm not. Want some toast?' She stood then, abruptly, and

moved toward the kitchen. He followed, found her scurrying about slapping slices of bread into the toaster, opening the refrigerator, pulling out butter and jam, shutting it, then opening it again to take out a carton of orange juice, which she shook vigorously before she put it back.

She dug out a tray from a cupboard, arranged a plate and silverware on it, poured him a second cup of coffee with a trembling hand, and though he'd drunk his first black she went to the refrigerator to fetch her creamer and added a sugar bowl from the breakfast table beside the door.

He watched in silence. This wasn't going to be easy; her wind-up-doll behavior told him that. Their eyes met, she turned away, then they both smelled the burning toast. She leaped back to the counter, yanked up the toaster lever and feverishly plucked out the burnt bread with a fork. She gazed at the remnants, flung them into the sink, then raced to the breadbox, grabbed up two fresh slices, stuck them into the toaster, plunged down the lever again and gave the machine a punishing slap.

'Forget the fucking toast, Lou. You're not going to put me off with that. I'll take the juice and the coffee and then we're going to sit. We got some things to talk about.'

She tried to lead him back to the living room, but this time he wanted to sit across from her, not side by side. He maneuvered her to the dining table and when they were finally settled she looked at him directly for the first time since he'd come into the house, and he could see that she was scared.

'What's the picture all about?'

'It's just Al and Tommy Wallace and Dale Hart.'

'I know who's in it. I didn't ask you that. I asked you what it's all about.'

'Where'd you get it, Frank?'

'I'm asking the questions, Lou. You asked me, as a personal favor, to find out if Al was working on a case. Okay, I did, and now I've come up with something and now you start acting like you're sorry that you asked.' He looked at her sternly. 'Time to cut the crap, Lou. You got something to say – spill it out.'

She glanced at him, then bowed her head. A shaft of light hit her face; her nose cast a triangle of shade upon her cheek. Janek thought he saw stored-up tears. He waited, silent. She glanced at him again. And then she began to pour.

As he listened he realized that although he had heard many stories in his life, many long confessions, he had never reacted quite like this. It was not that the things Lou confessed were in any way extraordinary, but that he felt aroused by them to an unusual degree.

'. . . they were grand friends, the three of them, Al, Tommy and Dale. They were pals, though Dale was a sergeant and Al was ten years older than the other two. We saw each other socially, six of us – me, the other two wives and the three of them. They had all been partners at one time or another – Al and Dale, then Tommy and Dale, and finally Tommy and Al. We had a lot of good times together before things went sour on account of what they found.

'I remember the day. More than twenty-five years ago, but I'll remember it till I die. Not just for what happened but for the way things changed. Al and I didn't know it then, but for us it was a terrible day.

'Fell sometime between the holidays. Very cold – one of those days when your cheeks sting and your fingers get numb inside your gloves. Al called me from a pay phone. I could hear the other two whooping it up. They were in a bar celebrating. "Found it, darling," Al said. "We're in the clover now." I must have smiled, because I'd given Al a four-leaf clover imbedded in a plastic disk to wear around his neck for luck so he wouldn't get shot or something on the job.

'Course it was a young cop's kind of thing, that stash they found. It was in a garage set behind a deserted house. There'd been some windows busted in the neighborhood, kids' vandalism, and it was just a routine call that had brought them to the house behind. There was a fence between the two backyards and part of it was curled back. Can't remember now why they crawled through. Maybe they thought the kids had a gang clubhouse back there. Anyway, they checked out the garage and through a crack they saw the car. It was a green 1940s Chevy convertible, perfect condition, clean and polished, stored up on concrete blocks.

'It was Tommy who wanted to go in and take a look. He always loved cars and he wanted to see this one close up. So they pried open the door, went in and Tommy jumped into the driver's seat. He started bouncing around and that's when the key fell into his lap. It was like some kind of miracle, they said, the way he shook it loose from where it had been hidden in the folds of the top. When it

141

didn't fit the ignition Al tried it on the trunk. It opened that up and there were two cardboard cartons in there tied up with rope. And of course they were curious and opened one to look inside, and soon as they saw the money they looked at each other and it was then they knew they'd made their score.

'Cash, lots of it, in old used notes, tied up in bundles, a thousand dollars in each. Left there for years, maybe, and they'd found it, more money than they'd ever dreamed, and they knew it was illegal money and that if they took it they wouldn't be doing anything bad because they'd just be taking it from another thief.

'I don't know which one thought of calling Dale. Think it was Al. They needed someone higher up to cover for them, and Dale was a friend and a slick operator too.

'The way they finally handled it, Tommy called in from a booth like a busybody in the neighborhood and said he'd seen two men carrying cartons out of that garage. Then the two of them, being practically in front of the place, radioed back they'd investigate. Later they reported a break-in. In other words, they reported the robbery they'd just committed and then they investigated it themselves.'

Janek imagined the icy glint in Hart's eyes when he thought of that nefarious scheme. 'How much was there?'

'Hundred twenty thousand. They checked around later and found out the house belonged to a guy who was doing time on a numbers charge. It was numbers-racket money, probably the guy's nest egg. They used to laugh about that, how he'd feel when he found it missing after spending years dreaming about it in his cell, using it, maybe, to keep himself going through the hard winters in Ossining. It was a perfect score, Dale said: soiled old bills, out of sequence, no markings on them, illegitimately gained, the sore of a lifetime, he said. They divided it in thirds, share and share alike. They were walking on air for a couple weeks after that.'

Listening, Janek had felt a growing chill: Al hadn't taught him that way of being a cop. Lou stopped talking and now Janek could hear a TV blaring from the house next door. Some kind of morning talk show: unctuous host, tittering studio audience and a guest plugging her new book on How to Feel Better, Show Your Feelings, Be Nice to Yourself, Be Kind to Number One. For an instant then Janek imagined Al sitting at the card table in the hall holding the revolver in his mouth, and it wounded him that maybe those had been the last kinds of human sounds Al had heard before he died.

Lou was staring at him, waiting for him to speak. She still was looking scared.

'So what happened?' he asked. 'You said things changed.'

She nodded. 'Not at first so much. I think at first it drew them close. They talked about it a lot and they made a pledge. They wouldn't flash the money around. And no matter what happened they would never reveal where they'd gotten it. And there was more. If one of them ever got in trouble the other two would be there to help.'

'And that's when the picture was taken?'

Lou nodded. 'Sometime that first week.'

'And after that?'

'They started to drift. They just couldn't seem to stay friends.'

'Why?'

'Their personalities. They were so different even if they didn't know it then. But with the money the differences began to show. And also suspicion, each of them feeling the other two knew something they might use against him someday.

'You remember how Al was such a worrier? He started worrying from the start. He'd wake up in the middle of the night. "What if someone finds out? I'd be cooked. Course we'd still have the loot. You could get along. Guess it would be worth it. You don't score like that except once in a lifetime. And maybe not even then."

'That was the way he was. He used to tell me how he'd worry over a case for a month, then you'd come in and see right into the heart of it. He always said you were a born detective, Frank. He said for you things were easy which were very, very hard for him. Well, that's the way he handled the money, like it was a problem he had to worry about. He was afraid to invest it, afraid someone would start asking questions if we used it to have a little fun. So he kept it in cash in a hiding place down in the cellar. And there's nothing in there now, because there's nothing left.'

'What did you do with it?'

'Spent it. A new dishwasher here, a new washer-dryer pair there. The porch extension. The barbecue. Down payments on the Dodge and then the Mustang. A little on the Honda too.'

143

'That doesn't account for forty thousand dollars.'

'Four years at Michigan for Dolly does. So she went there and majored in art history, got married, had three children and now she wants to get divorced and move to Houston and start all over again. You know, Frank, I doubt we had any fun out of all that money except for that two-week Caribbean cruise we took a couple years ago. But even then we had bad luck. We got seasick and it rained.

'Now, Dale – he was different. He knew what to do.' She smiled as if to herself. 'You know how people say he can afford to live on Park Avenue because he married a wealthy woman? Not true. Karen Hart never had a dime and she didn't inherit anything either. Dale took his share and invested it. He set up a brokerage account in Karen's name. He invested shrewdly the way he was shrewd about everything, planning for the long term the way he always did. That's how come he always ends up so far ahead of everybody else. The way he made CD, brown-nosing the chiefs, building up debt in the department.' She shook her head. 'He was always headed for the top.'

'What about Tommy?'

She smiled. 'He was the good-time guy who threw it all away. We all warned him, "Don't act flashy." He promised he wouldn't, but he couldn't help himself. He'd go on spending sprees. You know: "Set them up, drinks for everyone." Girls, gambling, stupid bets when he was drunk. He blew half his share in less than a year, then he got worried and invested the other half in a bar and grill. It failed the way everything he touched always failed – his cases, his marriage, and, considering what happened, I guess you could say his life.

'Finaly he quit the force, left his family and moved out to Newark, where he became some sort of salesman. In the end he had nothing. He talked to Al about it once and it was kind of touching what he said: "We each used our money like the kind of guys we were. I was always a sap, so, of course, I wasted mine." Never explain, never complain – that was Tommy Wallace. No matter how stupid or drunk he always had that smile, which was why we always liked him anyway.'

Janek understood it then, why they could not stay friends. Their score was their bond and also the mechanism that drove them apart. There was no falling out; rather a falling off. The money stood between them as an embarrassment, making them avoid one another until it came back to haunt them years afterward.

'It was last spring,' she said, 'that Tommy turned up. Didn't call or anything. Just came by and rang the bell. We were watching TV, me upstairs, Al down in the workshop he'd made out of his den. I answered the door and I recognized him right away. It had been ten years at least. He looked pretty bad, but he still had the smile. Al came up, the three of us stood talking for a while, then Tommy said he had to talk to Al alone and so the two of them went downstairs.

'He told Al he was in trouble. He owed ten thousand dollars, couldn't raise it and he'd been told that if he didn't he'd get broken legs or worse. He asked Al for a loan, and Al didn't hesitate. He pushed aside the workbench, reached into the hiding place and brought out all the cash he had left, about thirteen hundred dollars.

'Tommy was grateful but said that wouldn't be enough. For the people he was into he had to have the ten. They talked about it awhile, then Al called up Dale at home. You got to understand it was the first time they'd spoken in years. Al hadn't even gone in for the interview you're supposed to have when you retire from the division. Anyway, he told Dale about Tommy, then he put Tommy on and came upstairs to wait. A while later Tommy came up and he was bitter. "He refused, the prick," he said.

'But it hadn't been so simple. It seemed he and Dale had quarreled. Tommy made some threats and it got rough. He told Dale he'd go to the DA and tell about the money. Dale, he told us, laughed at that and said the statute of limitations had run out long ago. And then Tommy told him he'd better think it over because statute or no statute a story like that could cost him his job.

'Early the next morning Dale came to the house. It was his first visit here in twenty-four years. He tried to persuade Al they couldn't make the loan because they'd be giving in to blackmail and there'd be no end to it if they did. "He'll have us over a barrel. He's got nothing to lose while I'm CD and you're a pensioned cop. I know how prosecutors work our kind of threesome. Give immunity to the weakest guy so they can burn the other two."

'Al said he didn't see it that way, that he didn't think Tommy would blab. That he'd only made the threat because he was desperate and that if they made the loan they'd have fulfilled their pledge and they wouldn't have to help another time.

'In the end Dale agreed. He gave Al nine thousand in cash. Al put in a thousand of his own, then told Tommy to come by and pick it up. Tommy was very grateful. He confirmed he'd made an empty threat. "Dale's a shit," he said, "I wouldn't hesitate to squeal on him, but I know if I did I'd hurt you and Lou, and that's something I'd never do." So that was the end of it, at least we thought. And then, about three weeks later Al found out Tommy had been killed, his body found lying up in the trunk of a stolen car over in Jersey somewhere.

'When Al called Dale to tell him what had happened, Dale acted like he didn't care. "Got what he deserved," he said. "Took our money and spent it on himself. We can kiss our loans goodbye and be grateful too, because Tommy won't be coming around to hit us for any more." Al told Dale he was a prick to say a thing like that. Dale laughed and said he had to get back to work, that he didn't have time to discuss Tommy Wallace anymore.

'Al wanted to believe that's what happened. Maybe for a day or two he did. Then he began to worry about it the way he worried over everything. He started waking up in the middle of the night and after a week he couldn't sleep.

'So he went over to Jersey and got in touch with the detective handling the case. They struck some kind of deal, because Al started looking into it himself. It was then he came alive again, like I told you, Frank, before. I hadn't seen him like that since he'd retired. That case became his life. He thought about it all the time. And the more he thought about it, the more convinced he was that the syndicate execution was a fake and that Dale Hart had had Tommy killed.'

'Was that just his theory? Or did he have some real evidence?'

She shrugged. 'He kept it all to himself. He was like that, you know, a canny detective. But he did tell me how he felt, that it was the big case of his life. That the money they had found may have been the score of a lifetime but that if he could prove Dale had had Tommy killed that would be a bigger deal than any score.

'And that was very important to him, Frank, because when he retired he felt his life had been a waste. He'd always wanted to be a great cop, break a great case and become a legend in the division, but he never lucked into anything except that stash. Now suddenly, after he retired, and *on account of that stash*, he thought maybe he had.

146

'Thing was, he knew he was in a bind. If he could pin Tommy's murder on Dale he'd have a tremendous case. But if he did that he'd also ruin himself, because he'd taken a third of that money, had been in on the loan and because of that could be a suspect, too.

'I asked him how that was possible. He said that if Dale was pushed there wasn't anything he wouldn't do, including trying to make it look like it was us who'd had Tommy killed. "We both had a motive," he said, "we both had a lot to lose if Tommy talked." When I understood that, I begged him to forget it. Dale was too dangerous. If Al went up against him we could lose everything – the pension, the house, even our lives. If Dale was capable of having Tommy killed why would he hesitate to do the same to us?

'But Al was determined. He'd gotten it into his head that he owed this to Tommy, and also to make up for what the three of them had done. He got more and more obsessed with it until finally, when I kept complaining, he wouldn't talk to me about it anymore.

'I don't know what was going on with him those last few weeks except that beginning in August he seemed to be making up his mind. He was quiet and he was out a lot. I don't know where he went. I asked him to go see the department shrink or at least talk it over with you. He wouldn't. I think he was ashamed. He just kept getting quieter and quieter. He didn't sleep much and he spent a lot of time downstairs brooding in his den.

'He spent that whole Saturday night down there. When he came up to the kitchen he looked terrible. A little later – this must have been about eight in the morning – I heard him shouting over the phone. I stood at the top of the stairs and listened. I knew he was talking to Dale. He was threatening him, saying he knew he'd ordered Tommy killed. He was shouting all this vicious stuff and then suddenly he stopped, which made me think Dale had hung up in his ear.

'Al came back up to the kitchen. I saw something wild in his eyes. I started to beg him then, "Let it go." He didn't answer, just stared at me with those crazy eyes.

'He went back downstairs and I know he burned a lot of papers. I found the ashes later and I never found any notes about the case. Then he went outside for a while, just stood on the front lawn looking at the street. Then he came back in and said he was feeling better. He set up the card table in the hall and started whittling that flute. About an hour later I heard the shot.'

She sat back, exhausted. She'd been talking nonstop for an hour. As soon as she stopped she stared down at the table as if she couldn't bear to meet Janek's eyes.

'Why didn't you tell me this before?' he asked. 'Why all the crap about how Al was working on something and could I find out what it was?'

'I'm sorry, Frank. You're right to be angry. But, you see, I didn't want to tarnish Al. I was afraid if I told you about the money you wouldn't care about him anymore.'

'Then why ask me to look into it in the first place? If I discovered what he'd been doing why would my feelings be any different then?'

'It was stupid. I know. It was just that I had this idea.'

'What?'

She glanced up at him, a painful glance. 'That you might want to take over the case and bring down Hart the way Al wanted to do.'

'If that's what you wanted you should –'

'I know. I just thought that if I hinted around you might stumble on it on your own. But when you came by two weeks ago and told me there was nothing, I decided to let it go.' She exhaled. 'Tommy was dead and Al was dead and whatever Dale had done just didn't make that much difference anymore.'

'But I did find something.'

'Yes,' she said. 'Where did you get the picture?'

'Al gave it to Tommy Wallace's daughter.'

'Oh, I see. Yeah, I saw her at the funeral.' She looked perplexed. 'But how did you get to her?'

He ignored her question. It would require a complicated answer and he didn't feel like discussing his relationship with Caroline. But it occurred to him that Al's act of pressing the snapshot into Caroline's hand had been done with the same sort of ambivalent hope that had driven Lou to tell him Al had been working on a case and then ask him to find out what it was.

He thought about it. Al must have been brooding over suicide for weeks. Most likely he had prepared affidavits which implicated Hart. But at the last moment he lost his nerve, possibly because of something Hart said to him on the phone. So he burned his papers, his affidavits and his notes, preferring to go out as an inexplicable

148

suicide rather than as a cop too cowardly to make his case even if in the attempt he brought down ruin upon himself.

But still he'd given Caroline that photograph, hoping she would follow it up. The odds against that happening were astronomical, considering how strongly she'd resisted letting him talk to her about his agony. But astronomical or not, Al's last bet had been won. Janek had gotten hold of the snapshot, had pulled the story out of Caroline, Carmichael and Lou, and now he was in possession of a set of facts that he could pursue in a way that Al could not.

'Oh, Frank . . .' Lou was sobbing. 'I see now it was all my fault. I didn't understand. He wanted so much to be a great cop, to break open a great case and pull Dale down. But I wouldn't let him do it. I begged him to leave it alone. I was afraid we'd lose that stupid pension. I denied him his chance for – I don't know. Redemption, I guess.'

Or at least absolution, Janek thought. He turned to her and shook his head. 'It wasn't you. He was in a double bind. The more he investigated, the more evidence he found, the more likely he was to implicate himself. In the end he painted himself into a corner. And then there was only one way out.'

There were tears now streaming down her face. Janek pulled her to him, stroked her gray hair and let her sob. He wanted to comfort her but didn't know what to say. And then, suddenly, words came to him as he gazed around at the gold tassels on the cusions, the gold carpeting on the floor, the ornate veneer that had always made him feel uncomfortable, which Al and Lou had used to conceal the ambiguous virtue of their lives.

'You two had so much. I envied you. Always did. You had so much more than Sarah and me. I used to think about that whenever I saw Dolly, how barren we were, how much we missed.'

'All the pain . . .'

'Sure, but don't forget about the good stuff. You lived, Lou. The two of you lived. Sarah and me – we just cohabited. What a terrible way to pass the years.'

He knew he was being maudlin and he didn't care; he was doing the best he could. And then when she started arguing with him, denying that he and Sarah had not had a good and loving life together, he nodded in agreement although he did not agree. The important thing was for her to stop feeling guilty over Al. If he

149

could help her get over that he knew he would feel less guilty over Al himself.

Guilt: that was what Al's last case had been about. A struggle to stay incorruptible; a moment of weakness paid for by years of shame. Then a glimpse at redemption and the realization that there was no redemption to be had. And the knowledge that in his own special way he, Al DiMona, was also to blame for Tommy Wallace's death.

Glancing down at the table, at the snapshot of the three grinning cops, Janek understood the confusion that blemished Al's smile. *Even then he knew there'd come a day*, Janek thought. And thinking that, he grasped Lou harder and held her tight against his chest.

Narrowing the Focus

Early Monday morning Aaron called in: 'At the Museum of Modern Art. Looking up a couple things. I'll be in around eleven.'

Aaron had something – Janek could feel it, that he was the only one of the five of them to have come up with an idea. He told Stanger to check out Spalding. ('If he gives you any crap tell him he's a murder suspect and I want to see him down here with his lawyer.') He assigned Howell and Sal to interview friends and associates of Ellis. ('I think he's a homicidal sadist and see how they react.') Then, when the office was clear, he sat back in his chair to wait. He thought about Al and then about Hart's eyes and how cold they were and how he's always thought that Hart could kill.

When Aaron came in he was ready to sell. He took Karp's drawings of Ellis and Lane and tacked them to the wall.

'You and Karp see Ellis the same way,' Aaron said, 'a monkey, one paw clutching bananas, the other beating his chest. Suppose Karp's right, too, about my guy, Lane. Then what've you got? An owl, a nightbird, staring out waiting for his prey. Yeah, I know, Karp's a cartoonist. He may have better-than-average insights, but what's that got to do with the case? Nothing except that when I saw his drawing I thought, Wow, that's it, that's just the way *I* see the guy.'

'Did you talk to him again?'

'No.'

'Why not?'

'First time around I got enough.'

'So what have you been doing?'

'Checking him out.'

'And?'

'Well, I'll tell you, Frank, he makes movies about guys who stab whores and diddle around with cops.'

Janek waited, and when Aaron didn't add anything he sighed – there had to be more.

'Come on,' he said. 'I've heard that story. Ellis –'

'This is different.'

'I sure hope it is,' Janek said.

They ate lunch at the Taco-Rico, then drove to a repertory cinema near the Columbia University campus. Aaron insisted that Janek come; he said what he'd seen over the weekend was too subtle to explain. Janek said if it was all that subtle it probably wasn't going to throw much illumination on the suspect. Aaron said it might or it might not but that he had a very strong feeling and since the other suspects were more or less closed out what did Janek have to lose?

So he allowed himself to be dragged uptown, pleading reluctance all the way. He knew Aaron didn't have a bombshell and that he wasn't going to find out what he did have until he let Aaron soften him up.

The titles were spelled out on the marquee: 'TWO BY LANE: HAIRDRESSER and MEZZALUNA.'

'Two. Christ. You didn't tell me it was a double feature.'

'If you want we'll only stay for one.'

The theater was old and cavernous, nearly empty that weekday afternoon. A bearded wino, sprawled out on a rear-row seat, alternatively snored and gasped. A small contingent of young people passed a joint in a row near the screen. The place smelled of old popcorn and stale marijuana smoke. The usher, elderly and decrepit, wore a soiled uniform and a mismatched grey toupee.

'Not one of your fashionable first-run houses,' Janek said. 'And not exactly a couple of hits.'

Aaron nodded. 'A few critics love his stuff, but he's definitely

151

not commercial. More like a cult director with a small devoted audience.'

Hairdresser was about a killer named Seymour Trent who, after he stabbed his prostitute victims, lovingly gave them each a wash and a perm. He was pursued by a mean piggish cop named Templeton who staggered drunk when he wasn't speeding dangerously in his patrol car around the unnamed California coastal town where the story was set. There was an aura of corruption about everything in this town: cretinous deputies, hostile hippies, leering merchants, toothless hard-boiled whore-house madams. At the end killer and cop took part in an extravagant chase through a run-down amusement park. Trent escaped off a speeding roller-coaster by jumping into a murky river. Templeton swigged whiskey from a bottle and stared down at the oily water with the eyes of a bedazzled fool.

A crude low-budget film, probably an early work, Janek thought, employing inexperienced actors playing implausible characters in a story that didn't add up. But he also recognized energy: an atmosphere of menace; the way the killer's knife flashed in the light; and a hypnotic photographic style.

There was a brief break between the films. When the lights came on, the theater ricocheted with coughs.

Aaron leaned over and whispered into Janek's ear, 'Notice the cop didn't make his collar.'

Mezzaluna was stronger than *Hairdresser*, though in format pretty much the same. The murderer, Targov, a worker in a slaughterhouse, killed his whore victims with a mezzaluna, the Italian half-moon-shaped vegetable-chopping device.

When Targov slayed, the murder scene would dissolve into a memory: Targov as a boy watching his mother rolling her mezzaluna from side to side and smiling quietly as if with secret knowledge.

The detective was named Masterson and the location was Chicago. Masterson was slow-witted, walked with the heavy swagger of a street cop, slurred his words and rocked nervously on his heels when he stood still.

There was some sort of grim battle of wits between killer and cop; one felt that Masterson knew Targov was his quarry but for some unstated reason could not make an arrest. After numerous complications Masterson tracked Targov to a meat-packing plant, where he chased him amidst a maze of hanging carcasses, fired out his revolver, then lost him in the dark.

As Masterson shrugged, gave up and backed away the camera closed in on the shadows. When the detective opened the packing-house door a splinter of light penetrated, reflected off the mezzaluna and made it flash silver in the dark.

Janek was half nauseated. The story was unreal, the plot absurd, the ending unsatisfying. But still he felt that Lane was skillful; despite the shallowness of his work, he conveyed a vision, something bleak and miserable that stuck in Janek's mind.

'So you see,' said Aaron when they were out on the street, 'he makes movies about intense killers who use sharp instruments to cut up whores.'

'What else?'

'The same contrived, arranged style your lady friend saw in our photographs. The same studied artificial look.'

They got into the car. Aaron didn't start it up; he watched Janek, who stared out the windshield with his hands locked behind his head.

'You're right about the look,' Janek said. 'He works hard making the killings beautiful. They're really exquisite if you can stand to look at them. But I think there's more. The stories. That's what you wanted me to see.' He turned. Aaron nodded. 'The same strange logic, right? Like in our case. All that elaborate moving back and forth. Perfectly planned and executed, with a kind of artistic signature at the end instead of the mess and blood we should have found.'

They talked about it. Aaron said he felt the movies were a smirk. 'The cops are slobs, right? Templeton and Masterson. But the killers, Trent and Targov, are brilliant. Remember what you said the first day: "I'm superkiller and I defy you cops to solve my crime"?'

'I was just spouting.'

'Maybe so. But I get that same message from the movies. They give me a bad feeling, like that to Lane the killings aren't all that important, like the big play's the struggle between the killer and the cop.'

'What were you doing at the museum?' Janek asked.

'Using the library. They've got back issues of the scholarly film magazines.' Aaron unfolded a clipping and passed it to Janek. He had underlined several passages in an article entitled 'The Rage of Peter Lane':

... and when on the soundtrack we hear a chorale from a mass, the degraded crime-scene becomes a cathedral. Diabolic turns holy. The forbidden act of erotic murder becomes an artistic act of ritual sacrifice ...

The detective: he is inevitable, and in all Lane's stories more or less the same – a clown, a man to be taunted, to be broken and scorned as he fails to solve his case. The killer goads him, makes him mad, and when he charges wildly the killer steps nimbly aside and the detective stumbles, confused, at nothing, at the air ...

As they drove downtown he felt Aaron's stare.

'So why aren't you more excited, Frank? Usually when you get interested in a suspect you act a little more turned on.'

Janek exhaled. 'Who says I'm interested?'

'What's the matter? You saw it. The crime scenes in his movies look like ours, and the movies are about the same kinds of crazy homicides.'

'Too corny.'

'Okay.' Aaron pulled the car over and stopped. 'I dug around on this guy. He's given a lot of interviews. One thing he says again and again, that he'd like to make a picture that would inspire a real murder.'

'Grandiose talk. He's trying to sound gruesome. All the terror guys sound off like that.'

'But suppose it's a little different from what he says.' Aaron paused. 'Suppose what he really wanted to do was make a movie about a murder he first committed himself.'

Life imitating art; art imitating life: that did seem corny to Janek, but still he found Lane interesting.

Spalding was out of the case: for some reason the old man took a liking to Stanger, invited him into his apartment and confided his theory that the real target in the Ireland homicide had not been Amanda but her dog.

Ellis' friends were incredulous at the notion that anyone would think him capable of murder. His S-M fashion stills? Tongue-in-cheek. Orgies? Sometimes his guests got kinky and stripped. Homicidal sadist? You got to be kidding. Jack's a pussycat. Though, occasionally, he does overdo the hype.

Dr. Raymond Evans, Michael Hopkins and Nicholas Karpewicz were also out. And so was Hazel Carter: her weekend alibi had held up. But Cynthia Tuttle's records showed that on one occasion Brenda had joined a class just before Mandy's regular hour. Janek was intrigued. The girls had brushed very close, had likely seen each other, perhaps had even spoken in the changing room. He imagined the one suiting up, the other toweling off, as models and dancers gossiped at adjoining lockers. None of which, he knew, had much to do with the case, though he felt haunted by the possibility that they'd met.

That left the film director – if the window theory was to stand. Janek stared at Karp's sketch, the one that showed Lane as a brooding owl. He repositioned it on the squadroom wall so that Lane's eyes were on the row of crimescene photographs.

Tuesday morning he called the squad together. 'We're going to look at this guy real close. He hasn't met you, Sal, so you're the one to tail him. Covertly. No pressure. You lose him you pick him up later, right? Howell and Stanger: get photographs. There're plenty in the film magazines. Now, when you talk to the prostitutes you show them shots of Lane. Have they ever seen this guy? Is he a john? Aaron, you'll coordinate and start a background check. Usual sources – Defense Department, FBI. I want to know who he is.'

'Jesus,' moaned Aaron, 'another book.'

'Got to know him before I interview him. You think he likes to play games. Fine, we're stupid, just like the apes in his films. We're so stupid we don't even know we're in a game. Here's the strategy: we're looking at him, but no direct approach. When and if we find something, like that he made some memorable expeditions before he found his Amanda look-alike, I'll take a crack at him. And when I do I don't want to be a stupid cop.'

Aaron's greeting Thursday morning: 'I don't know, Frank. Are we throwing too much into this?'

Janek glanced around the squad room. The place smelled of coffee and cigarettes. 'Where are the other guys?'

'Sal's sitting in a car outside Lane's building. Stanger and Howell will be in later. The whores aren't up till afternoon.'

'So what's the problem?' Already he felt tired. He'd spent the night thinking about Hart. His hatred surprised him; it went beyond anything he'd felt in years.

'The problem, Frank, is Lane. He's top of the list by default. We're five guys. And now we're all working on him full time.'

'Thought you liked him.'

'I *do* like him. But . . .' Aaron shrugged. 'Is the allocation right?'

Janek sat down. His mind was whirling. There were Tommy Wallace and Hart, and Switched Heads and Lane. 'Got to allocate the way I feel, Aaron. May look like default, but I'm running on a hunch. I felt something at her window. Made me shiver. It's someone out there, someone who can see in. Lane fits. Right now I got to go with that. So – anything else?'

'Yeah. Sal's having trouble. It's not a one-man job. Even a normal low-key surveillance you're talking at least three guys and you're better off with five. But Lane's not normal. Doesn't keep regular hours. Doesn't go to a job, sleeps late, then stays out half the night. But the other morning Sal missed him. Doorman said he went out at dawn. Wanders around a lot, too. Like he'll take a series of subway rides, down to West Fourth Street, change to a Brooklyn train, then switch back to a train heading uptown. Or he'll ride down to City Hall, then walk across the Brooklyn Bridge. Quite a few times Sal's lost him. No way he can keep up.'

'Maybe Lane knows he's on him.'

'Yeah. That's possible.'

'If Sal's talking to the doorman –'

'Doormen know we're watching the neighborhood. Sal didn't let on he was particularly interested in Lane.'

'Still –'

'Sure. He could know.'

'So you want two more men.'

'Would help a lot.'

Janek shook his head. 'Hart won't give them to me.'

Aaron nodded and turned back to his phone. Janek watched him awhile, listening to him work. Aaron was good, a superb telephone investigator. Janek wished he could tell him why he didn't want to ask Hart for anything.

Lane didn't own a car. Which left the possibility he'd rented or leased one, or had used a stolen car that night. Which meant checking with all the car-rental agencies in the city, and the registry of stolen-car complaints going back three days before the homicides. None of which would prove anything, as Aaron and Janek knew perfectly well, since Lane could have rented a car in Philadelphia or Baltimore or anyplace within hundreds of miles. Or used fake ID to rent one. Or stolen one on Long Island or upstate. Or owned one he'd registered under an assumed name. Or had used a taxi whose driver hadn't responded to their call to check all destination lists. Or had taken a bus and hadn't been remembered because he'd carried the heads in a gym bag. Or had marched across Central Park carrying them in a backpack on an eccentric nocturnal urban hike. Which meant that a check of rental agencies and the registry of stolen-car complaints was hardly worth doing. Which didn't mean it didn't have to be done. Which it was. With the expected result. Which still didn't mean anything.

As Aaron put it to Janek as they shared another in an endless stream of pizzas at the Taco-Rico, 'Well at least we know one thing. He's got a driver's license. So we can assume he probably knows how to drive.'

At the end of each day Janek would drive uptown, check the mailbox at his basement apartment, take a shower, change his shirt, then drive over to Long Island City to Caroline's loft.

He'd become a short-haul commuter and, he decided, he did some of his best thinking on the road. He developed a little ritual: As soon as he swung from the access ramp onto the Queensboro Bridge he would glance back at Manhattan in his rearview mirror. Darkness was falling earlier; the twilight vision he'd enjoyed the first time he'd driven to her – the glow behind the buildings, the luminous city set powerfully against the fading sky – was replaced now by the spectacle of lit skyscrapers standing guard before the black impenetrable night.

The sight never failed to move him or to inspire some kind of idea. And when he arrived she would be there waiting for him, her loft filled with soft jazz music and softly dancing light, and he would take her in his arms and breathe in the scent of her body and her hair, and then they would drink wine and make love on her brass bed beneath her gently turning ceiling fan and sometimes he would feel less anger in himself and other times a tension he could neither fathom nor define.

Janek read Aaron's notes on Lane:

> ... won't go on talk shows. Rarely gives interviews. Conceals background by putting out contradictory stories on his past. At various times has claimed he was brought up: in Midwest; on Indian reservation; in rural community in California; that his father (named Jack Lane, Joe Lane, Harold Lane, etc.) was: barber (cf. *Hairdresser*), veterinarian, police officer (!), parole officer, and, alternatively, that subject doesn't know parents' names since he was orphan and brought up in foster home... As far as can be determined subject has never mentioned mother or siblings... Subject claims to have attended Princeton but name does not appear in college records. Claims that he studied filmmaking in Germany and worked as assistant to Munich-based director, Schoendorfer, check out...

Aaron managed to learn that neither the Defense Department, the Drug Administration nor the FBI had any knowledge of Peter Lane – a feat he accomplished informally on the phone by working through his network of law-enforcement friends. Old favors were reciprocated and new debts incurred, but answers to the most basic questions (names of parents, date and place of birth) eluded him. He could have obtained them if he'd been able to look at Lane's passport application, but that was protected by the Privacy Act of 1974. Lane had not been indicted for any crime, nor was he the subject yet of an officially sanctioned criminal investigation. And so, for all his brilliant telephone technique, his contacts, his coaxing and sweet talk, Aaron Rosenthal, to his immense surprise, could not manage to break through this single block.

One night on the bridge Janek thought about phoning Carmichael. And then he thought, *No. Not yet.*

He was worried. He sometimes got his cases confused. His mind would flash back and forth between them the way it had weeks before when he'd practiced switching people's heads.

Every case, he knew, had its solution. Switched Heads had a solution, and Wallace/DiMona had one, too. The trick was to find it, to look for it within the case, in the characters of the players, their weaknesses and strengths.

He thought, *There has to be a way to get to Hart, not to fight him on his terms but to make him fight on mine.*

Aaron summarized his Peter Lane material in a thickening looseleaf book he kept locked up with an extra yarmulke in the center drawer of his desk:

> Subject has had numerous 'girlfriends' but no long-term intimate relationships. Several informants speak openly of subject's detachment during, and quick loss of interest after, what they describe as 'perfunctory' or 'technical' sex ...
>
> Subject has no known close male friends ...
>
> Subject's reputation among technicians: businesslike and relentless. Among actors: 'exploitive,' 'brilliant,' 'unscrupulous.' Considered by those who have financed productions as extremely mercurial – 'friendly and seductive' when backing to be gained but 'indifferent and unreachable' once films completed and released ...
>
> On numerous occasions subject has expressed following view: 'The test of the ultimate murder film would be its power to inspire an actual murder.'
>
> Cinema critic and psychoanalyst Dr. David Lee writes: '[subject's] films seem driven by obsessions derived from undefined, heavily masked psychological conflicts in [subject's]) past: an over-powering matricidal rage in which all women are equated with prostitutes, and an unresolved early conflict with paternal authority symbolically represented by police.'

'"Heavily masked psychological conflicts"?' Aaron gripped the phone. 'What exactly do you mean by that?'

'Before I answer I'd like to know –'

'Listen, Dr. Lee –' Aaron met Janek's eyes and winked – 'this man's been quoted as saying he'd like to see his films inspire homicides.'

'But surely, you understand, he meant that in a certain spirit.'

'Like how?'

'Well, you know that several times when *The Deer Hunter* was broadcast some people got hurt playing Russian roulette.'

'Didn't know that.'

'Yes. I believe a couple of people were actually killed.'

'You're saying –'

'And there's the case of Mr. Hinckley and *Taxi Driver*.'

'We know about that.'

'Well, then you know that's what he means.' Aaron held out the phone and rolled his eyes. 'In a certain competitive spirit vis-à-vis other young film directors. And I don't believe you law-enforcement people should take such statements literally. Especially considering what I hear about the public-safety situation in New York City. I don't mean to tell you how to do your job, Sergeant. But, really, I find this dialogue rather...'

After Aaron delivered himself of the courtesies and hung up he turned to Janek and slowly shook his head. 'I don't seem to do so great with the academics.'

'But your question was very good.'

'I forget my question.'

'About "heavily masked psychological..."'

'Yeah. But he's masking the whole thing, Frank. I mean screw the "conflicts." Who the fuck is this guy?'

Aaron was happy. 'We got pay dirt. And these guys are terrific.'

He was speaking of Stanger and Howell, who had developed, contrary to everyone's expectations, into a first-rate prostitute-interviewing team. They were sitting in the squad room now looking a little smug as Aaron read aloud from their report:

'"According to informant, subject did nothing perverse. Informant describes subject 'a perfect gentleman.' Subject made no particular demands upon informant other than requiring her to perform fellatio upon him while postured on her knees. After which, according to informant, subject added a modest tip to informant's professional fee."'

Stanger and Howell's language was grotesque, but Janek knew what it meant: the discovery of a prostitute who recognized Lane from photographs was the first slim piece of evidence to support his theory of the switch.

'You got to hand it to these guys, Frank.'

Janek nodded. 'I love them. So keep at it, guys. Get me more.'

Sal was hollow-eyed. It was seven in the morning; Janek had
driven uptown to meet him in Amanda's apartment. Sal had
stationed himself there on the premise that if Lane had spied on
Mandy from his bedroom window, then he could spy on Lane
through the same two panes of glass.

The air in the room was close. There were dirty coffee cups in the
sink and crumbled potato-chip bags on the counter. A big glass
ashtray was overflowing. The room stank of a tired cop.

'Have to be careful, Frank. Move around too much and he
knows I'm here. Never turn on the lights. Just sit in the easy chair
and watch. Getting so I can find my way around in here with my
eyes shut. Know every inch of the place. Including the can. Just
love the can, Frank. I mean, it doesn't weird me out to go in there
anymore. Course I don't leave the shower curtain shut. Not the
way she did. Matter of fact, I took it down. I mean, who needs it? I
take my showers at home.'

Sal raised his eyebrows then in a particularly emphatic way to
show Janek he was talking about a lot more than personal hygiene.

'What's your feeling?'

'I've kept a log of everything –'

'Sal –' Janek placed his arms on the younger man's shoulders – 'I
know what you've reported. What's your *feeling* about the guy?'

'He knows I'm on him,' Sal muttered softly.

'What makes you feel that way? Does he look back a lot?'

Sal shook his head. 'It's not like that. It's hard to explain.' He
paused. 'He moves. He moves like he's conscious of me. But he
never looks back. *Never.* And that spooks me, Frank. He's so
controlled, you see. So incredibly controlled. And then the other
night he did something and I could swear . . .'

'What did he do?'

'Well, I was in here watching. He couldn't have seen me. The
window was closed. Christ, it was so bitching hot I could hardly
breathe. And I was still. Like a fucking stiff, Frank. I swear I was
sitting in that chair like a fucking stiff. And the lights were on in his
bedroom. He leaves them on a lot. Sometimes I got to wait hours
before I see him come in there, but the lights are always on. Okay,
he comes in, not self-conscious at all, and he starts to get

161

undressed. He pulls off his shirt. He likes those asshole shirts with the alligators over the nipple. So, okay, now he's stripped. He comes over to the window and I think, hey, this may be it, he's going to do something for a change, he's going to make a move. So I'm very alert and very still too. Just watching. And I can see he's doing this kind of deep breathing. You know, inhaling, exhaling, tightening up the stomach muscles, that whole trip. He's not a big guy, he's no body builder, but he's strong. Okay, then he tenses up and holds the pose, his eyes fastened on the window over here. I actually felt he was looking in. Knew he couldn't see me, but it felt like he could. So then he breathes out, relaxes, you know. And then he – you won't believe this, Frank. The guy throws me a kiss.'

A kiss. 'Show me how he did it.'

Sal demonstrated: he placed his hands on his hips, pursed his lips and kissed the air and at the same time thrust out the lower half of his face.

'Was it hostile?'

'Did I do it hostile? Didn't mean to, because it wasn't like that at all. It was almost – like, you know, he was wishing me good night. Sleep well. Happy dreams. Fuck you. Like that.'

Like that. The kiss bothered Janek. *Like how?* he wondered. 'Let's go out and get some coffee.'

'He's there now. Sleeping. Don't want to lose him.'

'You need a break,' Janek said. 'Come on.'

'But –'

'*Sal*, listen to me. I don't give a good goddamn about the stakeout. You're acting weird. Let's get out of here.'

They went to Aspen, the place with the copper pots and the waitresses with Finch accents where they'd met the night they'd done the walk-through. Janek encouraged Sal to talk, about baseball, the coming hockey season, the stock market, anything that interested him. Several times he noticed the younger man glance nervously at his watch.

'I'm thinking of pulling you off him,' Janek said. 'How would you feel about that?'

'Won't lie to you, Frank. These haven't been the greatest two weeks of my life.'

'You've been very conscientious.'

'Trying to do the job.'

'Not easy, I know.'

'I've worked plenty of stakeouts –'

'Alone's different.'

'Yeah. It is.'

'So, it didn't work. Looks like he may be onto you. And that's not your fault. So we throw it in on the surveillance for now.'

'What do you want me to do?'

'Got any ideas?'

Sal smiled. 'There is something. But I know you'll never –'

'What?'

'Let me do a wiretap.'

Janek studied him. Sal was wearing the shrewd conspirator's grin. 'No point,' Janek said gently. 'If he did this he did it alone, so there's no one he's going to talk it over with. No judge will grant us an order, and an illegal tap could backfire later on.'

'Still.'

'Forget it. That's one sure way to screw up the case.'

Sal lowered his eyes. 'I know. I'm sorry. It's just . . .'

'Tell you what,' said Janek. 'You want to do something extracurricular, I got a job for you, very covert.'

Sal looked at him. 'An investigation?'

Janek nodded. 'If you take this on it's between us. No one else must know, not even Aaron.'

'A job for my rabbi. You know I'll do it, Frank.'

'Anything, right, to get pulled off Lane? I'm pulling you off anyway. This other thing is optional. And no questions. That's the deal.'

Sal nodded. 'What do you need?'

Janek sucked in his breath. 'A full financial background report on Chief of Detectives Hart. All assets. Real estate. Bank accounts. Stocks owned and traded. Going as far back as you can dig.'

'Chief Hart?' Sal's face was suddenly motionless.

'And his wife, Karen. Particularly her. Because I think you'll find that most of what they've got is held in her name, not in his.'

Sal liked the project; Janek could tell. It appealed to the same part of him that wanted to put a wiretap on Lane.

'How do we keep this from Aaron?'

'You continue to file reports on Lane. You know the patterns, so you mix the stuff around a little bit.'

'And it comes out just the same.' Sal grinned.

Janek nodded and, for a moment, wondered if he was making a mistake. He had a major case, few resources, and now he was putting Sal on something else. Sal couldn't get hurt; Janek would protect him, absorb the blame, admit he'd given Sal an illegal order and take the consequences, the loss of his job and probably his pension too, if it came to that. He hesitated. Then he told himself he didn't have a choice. He smiled. This time he and Sal shared the shrewd-conspirator grin.

It was at Caroline's door that he remembered the kiss. When he entered the loft he went straight to the bathroom, stood before the mirror, pursed his lips and threw a kiss at himself just the way Sal had described.

'Good night. Sleep well. Happy dreams. Fuck you.'

Caroline was at the stove when he came out. They smiled at each other as he dialed the precinct from her desk. Howell answered – at least someone was working late. 'In my desk. Lower left-hand drawer. Mandy's diary. Couple of pages marked with paper clips near the end.'

While he waited for Howell to find the entry he threw Caroline a couple of kisses.

'Weird the way you're doing that.'

'Weird how?'

'I don't know. Mean. Grudging, I guess.'

Howell found the passage. Janek listened as he read it over the phone: '"A kiss good-night. A stingy, little kiss. If only it were real affection. Poor me here with Petti all alone..."'

He put down the phone. 'Hey.' She turned to him. He threw her three.

'What are you doing?'

'Being stingy.'

'Mean,' she said.

'Stingy little kisses?'

'Right.'

'Like "Fuck you," right?'

'Right.'

He thanked her as he dialed Aaron.

'... Here I am, Frank, just sitting down to dinner with my four

164

beautiful daughters and my lovely wife, and you call me about a
kiss.'

'That's it, Aaron. A stingy little fuck-you kind of kiss.'

'You crazy or something?'

'I don't think so,' Janek said.

'Got to be him,' Janek said. They were in bed. The fan was milling
above their heads.

'So what are you going to do now?'

'See him,' he said. 'I think it's time.'

'How will you handle it?'

'Oh – play it by ear.'

She took hold of his face, turned it so she could see his eyes.
'Bullshit,' she said. 'You're going in there with a plan.'

He nodded. 'I'll probably slap him around a little. The way you
think cops like to do.'

'*Janek.*' She punched his arm.

'Okay, I'm going to patty-cake him a few times, mentally, of
course, in a couple of different places. The way I figure it he'll play
it like a tar-baby, try and sucker me in, get me mad, try and tie me
up. Then, depending on how I feel, I may haul back and clobber
him one. Just to see how he takes it, to see if he's breakable or not.'

She shivered. 'What if he isn't breakable?'

'Then I'll know what I'm up against. And he'll know something,
too. He'll know I know it's him.'

Criminal Conversation

It's his eyes, Janek thought. Empty eyes, shiny and hard like wet
gray stones. Unwavering eyes, utterly still. Eyes without effect.

They sat facing one another on long black leather sofas, a large
square glass coffee table in between. Nothing on the table. Nothing
on the walls. The apartment cold, pristine, the floors painted a
hard-gloss white, the young man sitting silent, still – watching,
appraising, waiting for him to begin.

Janek had puzzled over photographs before the meeting. Peter hadn't looked like the sort who would make the kind of films he did. No brooding countenance, no tormented brow. Rather a regular, bland unlined face, light brown hair cut short like a college boy's, the features empty, inexpressive, blank like a sentry's. Like a marine sentry, Janek thought, on duty, on guard.

'Detective Rosenthal tells me you're interested in the Ireland homicide.' No reaction, no anxiety, just that blankness in the eyes. 'The investigation's bogging down. Thought I'd drop by and pick your brains.'

Peter smiled, as if to say: 'Okay, go ahead. Pick.' The photographs, Janek realized, did not do justice to his eyes. Or to his stillness, the guy just sat there, didn't move.

'Have any theories?'

Peter cocked his head. Theories? Was Janek serious? 'Told Rosenthal I saw the girl. Couldn't have missed her if I'd wanted to.'

Janek leaned forward. 'Tell me,' he said. 'What did you see?'

Peter stared straight ahead. Finally, he spoke. 'She did these stretch deals, bare ass, around eleven every night. Wondered what she was up to. Whether she was asking for it. Or what.'

'Asking for what?' Janek asked. He shifted position. Lane had seated him so that a ray of the late afternoon sun was shining directly into his eyes.

'That's what I wondered: "Or what?" That's what I wondered about.'

Janek shook his head. 'That's not what I meant.'

'What did you mean?'

'What did you think she might be asking *for*?'

'Oh, I see. Well, *that's* what I asked myself.' He spoke in a maddeningly laconic tone of voice, then sat back. He smiled the small cool smile of a man who'd just delivered a message: *Push and I'll concede you nothing; press and you'll find I'm made of stone.*

The shaft of light fell between them now, cutting across the room like a sword. Watching his suspect through the curtain of sparkling dust Janek was struck again by Peter's stillness. No fluttering, no nervous energy, just an inappropriate tranquility. Janek had seen that same calm before in certain Vietnam vets he'd met. A quiet that screamed. A hush that roared. It was there in Peter's eyes.

'You were fascinated by her?'

'Interested. Thought it could make a brilliant scene. The girl so provocative, offering herself. But holding back too. She didn't wiggle her boobs.'

'What was she like?'

Lane thought about it. 'Hard to say.'

'She was practicing for her exercise class.'

'She should have pulled the blinds.'

'Suppose she had? You think she'd still be alive?'

Peter ignored the question. 'There were reflections. Stuff going on. Interesting, the way she'd be there stretching and then she'd turn off the lamp and the scene would change and suddenly you'd see what was happening across the way.'

Peter was speaking now like a director explaining a scene, but his animation rang false to Janek – as if he were feigning emotions he didn't feel but thought he ought to show.

'. . . kind of superimposure.' Lane squinted as if imagining it. 'Connections. Opposites. Great visual idea. Filed it away. Then, when I read she got herself killed, got to thinking about it again . . .'

He lowered his eyes, pausing as if weighing whether to go on. *Mind-fucking me*, Janek thought.

'Could make a powerful opening. Knew that. But knew there had to be someone else. Man. Watcher. Voyeur. Guy like me. Guy living across the yard. Ever see *Rear Window?* About this photographer, Jimmy Stewart. His leg's –'

'Seen it.'

'– in a cast. Pure cinema. Lock yourself up and see what you can do. You're in this one room with your camera. Got to tell your story from there. Got to play fair. Can't show anything the guy can't see. Can't take the camera into the girl's apartment. Rules of the game.'

'Rules? Play fair?'

'Fair with the audience. That's the challenge – can you tell your story from that room across the yard? Can the guy looking into the victim's apartment plan the crime just from what he sees?'

'Plan the crime? I thought Jimmy Stewart solved it.'

Peter shrugged. 'Well, there's the difference.' He stopped talking then, as abruptly as he'd started, peering closely at Janek, waiting for him to take up the thread. And as he let the silence hang between them Janek was struck by how shrewdly he'd reversed their situation, from one in which a detective had come to measure a suspect to one in which the suspect signaled he didn't care.

'Well,' Janek said after they had sat in silence for a time, 'suppose you put in a cop.' Peter looked at him. 'With a suspect, a film director, in whose movies he's noticed similarities to the crime.' Peter nodded. 'Now suppose this cop decides to try and trap his suspect by turning the script around.'

'How do you mean?'

'Making it come out opposite from the way it always does in the suspect's films.'

Peter studied him. 'This is a pretty highfalutin' cop you're talking about.'

'Well, what do you think?'

Peter squinted. 'Needs complications. Psychological dimensions. The cop's fear of failure and of being made to play the fool. And physical violence – something that could happen to him or to someone he cared a lot about.' Lane paused. 'Still, the real drama would be the struggle between the two. Not who wins, who loses; that wouldn't matter much. But the struggle, the confrontation. The killer taunting the cop. The cop doing a terrible burn. The killer calm as rain...'

It was the master bedroom window which had the perfect view of Amanda's apartment. Lane brought Janek to it last. They stared down at her window together in silence; though a good hundred feet away it looked much closer in the gathering dusk.

If Janek had had any doubts about his voyeur theory all of them were settled now. Amanda had been so close, so clearly visible, and the ladder from her roof stood there begging to be climbed.

Peter spoke first. 'What do you think happened over there?'

Janek turned to him; Peter was searching his face.

'I'll tell you,' Janek said, 'I think the killer wanted to murder a hooker.'

'She didn't strike me that way.'

'She wasn't like that and her killer knew it. So he had to work things out.'

'If he wanted a whore why pick her in the first place?'

'You've put your finger on it. That's the crux of the case.' Peter's gaze on him was steady now. 'His script demanded a whore but no matter how hard he tried he couldn't make Amanda into one. The challenge, remember? Trying to shoot an entire picture from a window?' Janek turned back toward Mandy's building. He spoke slowly, rhapsodically, wanting to hold Peter's attention now. 'I imagine him watching her night after night, standing at his window the way we're standing now at yours, peering out, studying her, working up hatred for her on account of the way she refuses to play her part. Days go by. Weeks. His rage mounts up. He wants to degrade her. Knock her down. Make her dirty. Make her crawl. Then, at last, an idea. Comes to him in a flash. As satisfying as it is brutal. A way around the dilemma of the prospective victim who has refused the coveted role. If Amanda won't be a whore he'll make her into one. He'll find a real whore, one who resembles her, kill them both and then exchange their heads. That way, in a single stroke, he'll double the magnitude of his crime. He'll create two dead and mutilated sluts instead of one, and turn his act into a puzzle that will taunt and defeat the police.'

He turned back to Peter before he finished speaking. The curiosity was gone. Peter's face was still again.

'Well?'

'That's a truly incredible story.'

'Don't believe it?'

'You got enough going on over there without dragging in a second girl.'

'What's wrong with a second girl?'

'Farfetched. Grandiose.'

'Funny,' Janek said. 'I've seen a couple of your movies. Compared to them I'd say my story's pretty solid.'

Lane looked at him. 'What did you think of them?'

'What?'

'My movies.'

'Oh.' *Finally, a soft spot.* 'Found them disturbing, to tell the truth.'

'They're meant to be.'

'Sure. But I don't mean the way you think.'

'How do you mean?'

'Oh, I don't know.' He worked to keep his tone mild and free of rancor. 'Felt that for all the blood and gore in them, in the end they lacked real blood.' He waited a moment for Lane to respond, but the director's eyes remained blank. 'Your characters are made of cardboard, Peter. And most of your visual ideas are borrowed from

169

Hitchcock. I know there're critics who say you have a powerful vision but, frankly, I don't think you do. You see, when I looked at your stuff all I could feel was the wounded little guy who'd made them up. A cop-hater with a chip on his shoulder serving up a pathetic little rage.'

It was an enormous insult. As Janek delivered it he carefully studied Peter's face. His eyes were empty and his body still, like a sentry guarding a vault.

An Accumulation of Regrets

'You'd have liked it,' Janek said. 'Real aggression. Two boxers feeling each other out, then, suddenly, they start to punch. He didn't do the tar-baby bit. Wanted to show me his fancy footwork from the bell.' He stared up at the ceiling, the fan slowly revolving above the bed. 'He's crazy, of course. And also very smart.'

They were lying together, their limbs entangled, the bedding pushed to the side. It was nearly midnight, a hot, humid evening, last gasp of the sultry summer weather that still lingered upon the city although the calendar said its time was past.

After leaving Lane's apartment he had driven straight to the loft, filled with a great need to hold Caroline close. An hour of lovemaking had restored him. He now knew the man he had to beat. The sickening feeling that came from facing madness was replaced now by a detective's need to understand.

'Nothing there to sympathize with. No visible agony or passion. About the only human thing he showed me was a sour vanity about his work.'

'Why do you think he did it?' He could feel her body tremble.

'Don't know. My theory of the disturbed filmmaker, the genius in torment, didn't hold up. He's so much colder than I thought. So much more furious and controlled. I'm not even sure that making Amanda a whore was all that important to him in the end.'

She pulled back to look at him. 'Then why?'

He studied the fan, the blade turning, turning, becoming a disk.

'I got a feeling from his movies that he uses people the way an artist uses paint. Plays with them, arranges them into unusual patterns, to make something he wants to see. A design.'

'You're saying –'

'That maybe he wasn't *driven* to this. That he simply did it willfully. If that's true, then the victims were irrelevant, just actresses forced to play gruesome roles.'

'He must have had a motive.'

'Sure. But it doesn't have to have anything to do with them. He could be trying to impress somebody. Or just playing some kind of game.'

She looked at him. 'I'd think that kind of game would be pretty dangerous.'

He nodded. 'That's what he likes about it. The danger – that makes it fun. And now that he's met me he's got someone to play against. I could feel him sizing me up, trying to decide whether I'd made a tough competitor or be a typical easy match.'

She traced her finger upon his face, exploring the lines, the wrinkles, gently touching him, her fingertips speaking eloquently of her love. 'What are you going to do now, Frank?'

'I'm going to nail him.'

The next morning, as he made coffee, feeling clearheaded, his thoughts turned again to Al and Lou. He and Caroline had discussed Lou's story casually for two weeks as if mere knowledge were enough and no further action were required.

'Hey,' he said, shaking her awake, offering her a mug of coffee. She opened her eyes. 'How do you feel?'

She stretched her arms above her head. 'Great.'

'Sleeping with you restores me.'

She sipped her coffee. 'Yeah. I notice that.'

'Been thinking about the way Hart acted in the car.'

She drew her brows together. 'When?'

'Driving back from the cemetery. When he assigned me the case. That was when he told me he hadn't known Al personally. A lie. We know that now.'

She took another sip. 'Well?'

'When I spotted you at the cemetery I thought you looked out of place. I got this idea you might have been Al's mistress and since

171

I'd promised Lou I'd find out what he'd been doing, I made a move so I could catch you and get your name when the group started breaking up.'

'Sounds like fairly standard detective practice.'

'Yeah. But just then I saw Hart whispering to his sergeant, who hurried over and interposed himself.'

'Between you and me?'

Janek nodded. 'He said Hart wanted me to drive back with him. I did and that's when he gave me Switched Heads.'

'So what's the insight?'

'Say he recognized you as Tommy Wallace's daughter. He also knew Al had been my rabbi. Al kills himself and doesn't leave a note. It would be natural for me to try and found out why. Hart doesn't want any trouble. He's come to the funeral to check me out. He spots you and, worse, notices me watching you. I make a move toward you. He gets worried. So he sends over Sweeney to intercept.'

'Sweeney's the sergeant.'

'Right. So now he's got me in his car. He wants to distract me really good. So he gives me this crazy case to tie me up, the kind of case that can destroy a detective's brain. Maybe he figures by the time I'm done with it, solved or unsolved, Al's suicide will be very old news and if anything ever turns up about Al's investigation into your father's death it will look more or less like what it was, namely a farce.'

'You don't think he was going to give you the case anyway?'

'Maybe. He certainly had it in reserve. But what makes me think he hadn't thought it through was the mistake he made, that lie about not knowing Al.'

She'd been watching him closely. He had the feeling she was struggling to keep something in. 'Quite an improvisation. Is Hart that slick?'

'To get to be Chief of Detectives you got to be very slick.'

'Well,' she said, 'what are you going to do about it?'

'Haven't decided yet. Al couldn't do anything, could he? Except make a lot of empty threats.'

'I don't understand.' She looked angry. 'You just finished telling me Hart played you for a fool.'

'He even called me in after a week on the pretext of discussing

172

Ireland/Beard. Then the first thing he does is ask me was how Lou is getting along.'

'You told him –'

'That she was coming along all right. Now that I think back on it I remember he lost interest after that.'

'But that's outrageous.' She was full of indignation.

'I'd say less outrageous than the rest of it. Wouldn't you?'

'So you're just going to let it go at that?'

He stared at her. 'I didn't say I was going to let it go.'

'You have to do something.'

'Sure, I do. So, tell me – what would you suggest?'

She pulled herself up, sat still by the side of the bed, then pulled on her robe and walked toward the galley. Halfway there she stopped and turned. 'I don't get it. Last night you tell me you're going to nail Lane. But that's just a case you were assigned. Now, this morning, I don't hear you saying anything about nailing Hart even though it seems he killed my father and drove your best friend to suicide.'

There was something marvelously confrontational in the way she was standing – defiant, angry, outraged.

'The first rule for a detective,' he said as softly as he could, 'is don't take your cases home.'

'*Oh, screw that shit!*' She was furious now; the explosion had finally come. 'That may be the first rule for you. But I'm not a detective, thank God.' She paused. 'Think I'll go to Hart and confront him. Fling Lou's story in his face. How would you like that?' She turned on her heel.

He walked up to her in the galley, stood behind her, put his arms around her and grasped her. She struggled to get away.

'I've been waiting to hear you say that.'

She continued to twist and squirm. 'What are you talking about?'

'To hear you come after me, mad, and push.'

She stopped struggling. He loosened his grip. She turned. 'You mean this was a setup? You were trying to get me mad?'

'Something like that.'

'Then you *are* going to do something?'

He nodded.

'Then that was bullshit about how you haven't decided yet?'

173

'Yeah,' he said. 'But I'm not going to do it alone. You're going to help me. Because if it isn't important enough to you it's not important enough to me.'

Later, when she was dressed, he escorted her to the tennis club. He carried her rackets; she walked her bike.

'Al had a great case,' he said, 'tie the CD to a murder. But he botched it. Hart had a hold over him because Al had taken money, too. That's what they mean when they say a good detective doesn't get personal. When the guy you're after has that kind of leverage on you there's nothing you can do.'

She glanced at him. 'Are you all that free of leverage?'

'The job's the only thing he's got over me and I don't want the job if it means he gets to Yo-Yo me around.' He paused. 'Remember how we got to the point one night where you admitted maybe you were hiding from certain things? Well, I've been thinking about that and I've decided I've been hiding, too.'

'Behind what?'

'My shield, my profession. Playing the detached detective. And, you know, I'm getting tired of telling myself we're all criminals at heart and that the only worthy feeling I can have is to be filled with pity for us all. Maybe my dear ex-spouse was right – it's an awfully heavy burden I've been carrying around. Maybe that's why I've felt so tired the last few years, as if every new case was just an added weight.'

'Oh, Janek, what brought all this on?'

'Lane and Hart. Hart especially. I really hate that son-of-a-bitch. I'd like to get *very* personal and stick it to him. It's been years since I felt anything like that.'

'But still you feel funny about it.'

She was right, but he found it difficult to explain. They walked a block in silence. 'Maybe I feel you won't like me so much,' he finally said.

She looked surprised. 'I don't understand.'

'That afternoon it rained –'

'When the loft turned dark while we were making love.'

He nodded. 'I told you about the burden then.'

'Yes?'

He glanced at her, then turned away. 'You said it was the thing you loved about me most.'

'Yes. But that doesn't mean –'

'I was wondering if you'd feel that way if you found me full of hate.'

'But you're not full of hate. You just hate Lane and Hart.' She searched his face, then reached out to him. He gave her his hand; she took it and held it tight. 'Don't be afraid I'm not going to care for you because you're a human being.' She stood on her toes to kiss him. 'That's wonderful, you see. Makes you fuller, a man struggling with a contradiction. If anything it makes me love you even more.'

When they reached the tennis club he waited on the terrace while she went to the locker room to change. Her opponent, the tall woman he'd watched play with her the other time, had called to say that she'd be late.

'You said it's been years since you felt the way you're feeling now.' Caroline, looking good in her tennis clothes, settled down beside him. They were the only ones on the terrace. 'What made you change – way back then, I mean?'

'I went into the deep-freeze when I killed my partner.'

'You mention that a lot, but you don't talk about it.'

'Because that was the turning point: After that I *had* to feel detached.' He paused. 'Was either Terry or me, you see. Terry Flynn. My partner and my friend.

'He was a very good detective, had a sixth sense that made him extraordinary. But he was crazy too, full of anger, and he hated the criminal-justice system with a passion. What happened was that we were being taunted by this minor hood, a creep named Tony Scarpa, a "scumbag," as Terry used to say. And Terry got it into his head that we were going to execute the guy, take the law into our hands, become rogue cops and take him out. I didn't think he was serious. He'd talk about it and laugh. But he was serious. I found that out too late, one night in a coffee warehouse on Desbrosses Street where we cornered Scarpa with enough dope to make a fairly decent case. But Terry wasn't interested in making a case; he was out for blood. So there was Scarpa down on his knees and Terry pressing a revolver against his head, a clean gun he'd gotten hold of, and I was yelling at him to stop before he pulled one off. Then I knew he wasn't going to stop, that he was going to kill the guy, and that if he did he'd ruin his life, so I knew I had to take that gun away. I tried. He fought me off. Then he pointed it at me and I

175

could see he was way out of control. He started firing. I had to shoot him. Unfortunately I aimed too well. Tony got Scarpa in the head, but the creep survived. I got Terry in the chest. He was dead before the ambulance came.

'Funny – for years I wondered if I'd chickened out. Took me a long while to realize I hadn't. It was later that I acted like a coward, when something closed up inside. That thing with Terry held me back, so I had to work up my pity-us-all theory which I've been using ever since as an excuse not to feel – anger, rage, revulsion, even love. You see, it's been more than Switched Heads and the thing with Al that's brought me back. It's been you. I know now I started to really feel again when I began to fall for you.'

She'd been watching him as he spoke, peering at him, as if he was an exiled king restored to a stolen throne. Just seeing that look on her, of admiration and awe, filled him with courage.

'I have to tell you something, Frank,' she said. 'I think you and I are alike.'

'How do you mean?'

'I love to hear confessions. At least the kind in which I'm the rescuing heroine.'

Stalemate

The restaurant wasn't a cop place. It was an expensive seafood restaurant in the South Street fish-market area, a stockbroker's paradise full of guys yapping about liquidity and arbitrage. They knew Hart, greeted him as 'Chief' when he and Janek walked in. The headwaiter seated them in a booth.

Hart ordered Manhattan clam chowder, grilled sole and a bottle of white wine. 'Lovely wine,' he said after he chewed it awhile. Then he signaled the waiter to pour.

While Janek talked he watched Hart eat his soup. There was a rhythm to the way he dipped his spoon. Janek tried not to let that annoy him as he toured the perimeters of Switched Heads and Peter Lane. Just as he was finishing the waiter brought their fish.

'That it?' asked Hart as he began to bone his sole. He fileted it like a surgeon.

'Isn't that enough?'

Hart looked up from his handiwork. 'No, Frank. Not nearly enough.'

'You heard what I –'

'I heard every word. You got a goddamn kiss and some alleged artistry you think you saw in the crime-scene photos. And then you got a lot of psychological mumbo-jumbo that adds up to exactly zilch. You got no physical evidence, no witnesses and no plausible motive. Your suspect is a famous film director. The only connection between him and one of your victims is that he happens to have a view.'

'We know he goes to whores.'

'Screw the whores. So what that this guy Lane goes to whores? Half the men I know go to them and the other half are married to them. Take that to the DA and he'll puke all over it. What's worse, Lane will sue us for harassment.' Hart lifted the skeleton out of his fish and laid it carefully on his bread-and-butter plate. 'It's crap, Frank. A real crock. So tell me – what do you want?'

'Extra men.'

'How many?'

'Enough to watch Lane full time.'

'That's an awful lot of detectives. I don't know. If he's as smart as you say he is he's not going to do anything anyway.'

Janek didn't argue or nod. He watched Hart eat for a while. There was something disgusting about the way Hart chewed his fish. And the look on his face – the look of a man who had the world by the tail. Janek reached into his pocket and pulled out the snapshot Al had given Caroline. He propped it up against the salt and pepper shakers.

Hart glanced at it. 'So what's that?' He squinted at Janek to show he wasn't impressed.

'Another case.'

'Looks like three young cops having a laugh.' There was a sneer in his voice. He turned back to his food.

'Three young cops. Except now two of them are dead.'

Hart shrugged.

'You told me you didn't know Al when we drove back from the burial.'

'So I bullshitted you. So what? I invited you into the car to give you a case, not reminisce about the past.'

'Why do you think he shot himself?'

Hart puffed out his cheeks. 'Beats me.'

'What do you mean it *beats* you? He called you that morning. What did you say to him?'

'I didn't say anything. He started telling *me*.'

'Now, *look* –'

'*You* look. Guy shot himself. No doubt of that. *He* did it – not me or anybody else. Whatever I said or didn't say, *he*'s the one who pulled the trigger.' Hart picked up the snapshot, squinted at it again, laid it down on Janek's side of the table, then gazed steadily into Janek's eyes. 'You know I think very highly of you, Frank. Consider you one of my best detectives. There's a precinct command coming up in Brooklyn. Ever think about a captaincy?'

'Sure, I'd like to be a captain. But I don't want a precinct command.'

'What do you want?'

'I like to work cases.'

'Everyone likes to work cases. But if you're going to be a captain you have to do administrative work.'

'Then maybe I'm not ready yet.'

'Not ready to be a captain? Why the hell not?'

'Just don't see myself shuffling papers.'

'There's retirement. You'd do a hell of a lot better if you went out at a higher grade.'

'The pension's important, but I'm a detective. Do I get extra men or not?'

Hart gazed at him. 'Never let go, do you? Get an idea into your head and hold on to it no matter what. You got some mystical idea about detective work, you some kind of metaphysician, Frank? I've heard that before and I don't respect it. A police career's about power. You either get more power or you stall in place.'

The waiter asked if they wanted dessert. Janek shook his head. Hart ordered pumpkin pie. 'Reminds me of Halloween,' he said. 'Tricks and treats. Jack-o'-lanterns in the windows, then mashed pumpkin on the streets. Heard about this case where this guy slipped in some pumpkin, broke his back, sued the city, said Sanitation was "irresponsible and derelict." City attorney I know handled it. Told me he looked for precedents. "Basically," he said, "what we were dealing with was a classic slipped-on-the-old-banana-skin case."' Hart laughed. 'Okay, so you like to work cases. Then stick to the case you got. You think Lane did it, go ahead and prove it. Or start looking at someone else.'

They sipped coffee in silence. Much as he hated Hart, Janek couldn't help but admire his cool. He appeared unshaken, and it occurred to Janek that maybe that was what had finally discouraged Al. There was no way to reach such a man; the smart move for Al would have been to put the case aside. But he couldn't do that, so he ate his gun.

After Hart paid the check Janek saw his cold little eyes turn appraising once again.

'I know your trouble. You think taking a captaincy would be selling out, like you're important enough to be offered a pact with the devil and so pure you can refuse it on the spot. Well, I got news for you. Enlisted man's pride – that's all the fuck it is. You and all the other assholes who like to work cases. Where does it get you? A stinking house in nowhere Queens and a stupid cow of a wife and a barbecue pit. Be smart, Frank, and think it over before you turn down what every detective in the division would give his left ball to have.' He paused. 'You got till the end of the year on Ireland/Beard. After that the only extra personnel you're going to see is the guy I put in your place.'

He stood, picked up his raincoat, then bent down very close to Janek and whispered harshly in his ear.

'Like I said, Frank, you think you got a case. *But all you got are photographs.*'

Getting Personal

'Okay,' he said, 'first the record thing, then the mail thing.'

'The mail thing's much worse,' she said.

'Let's look at them one at a time.'

'I could be wrong about the record.'

'We'll see. Take me through them both again.'

They'd been listening a lot to an old Stephane Grappelli record. Caroline had one of those sleek Danish stereos done up in redwood and black with a hand-sized 'control module' she could use to turn it on and off. When they decided to go to sleep she'd carry the module with her and place it on the little table on her side of the bed. (He kept his wallet, keys and thirty-eight on his side.) They'd settle in, turn off the lights, continue listening and when they were ready to sleep she could click off the system without getting up.

'... Okay, the next morning we didn't play music. You were in a rush and I had a tennis date. You left, I got my tennis stuff and left, and, yes, I locked the door. I came home around noon. Then I went out with my camera for a couple hours. I got home at maybe five o'clock. I remember I turned on the radio to listen to *All Things Considered*. I went into the darkroom, and when I got tired of the news I came out, clicked the phono button on the module, and that's when I started to hear that old *Marriage of Figaro* album I hadn't played in years.'

She looked at him and shook her head to show how crazy that had seemed.

'So then?'

'I came storming out. The Mozart was on the turntable, the album was where I usually leave an album, and the Grappelli was back on the shelf.'

'And as far as you remember you hadn't touched the stereo since the night before?'

She nodded.

'So how did it happen?'

'Either I put the Grappelli away and pulled out the Mozart and put it on, *which I absolutely do not remember doing*, or someone else did it, which is very weird.'

'Me?'

She nodded. 'That's what I thought.'

'Why didn't you ask me?'

'Forgot.'

'Forgetting's consistent with forgetting you changed it yourself.'

'That's why I wasn't sure. Until this afternoon, when I began to see the pattern.'

The mailbox incident was something else. She'd come home early that afternoon (she'd been photographing football scrimmage at an all-black high school in Brooklyn), unloaded her camera and started opening her mail.

First she found a letter she'd received a week before, which she remembered placing on her desk to be answered. It was just the way she'd left it, still in its envelope, slit. Then she found two old phone bills from the summer which she'd paid, missing from the side drawer where she threw everything to do with business. And she found a plain envelope, white, business size, and in it, carefully wrapped, its edges Scotch-Taped so there would be no chance she could cut herself, a used razor blade. That sent her rushing to her bathroom, first to check Janek's razor, then the one she used to shave her legs. From which, she discovered, the blade was missing, which sent her rushing back to her desk to phone Janek at the precinct in a panic.

While she waited for him she went through her business files, all her old bills and canceled checks. She couldn't find anything else missing but felt certain that there was. The person who'd done this, and who, she was sure, had also changed the record, had searched her home carefully, then helped himself to things she wouldn't miss. So that even as she was searching for more such things, she was shaking on account of her sense of this person's cleverness and power. There was a bold and fiendish intelligence behind his acts: an ability to understand her and then exploit her fears.

'Felt like I was going crazy,' she told him. 'You know – currents of terror and rage. It felt like the worst kind of male aggression. Penetration against my will. Really the worst.'

Nothing had actually happened to her, she had told herself; the two incidents were a kind of prank. Except, of course, she knew they weren't. There was something insidious behind them and she had tried to think of what it was. *Intimacy*, she decided, the *intimacy* of that razor blade, and also the threat of it, for it was sharp and cutting, and the threat was somehow worse on account of the fact that the dangerous sharp cutting edges of that intimate item had been taped. As if to say, 'They *needn't* have been taped.' As if to say, 'I, who did this, *could* have booby-trapped you if I'd *wanted* to.' As if to say, 'There *could* be other traps set around, other blades perhaps hidden in your gloves or shoes, places you wouldn't ordinarily look before you plunged in your hands or feet.'

So she had looked through everything carefully, found nothing else out of place, but now that he was with her she began another search. Since her violator had chosen to demonstrate his power by

181

attacking her so intimately, then, she believed, it would be in intimate regions such as her drawers of underwear that he would have made further demonstrations.

'But how do I *know*?' she asked, turning to Janek, her voice shaking, one of her bras dangling pathetically from her hand. 'He could have taken some of them. God! I don't count the damn things. Some could be missing and I wouldn't even *know*.'

Struck by her expression of helplessness, he took her in his arms. When her trembling stopped he sat her down, then phoned a locksmith he knew who did contract work for the NYPD. He asked the man to come to the loft immediately with his best, newest, most impregnable lock, and while they waited he carefully examined the locks already on her door. With his own set of keys he tried each one of them in turn, then squinted and looked closely at the cylinders. Her security lock was the only one that would have given a housebreaker any trouble. His inspection confirmed what he already knew, which was that either it had been opened with a key or there was another way into her loft besides the door.

He went downstairs and inspected her mailbox, one of a set of vertical compartments imbedded in the wall. The mailman's lock on the top looked reasonably secure, but the small lock to her box could have been opened by a child.

Upstairs again, he paced the walls, checking each window in turn. He opened them, stuck out his head, looked up and down – the building walls were sheer.

He knew there had to be a fire escape, since the building had no separate fire stairs. But for some reason he had never noticed it and when he found it he realized why: the entrance to it was through the window of her darkroom, which she kept covered with a black shade and then a double set of black velour drapes.

He pulled the drapes, raised the shade, found that the windowpanes had also been painted black. The clasp was not secured; he raised the sash. The fire escape led down the back of the building, a side he'd never seen.

When he came out of the darkroom she was sitting on the couch. She didn't say anything, just followed him with her eyes.

'The window wasn't locked in there,' he said. 'Anyone else have a set of keys?' She didn't answer. 'Super? Friends?' When she didn't reply he took her face in his hands. 'Look,' he said, 'I'm a detective. I love you and I want to help.'

She gazed at him, then held out her hands so he could see them shake.

It could have been Lane, he knew, and also, possibly, Hart, but he didn't tell her that as he lay beside her staring up at the fan, admiring its slow revolutions, its slow inexorable strokes. After a while the even regularity of her breathing signaled she had finally fallen off to sleep. It had taken him hours to relax her. Now he lay on his back watching the fan cut slivers of light, putting everything he knew through the mill of his mind, grinding, pulverizing, then searching for signs and meanings in the dust.

It was the same sort of fire-escape entry made into Amanda's except for the striking difference that this time it had been made during the day. A very risky venture and also diabolic. Janek was sure Lane was capable of it. But would he bother? Why take such a chance?

On the other hand a surreptitious entry smacked of a professional job. Janek knew men who could have done it, and Hart knew such men, too. Knew even more of them, had all sorts of slick old detectives in his debt, men he could ask to do special favors, anything for a chance to please the Chief.

He watched the fan, angry now he'd pulled off Sal. Even if Lane had shaken Sal the day of the entry at least Janek would know that he had. And if Sal could account for Lane's movements that entire day, then Janek could be sure that it was Hart.

Sal was busy backtracking through Hart's finances. What if he messed up and Hart found out? How badly would Hart feel threatened? Badly enough to do this? But a designed policy of slowly applied terror was not at all Hart's style. His style was a bullet in the head. And now there were too many: Janek's, Caroline's, Lou DiMona's, Carmichael's. Hart couldn't execute them all.

He felt sticky, pulled away the sheet, lay naked to the breeze generated by the fan. Caroline was right: there would be other traps. He grew tense as he contemplated what they might be. *It had to be Lane.* Now the Switched Heads case had turned personal just like the case of Tommy and Al. But he had no proof. He didn't even have enough to convince anyone Lane had done anything at all.

*

He hadn't counted on their finding Nelly Delgado.

Stanger and Howell brought her in late on Thursday afternoon, a short slim actressy redhead with sparkling dancing eyes. They had found a total of four prostitutes who could identify Lane from photographs; interesting information, inconclusive though suggestive of a pattern. But Nelly was different. She had a real tale and she told it to the five detectives from the center of the squad room, all ninety-seven pounds of her packed into an office swivel chair which she used to heighten the effect of her recitation, whirling herself around in it to dramatize important points.

It had happened five years before; she couldn't remember the exact date, though she knew she would never forget the man. He'd come to her several times for ordinary sessions. Nothing remarkable until one day he asked if she'd be willing to enact a special scene. Sure, why not, she'd said; in those days she still aspired to be an actress. They made a deal (five times her normal fee); he instructed and rehearsed her and arranged to pick her up the following night.

'The pickup,' Nelly said, 'was on the street. He wanted me to play it like a hooker. Dress cheap over black satin underwear, wear high spiky heels, chew gum and swing my ass. I was to march up and down Eighth Avenue, Forty-second to Forty-sixth and back. He'd cruise, follow, watch me reject a couple johns. Then when he approached I'd tell him my fee, we'd strike a bargain, he'd hail a cab and take me off.'

Nelly stood up from the swivel chair to show them how she'd paraded, the exaggerated high-stepping haughty strut of a cartoon prostitute.

'He emphasized that I had to act really cheap. Wear too much makeup and be insincere. He wanted a real Times Square trull.' She demonstrated her harlot's smile.

He had asked specifically that she not disguise her contempt, that she feign interest but make her indifference manifest. Under no circumstances was she to become sexually aroused. The entire encounter was to be flagrantly commercial; indeed, that seemed to be its point.

So they met as Lane had prescribed, drove to a nondescript neighbourhood and stopped before an ordinary apartment house.

'It was a walk-up. Six flights. The stairwell stank of roach spray.

184

When we reached the top he unlocked the door. Then came the part that we'd rehearsed. When he turned on the lights I was supposed to look around like I thought the joint was a dump. And in a way it was, though it was also kind of cute. All this crummy furniture arranged just so, like somebody's fancy parlor. A woman's room – old-fashioned lampshades, doilies on the chair arms. Kind of place makes you feel uncomfortable because it's set up just for visitors.

'He watched me while I sniffed around. I was to look at everything and make faces to show how gross I thought it was. He sprawled out on the couch and loosened his belt. I took off my clothes except for my underwear and shoes, then walked around again telling him how cheap the furnishings were. Ugly, tasteless, dreary, dull. There were these framed photographs of people set up on the side tables. I was supposed to pick them up, stare at them, and tell him how stupid and low-class they looked. So I started doing that and he couldn't take his eyes off me. I'd look back at him every so often to see if I was doing it right. He nodded to encourage me. The harder he nodded the rougher I got. Like I'd pick up this wedding picture and tell him what crud it was. I was supposed to make fun of everything, call the people names, work my way around the room doing crazy stuff like that.

'It turned him on, I could tell. It was weird the way he ate it up. Every so often I came back to the couch and gave his cock a little tweak. But what kept the scene going was the way I acted toward the photographs. I had to keep insulting them, saying what total pieces of shit the people were. When finally I started spitting at them he really began to writhe. There was one of this woman and when I said she looked like a stupid slut he moaned and gasped and came. That was it. The scene was over. He thanked me, paid me, gave me extra money for a cab. I left. I guess I must have been up there total maybe half an hour.'

The story was so bizarre that when she finished telling it the five detectives stared at her amazed. Aware that she had held them spellbound, she swiveled herself around twice and beamed.

'Ever see him again?' Janek asked. Nelly shook her head.

'Think you could find that building?' asked Aaron.

'All I remember is the top-floor apartment and how we had to climb up all those stinking stairs.'

'Was he rough or threatening?'

185

'Not at all. Fact, he was kind of sweet.'

'You're sure it's the same guy in the picture?'

'Long as I live' . . . she crossed her heart – 'I'll never forget that face.'

They wanted to know whether she'd been curious enough to look at the names beside the downstairs buzzers when she left.

'That's funny,' she said, 'I remember now I did. There wasn't any name beside his buzzer. That struck me because at my place I didn't put out my name either.'

They questioned her into the early evening, making her repeat portions of her story. They showed her other pictures of Lane taken at other times, trying to shake her confidence. Aaron worked to elicit details of the neighborhood; Janek was interested in the nuances of Lane's behavior. Had he actually told her to spit at the pictures or had she gotten carried away and done that on her own? She shot back her answers. The spitting was her idea. She retold segments as best she could. She stood firmly by her identification and swore she'd only done what Lane had asked.

They sent out for pizzas and coffee. Did Nelly recall if there'd been any knives around? Pairs of scissors? Swords? Vegetable-cutting devices? She stared at them from her chair, her hair a flame against the gray. No, she didn't recall anything like that. And why were they asking her all these questions anyway?

The double feature uptown had closed, so it took them until the next afternoon to arrange a private screening of *Mezzaluna*. Janek and Aaron sat on her either side, watching her as she watched the movie, noting how she began to twitch when the scene came on in which the prostitute insulted the furniture in the parlor of Targov's mother's house.

'It's the same,' Nelly whispered, 'the same room, the same stuff!' She stared intently at the screen. 'Can't believe this. The same fucking pictures too!'

Janek kept his eyes on her face, observing her wonderment as the scene unfolded. He believed in the authenticity of her gulp when the screen prostitute began to spit at the framed photographs. And when things progressed further, when Targov slowly and lovingly drew the mezzaluna across the distracted girl's throat, Nelly began to scream. Janek knew she'd never seen the movie before.

*

186

Sal had tried hard, but it was tough. 'Hart covers himself real good,' he said. Janek sighed. 'But still I got you stuff.' Janek looked up. Sal was grinning.

'Bastard.'

'Shit, Frank – you pull those deals on me all the time.'

They were sitting in Janek's favorite Greek restaurant on Howard Street. Between them a basket of pita bread, a plate of stuffed grape leaves and a bottle of retsina wine.

'So what did you get?'

'At least let me tell my story first.'

Janek sat back. Getting to tell the story was Sal's payment for doing the job.

'Knew right off there was no way to get a reading on Mrs. Hart's finances short of pulling a black-bag job on the residence or the mail. Since I knew your attitude toward that kind of maneuver plus that this had to be a very quiet dig, I thought about it awhile before I came up with a plan. Sort of sex plan, actually, Frank –'

'Sex!' Janek laughed. 'What did you think you were going to do? Screw old Karen Hart?'

'Better than that. Screw a certain girl who's been eyeing my ass.'

Janek listened, throwing in obscenities at appropriate moments, nodding enthusiastically as Sal recounted all the splendid lovemaking that had weakened the high moral posture of the sex-starved records clerk who had access to the computer that guarded the financial statements required of all the division chiefs. It was a good story, too, he thought, full of drama and moral quandary. And the assignment had inspired a mobilization of all Sal's resources: the persuasive powers of a narcotics detective honed on addict informants, the hours he'd spent in the gym keeping his body hard, years of experience dating and laying siege.

'See, she's the type who wouldn't fiddle with her income tax even if she knew she could get away with it. So I had to pitch it to her like there was this sort of, hmmm, higher morality involved.'

Exactly how he'd done that remained obscure; Sal couldn't remember the sequence or the words. But he did recall that the Roman Catholic faith had been invoked (helpful since the girl was also an Italian-American), that IAD (acronym for the much feared Internal Affairs Division) had been mentioned, and that he had exhibited a malaise appropriate to a young officer forced to work

187

undercover against men to whom he felt bonded on account of the shared dangers of the job.

In the end she'd yielded, giving Sal the printout, knowing he needed it to break a case so sensitive that even he had no clear idea what it was about. And, of course, he felt rotten knowing how cruel it would be to dump her now. She'd gone all the way for him, sure, he'd given her great sex in return. But still he'd manipulated her principles, for which, he felt, no number of good screws could fairly be exchanged.

Janek looked at him. Was he serious? 'You were a narc, Sal. A detective manipulates. You know that. That's what we do.'

'Sure. But in bed, Frank?'

'In bed. On the street. In a shit-house interrogation room. We extract what we need. We make our cases. We investigate. And if you're a decent human being you hate yourself sometimes. But you do it anyway because that's the job.'

More wine. A big Greek dinner. Lots of soul-searching, good advice, and soon Sal Marchetti came to terms with what he'd done. He'd completed his assignment and pleased his rabbi. By the time dessert arrived he was feeling proud.

The printout didn't tell where Hart had gotten his money, but it did confirm that he was rich. He and his wife jointly owned a Park Avenue apartment and three investment properties in Queens. In addition Karen Hart held a portfolio of stocks, bonds and various other forms of government and commercial paper worth, at the end of the previous year, approximately $475,000.

So – Hart had turned forty thousand in cash into an estate of nearly three quarters of a million dollars and, in the same twenty-five-year period, had risen from sergeant to CD. An astonishing dual accomplishment, Janek thought; he wondered how many other dirty little deals Hart had done.

'Want me to go further on this thing?'

Janek nodded, brought out a card and laid it on the table. 'Know anything about this?'

Sal picked it up. 'Sweeney's brother-in-law's garage.'

'What do you know about it?'

'Hear they give a good discount to cops.'

'Anything else?'

'That sometimes they get sloppy. That maybe going there's not worth the hassles.'

'Suppose you look into that.'

Sal smiled. 'First Hart. Now Sweeney. This thing must be big. Know you can't tell me what it is, but do you ever win with guys like that?'

'We'll see who wins. Here's what I need. First, who really owns that garage? Second, just what kind of operation is it? Third, who works there? Fourth and most important – just how "sloppy" do they sometimes get?'

A stalemated case: he knew he had the right man, but he didn't know how to get him. Nelly Delgado was good, but she wasn't nearly enough and now they were all behaving like treadmill detectives going through the motions. Stanger and Howell had reverted to their former sluggishness, and on several occasions Janek had caught Aaron reproachfully searching his face. On an autumn afternoon in mid-October as they were preparing to go home he asked Aaron to stay on. They talked over the case for an hour, shared a paella at a Spanish restaurant on Bleecker Street, then returned to the precinct house to talk about it some more.

'When you get down to it,' Aaron said, 'all Nelly tells us is that Lane's a very freaky suspect. We read the crime-scene photos a certain way and we get a bad feeling from the guy. But Hart's right – DA'll take one look at that and puke. Bad odds on turning up hard evidence, which means there's only one way to make this case and that's to get a confession. If the suspect stonewalls, our tough luck. That's the way I see things, Frank, and that maybe it's time to start thinking someday we're going to have to close this down.'

Janek nodded. 'That what you want to do?'

'Course not. But Lane's not going to confess. We can keep watching him, even apply some pressure. But he strikes me as the kind who'll thrive on treatment like that.'

'Because it makes his game all the more exciting.'

'And because he's a sociopath who doesn't feel guilt. Without evidence, pressure or guilt there's no incentive for him to talk.'

Janek had thought these things himself and also that Switched Heads was not a case from which he could walk away.

'We both know these kinds of cases,' Aaron said. 'And we know what happens to detectives who try to break down unbreakable guys. Make you crazy. Years pass and you get to be one of those haunted types who prowl the corridors downtown. "Oh, him?

189

Rosenthal? He's a one-case guy. Obsessed. Been after this joker for fifteen years." People don't like detectives like that. They back away when they see you coming. The wife walks out and the children turn against you. The crime ruins not the criminal but the cop.' Aaron paused. 'You want my gut feeling? Still too early now to throw it in, still got to go through lots of motions. But it's getting time to withdraw from it in our heads. Just a question now of owning up to that and taking the necessary mental steps.'

He stood, stretched, then sat down again, this time more resigned. 'Sal's doing a side job for you, isn't he?' He looked at Janek, then turned away. There was silence in the squad room then, both men sitting very still, as still as Lane, Janek thought.

'That's right,' Janek said.

'Well...'

'Doesn't have anything to do with Lane.'

'So the rest of us just bust our asses, right?'

'Lane was onto him, Aaron. The stakeout wasn't any good.'

Aaron nodded. 'I get it. So now you guys are in business for yourselves.'

'I'd like to tell you about it. I really would.'

'I understand. Rabbi stuff. So, okay, tell me this: Why won't Hart give us extra men?'

'That's complicated.'

'Well, shit, you know me, Frank. I can barely grasp...'

Aaron was hurt and Janek was angry with himself; he should have seen what was happening, should have read those anguished reproachful stares.

'Has to do with Al,' he said. 'Even Sal doesn't know that. He's working for me blind.'

Aaron shook his head. 'Three rabbi generations. Jesus!'

'It's all connected. Something between Hart and Al. When I let on I might know about it he dangled a precinct command. When I didn't bite, he gave me a deadline, the end of the year, and told me to screw off on the extra men.'

'Well, you sure picked a great guy to have a feud with. Now I understand why you couldn't ask him for favors.' Aaron paused. 'I'm a good solid detective. I like to think I'm sometimes very good.'

'You are.'

'Sure. Maybe. But nowhere near your league. Potentially you're a great detective. You look deeper, see things, connect things up.' Aaron stood, walked over to the wall and stared, as they had both done so many times, at the crime-scene photographs. 'It was you who understood this case. Don't know that anyone else could have done it. Sure, someone might have thought of the window. Maybe I would have come up with that. But to know what to look for, to focus the search so that I was able to pick up on Lane so fast. And the way you figured out the meaning behind the switch – that was a stroke of genius.' He turned from the wall to face Janek. 'Okay, so we're going to get this guy.' He smiled. 'So how are we going to do it?'

'Back to the beginning. Re-examine the fundamentals.'

Aaron nodded. 'Yeah.'

It was late when they left the precinct. Janek drove Aaron home. In the car his thoughts turned again to Hart.

'Suppose,' he asked Aaron, 'you had a case like Ireland/Beard but different in one major respect. No possibility of getting a confession, no physical evidence, but the certainty there were accomplices. How would you attack?'

'Pretty basic stuff,' said Aaron. 'Locate the accomplices and turn them around.'

'Suppose you're not in a position to offer a credible deal.'

'Never knew a prosecutor who wouldn't deal.'

'Suppose this isn't that sort of case.'

Aaron thought about that. 'It's the same situation even when you're in business for yourself. You get something on A you're willing to ignore if he'll help you by squealing on B. It's only tricky because it's not official, which means the deal depends on trust. It's like those wartime intelligence interrogations where they dangle a guy out of a plane. If he talks he comes back in; if he doesn't they let him go. An approach that only works if he's convinced the bargain will be kept both ways. To create that kind of conviction you got to believe in it yourself. But once you go that route, seems to me, there isn't any turning back.'

When they arrived at Aaron's house in Brooklyn, Janek lightly touched his arm. 'You think I'm getting in too deep.'

'Going up against Hart.' Aaron shook his head. 'I don't know, Frank. That's a very heavy guy.'

*

It came to him as he crossed from Brooklyn into Queens, Hart's sneering 'all you got are photographs' ringing in his ears. A switch snapped between the two cases. Lane's films: something in them he'd felt but hadn't seen, something that had been haunting him for weeks.

Cinema Studies

They viewed the complete works of Peter Lane in a shabby Times Square building filled with second-rung prop and costume houses and seedy rehearsal halls. A stale smell in the corridors of greasy take-out food and sweat. 'It's either this,' said Aaron, leading Janek into the screening room, 'or our spotless Police Academy auditorium.'

Ripper; Magenta; Hairdresser; Mezzaluna; Winslow Road; Film Noir: the movies flickered by in a twelve-hour marathon that included short breaks for coffee, quick trips to the lavatory, a fifteen-minute lunch at an eggroll place across the street. 'We're going for total immersion,' Janek announced, which was what he and Aaron got.

The movies exhausted them and hurt their eyes. Axes, razors, shears employed at pounding rhythms with repeated strokes. Moans of pain. Pants of ecstasy. Agonized stalking released in sudden vicious assaults. Janek couldn't reconcile the stony language of the critics with the gruesome stuff he was seeing on the screen. And he noticed Aaron becoming strange, sometimes mumbling to himself.

'See, basically there're two kinds of spatter films. The crummy obnoxious drive-in stuff, like someone's got rabies and is going around biting people in the neck, and the class acts by Hitchcock, De Palma, guys like that. Thing about Lane you got to remember, he's in the second category. Has his following, almost like a cult. His stuff gets shown at festivals.'

The next movie was *Winslow Road*. The killer kept a garden

behind his house on a middle-class suburban street, where, it turned out, he grew exemplary vegetables fertilized by the remains of the whores he lured to his potting shed and killed. There was a long sickening sequence set during a lightning storm during which he sliced up a girl with pruning shears, and lovingly ground her into compost.

'There! Hear it on the sound track?' asked Aaron in the middle of the scene. 'There's a chorus singing behind the thunder. Guess what? We're in a *cathedral*, Frank.'

In the end, Janek decided, the stories were pretty much the same. A ritual set of killings. A cat-and-mouse game with a stupid cop. An elaborate chase and an inconclusive finale – the killer disappearing, the cop left looking like a jerk.

But there was more. He sensed something deeper, a basic cryptic tale that stood behind these stories and gave them weight. Strange long silent looks between killer and cops, peculiar references to unexplained past events. It was as if there were some kind of *back* story known only to Lane, as if his characters shared the burden of a traumatic past.

Janek leaned forward trying to concentrate. Perhaps it would be possible to enter Lane's mind. If he relaxed, just let himself slide into the films, then he might catch it – the same coiled anger he'd felt in Amanda's tub behind the curtain, the fury he felt some nights at Hart, the mad-dog killer part of himself he'd always feared and had tried to kill when he shot Terry years before . . .

Late that night, his mind still cluttered with murderous images, there came a searing thought: that the movies were about the past – guarded, stylized, heavily masked renditions of an old and haunting crime. A real crime.

He crawled out of bed, went to Caroline's darkroom, picked up the wall phone there and dialed Aaron at home.

'Couldn't sleep either,' Aaron said. 'You got an idea?'

'He's concealing.'

'We know that.'

'Remember how much trouble you had getting the basic facts.'

'Still don't have them.'

'He's covering up.'

'Sure. So what else is new? All psychos have backgrounds and try to conceal them.' Silence. He could feel Aaron's resistance. 'You sure this isn't just desperation, Frank?'

'No, I smell something real. And that it's the subject of the films.'

'Well, they got to be about something, don't they?'

'Right. So let's find out.'

'You talking about a deep background check.'

'The deepest. Track the past, Aaron. There's a crime back there. In the movies he tries to tell us about it but can't quite get it out. What we got to do is find out what it is. Then, maybe, we can use it to open him up.'

The Hunt

He decided to take the subway – it would be quicker than his car. He ran to West Fourth Street and jumped on an F train before the doors slammed shut. 'Stalking me,' she'd said over the phone. 'The same one, you know – the mind reader.' Janek knew; the man who'd changed the record, the one who'd stolen the razor blade, the one, she'd said, who'd psyched her out.

A delay on the tracks. The train halted at the Fifth Avenue station. The doors jammed and people on the platform stared in with anger and disgust. He'd known that that razor blade was not going to be the end of it, that something else would happen and when nothing had happened he'd been relieved. A mistake. The subway doors opened and slammed during an incomprehensible public announcement. The train jerked forward. *What's that bastard done?*

She was better composed than he; he was panting from running up the stairs. 'It's so stupid,' she said. 'But I wish you could find him, Frank. Find out who he is and make him stop.'

Though she always made her prints herself, she sent out her exposed rolls to be developed. When she accumulated a lot of film, say thirty or forty rolls, she'd drop the stuff off for processing and a day or two later she'd pick it up.

Which was what she'd done that morning. And around noon she'd begun to examine the contact sheets. And then she'd found the extra sheet and then she'd called the lab. They checked. She'd brought in forty-one rolls and gotten forty-one back, and nothing she'd shot was missing from the shipment, which meant she'd brought in the extra roll herself. Which meant it had been placed in the basket on the counter in her darkroom where she left her exposed rolls to pile up. Which meant it had been planted on her by the intruder, probably at the same time he'd changed the record and stolen the razor blade.

There was more. 'What's on it?' he asked.

She swallowed hard and handed him the contact sheet.

He examined it with a magnifying glass, his heart sinking as he did. Thirty-six amateurish telephoto shots, some of them shaky, some not focused very well. But all of Caroline – walking, bicycling, shopping, playing tennis, coming out of her building, returning to it at the end of the day, buying a newspaper, scratching her ankle, raising her camera, living her life.

The prick.

'Has a thing for me, doesn't he, following me around?' she said. 'But I reconstructed the time frame from the locations and my clothes. All those shots were made before he changed the record. So, you see, Frank, that's not so bad. I mean, he hasn't really done anything at all since then. It's sort of like a time bomb. And today it just happened to go off.'

'Know something, you're terrific. You've got every reason to feel scared.'

'Maybe I am. A little, anyway. But then I feel it's not all that bad, not really all that aggressive. More like a game by one of those phone-freak types.'

Janek took her hand. 'You're right, the game-player's usually harmless. Aggressive, sure, but sneaky. And underneath a sneak's more scared than you.'

She smiled. To his amazement she was managing to shrug it off. But to Janek the message was stunningly clear; *I've been tracking your girl; I could have gotten her thirty-six times.*

Aaron made a breakthrough.

Through a cop he knew who worked crowd control on movie sets he found a German-born script girl who'd lived briefly with Peter Lane. Her name was Elga Becker and this living together had occurred in Munich. Now Elga told Aaron, 'I'd like to see him crawl through broken glass.'

According to her, when they'd been lovers in Germany he'd confided that 'Lane' was his mother's maiden name, that his real name was something else and that he'd been brought up in Cleveland.

Why did Elga hate him so? Seems when she came to New York and was looking for a job she called Peter for help and advice. He heard her out, then told her he didn't remember her very well. He hung up on her and she could never get through to him again.

'Nasty little thing,' Aaron reported. 'Bad breath and she sprays when she talks. Says when they made love he "used his pecker like a dagger." Then, she says, he'd lay his head upon her breast and sigh.'

'Real romantic. You believe her?'

'Sure,' Aaron said. 'At least the part about the name.'

'Then you better go out to Cleveland,' Janek said.

Aaron left that afternoon.

He was counting days now. Halloween was uneventful: the usual number of 'treats' that turned out to be drug-soaked brownies, and 'tricks' that turned out to be razor blades concealed in fruit. He pondered his cases. Was Caroline in real jeopardy? He wasn't sure and the possibility worried him; he carried it around.

He grew tired of waiting to hear from Aaron and began to drive aimlessly about the city. He revisited the crime scenes, asked himself if there could have been something important that he'd missed.

He found himself acting nervous in the squad room, irascible with Stanger and Howell.

'I need more Nelly Delgados,' he shouted. 'So find them, dammit, before this case turns to total shit.'

Sal called: 'The garage belongs to Sweeney. *Not* his brother-in-law like he says. They do a fairly decent job, maybe not the best in town, but you could pay more and do a lot worse without trying very hard. The guys who work there, they seem like competent mechanics. But a friend of mine says he's spotted hoods.'

'What kind of hoods?'

'That's what I'm going to be checking out. And also into a sort of parallel operation that seems to be taking place around the back.'

Indian summer: warm air, hazy skies, comfortable lazy days. The parks were filled with joggers, the museums with European tourists. Skaters on the rink at Rockefeller Center cut flowing figures in the ice.

Always, when he drove across the bridge, Janek would look back at the city and wonder at its beauty and its power. And then as he came off the ramp in Queens he would think of Caroline, how much he loved her, her vulnerability, her smile when she greeted him and how being with her and staring into her soft brown eyes would soon relieve his stress.

He kissed the side of her neck that pulsed after they made love, the place where she said she thought her skin was weak and a vein or an artery was perilously exposed.

'Think it's over?' she asked.

'All those things grouped together, and nothing more since then.'

'Sometimes –'

He kissed her neck again. 'You know no one can get in here now. This loft is like a vault.'

She was quiet and after she fell asleep he slipped quietly out of bed and walked along the walls, pausing at each window, leaning forward and peering down through the blinds at the empty streets.

It was 2 am. There'd just been a terrific rainstorm. Janek pulled off the Major Deegan onto the East 134th Street exit ramp. As he approached the traffic light he locked his door. When he stopped, an elderly black man with desperate eyes approached with a bottle of Windex and a rag.

Kind of pointless since it had just rained, Janek thought. But the man started to clean the windshield anyway. Janek shrugged, waved him around to his side of the car, rolled down his window and handed him a buck.

He spotted Sal's Chevrolet a block short of the Third Avenue Bridge. He pulled ahead of it and parked. A few seconds later Sal slipped into his car.

'On time even with the rain. What do you want to do? Look, or talk it over first?'

'Let's look,' Janek said.

197

They got out. Janek followed Sal up the street past a closed tire-repair shop, a string of junk stores, through the debris of discarded rubber treads and bent-in hubcaps that cluttered the way. The ramp to the Third Avenue Bridge loomed before them in the night. The air was sticky. Manhattan glowed across the Harlem River, the tops of its towers shrouded in fog.

Sal led him across a yard of broken bottles and smashed bricks, then to the door at the back of an abandoned tenement. 'Stay close,' he whispered. Sal stopped, listened, then turned back to Janek. 'Pushers operating here. Should be clear this late, but you never know. Better follow in my footsteps. They lay booby traps sometimes.'

Janek watched while Sal pried the door. A sliver of light caught the pry-bar and made it shine. Inside there was gloom. All the windows of the building had been covered with sheet aluminum. Sal switched on his flashlight, and Janek followed him closely to the stairs. There was rubble – broken doors, beat-in stoves, burned-out timbers – but the stairs, surprisingly, were intact and were clean as if someone had recently swept them with a broom.

They moved up, a flight at a time, pausing at each landing, listening. Once Janek thought he heard the rustling of rats. There was the sound of water dripping, residue of the rain still seeping in.

Sal led him out an open door onto the damp black asphalt roof. They had climbed four stories and now had a view of the surrounding territory – more abandoned residential buildings, ruins of still others which had burned, and access to the roof of a neighboring structure which Sal, crouching beside him, pointed out. 'That's it.'

'What?'

'Back shop,' Sal whispered. 'The legit setup faces the street and it's open all day. Then there's the alley – used for deliveries. Then this other structure where they only work at night.'

'Men working in there now?'

Sal grinned.

'How'd you find it?'

'For starters had some work done on my car. Then I hung around. Local pushers clued me in. Could have made some collars if I hadn't traded back my evidence.'

Sal was good: a narc detective who knew how to shake down pushers and trade for information.

'Frank, you ought to see the parade of cops coming around here with their fancy foreign jobs. Porsches. BMWs. Mercedes. Got to wonder where they get the dough.'

They moved carefully to the side of the roof. There was a rickety ladder lying against the low roof wall. Sal pulled it up and lowered it over the side. 'Only a seven-foot drop,' he said. He held the ladder until Janek got off. The roofing over the back shop was slippery. Now that Janek was on it he understood the setup. There were two buildings, the one they were on and the front building, which had a slightly lower roof. There was a twenty-foot gap between the structures. To move a car from one garage to the other it would be necessary to open a set of sliding iron doors in each.

Sal led him to the skylight, a low walled hut with a pitched roof composed of safety glass. The panes had been painted black on the inside, but there was a patch that had escaped the brush, small, less than an inch in diameter, but large enough to peek through when they brought their faces close.

It looked busy down there: a dozen men wearing safety masks, with wrenches, bolt clippers and acetylene torches, stripping and chopping cars. The vehicles were arranged in parallel rows like corpses in a morgue. The mechanics played the role of forensic pathologists methodically dismembering the vital parts.

They crept back to the ladder, climbed back onto the tenement roof, then Sal pulled the ladder up and placed it back against the wall.

'What do you think?'

'Begging for a raid.'

'But you're not going to call a raid, are you, Frank?'

Sal led him back down, using his flashlight to point out debris. Regrouping by the exterior door, he paused to light a cigarette.

'Not bad, huh?'

'How long have you known?'

'Four days.'

'Why didn't you tell me?'

'Had to link it to Sweeney first.'

'*Did you*?'

Sal smiled. 'Better than that, I think. The way I figure it the front shop, Sweeney's shop, makes an enormous profit. They got to, since they're billing customers for what are basically free parts. Knock off the special discount to cops and the profits still are huge, since their only real costs are overhead and labor. It's a classic. The stolen cars are trucked into the alley and the leftovers are trucked out at dawn. They move the good parts over to the front garage and for all I know they got a wholesale business to get rid of the surplus too. Okay, that back shop, that's a separate operation. Different ownership, different business name. Owned by a company owned by another company owned by still a third. We'd have to subpoena records to be sure, but funny thing – since I had that printout on Hart I knew his wife's holdings, and that third company was on the list.' Sal's voice turned cocky; he knew he was onto something good. 'Now, everyone knows Sweeney's Hart's man, and if you mess with Sweeney you mess with Hart. So it figures they're in this together, with maybe Hart acting as banker through his wife. Chances are they can both wriggle out of it in case the operation blows. Neither one is stupid. They'll have a story. Claim they didn't know there was work going on at night. Claim they didn't know anything, that the back shop was just for storage. You know: "I think we got just the part you need, Sergeant Maloney, in the storage room on the shelf." They only own the building, after all – they're not responsible for an illegal business some crook's set up in back. Doubt either one of them's even been in there with witnesses around. Still, if you ask me it's kind of stupid having the two operations so close.'

'No, that figures,' said Janek. 'Just like Hart. So *arrogant*.'

'Yeah.' Sal looked at him, perhaps a little surprised by his intensity. 'I know this is really important to you, Frank. That's why I've been busting myself.'

'You've done a terrific job. Now what about those hoods?'

'Going to start on that tomorrow. I'll park opposite the end of the alley and see who comes out the door.'

'Be careful. I'm looking for muscle, guys Sweeney could order to do very bad things.'

'Going to burn them, aren't you?'

Janek nodded. 'Sweeney, probably.'

'Not going to be easy.'

'Don't worry.' He clapped Sal on the shoulder. 'I'll think of a way.'

He told her, 'It's always tough when you take a stance, because then there're lines you have to cross. It's a dangerous territory on the other side. Terry wanted to go in there and when he finally did he couldn't return. For years that was a lesson to me. Don't stray across, you might get caught. But now I know there are times when you have to go in no matter the fear of no return. The thing I fear most of all now, you see, is that I might blow out my brains one Sunday morning because I knew I'd been afraid.'

'He's going to whores again, Lieutenant.'

'*What*?'

Stanger and Howell had entered the squad room with wild eyes.

'You didn't know?' Stanger asked.

'How the hell would I know that?'

'We thought Marchetti –' Stanger was glowing.

'Sal's been off Lane for weeks. He's been working another angle.'

'Oh. We just kind of figured...' Janek understood: Stanger thought he'd found something that would show Marchetti up.

'Well, don't just stand there. Find out what the fuck he's doing with the whores.'

Aaron finally called from Cleveland.

'Found the house. Ticky-tacky. West Side neighborhood. Run-down. About what you'd expect.'

'What would I expect?' Janek asked.

He could hear Aaron trying to control his breathing, getting ready to spring a surprise.

'About what you'd expect for a cop. Ohio state trooper, name of Jesse Dill.'

Janek's heartbeat quickened. 'You're not –'

'No bullshit, Frank. So maybe you were right, goddammit. Maybe the films are connected to his early life. Tell me something – how do you come up with stuff like that?'

'I'm just a detective. Stop stalling. Tell me more.'

'Give me a couple days. It's been years. Most of the neighbors are different. I only found one person so far who remembers them as a couple. But there's something here. I can smell it.'

'What kind of smell?'

'Bad. Very bad.' Aaron paused. 'Detail you ought to know

about. It's a normal house, one bath, working-class with add-on garage. And the people who own it now don't have any kids. But I see this rusty old basketball hoop set up on the garage, so I ask them why they put it in. Say they didn't, that it was there when they bought the place, and they bought direct from this guy Dill.' Aaron paused again. 'You hear what I'm saying, Frank. Our friend Peter – he had a normal childhood. The great devil, the whore-killer – he practiced lay-ups in his driveway. Jesus . . .'

Stanger and Howell reported back. Four prostitutes visited over the past two weeks. Normal sessions. Nothing unusual. Except afterward Lane had asked them about their friends. Said he was interested in locating a certain type. Actually showed them a photograph. Wanted someone who looked the same, five feet seven, slender, good legs, chiseled features, and he was very particular about the hair and eyes. Eyes had to be deep brown. Hair had to be lighter, layered, and graduated longer toward the back. The hair, Lane had told them, was very important. Emphasized he was turned on by that kind of hair.

'Girls were freaked,' said Howell. 'Weird situation. We show them photos of a guy. He shows them photos of a girl.'

Janek felt a sharp chill. 'I want to talk to them. Bring them in.'

He interviewed the women privately in the tiny interrogation rooms in back. He showed them several pictures of Caroline. Two of them were vague – Caroline could have been the one; two were certain that she was. After they left he sat for a long time, his elbows planted on the table, his head resting in his fists.

On a cold and glittering Sunday afternoon early in November, Janek packed up most of his clothing, then drove over to Long Island City and stowed it in a closet that Caroline had cleared out specially for his use.

'Well, you finally did it, didn't you?' Caroline said, watching him, greatly amused. She was standing in a pool of sunlight by a window. 'I guess what we're seeing here is "commitment to a relationship," as they say.'

'Commitment to convenience too.'

'Oh, sure. And you still got your basement across the river, your refuge in case things don't work out. I understand, the apartment situation being what it is. But they still have those bunk rooms at the precincts, don't they? For the double-shift guys and for when things get rough at home.'

He looked at her. Her skin glowed and the autumn light split up, fractured, in her eyes.

'It's because of the photographs, isn't it?'

'What?' He stopped stowing his clothes. *Did she know? She couldn't.*

'The guy who took the pictures. You're worried about him.'

'You think that's why I'm moving in.'

She nodded. 'Part of the reason. Sure.' She turned away. 'You know, I've been thinking a lot about that guy, why he took those pictures, what he was trying to do. Made me think of Lane and what Hart said to you at lunch. Remember: "All you got are photographs." Well, photographs are plenty. They can be enough.' She turned back to him. 'Find the photographs, Janek. The ones he took of the girls.'

'What makes you so sure he took photographs?' When she'd said 'Lane' his heart had skipped a beat.

'Came to me this morning, don't know why. I thought: He needs to have pictures; that's how his mind works, like mine.'

'Why? What does he need them for?'

'Don't know. Some sort of proof, I guess.'

Could she be right? 'Proof of what?' he asked.

There was a long silence before she answered. 'Maybe just proof to himself that he was really there.'

'There was a murder, Frank. Double homicide. Peter's mother, woman named Laurie Dill, originally Laurie Lane. And her lover, guy named Norman Baxter. Both of them found slain in a trailer Baxter leased in a Cleveland trailer park.'

It was Aaron's first call since he'd found the house. Janek could feel the tension. It was finally unraveling, that thing he was looking for, the shared past he'd discovered in the movies, the dark and terrible ancient crime.

'Baxter owned a filling station across from a shopping mall. He was a womanizer, kept the trailer for assignations, matinees. Anyway, Laurie was carrying on with him like she'd been doing with various other guys. The father, this Jesse – seems he was a shmuck. Mushy type, fat, not too bright. Laurie was younger and hot-tempered. Would ridicule him, in front of people, too.'

Janek recognized them: a recruit to the force married to an ambitious girl initially attracted to his uniform. She soon discovers he isn't going anywhere and, worse, is boring in the sack. The cop quickly resigns himself to mediocrity; his muscles turn to lard, his features become lost in fat. The wife turns contemptuous as the marriage becomes a bitter drone. She starts looking around at other men. Begins to flaunt herself. Starts a string of affairs.

'... Killings very bloody. Multiple stab wounds. *Jesus*. Big story around these parts. Being the cuckold, Jesse is suspect number one, but he's got an airtight alibi – he's patrolling the Ohio Turnpike all afternoon giving out tickets right and left. Gets the call on his car radio and rushes to the scene. Freaks out. Bursts into the trailer and starts throwing stuff around. Before they can restrain him he's screwed up everything, including what might have been important forensic evidence. Then he goes crazy. Starts drinking. Pays no attention to his kid. Laurie's brother, a veterinarian name of Harold Lane, takes Peter in. Lots of police theories. Maybe another one of Baxter's women surprised them. Or one of the husbands. No one knows. Bottom line – the case is never solved. Meantime Jesse quits the force and disappears.'

'Find him.'

'What?'

'You've done a great job, you found the crime. Now go for the father.'

'You kidding, Frank?'

'I'm not. Go for the father, Aaron. Find him. He may be the key.'

'Yeah, there's muscle, Frank, guys who've done time – they're the ones driving the trucks in and out. Now, whether they're buying stolen cars off thieves or they got their own people out is something I can't tell you – to do that I'd have to start following those trucks.'

'Don't risk it, Sal.'

'Okay, but to really ID these creeps I'd have to bring in some friends. Figure you don't want that done, at least not yet. Another thing, you asked me to check up on rumors the garage gets sloppy. I managed to track one down. A black homicide detective name of

Beau Jones – been in the department for years. He owns a Mercedes, took it in there once and got it back with a beat-up old carburettor for which they billed him eight hundred bucks. Got mad. Went straight to Sweeney, told him he was going to file a complaint with Consumer Affairs. Sweeney promised he'd take care of it, got Jones a brand-new carburettor free. But next thing Jones is out of Homicide and assigned to transit-yard security at Gravesend. Now this is one very bitter detective, Frank. Takes him an hour and a half just to drive to work. Spends his time chasing graffiti artists but he doesn't gripe, because he got the message. Don't mess with Sweeney and don't make threats.'

Janek and Caroline went to see *Dreamgirls*, third row orchestra, eighty bucks. During intermission they collided with Sarah Janek and her date. Awkward introductions. Sarah and Caroline braved it out by shaking hands.

'Great musical.'

'Terrific. Yeah.'

The other man was Sarah's boss, head of the accounting department at Macy's in Queens. Older than Janek, maybe fifty-five. He and Caroline talked about the show.

Sarah smiled. 'You look good, Frank. Real sorry about Al. Wanted to call you when I heard.' She paused. 'How's Aaron? Sal?'

'The three of us are working a case. Both of them are great.'

She gestured toward her date. 'We're going to get married.'

'That's terrific. Congratulations.'

'Was going to call you. Don't have to now, I guess.'

'Going to keep the house?'

'Sure.' She glanced over at Caroline. 'Nice-looking girl. Hope things work out for you.'

After the show Janek rushed Caroline out of the theater. Driving back to the loft she asked him what was wrong.

'Nothing.'

'She said something.'

'Going to marry the guy.'

'Is that why you're mad?'

He didn't answer.

'How do you feel about it?'

'Different ways.'

'What kinds of different ways?'

He glanced at her. 'Dammit! Took me years to pay off that house. Now *he's* going to live in it.'

She glanced back at him. 'Look, it isn't your house anymore.'

'I know.'

'Belonged to another guy. Another Janek. Same name but different. That house is from your other life.'

At a traffic light on Northern Boulevard she leaned over and kissed him on the lips.

She came out of the bathroom smiling, her hair wet the way he liked it from her shower. He loved making love to her after she washed her hair, running his fingers through it when it was wet, staring into her eyes as, mysteriously, she stared into his, feeling her holding him tight inside her as she smiled.

Just then the phone rang. Janek picked it up. It was a quarter to twelve on a Saturday night.

'Sorry to bother you, Lieutenant.' It was Stanger.

'What's the matter? You lost him? Don't apologize.'

'No, we got him in sight down here on Eighth near Forty-fourth. The same area he met up with Nelly.'

'What's he doing?'

'That's the funny thing, Lieutenant. We think he's photographing whores.'

'You *think*,' he looked at Caroline. She was getting into bed beside him. 'Dammit, what *kind* of whores?'

'Maybe the same kind he told those girls he was looking for.' Stanger paused. 'Give us a break, Lieutenant. It's hard to see from here.'

Janek hung up without saying goodbye.

'Who was that?' she asked.

'One very tired detective.'

'Important?'

He shook his head.

Sal wanted to be there for the kill. He was adamant. 'I want to see Sweeney burn.' When Janek told him that was out of the question, Sal turned sullen. 'I think you owe me, Frank. Considering everything.'

206

'Things may not work out. It's for your own protection.'

'I can take care of myself.'

'That's not what I meant. The danger's to your career. You're a young guy with a big future. Stupid to risk it over this.'

'What is "this"?' Janek was silent. 'I'm already involved. I feel almost insulted.'

'Don't try and get to me like that, Sal. I did a lot of things for Al and he protected me. And a lot of the time he protected me from myself.'

'Okay, give me one good reason. Just convince me that you're right.'

'It's personal. That's it. There's nothing else to say.'

'No leads on Dad yet. But more goodies on Peter,' Aaron said. Janek was silent.

'First place, remember that scene he did with Nelly? Well, get this. Liz Lane, the vet Harold's widow, the survivor of the couple, remember, who took Peter in – she swears up and down that the furniture Peter used in that scene was the actual stuff from his parents' parlor and that the photographs were photographs of Jesse and Laurie Dill. Now, isn't that a little creepy, Frank? Hiring a whore to spit at your parents' pictures. Isn't that sickening? I mean just a little bit?'

Before Janek could respond, say that sickening though it was he had suspected it for some time, Aaron was onto something else.

'Found this guy, Chuck Brubeck, used to be a neighbor of the Dills. Peter's best boyhood friend. Seems our little Peter used to torture animals.'

First there was the story of the cat, then the story of the birds. The cat thing happened when the kids were eleven years old. Peter's Uncle Harold was performing a hysterectomy, the boys were playing over at his house and he asked them to help by holding the animal down. No anesthetic. Chuck Brubeck was horrified and threw up. But Peter's gaze never left the operating table. He could talk of nothing else for days.

'Couple of weeks later he kidnapped a cat belonged to a neighbor, took it into the garage and tried to perform the operation himself. Made a mess of it. Wanton cruelty. Cat bled to death. Afterward Chuck's father found out and gave his son the beating of his life. But when Mr. Brubeck called trooper Dill, Jesse was preoccupied. It was clear he didn't care.' A pause. 'You listening, Frank?'

'I'm listening.'

'Torturing animals – we've heard stuff like that before.'

They had. Over and over in the childhood of sociopaths. 'So what's the story with the birds?'

'That happened maybe four years later, when the kids were around fifteen. Another neighbor, an amateur ornithologist, kept these birds tethered in his backyard. Golden eagle chained up to a stump, raven in a cage and a couple of owls. One night, this was in winter, Peter attacked them with a rake. Asked Chuck to help, but he refused. Peter went ahead anyway. Real massacre. Big story, too. Got national attention in the press.'

Again Janek recognized a phenomenon, people getting more upset about cruelty to animals than when human beings were abused.

'Neighborhood in an uproar. Talk of a madman loose in the suburb. There were bloody tracks in the snow, but they didn't lead anywhere. Chuck was the only one who knew and he kept quiet. I asked him why. Said he was scared – which is understandable. So then I asked him why Peter had done it. Said he asked Peter the same thing and Peter answered he just wanted to see. See what? I asked. See if he could get away with it, Chuck said.'

After they hung up Janek asked himself, *Had Peter really wanted to get away with it?*

Now it was cool she rarely turned on the fan; the four blades hung silent and still above the bed. Often after she went to sleep he stayed up sitting on the couch, his thirty-eight beside him, an accordion in his arms, silently fingering the keys, waiting... perhaps for Lane.

He heard her move, turned to look, saw that her eyes were open and that she was watching him.

'What are you doing, Frank?'

'Just sitting here.'

'Thinking?'

'Yeah.'

She smiled and closed her eyes.

I am her guardian, he thought. *I must protect her from knowledge of her jeopardy.* And thinking that, he realized that he had finally, truly, entered into the madness of the case.

Later he saw her watching him again. 'It's Lane, isn't it?' she asked.

Their eyes met. He could see that she knew, perhaps had known ever since the first intrusion.

Hart called. 'What's going on with Switched Heads?'

'I got feelers out.'

'Feelers. What the hell are "feelers"?'

'We're investigating,' Janek explained.

'Yeah. Right. Well, you investigate. Investigate the hell out of the thing. Because I wasn't bullshitting you about that deadline, Frank. You're warned. Your time is running out.'

He watched Lane's windows from Mandy's chair, saw the lights go on and off. Another time, when Lane didn't come home, he watched one of Ellis' parties and saw a girl with long straight black hair do a bump-and-grind striptease to the unison clapping of the other guests.

Aaron was onto something. He called to say he was leaving Cleveland for New Jersey in the morning.

Find me Jesse, Aaron. I need him now.

He told her, 'He lives on a knife's edge. The movies and homicides come out of the same stuff. He sees his mother as a whore and kills her over and over again. When he does it in a film he's acting fairly healthy. When he kills and switches heads he's monstrous. But his films are shallow – he never became a first-rate artist because he could never get beyond his mother. He got stuck. The old crime was always there. And he committed it, didn't just fantasize it like other kids. So now when he relives it the only thing he can do is try and make it puzzling and beautiful. Switched Heads is his latest design, very complicated, requiring lots of concentration, which spared him from having to face what it was really about. More than anything I want to see him put away.'

Thanksgiving was cold; December came in with a chill. One

afternoon early in the month Janek went to his old apartment on West Eighty-seventh, took off his pants, hung them up carefully, pulled out an old accordion, sat down on his bed and filled the room with sound.

She was shooting on Sixth near Thirty-ninth when suddenly a streak of pain leaped across her throat, a terrible white-hot searing pain that made her yell.

'For a second or two I was in shock,' she said. Then she saw a kid running away from her down the block. She reached up, found that the small gold chain she wore was gone. The kid had ripped it off her neck.

Janek moved his fingers to the place where the chain had been torn, a thin red line, a bruise. 'I thought. Well, baby, this is it,' she said. 'It was *him*, I thought, measuring me, measuring my neck for –' she shook her head and smiled – 'dismemberment.'

They were lying together on the bed. The whole evening she'd been pensive. Janek had had the feeling something had happened; he'd waited patiently for her to bring it up.

'Then it came to me, that it was just street aggression, just a kid stealing a chain. And I knew then I could handle it. I could shoot aggression and live with it, too.' She kissed him. 'You know, Frank, I've changed these last few months. I'm stronger than I was. And I know the reason. You've been so gentle with me and strong. You were there when I was scared. You moved in here to protect me – of course I knew that. And by doing that and being the guy you are you've helped me work this through.'

She kissed him again, then wrapped her arms around him and pulled him upon her. 'God, I love you, Frank.'

On December tenth, at nine-thirty in the morning, Aaron Rosenthal called.

'Got him, Frank.'

At last! The model for all the blundering cops in all the awful films.

'Living in a shack down here in rural Jersey. You wouldn't believe the place. Got a job, too. Typical old-cop job. Night watchman at this abandoned car racetrack.'

'What's he like?' Janek could feel the excitement rising through his chest.

'Strange. Very strange. I don't think he's what you're expecting. For one thing, he's not fat anymore. Jesse's a very thin man now. Looks like Abe Lincoln until he opens his mouth. But then, Jesus, there's nothing there.'

Jesse

He took the Metroliner to Philadelphia, was met by Aaron at Thirtieth Street Station. Then they drove south in a rented Toyota Aaron had been using for a week.

A voyage from ignorance to knowledge, Janek thought; or so he hoped – impossible to know until he met the man. They drove in silence across the girder bridge into Camden, through a petrochemical maze, past industrial parks and finally, when they reached the suburbs, past half-empty sterile shopping malls.

A cold day, below freezing with a harsh northwest wind that amplified the chill.

Aaron handled the car well, his bulky detective's body awkward in the seat, his hands resting lightly on the wheel. They didn't talk much, a few words in the staccato shorthand they'd been using with each other for months. Janek stared out the window at flat fields crusted lightly with snow and drifts caught in fences that showed the power of the winds that buffeted the hibernating farms. There were deserted barracks built of rotting planks set in clusters by the road, homes to the migrant workers who lived here through the picking season, moving northward with the harvest, ending up in the potato fields of Long Island, sustained by high-starch meals.

It was a bleak terrain.

At Millville they crossed the Maurice River, which they'd been following on and off, then took a secondary road that led them to Port Norris, a town set on a cove of Delaware Bay. Half a mile down a back street to a place called Bivalve on the map. Aaron said the locals called it 'Shell Pile' on account of its huge piles of oyster shells, twenty and thirty feet high, encrusted now with snow.

211

A vision then, behind the piles, of a shantytown out of a nineteen-thirties photograph.

'How did you find this hole?' The first words Janek had uttered in ten miles.

'Asked around,' Aaron said. He wasn't going to tell. Already known as a superb telephone detective, now he would become a legend – he had tracked a man who'd been missing for eighteen years to this hellhole in the Jersey mosquito country, this dead end of dead ends, this frostbitten wasteyard for human junk.

Across a landfill, then down a rutted road that hadn't been shoveled, the ice cracking beneath the tires. Aaron stopped the Toyota. They'd reached a dead end. There was a path leading off into a stand of pines. Aaron pointed. Janek nodded, got out of the car and walked forward alone.

A cabin in a clearing: it was not what he'd been expecting. He thought he'd find another wretched shack, the sort that dotted the landfill behind the shell piles. But this cabin was idyllic – built out of logs, well kept up, the firewood stacked neatly along one side, a curl of smoke rising from the chimney perfuming the frigid air.

Jesse was waiting for him. Aaron had told him another detective was coming from New York, and so evidently the old man had spent the day in his easy chair beside his wood stove, thinking, wondering, expecting . . . he did not know what.

Janek searched his face for Peter's features, discovering them slowly in an unexpected form. The same hard gray eyes, same lips and ears, but the skin was different, like leather stretched over his cheekbones and warmed by something powerful within. It was a beautiful face, he thought – great sadness in it, marks of past misery, but beatific too, as if it glowed with some special brand of knowledge.

Later Janek would understand that he had mistaken the nature of that glowing – that Jesse's face was enlivened by a long slow-burning pain.

He felt at home there and didn't know why: the cabin was different from any place he'd ever seen. The man was special too; he reminded Janek of drunks he'd seen on the Bowry when he'd been a boy, or the old man who'd tried to clean his windshield in the rain the night Sal had showed him the back shop behind Sweeney's garage. It was a face Caroline would want to photograph – something in it broken but also strong.

There was a chair waiting on the other side of the stove; Jesse, he knew, had put it there for him. And then when they began to talk, in the strange, slow, intuitive way that came spontaneously to them both, he found himself riveted by Jesse's voice, the deep throaty hoarseness of it and a metallic quality too, an iron sound that gave every utterance an edge.

'Aaron told you why I've come?' The old man nodded. 'Then you understand.'

When Jesse shook his head his throat quivered like a turkey's gullet.

'What don't you understand?'

'None of it,' the old man said.

Janek kept having to remind himself he was a detective interviewing an informant with special knowledge of a suspect in a murder case, because that role kept seeming wrong. He wondered how Jesse viewed their meeting: a detective from the city on a hunt, face to face with a ruined former cop.

As they talked it became evident they both thought Peter was evil.

'... Spent years trying to get my goat. Tried everything. Wickedness after wickedness. Wanted a lickin', I always thought, though it was guidance he needed – see that now. He didn't get it. Wouldn't give it to him. So he floundered, that boy, *had* to flounder. On the rocks, you know. The rocks we put there so he would break himself.'

It was a kind of poetry he was speaking, an amalgam of simple words, clichés, and penetrating insights too. Janek listened, his eyes locked into Jesse's, his mind seeking to fathom the strange poetry. He began to view Peter's childhood then as an enormous struggle – the harder he pushed, the more Jesse withdrew into ineffectuality. Except it was not his son from whom he was withdrawing; it was his rage, his enormous rage at the woman, the boy's mother, Laurie, his wife.

'... She whored. Goddamn she did. And he knew it. Had to. We both knew and couldn't say nothing. Because it was there, between us, always. Always there. Always between us. He looked to me for what to do and I told him. Showed him she was ruining me. By my face. My look. My silence too. He saw and knew. I told him. Though we never talked.'

In the end something had to give. Jesse knew that, realized now

213

he had conveyed that to Peter, that the strains had grown too great for the boy, the pressure built too high. Peter could not sustain the mediative role – rage at his mother for what she was doing to Jesse, and contempt for Jesse for permitting her to ridicule him, cuckold him, play him for the sucker, for the fool.

'... Wanted to kill me. Sure of it. Saw it in him lots of times. So okay, I told him, kill me, go ahead. Won't make no difference. I'm dead inside anyway. But soon as I told him that, with my eyes, mind you, never out loud, he'd turn away and then he'd think of killing her. Which was what I wanted deep in me. Always. Use him, see, to get rid of her. Those were the rocks we put there for him. Couldn't swim his way out. Not from what we put between us and him. And what we *didn't* put there, either. The channels we left open, I mean. Had to drown, that boy.'

The afternoon wore on, it grew dark, until Janek could barely make Jesse out. The old man left his seat to fetch a Coleman lantern. He pumped it up, lit it, then set it down beside the stove.

He moved gracefully, a strong lean old man, very thin as Aaron had said, the blubber accumulated as a failed cop burned away by years of wandering. Now, at last, he was back working at his first love, security work. He was a night watchman who guarded a worthless place. He laughed when he told Janek that. A perfect ending for a broken cop, his laughter seemed to say.

That Jesse understood the family conspiracy so well seemed to Janek a kind of miracle. Except that he had had eighteen years to brood upon Peter's matricide.

'... Wanted punishment. Know that. And my way of punishing him was always to ignore – which was, mind you, what he wanted, too. Pushed him further, see, to worse and worse. And when he finally did the worst of all – then *nothing*. No punishment. I messed things up so he'd be safe. My fault, I thought. Pushed him to it. Knew she did, too, but blamed myself. Because that's what I'd wished, see. *Wished*. Drove him by that, by what I *wished*...'

There was magic here, belief in the power of wishes, killer thoughts, telepathy, unspoken conveyance of desires and all the guilt that accrues from such beliefs. Janek recognized the guilt, smelled it in that cabin with the Coleman lighting one side of Jesse's troubled face, leaving the other side lost in darkness.

He described Switched Heads then, one cop to another. It didn't

214

take him long; the story was much simpler than he'd thought. Which surprised him. He'd always believed it was fiendishly complicated, that the case was nearly intractable on account of its web of complications.

'"Stop me,"' Janek said. 'That's the message of everything, the cat, the birds, the killing of your wife and Baxter and my two girls in New York. He wants to be stopped, he needs to be. And the only way I can do that is to come at him in a way you never did.'

'Yeah,' the old man said, 'all those girls he carves up in his pictures – thinks he can get to me with them.'

Janek saw a glimmer then in Jesse's eyes, saw it burn there a moment, then die away. The old man shrugged, a great and final shrug of impotency. Aaron was right – he was too far gone to care.

It was dark when Janek returned to the car. Aaron had kept the engine running so he wouldn't freeze. They started driving back in silence, the snow a black crust upon the fields, an occasional truck roaring toward them out of the night, headlights shimmering off the ice upon the road.

'Well?' asked Aaron finally.

'Didn't work out,' Janek said.

'What was supposed to happen?'

'My crazy idea that he might want to tell his father, that the movies were somehow addressed to him. That they said, "Come on. Wring it out of me. Here's what I did. Now do something. Capture me. Don't let me get away." And that if I could enlist the old man I might be able to break through. Look, the hell with it! He's useless. You were right – there's nothing there.'

They drove a while longer. 'He's shrewd, though.' He glanced at Aaron, 'I thought you told me he never saw any of Peter's movies.'

'That's right,' Aaron said.

'You're sure?'

'He told me he didn't.'

'Then how –?' Janek paused. 'Aaron, please stop the car.'

'What?'

'Stop a minute. I need to think.'

Aaron pulled over to the shoulder. A truck rushed by. Janek thought. *If he saw the movies he would have said so. If he didn't see them, then what did he mean when he said, '... those girls he carves up in his pictures – thinks he can get to me with them'?*

'Listen, we got to go back. I think I missed something back there.'

Aaron nodded, turned the car around. They sped back through the night.

Though it had been an hour since he'd left, it seemed to Janek that Jesse had scarcely moved. He was still sitting in his chair beside the stove, and his expression, that look of fright and gloom, was still the same. The old man didn't even seem surprised that his visitor had returned. When Janek came in he motioned him again toward the second chair.

'What do you know about Peter's movies?'

'Don't know nothing. Never saw one.'

'But you spoke of the girls he carves up.' Jesse shook his head. 'You said –'

'The girls in the pictures. Yes.'

'What pictures?'

'The ones he sent.'

'Pictures?' *Was Caroline right?* 'You mean photographs? He sent you *photographs*?'

Jesse nodded.

'Where are they?' Jesse looked at him curiously. 'You have them?' Janek held his breath.

It took more than an hour to extract the story, how over the years Jesse had received envelopes containing still photographs of murdered girls. Awful grotesque pictures but prettied up too, as if an effort had been made to make them look beautiful in death. Jesse could see that they were faked and knew they came from Peter, but he'd no idea how Peter had found out where he lived. Which was why he'd moved so many times, covering his tracks – to escape those envelopes which were reproaches, to escape the reproaches of his son.

He thought, finally, he'd succeeded; it had been two years since he'd come to Jersey, two years since he'd received a set of stills. But then a couple of months ago he'd received an envelope with four pictures inside – two of dead girls and two more in which each girl bore the other's head. Crazy, sickening, crazier and more sickening than anything he'd received before. They looked real too, though Jesse knew they couldn't be – that Peter had faked them up, that

216

they were trick shots done with models just like the others. He didn't even examine them. Just threw the damn things away.

On the way back to Philadelphia for the second time that night Aaron tried to give Janek consolation.

'Well, one thing anyway, at least now we understand why he prettied up the crime scenes. But, I tell you, Frank, the deeper we get into this the less I understand the case.'

They stopped at a gas station. While the tank was being filled Janek called the precinct from a pay telephone. Howell answered and he had something to report:

'Peter's found a whore, Lieutenant. Looks kind of like the one in those pictures he was showing around. Sal talked to her. She told him Peter's been back three times and that he likes to do it on a rubber mat. Now we're thinking maybe he's going to try and switch her with the girl in the photo. But we got a problem. We don't know who that other girl is.'

When he put down the phone his head was reeling. Was Peter bluffing, taunting, or was he really setting up to go after Caroline? He worked to calm himself, then phoned the loft. Three rings before she answered. 'Listen,' he said, 'this isn't meant to alarm you but you know me – I like to play things safe. I've got an extra revolver and a box of bullets in the closet, upper shelf on the right. Make sure all the windows are locked and stay inside till I get back. Whatever you do don't open the door for anyone. Anyone tries to break in you shoot. No, I don't expect anything to happen, but still I want you aware. I'm on my way now. Should be there in a couple hours. Don't worry. It's going to be all right.'

Back in the car he couldn't contain himself; he spilled the whole story to Aaron – of Caroline, the intrusion, the razor blade and the stalking photographs.

'I suppose if I were a real hard-case I'd think of some way to use her for bait,' he said.

'No way, Frank. Not you. Look – we'll get more guys and put them on her. Meanwhile we'll crowd Lane. We got to stop this guy.' Suddenly enraged, Aaron banged his fist against the steering wheel. '*Real evidence*. In a cop's hands, too. So the old fart does just what he did before. Throws the fucking stuff away. Jesus!'

It was five minutes before Janek answered, for it took him five minutes to understand his idea. He caught a glimpse of it, wasn't sure he liked it, set it aside to germinate awhile. When he brought it out again for another look it sprang forth fully made, a flower emerging instantly from a seed. And the flower was beautiful, perfect, symmetrical and so frightening too that Janek shrank back from it, afraid. But its beauty enticed him to look again and when he did the petals beckoned. And when he touched them he knew he must have seen that perfect flower before, perhaps one night in a dream.

'Peter doesn't know he did.'

'What?' Aaron glanced at him.

Janek nodded slowly. 'Peter doesn't know Jesse threw the evidence away.'

Dumbshow

He announced himself from downstairs; he knew she wasn't trigger happy but he'd seen too many mishaps to want to come charging through her door. As it turned out she was lying in bed calmly watching TV.

She looked up at him. 'Hi. I'm fine,' she said. She turned back to the screen. 'Now that you're here I can get all feminine and nervous again.'

He leaned down to kiss her. Bogart and Bacall were exchanging heated sexual innuendoes; the movie was *The Big Sleep* and Caroline was totally engrossed. He noticed his extra revolver next to her camera on the bedside table. He sat down beside her. 'Going to try to bluff Lane out.'

Several seconds passed before she turned and looked him in the eye. 'God, that's a terrific line.' She shook her head, got up and switched the TV off. 'Bogart's fine, but you're better, Frank.' She reached for him. 'He's a good detective but you're the best.'

In the morning he explained it to her, how the bluff would work, the role Jesse would play and the chances of success. 'A gamble,' he said. 'Except if I lose I'm no worse off than I am right now. Which is loser-city. Because without a confession I'm never going to make the case.'

218

'What makes you think it'll work?'

'I feel something explosive in the father-son relationship,' he said, 'that's maybe strong enough to blow Peter apart. He's too controlled to be really stable. That's his weakness – all that control. Switched Heads was perfectly done, but then he went ahead and took those pictures. Why? You said maybe he needed proof, for himself, to show himself he'd really done it. I read it differently. To me it's like he needed to create evidence. Something confessional there, something to exploit. Suppose I could freak Peter out, put him in a deranged frame of mind. Then things could get really interesting. Under the right conditions maybe he'd break and spill . . .'

An icy day a week before Christmas, a perfect day, Janek thought. Too cold and windy for Peter to want to go out, but the air so clear he'd see everything – if he looked.

The first step was to attract his attention. They'd planned that part carefully. A burst of activity, squad cars parked in front of the building, detectives coming and going, assuming energetic poses, conferring urgently in Amanda's studio, behaving as men do when a change is imminent.

'I don't know, Frank. It's a cute idea. But I'd say the odds are one in four.'

'Well, you know me, Aaron – I never play the odds.'

They were standing around Amanda's bed while Janek conspicuously framed it with his hands, as if he were taking photographs or trying to match up imaginary shots with real ones. He tried not to overplay; Peter knew acting, could read a false performance. But even if Peter thought it was a performance Janek felt certain he'd be tantalized, if only out of curiosity and for the pleasure of watching them bungle their show.

The only important thing was that Peter watch.

They spent the early evening standing around, waiting for the night. When darkness came they were well illuminated – all the lights in the studio were on.

Finally Sal went to the window and peered out. 'He's there,' he said, 'I know it. Sitting in the dark, watching from darkness the way he likes.'

'You sure?'

'Positive. He's an owl, Frank.'

Janek nodded, then looked at his watch.

Jesse was the dummy. Howell, assigned as handler, had cleaned him up, brought him to New York, kept him fed and occupied. Jesse didn't know what he was doing or why, which was how Janek wanted him. If Jesse didn't know what he was doing, then there was no conspiracy to entrap. If Janek's plan happened to work he didn't want the results to fall apart in court.

The old man looked good in his night watchman's uniform, tough and skeletal, almost frighteningly intense. A specter from the past, the single flaw in Peter's flawless crime, turned up unexpectedly with evidence in hand.

Janek introduced him to Sal them marched him past the window several times – it was important the old man be clearly seen. It was possible, Janek knew, that Peter would not recognize him at once, but he would know he was watching a figure of importance, a man for whom the detectives had been waiting many hours.

Janek took him into the bathroom where he explained the stabbing in great detail, wondering, as the old man nodded, whether he understood how he was being used. Then, when he thought sufficient time had passed for Peter to have begun to grow unnerved, he brought the old man back into the studio and then to the side of Amanda's bed.

There he conspicuously pulled out four Polaroids. 'Look familiar?' Janek asked. Jesse squinted at them hard. Ostensibly he was there to study the crime scene and say whether he recognized elements from the background of the photographs he'd thrown away. 'Like the ones you got, right?' Janek nudged him. 'Right?' Jesse nodded slowly like an old cop dumbly matching the pieces of a puzzle.

The object was to make Peter think his father had kept the shots, though Janek had resolved never to tell him that he had. It had to be unspoken; Peter had to *think* Janek had the proof. However successful the interrogation to take place later on, Janek wasn't going to be accused of inducing a confession with a lie.

His last move, the one he hoped would make Peter crazy, was to take Jesse to the window, open it and place him there facing out. It would be from this display that, hopefully, the realization would sink in. Peter could choose not to believe in Jesse, or to believe in him and still not care. The third possibility, the one Janek was counting on, seemed sometimes, when he thought about it, not plausible at all.

So he placed the old man in full view, on the very spot where Amanda had once set her exercise mat, then stood beside him feeling the cold night air wash across his face. Did he also feel something else, that same shiver that had brushed him on a night so many months before? He stared, wanting to penetrate the darkened window across, willing himself to make out the face he knew must be lurking there behind the glass.

For an instant he thought he saw it. A movement... or something. He stared harder, feeling Jesse beside him, hearing the old man's breathing, wondering if it matched the worried breathing taking place across the yard. Then, he didn't know why, he felt the connection suddenly broken. And just then, as he asked himself if he was imagining things or whether his scheme was going bad, he heard a noise and turned around in time to see Stanger come rushing through the door.

The detective was panting. He'd run up the stairs. 'Charged by me,' he gasped, trying hard to steady himself. 'Came tearing out, Lieutenant. Too fast.' Stanger let his arms fall to his sides. 'Sorry, Lieutenant. He's gone...'

The Room

'Well, at least,' said Sal, 'you ran him to ground.'

'But where's the ground?' Aaron asked.

It was Christmas Eve. They were sitting in their squad room. Sal and Aaron had been roaming the city checking out Peter's haunts. Aaron was wearing his yarmulke. Carols, played over the precinct-house p.a., wafted to them through the walls.

The Jesse plan had certainly worked, but not the way Janek had hoped. A week after the dumbshow at Amanda's and Peter had not reappeared, had not returned to his apartment, although Janek still had Stanger posted there.

221

'It being the holidays, maybe he's gone home.'

Aaron looked at Sal and laughed. 'That dump down in Jersey?'

'Home is home.'

'This guy's not sentimental.'

'So where the hell does he hide out?'

The two detectives looked at Janek. The three of them had been puzzling the problem for a week. It seemed logical that Peter was hiding; spooked by the appearance of his father, he had figured the game was up and fled. Jesse was now ensconced back in his cabin with Howell as companion and guard. Peter had known where to address the pictures but Janek didn't think he would head down there; faced with his father, he had chosen to run.

'It being the holidays, why don't *we* go home?'

'That,' Aaron said, 'is a great idea.'

They went downstairs together. There was a Christmas tree set up in the lobby, a pathetic little spruce laden with tinsel. An old sergeant in a Santa costume sat grinning on a bench reserved for drunks. Police officers' kids crowded around and giggled.

Light snow was falling when they stepped outside. The sky was dark and people hurried along the sidewalks clutching packages. The three detectives stood together for a moment, then headed for their cars.

On his way to Long Island City Janek found the traffic almost sweet. Drivers were polite and the Queensboro Bridge seemed magical, the snow clinging to its girders like a fringe. He listened to Bing Crosby sing 'White Christmas' on the radio, thought of Lou DiMona and wondered if she'd flown to Houston to spend the holidays with Dolly.

He parked outside Caroline's building, retrieved his presents and carried them up the stairs. Climbing, he felt like a very weary detective, but when he opened the door and she ran into his arms he felt himself shedding all fatigue. They ate, drank, listened to music, made love, lay touching each other until they fell asleep. In the morning they exchanged gifts. He gave her a new gold chain and an oversize graphite tennis racket. She gave him a soft gray button-up sweater and a waffle iron – he'd once told her he was sometimes seized with irrational cravings for waffles.

Watching her make breakfast, he wondered why he was so happy. For years Christmas had filled him with gloom. It had been

222

a day that never passed quickly enough, but this year – a unique sensation – he hoped it would go on and on.

'That's because you're not alone,' she said. 'This year you have a home.'

'But I didn't feel this way when I had a home before,' he said.

'You didn't have a home,' she said. 'You had a house.'

In the afternoon they went for a walk. The snow had stopped, the sun was out, the air was clear and sharp. She carried her Leica. He watched while she stopped and took pictures. He never tired of watching her or of the intensity she transmitted when she worked.

'Funny how the last few months have been filled with so many photographs,' he said. 'Yours. Then the crime-scene shots. Then that old snapshot of your father with Al and Hart.'

'And Lane's shots of me, too. Don't forget them.'

'And the pictures he sent Jesse – the ones you told me must exist.' He looked at her. 'So where is he? Sal says he'd head for home.'

'Sal's right.'

'Not the cabin. Howell's down there, anyway.'

'Maybe there's another home.'

'Where?'

She shrugged. 'Everyone's got a place.'

They walked. A boy rode toward them on his new Christmas bicycle. An old man stood on the corner tossing seeds at a flock of pigeons. Another home . . . So many photographs . . . Janek looked up. A plane cut across the sky, leaving a trail of vapor. He stopped. He looked at her. 'The parlor,' he said.

'What?' She stopped too, to search his eyes.

'The place where he put his mother's furniture.' He could feel his voice rising. 'The chairs with doilies on the arms. The side tables holding the family photographs. The place in the movie. The place he took the girl.' He paused, still looking at her. 'The room.'

He knew all about secret rooms, had been in them before. We all have them, he often said – secret hiding places like Mandy's stash, chambers in the mind, and, sometimes, actual rooms. They are the places where we store our demons and our fears, the props of our childhoods, the memories that control our lives. Aaron had long recognized Janek's fondness for uncovering secret rooms. He called it, 'Frank's speciality.' 'He loves the process,' Aaron said.

It was the day after Christmas. The squad room. Eight am. Janek had called Aaron and Sal at home the night before: 'That's where he's holed up. So now we got to find the place.'

He had ordered Sal to cover for Stanger while Stanger located Nelly Delgado and brought her in. She was sitting with them now swearing she could never find it, sniffing on account of a cold, angry at being hauled out of bed. Janek tried to soothe her. Certainly she could remember if she tried. The two other detectives were busy, Sal on one phone trying to locate the prop man who'd worked on *Mezzaluna*, Aaron on the other talking to Peter's aunt in Cleveland, begging her to remember where she'd shipped the furniture when Peter had asked for it when he'd first moved to New York.

'Guy takes you from Times Square to Brooklyn in a cab,' Janek said, 'he's got to take a tunnel or a bridge.' Nelly nodded. 'There's three bridges. Williamsburg, Manhattan, Brooklyn.' He looked at her. 'Or did he take the tunnel?'

'No. It was a bridge.'

'There, you see – it's not so hard.'

'But I don't know which.'

'Of course you don't. That's why Sal's going to show you all of them. Sooner or later it'll start coming back. Would you be willing to be hypnotized? We have a police hypnotist.'

Nelly glared.

By ten o'clock Sal had found and spoken with the prop man, the set decorator and the production manager. They couldn't remember much except that the scene between Targov and the whore had been shot on a set Peter had ordered built. So where had they gotten the props? Peter had chosen them, the set decorator said. Where? He didn't know, though the propman vaguely remembered a truck. A union truck driven by theatrical teamsters? No, the picture had been made nonunion; Peter had employed film students. They'd used a rented van. When the set was struck they'd hauled the stuff away.

'Back to where he kept it,' Aaron said.

'Unless he gave up the place and put the furniture in storage.'

Janek didn't think he had. 'It was his refuge. He needed that room. You don't give a refuge up.'

'Refuge against what?' Sal asked.

'Anger. Madness.' Janek paused. 'That's always the curious thing. The place where the fury was forged becomes the place where the fury is relieved. If Peter went to such pains to recreate his mother's parlor he's still got the place and that's where he is.'

Sal was assigned to drive Nelly to Brooklyn. They would try to locate the neighborhood, then explore it block by block. She remembered that the building wasn't on a corner, that it didn't have an elevator and that it was six stories high. So maybe, Janek admitted, there're five thousand such buildings in Brooklyn. So we do the legwork, he said.

Aaron booked a flight to Cleveland. Liz Lane hadn't kept her copy of the mover's bill of lading and had no record of Peter's old address. She didn't even remember the shipper's name. She'd found it in the Yellow Pages, had chosen it from an ad.

Janek drove him to the airport. He enouraged him while they waited for the plane. 'Get her to remember the year and then the season and then get the phone company to find you a phone book from that year. Go through it with her. She might remember whether the ad was on the right or left. Worse come to worse, call the interstate shippers. Make a list and work your way through.'

When he returned to the precinct he phoned the city rent commision. Was there a way to locate a tenancy if all you had was the tenant's name? He got the answer quickly enough: 'Sorry, Lieutenant – no.'

After four days Sal asked to be relieved. He was sniffling; he'd caught Nelly's cold. 'She's a good kid, but it's hopeless, Frank. Miles and miles of tenements. Everything starts to look the same.'

Liz Lane spent three days pondering an old edition of the Cleveland Yellow Pages before she phoned Aaron at his motel in the middle of the night. She said she thought the shipper's name was 'from the Bible or maybe from a myth.' Aaron drove over to her house. For the tenth time they went through the phone book together. She narrowed it down to the Atlas, Hercules and Samson moving companies. The next morning Aaron contacted all three and cajoled them into searching their dead files. It took two more days before Atlas found the papers and could give him the address and consignee. Aaron phoned it in from Cleveland, Janek and Sal rushed over to the place. There was nothing there but a vacant lot.

Ten years before, the building had been demolished.

Aaron flew back to New York.

At two o'clock in the afternoon on December thirty-first Janek interviewed Nelly Delgado again. He took her through her story step by step – the drive to the tenement, the walk up the stairs, the layout of the apartment, the scene. He was looking for something, anything, a detail she didn't realize was important, a small thing that had slipped her mind that could help him find the place. Her impressions were less than vivid. Had she seen a telephone? No. Had she used the bathroom? No. Did the windows face the front of the building? She didn't know. Why not? The curtains had been drawn and also there'd been shades.

From her description Janek drew a floor plan, then located the positions of the couch, the chairs, the side tables, the buffet.

'What happened when you reached the door?'

'I waited while he took out his keys.'

'Then he unlocked it?'

'Yes.'

'Then what happened?'

'We went in.'

'You first?'

'No. Him.'

'Then?'

'He turned on the lights.'

If Peter had lights he had electricity. If he had electricity he had an account with Con Edison. Perhaps the account was under an assumed name, but Nelly remembered there'd been no name beside the buzzer. What about the mailbox? She didn't remember the mailbox. But the electric company had to send bills somewhere. Janek picked up the phone.

By five o'clock they were running computer checks. Janek fed the Con Ed girls names. Peter Lane: the only account was the one on Eightieth Street. Peter Dill: there were two; Sal and Aaron left to check them out. Janek tried all sorts of variations on Lane and Dill, and then when he'd exhausted those he started with the names of the killer characters in the films. At 8 pm he was sure he had it: Targov, Ivan; 12309 Oakland Avenue, Brooklyn, in Greenpoint near McCarren Park.

He drove there alone. An ordinary street. An ordinary working-class neighborhood. A polish delicatessen on the corner, then a dry cleaner's, a shoemaker's shop, an oculist. Hanukkah candles visible in many apartment windows. A Christmas tree blinking in a bakery.

He entered the building. No name beside the buzzer for the top-floor-rear apartment. He rang for the super. The inner door clicked open, a white-haired woman with glasses stepped into the hall.

'Yeah?'

Janek showed his shield. She frowned, motioned him in. There was the smell of garlic on her breath. No, she didn't know 6B. No, she didn't have an extra key.

Janek climbed the stairs, resting at each landing. The odor of roach poison, apparent in the lobby, was nearly overpowering by the time he reached the top.

He pulled out his revolver, cocked it, held it ready. He knocked. No answer. He pressed himself back against the wall, turned the knob and pushed.

The door swung open slowly. At first he thought the room was empty. But when he moved to the doorway and stared into the gloom he met a pair of hard gray eyes.

A Long Night's Confession

He had been inside Amanda's apartment nine times before he killed her. Nine times! Could Janek believe that? *Nine! Nine!*

Think of the risk. Incredible! An absolutely impossible feat. But those expeditions had been necessary, first to case the place, plan, rehearse. But even more important (and he doubted Janek had considered this) on account of the single great imponderable: the dog.

That awful dog, that snarling Petunia – she'd been his biggest worry. Because if he was waiting for Mandy, waiting for her behind the curtain in the shower, the dog might sense his presence, warn her off, and that could blow everything, cause her to scream, force him to rush out into the living room and attack her there. Then there would be a struggle. He would have to kill her without the advantage of surprise. And that could lead to variables. He might be forced to improvise. And unless he carried out his script exactly as he had written it he could put himself in jeopardy. Worse, he could risk the perfect symmetry of his design.

Anyway...

Later, when it was over, Janek would recall how easily it had come, entering the dimly lit room, seeing him curled up on the shabby vintage-World War II sofa. 'Hello, Peter,' he had said gently, putting away his thirty-eight. Then he had sat down very quietly in a chair with lace doilies on the arms.

It took no prompting on his part to encourage Peter to begin, and, once he did, Janek felt no need to urge him on. They sat in silence for a while in that strange and gloomy room, lit only by an old-fashioned lamp whose shade bore a ragged lacy fringe. And then Peter started talking and Janek listened, nodding, as the story tumbled out. Peter seemed smaller now, boyish, without his former menace, and all the while the framed photos of Laurie and Jesse Dill sat perched on the side tables like silent sentinels to the extraordinary discharge of their son.

Peter, Janek knew, was not confessing particularly to him, but to Jesse, perhaps, or to some fantasy father by whom he wished to be absolved. In the end, Janek felt, it didn't matter: he was there, a detective-confessor, an empty vessel waiting to be filled. As soon as Peter made his proud boast that he had been in Amanda's apartment *'nine times!'* the crime was as good as solved and the only understanding issues were the details Janek hadn't figured out.

The rage he had figured out long before.

And so he listened, glancing from time to time at Peter slumped on the couch, eyes half closed, blank, vacant, speaking in a soft but passionate whisper, directing his words not particularly to him but more generally to the room.

As if, Janek thought, Peter was describing a story he'd made up for a film.

The tale was told that coldly, he thought.

The dog was unpredictable, hated strangers, snarled at everyone, so he had to figure out a way to neutralize her, and the way he

228

thought of was to make her familiar with his scent. If he left his scent in the apartment (which is what he'd done by going there so many times) and Mandy came home with Petunia from a walk, and Petunia began to act funny, to rush around squealing and snarling looking for the stranger she could smell, then, well, obviously, since there would be no one there, Mandy would order the little monster to shut her yap, and the next time it happened she would recognize the pattern and would disregard the warning which would be the only warning she would ever get.

And still, he knew, it would be dangerous.

Brenda, on the other hand, was a cinch. Vulnerability was the way to court a whore. He had known that for years, had known that all his life. All you have to do with a girl like that was be nice to her to have her eating from your hand.

He hadn't met Brenda before, hadn't thought of bringing in another woman. That idea came later. But he was getting ahead of himself. Back to Mandy. She was the spur, the cause.

He had studied her for months. He'd been at home a lot licking his wounds. His last picture, *Film Noir*, his finest work, he thought, had failed, played two weeks at a crummy theater in the Village, hadn't even made it onto the drive-in circuit, and after that debacle all his sources of financing had dried up.

So he was home a lot, and he noticed her, and then he started to watch her carefully. Her window, lit up at night, became a screen upon which he could fantasize a tale.

Studying, fantasizing, he discovered the way into her apartment – that ladder down from the roof, that apparently unlatched window grill. One night when she went out to a movie – he knew because he'd been following her – he got into her building, went up onto the roof, climbed down the ladder, looked through her window and tested the grill to make sure it wasn't locked.

He didn't go in on that occasion, so that was not one of the nine. So maybe you could say he'd been there nine and a half times before the final night, because you'd have to count that first expedition since it broke the barrier between fantasy and fact.

He spent hours drawing story-board sketches of how she might be killed. And the more work he put into them the more exciting the idea became. And then he started following her and then he was caught up. And the more caught up he was the more definitely she was doomed, for once an idea took hold in him he felt compelled to carry it out.

For weeks he followed her, watching, studying, learning the currents of her life. He knew when she woke up, walked her dog, the time and place where she waited for her bus, her route to the school where she taught, the supermarket where she shopped.

She'd come home from work and change, right there, in the living room, without even bothering to close the blinds. Like she didn't care. Like she was flaunting herself. Like she was saying, 'Hey, look at me, feast your eyes and eat your heart out, jerk. Because I'm a perfect little princess and you'll never touch me. *Never never never.*'

The cunt!

He followed her up and down the aisles of the supermarket, watching her pluck items from the shelves. And thus he came to know her favorite brands of scouring pads and laundry soap (biodegradable, that kind of crap). He learned how often she replendished her pantyhose, her impulsive purchases of raisins and nuts, that she liked skim milk, unsalted butter, pink grapefruit and the goody-goody stuff like yogurt and wheat germ and whole-grain bread.

Her life was measured, her habits were predictable – even her variations held no surprise. A visit to the dentist. A splurge at a bookstore. Dinner by herself at the Chink joint on Third near Seventy-ninth. An occasional evening out alone, at a concert or a film. (She had no taste in cinema; like the arty foreign stuff, those *sensitive* French pictures in which the girl shows so much sweet agony you feel like strangling the little bitch!)

A stop at the library, the bank, the wine store. Lunch with a colleague, that fag art teacher she aways dragged around. Clothes to the cleaners. Then off to her exercise class, as if getting into shape meant anything since nobody would ever get to touch the precious tuned-up flesh.

She did not go out with men. He wondered why. She was decent enough looking, slim, a little drab perhaps, but her features were nice, occasionally even beautiful, when she wasn't looking sappy at some children or walking around smiling smugly to herself. He supposed it was her aura, the image she projected that she was content, that she wasn't sensual or open or worth another person's time. She held her elbows close, avoided eye contact, parted her hair in the middle and let it hang. Still, he saw, people liked her: she acted meek, pretended sweetness, and it was enraging the way she got away with that, since she was so clearly hostile, especially to males.

The monotony of her life became a drama. How long, he wondered, could it go on? He could not imagine how she could endure such a tiresome routine: get up, make coffee, read the paper, walk the dog, go to work, come home, walk the dog again, stop at the store, cook dinner, grade papers, walk the dog a final time, return, bathe, listen to the radio, stretch-exercise, turn off the lights, resign herself to emptiness, fall into dreamless sleep.

That was the suspense: would she break out of it, do something, finally, to shatter the design? He felt that she might, that she was a bomb waiting to go off. And so he waited. And nothing happened. And that made him angry, too.

He could predict when her periods was coming. She would grimly buy a small bottle of aspirin and an econo-pak of sanitary pads. She'd grimace waiting for her bus, speak with irritation to her building super, yank back on her dog, greedily munch sunflower seeds on her walks. You'd think those damn periods would do something for her, make her conscious she had a twat. At least cause her to own up to having one instead of pretending she was this porcelain doll. Then, maybe, he wouldn't have hated her so much for being such a little hypocrite. But she didn't own up to anything; the longer he studied her the greater his hatred grew.

Because she was a fake. Mean. Nasty. Not generous and sweet the way people thought. She was a fuckless bitch and she was asking for it. For something. Begging for it, he thought sometimes.

So maybe that was just the way he looked at it. Maybe other people would have drawn different conclusions. So what? He was burning up with hatred. He had this itch to *despoil* her. Cut her down.

If, he decided, he could not finance a new movie to siphon off his rage, then he would kill her and that would be better than any movie – more difficult, complex, brilliantly planned and executed, unsolvable and ultimately more satisfying; by comparison his stabbing of his mother would seem like child's play.

(Oh, yeah, he'd taken care of her. And that Neanderthal she was sleeping with. Assumed Janek had dug that up. No point in bringing Old Jesse round if Janek hadn't figured out the connection first.

Their eyes met twice. She was on her way to work, on her bus, and he was on it, too, across the aisle. The driver stopped suddenly and some of the standing passengers were thrown. She glanced up, saw him staring at her, creased her brows as if struggling to remember him and, failing, turned back quickly to her book.

The second time was when he tracked her to a movie, a revival of *Les Enfants du Paradis* at an upper Broadway theater that from time to time had played his own old films. The movie was long and she had gone to the last performance. It was raining hard when she came out. She paused a moment, made a decision, ran into the street and flagged down a passing cab. He watched her slide into it, lean forward, speak to the driver, then suddenly turn and stare panic-stricken out the back. As the taxi pulled away he had no doubt she saw him, a receding figure staring after her, standing alone in a belted raincoat beneath a dimly lit marquee.

It was around that time that he got the idea of turning her into a whore. He began to plan in earnest and came up with the notion of the switch.

He started going to whores, looking for one who resembled her. ('Yes, you were right. I was impressed – I didn't think you'd get that far so fast. They were look-alikes, but not in an obvious way; only in a way that suited my purposes.') And checking out the whores was fun because they didn't pretend to be anything but what they were. Which was trash, of course, but at least they knew it. Not like Mandy. She didn't know what she was.

Anyway, Brenda turned out to be very important because it was the switch that made his crime a work of art. It seemed impossible in practice, if so beautiful in concept, and yet he felt he could do it, that he had the brains, experience and temperament to bring it off. So the plan became a puzzle that filled his days, a game he would play out with flesh and blood. And in the end it was the blood that almost got to him – he nearly swooned when he cut off Amanda's head.

The blood.

He had always loved blood, from way back, early in his

childhood, when he'd watched his Uncle Harold operate. Something about it was beautiful, the color, sure, but also the way it moved. Spurted sometimes, or flowed slowly, spreading out into puddles, rich and thick.

When he made movies he always fussed around with the blood. He was famous for that, the way he insisted on applying it to his actresses. The make-up people could do the faces, but he always did the blood. It had to be just so, the way he remembered it from those primitive operations, and from the way it flowed out of the whore back in the trailer years before.

But it wasn't as if he were some kind of vampire. Janek should not misunderstand. He didn't actually like the stuff. What he liked was the way it *looked*.

So when he planned the crime (and he did consider it a single crime; sure, there were two parts to it, but each one by itself was meaningless – it was only the combination of the two that made the sense) he thought a lot about how he wanted the blood to look and how he didn't want any of it to get on his skin and clothes. So he used the shower curtain to protect himself with Mandy, and the rubber sheet with Brenda, which he'd told her was just 'his little kinky thing.' (She'd fallen for that easily; nothing surprises a whore; they know all about fetishes; from the start he'd palmed himself off to her as a 'mild rubber freak.') And he had worn plastic clothes and gloves even though it was hot. And used plastic bags to carry the heads, and still he'd nearly swooned.

So, anyway . . .

Peter stopped talking after a while; Janek guessed he was exhausted. It was three in the morning. Sometime during the tale the new year started. There was a sputtering of fire-crackers. Then the thunder of many fireworks at once, then an occasional squealing of tires out on the street, a burst of drunken singing, a siren wailing on a distant avenue. Laurie's reconstructed parlor was growing cold.

'What did you use?'

'Huh?'

'To cut off the heads?'

'Oh.' Peter pulled himself out of his reverie. 'Couple of old Jap swords I had around.'

233

'Where did you get them?'

'Antique store in San Francisco. That was back five years ago.'

'And the knives?'

'What?'

'You killed them first, before –'

'Yeah. Kitchen knives. Standard stuff. Paid cash at a cutlery shop. They won't remember, of course.'

Of course. 'The vehicle?'

'God sakes, Janek. "Vehicle"! Next thing you'll be calling me "the perpetrator."' He laughed scornfully. 'You mean how did I get around? Motor scooter. Carry-box mounted on the back for the heads. Kept the swords in a guitar case. The changes of clothes and gloves and stuff in a backpack from an Army-Navy Store.'

'So what did you do with all of it?'

'Deep-sixed it, naturally.'

Naturally. 'The scooter too?'

He shook his head. 'Abandoned the scooter. Figured someone could use a decent set of wheels.' He paused. 'You need all this for the file, right?' Again that withering scorn. But then, in a new voice done with scorn, filled with resignation, 'What difference does it make? Sure. I'll tell you. I'll even show you. How's that? I'll even take you there.'

Walking across the icy deserted street toward Janek's Volvo:

'How did you get into my girl's loft?'

Peter smiled. His breath was steam. 'Wondering when you were going to ask me that.'

'Well?'

'Fire escape.'

'In daylight. Lucky you weren't caught.'

'I went in at night.'

Janek turned; they'd reached his car. His hands trembled as he unlocked the door.

'. . . Yeah. Went in there when you were sleeping. Could have killed both of you in the bed. Spent half the night in her darkroom crouching on the sill. Heard you fooling around in the morning. That's a pretty high-strung girl you got there, Janek. Thought I could spook her pretty good.' He laughed then, his voice filled again with resignation and despair: 'Wanted to make you crazy. That's all.'

Driving to Manhattan across the Williamsburg Bridge, the river black beneath them, black like roiling oil:

'What do you care about this crap? You solved it psychologically. So tell me, how did you find the old Greenpoint hideaway? How'd you even know I had the place?'

When Janek told him about Nelly Delgado, Peter blinked – he couldn't remember who she was. Then, when he did remember, he shook his head. 'Been years. Completely forgot. But she didn't. Should have thought of that.'

Janek glanced at him. The inference was clear: If Peter had thought of it he would have done something about it. Found her and killed her – that was what he meant.

Janek drove to the crime scenes. He wanted to know every detail: the way the wind had felt on his face as he'd raced through the park that sultry night, whether he'd grasped up the heads by their hair, the sound he'd made when he'd brought down the sword, whether he'd stared into or avoided the girls' lifeless eyes ... He wanted to know these things in the belief that if he did he would finally understand. But the details didn't help. He didn't understand. All he could feel was the coldness and the rage.

Driving downtown on Ninth Avenue, the same route Peter had taken after he'd completed the switch:

'Those pictures you sent Jesse ...'

'Stills from my films. Except, of course, for the final set. Thought he'd like them. Thought they'd make a good reminder. *In case he let himself forget.*'

'You were trying to torture the old guy.'

'Wanted him to know I was still around.'

'So you tracked him down where he lived?'

'You did, too.'

'Took my best detective three weeks.'

'Big deal. Every time the fucker moved it took me three months.'

'So' – Janek turned to him – 'you wanted him to remember. Was that what it was all about?'

Peter glanced at him, then stared out, then he shook his head.

On West Street, crossing Fourteenth, New Jersey across the river lost in whorls of blackening mist:

'What was it then?'

'Much more than murder. I don't expect you to understand.'

'Try me.'

Peter smiled. 'Okay, Janek. Call it art.'

'I don't buy that. You were a film director. You made movies. You had an outlet. That should have been enough.'

Peter shrugged. 'Film's imitation.' And then, his voice level, his eyes half-closed, his mouth dead serious: 'Tell you a little secret, Janek. Even the real thing is not enough.'

It was important now to find the knives.

Peter was bored. He waited in Janek's car, stretched out on the back seat, handcuffed, his coat thrown over him like a blanket. Janek rubbed his hands together as he paced the Bank Street Pier. The fog was heavy, wet. Janek stopped from time to time to stare at the water lapping the pilings beneath the rotting planks.

Finally, at dawn, the police boat came. He stood watching the divers while they struggled into their wet suits, checked their canisters and underwater lights. They were happy to come, even so early on New Year's Day. They knew Janek and they knew about his case.

When they were ready, he showed them the place where Peter had said he'd ditched the stuff. Then he took Peter back to the precinct, got the skeleton of his confession onto video-tape, returned with him to the pier, checked on the underwater work, then walked up to Fourteenth Street looking for a diner.

It was nine in the morning on New Year's Day, but he found one open, no customers, the waitress's hair done up in a beehive, the counterman in a grease-stained butcher's apron, a streamer of bunting hanging over the cash register and trailing to the floor.

He ordered a mug of coffee, carried it to the pay phone in back, woke up Aaron and Sal, told them what had happened, then picked up a coffee-to-go to take back to Peter in the car.

Aaron was the first to come. He'd called Stanger; Howell was too far away. Sal arrived a few minutes later. The two detectives wore nearly identical three-quarter-length black leather coats.

The fog was even thicker now and they could hear boat horns calling and answering off the Battery. The police divers worked steadily, bringing up objects covered with muck. The radio crackled on the boat while a mound accumulated: empty liquor bottles, a discarded pail, hunks of glass, bricks, a tire iron, the carcass of a bicycle – all coated with a black ooze that made them shine beneath the harsh quartz lights.

Stanger came and stood with them. He too wanted to be there for the finish. None of them paid any attention to Peter – it was as if the knives were now the most important thing, the evidence more important than the man.

The sun finally broke through, a gray and noxious hazy sun that reminded Janek of the day they'd buried Al except that that day had been hot and this one was very cold. Aaron, nudging him with his elbow, motioned for him to turn around. When he did he saw the patrol cars, a half dozen of them parked at odd angles in the lot behind the pier, lights on, silhouettes of cops visible through the windshields, waiting, watching, silent in the mists that rose from the pavements all around.

'What's going on?'

'Guess our show's on the air,' Aaron said.

'Who knew?'

'Jesus, Frank *everybody* knew.'

He shook his head. The case had never been in the papers, not the part, at least, about the switch. But in the department it had become a famous case, and now, on this New Year's morning, word had gone out on the police radio band that it was nearly done.

At eleven o'clock the divers brought up the first of the two Japanese swords. By noon the dredging was complete. They had both swords, both knives, a rotted-out guitar case, a water-stiffened backpack, plus assorted plastic garments, bags and gloves and two sets of apartment keys. From an investigative standpoint the case was finished. All that remained was to take Peter downtown, book him and turn him over for prosecution.

When Janek left the pier more than fifty patrol cars, including some from precincts in other boroughs, had assembled at the foot of Bank Street. He walked among them recognizing faces, greeting officers he knew, accepting their homage to him and to his special squad for having solved the unsolvable Switched Heads.

Aggression

They watched the 11 pm news wrapped naked in each other's arms.

Manhattan District Attorney Francis Semple announced the indictment of Peter Lane and also, for the first time, publicly linked the killings of Amanda Ireland and Brenda Beard. Semple sat at a table in front of a battery of microphones beside Chief of Detectives Dale Hart. Janek stood in the background along with his squad waiting to be introduced.

'... revealing certain gruesome details concerning the Ireland/ Beard double homicide,' said the pert and breathless female reporter, 'which, according to Chief Hart, were kept confidential until the investigation was complete. It was revealed this afternoon by sources close to the Chief's office that for months this case has been known informally as "Switched Heads." Chief Hart gave no special praise to individual detectives but chose to emphasize the awesome responsibilities of his division. A division which builds hundreds of important cases a year, he said, out of old-fashioned legwork performed day in, day out, by thousands of dedicated men...'

Janek slipped out of bed to switch the TV off. Then, standing naked before the set, he turned and faced Caroline.

'God, didn't you just want to slug him?'

'Told him I wanted a transfer to Internal Affairs.'

'Hope that jolted him some.'

'Some. But not enough.'

He walked into the living area, went to the table where she kept her liquor, poured out two glasses of Scotch, handed one to her, then sat down on a hassock.

'You're a great detective, Frank. Everyone says you are. Aaron told me no one else could have gotten Lane.'

He sipped his Scotch. 'We could get Hart too, you know. The two of us. I couldn't do it alone.'

She slipped into her robe, picked up his, placed it over his shoulders, then knelt before him and tied the belt. Then she leaned against his knees. For a while they drank in silence. 'Okay,' she said finally. She looked up at him. 'Let's, the two of us, nail the prick.'

'When Carmichael told me about the car being filled with junk what struck me was how Al had gotten so excited hearing that. Soon as Lou told me Al was after Hart I put the two things together. Hart obviously didn't kill your father himself. He ordered it done, which meant a chain of command. It all snapped together. Hart tells his henchman, Sweeney, to get rid of Tommy Wallace. Sweeney, in turn, passes the word to a couple of the goons who work at his garage.'

'How did you know about the garage?'

'Sweeney's been bugging me to bring in my car ever since he drove it back from the burial. For years I've heard about the fat discounts he gives to cops and all the little courtesies he extends. I've also heard about shoddy parts – getting your car back, then later finding something wrong. I put Sal on it, and when he found the back shop and I could see them stripping cars it was pretty obvious how the thing had worked. Sweeney told his goons to make it look like a New Jersey gangland slaying. But they got sloppy – out of greed or incompetence or both. You know: "Why waste a stolen car? Let's get double use out of it. Strip it first, the stereo, the tires and all the easy stuff. Then slap on some crud and use it to stow the corpse." Al must have known he'd hit pay dirt when he heard about that car. But then he blew his case. He had no real proof, but he went ahead anyway and threatened Hart. Big mistake. He should have concentrated on Sweeney instead.'

'Why Sweeney?'

'Because Sweeney's the weak spot, the link between the executioners and Hart. He's the insulation, and the insulation's always weak. He had no stake in your father being killed and he doesn't go around shooting people in the head. The way he sees it he was just the broker, and he's not going to want to burn alone for that. Still he's a strong-arm guy and that's important to know because you can break a strong-arm guy if you handle him right – show him superior force.'

'So what are we going to do?'

'Make him squawk.'

'How?'

'Leverage. I send him to prison for the garage unless he gives me Hart.'

'Is that really going to do it?'

'First you're going to have to scare him.'

'Me?'

'You' – he leaned over and kissed the top of her head – 'with your crazy-daughter-of-the-man-he-killed routine. Now, don't worry, I know you can do it. It'll go something like this: If Sweeney doesn't tell me what I want to know I threaten to cut you loose. He'll believe in your fury if you show him furious eyes. If you do it right you'll scare him and he'll break.'

'Well,' she said, 'sounds like we're back to aggression.'

'Yeah,' he said. 'But this time it's yours.'

The first hard part would be to lure Sweeney out. Janek decided to use his car.

It was a late 1960s Volvo, the classic Model 122, battered and only shiny when it rained. But it ran well, never failed to start, and it could use a tune-up, he thought.

He drove it over to the Bronx and into the garage, then stood beside it, stupid, while Sweeney's chief mechanic checked it out.

'Needs all new shocks. The pinion on the differential leaks. Needs a new slave cylinder. Tune-up and ring job like you say. And there's an oil leak. New oil-pan gasket. Run you eight or nine hundred, but when we're finished it'll be perfect.' The man glanced at the body. 'Mechanically speaking, at least. I notice some rust on those fenders round the lights.'

'Let's just stick to the insides,' Janek said. He showed his discount card.

She spent two weekends working with Jamie Sullivan in the garage behind Jamie's house in Bayside, Queens. Janek watched her. She and Jamie got on well. He showed her how to handle explosive, mold it around caps, how to strip and curl wire, connect caps to wire and wire to batteries and then bring all the wires to the terminals of the switch.

'You got to do it like you've been doing it for years,' Jamie told her. 'It's the way you handle the plastic. There's a touch. You can always tell a good demo man by the lightness and sureness of his hands. You train yourself by playing with clay. Your fingers get good. You always flutter them first before you begin. And in weather like this you always wear gloves. The way an old safecracker does, to keep his fingers warm and loose.'

They left her to practice, went to the kitchen, opened beers, sat down and drank.

'She'll make it if she doesn't panic,' Jamie said, 'and she won't panic if she concentrates.' He was an ex-cop, a Vietnam vet who'd been a member of the Bomb Squad for five years. In that time he saw four men he loved get blown to bits. He quit finally because he began to shake; he'd be shaking in the morning before he left for work. He got a full disability discharge and grew a beard. It was half a foot long now, black and curly tinged with gray.

'She says she plays tennis. Is she any good?'

'Excellent player,' Janek said.

'She and I should play this week. It'll help her concentration.' Jamie paused. 'She might even pay more attention to me if I win.'

He told her, 'At first he'll think I'm pissed about the car, he'll know there's got to be more, but he won't put it all together till the end. I won't talk much and you won't talk at all. You'll do everything with your eyes. Don't grimace or make faces. Just feel your anger and it'll show. Don't try to act and don't forget: this guy got your father killed. You want him to die hard. I'm the only one who can control you. When I tell you to do something you nod and do it right away. That way he knows I can stop you. You're my creature until I cut loose and then you're an icy maniac. Try and be like Lane. Cold like that. Full of ice-cold fury. Let him catch a glimpse of the beast, but only just a glimpse. Remember: the two most effective tools we got are silence and the way you handle yourself. The more silence the better – that way he makes all the noise. If you make a mistake just go on like it didn't happen. It's important that you keep your movements clean and sure. A lot depends on the determined way you go about the thing, like you've thought it all through and there's no way once you start you're not going to take it to the end. That's what'll make him know we're dangerous. I'm a guy who doesn't give a shit and you're a woman who's willing to go all the way.'

He was delighted with his car; it purred better than it had in years. It performed exceptionally well as Caroline drove it out to Douglaston then past Sweeney's house, an expensive split-level on three-eighths of an acre with a two-car garage facing the street and an Audi 5000 parked in the drive. Janek told her to turn the corner and come around again. It was an exceptionally warm February evening, a kind of false spring evening, he thought.

He knew that Sweeney's wife was in Florida for the week and his kids were away at college. If they were going to do it they would have to do it now. He knew she was ready and feared if they waited she would lose her edge.

She turned into the drive, blocked the Audi the way he told her. He liked the way her hands were steady on the wheel. He got out fast and moved quickly to the front of the house. By the time Sweeney opened the door he could feel adrenaline pumping through his heart.

'Janek? What the hell –?' As predicted, Sweeney was surprised.

'Took my car into your so-called garage.'

Sweeney squinted at him. 'I rate a house call 'cause of that?'

'Going to ask me in?'

'You look pretty upset.'

They stared at each other. 'Fuckin' right I'm upset. Rotten parts. Car's been filled with crap. Came to tell you that and that tomorrow I'm reporting you for fraud.'

'What you talking about?' Sweeney's face turned red.

'Come out and take a look.'

'Calm down, Janek. I'll see you're satisfied. And no charge, either. The whole job free. How's that?'

Janek ignored the offer. 'You want to look?'

Sweeney paused, trying to decide just how angry Janek was and how dangerous he could become if he didn't look at the rotten parts and sympathize. 'Okay,' he said, 'let me get my jacket.'

'Never mind the jacket, Sweeney. Come out and see the damage.'

Sweeney shrugged and stepped onto the stoop. He glanced at the car and spotted Caroline. The sight of her seemed to relax him. A girl in the car meant Janek wasn't totally crazy, though it was strange he'd come all the way out to the suburbs to bitch to him at night.

'Look, Janek, if there was a mixup on parts don't worry – that's no big deal. You know me. I'm not going to let my brother-in-law crew a cop. Too much to lose. You guys are my bread and butter.'

They were beside the car now. 'Hands behind your back.'

'*What?*'

Janek pressed the barrel of his Colt into Sweeney's side, then jammed it hard into his kidney. 'Your hands. Fast. Before I blow you away. Move it, fuck-face. *Now.*'

Sweeney muttered something that sounded like 'Shit!' and Janek jabbed him again. This time Sweeney put his hands behind his back. Janek snapped cuffs tight around his wrists.

'What the – ?'

'*Shut up.*' Janek pulled open the back door and shoved Sweeney into the car face-first. Then he came in on top of him, grabbed hold of his hair, jerked his hand back, then smashed his face down as hard as he could into the seat. 'Listen, scum-bag. I only say this once. Try something and you're gone.' He gave Sweeney's head another brutal shove. Sweeney blubbered against the vinyl while Janek patted him down.

No gun, no knife, nothing. He pulled off Sweeney's shoes and threw them into the front. Then he tied his ankles together with rope, forced his legs back, connected the handcuffs to the ankles so that Sweeney was hog-tied face-down on the seat. Then he got out, came round to the front and got in beside Caroline. 'Go,' he told her. She nodded crisply and backed out of Sweeney's driveway fast.

He figured it would take a minute or so for Sweeney to comprehend his predicament. He'd been forcibly kidnapped by a fellow police officer from in front of his house at night. He was bound up now, very uncomfortably, in the back of that officer's car. A girl he didn't know was driving. They seemed to be heading somewhere. There'd been a crazy look in Janek's eyes, but he'd acted like he was carrying out a plan. Janek could lose everything for this; if Sweeney filed a complaint Janek would go to jail. Unless this whole thing was official somehow, which seemed highly improbable. Or unless Janek had planned it so he, Sweeney, wouldn't be around at the end to file a complaint.

'Janek –'

'Okay, here it is. Got an airtight case. You're running a chop operation behind your garage. Been watching the place for weeks.

243

You're going to Attica. You'll do hard time. Five years, probabl) ten. For a big-shot police sergeant, that's going to be rough. I'm *glad*, Sweeney, because I always thought you were a piece of shit

That, Janek figured, ought to hold him for two to three minute long enough for them to get out of the suburb and onto the Lon Island Expressway. From now on silence would be their weapon Sweeney had to talk himself into a state of panic.

'Janek –?'

Janek didn't answer.

'Look, Janek – this is no kind of good arrest.'

Silence.

'You can't make anything stick you take me in like this. This i fuckin' kidnapping, Janek. You'll do big time for this.'

Janek laughed.

'Think it's funny, huh? You're stupid, really dumb. Who's thi bimbo driving? She some kind of police officer, too.' A pause. 'Yo) got to be crazy. All this on account of some parts. Tell you th) truth, this jalopy's sounding pretty good . . .'

He went on like that, calling names, complaining about hi discomfort, appealing to reason, making threats. It was when he') try to bargain that Janek would hit him again, so he glanced a) Caroline, shrugged, and she drove on.

The Long Island Expressway to the Suffolk County line, then) U-turn and back again. Then the Brooklyn – Queens to th) Verrazano Bridge. Then around Staten Island for a while:

'Where we going, Janek? Christ, my legs are cramping up. The fuck you taking me?

'Jesus, Janek – what do you want? Tell me. *The fuck you want?*

'Janek – you can't do this. You'll be up shit creek for sure.

'Janek – let's settle this thing. The car? Christ, I'll give you) Mercedes if you want.

'Janek – you want to kill me count of some stupid parts? You're fucking *crazy*. You're a cock-sucker, Janek. Wait till Hart – he'll ream your ass for this.'

Janek turned and looked down at his prisoner. There was a line of sweat on the back of his neck. Janek stuck the point of his Colt into the crease at the base of his skull. 'What about Hart?' he asked.

He was surprised at the harshness of his voice; his whisper, he thought, grated like a saw. Sweeney didn't answer right away; he was calculating, Janek knew, trying to figure out what Janek wanted. It had something to do with Hart; now that message had been delivered. Janek worked the gun barrel in, slowly, methodically, twisting it in the sweaty crease of flesh.

'Calves starting to hurt bad.'

'Sure they are.'

'What do you want?'

'Tell me about the garage.'

'What about it?'

'The chop-shop operation – Hart's the banker, isn't he? What's the split? Who else's involved? Who you paying off?'

Silence.

'Okay, have it your way. It's all the same to me.' He liked the way he said that; there was the proper degree of resignation in his tone. 'Meadowlands,' he said to Caroline. She juiced the accelerator. The car leaped ahead.

Frighten him by their relentless silent fury – that was the plan. When Sweeney started sputtering again, Janek took a long strip of sheeting, yanked up Sweeney's head, then wrapped the cloth around his lower face till he was gagged. 'Now we don't have to listen to the creep,' he said.

Caroline said, 'Good, I like it better that way.'

He would be thinking, *Why the Meadowlands? The Meadowlands is where you dump guys you put away. Janek's going to do me. The girl's in on it, too. It's got to be more than the garage? But what? They're bluffing. Got to be.*

He would figure he could call their bluff but would think, too, that, worse came to worse, he'd spill on the garage because the way Janek coerced him no one could ever make that stick. But Janek would know that, too, so there was something deeper going on. He'd worry about that, worry about it a lot. He'd tell himself he was going to get out of this but it would cost him and when the time came he'd have to think fast about how to limit the damage.

He would decide that until he knew what Janek wanted there was no way to know how to deal. So the next move was up to Janek. For now all he had to do was keep calm and wait.

They passed Newark Airport, crossed into Hudson County, took a turnoff that followed Sawmill Creek. The Meadowlands: a huge rubble-filled swamp between the Hudson and Hackensack

Rivers, a place of oily desolation, a place where you got rid of stuff you didn't want, where you shot people, then dumped them, left them to bloat and rot.

They reached the spot Janek had picked, a flat between mounds of smoking debris. The light was strange; there was something in the scrub that luminesced in the night.

'Get your stuff,' Janek said.

She cut the engine, got out, slammed the door. He liked the way she moved, as if she had a job to do. The car shook when she slammed the trunk door down.

'Got it?'

'Everything.'

'Okay, let's get this over with.'

All the dialogue and sound effects were for Sweeney's benefit. Now the back of the sergeant's shirt was soaked. He knew the crunch was coming, the moment of truth. His mind would be working now at triple speed, and Sweeney, Janek knew, wasn't dumb.

'Want to talk about it?' Janek asked. The same diamond-hard whisper he'd used before. Sweeney struggled to nod. 'Then talk,' Janek said. Then: 'Oh yeah, the gag.'

He got out, went around to the left back door, opened it, grabbed hold of Sweeney around the knees and pulled him roughly off the seat and halfway out. When his face was resting on the edge of the car floor he eased him onto the ground, because he didn't want to injure his head.

He nodded to Caroline. She was sitting, door open, in the driver's seat, busy stripping wires. Janek set Sweeney so he could see her, then reached around and untied the gag. He unwrapped it slowly. When it was off Sweeney was panting hard.

'You got about six minutes,' Janek said. 'You can start talking now.'

'I don't –'

'Listen, Sweeney. This is it. We're through fucking around.'

'Put him on his back,' Caroline said. She said it perfectly, like she didn't care if he talked or not. Her eyes were perfect, too – cold hard points gleaming in the night.

Janek rolled Sweeney over so he was lying parallel to the car, then squatted down beside him. If Sweeney wanted to look at

Caroline he had to turn the other way. The idea was to make him twist back and forth as he struggled to watch them both.

'So, tell me.'

'Won't stand up.'

'Who gives a shit about that?'

'Who's she?' he gestured toward Caroline.

'She's a person who wants to blow you up.'

Sweeney stared at her. 'Seen her before. Where?'

'My rabbi's burial,' Janek said.

Sweeney shook his head. He couldn't figure them out. 'You're bluffing. This is some kind of bullshit stunt.'

'Suit yourself.' Janek nodded to Caroline. Sweeney twisted his head to look at her.

'Okay, what do you want?'

'What's Hart's connection to the garage?'

'No connection. My baby all the way.'

'Fine. Then you can burn alone. She's going to blow you up little piece by little piece.'

Sweeney twisted around to look at her again. She was molding the explosive now.

'Little charges,' Janek said. 'Maybe your thumbs first. Then a couple fingers. Then maybe your balls. Then, when she gets tired of the screaming, she'll go ahead and do your guts.'

'*You're fucking crazy,*' Then: '*Why?*'

'Really don't know who she is?'

Sweeney shook his head. She had placed the caps in the explosive. Now she was looking very competent the almost loving way she was closing the plastic around the caps.

'Tommy Wallace's daughter.'

'So what?'

'You ordered Tommy killed.'

'Bullshit I did!'

'See.' It was Caroline who spoke this time. 'Told you, Frank. It's okay, too.'

'*You're both crazy.*'

'Sure we are. She said you'd deny it. That's why she wants to blow you apart.'

'You're a cop, Janek.'

'So?'

247

'You can't let her do it.'

'All the same to me.' Janek stood up.

'Wait a minute. *Why?* Just tell me *why.*'

'Because it's personal and I don't interfere in personal stuff.' Janek paused. 'Well, so long, Sweeney.' He walked over to Caroline.

Her charges were ready. She was attaching the wires to the switch. 'I'll move the car,' he said. 'Blow that up, too, we're really stuck.' They laughed. She got up, brought her charges and wires over to Sweeney, stood staring down at him lying hog-tied face-up on the ground.

Janek started the ignition. This was the turning point. If Sweeney believed them he'd have to deal. If he didn't, if they'd lost him ... Janek didn't want to think about that.

Call me now, mother-fucker.

'Janek!'

He turned. Sweeney's eyes were panicked. 'Yeah?'

'I'll give you the garage.'

'Already got it.'

'You said –'

'Tell you what – I'll trade you.'

'*What?*'

Janek got out of the car, came over, stood beside Caroline. Sweeney looked helpless writhing in his bonds. 'Don't care about the garage and neither does she. What we care about is Hart. Hart ordered Tommy Wallace killed. Wanted him out because he thought he was being blackmailed. Supposed to look like a gangland execution but wasn't done that well. And now there's a Hoboken detective who can show that Wallace's body was stashed in a stolen car stripped in your back shop. You think your goon mechanics will keep quiet, but they won't – not when they find out we're talking homicide. You got one chance, Sweeney. Come over to Hoboken with us now, give evidence against Hart and I'll see you get a deal on Wallace. About the same as you'd get for chopping cars, four to five, something like that. But meantime the garage carries on, it's yours, still making money, making plenty for you when you get out. You'll do hard time, sure, but not like Hart. He's Chief. He'll really get it. You'll be lost in the shuffle. Hart ordered the killing, so he's the guy who ought to pay. That's the deal. The garage for Hart. Take it or leave it. Up to you.' Janek glanced over at Caroline. 'She's got a grievance and far as I'm concerned she can take care of it any way she likes.'

Sweeney looked into Janek's eyes and then into Caroline's and then at Caroline's hands. She was fluttering her fingers the way Jamie Sullivan had taught her.

'Forget it, Frank,' she said.

Janek nodded. He looked at her charges. 'Never mind the little ones. Tape the big one to his belly and do it all at once.'

And then it happened, so fast Janek could hardly believe it. Burned, broken and bluffed out, Sweeney began spontaneously to talk.

What was strangest of all, Janek decided later, was the way he addressed himself to Caroline. As if he owed her the story, as if he needed to justify himself to her, as if it was very important that she understand his relatively minor role in the execution plot.

Janek tape-recorded everything, breaking in to ask questions, pinning down times and places, getting details so that if Sweeney decided to recant he'd still have enough to make a decent case. But he didn't think Sweeney would recant or claim they'd forced him to confess. The garage deal was too good and, more important, Janek thought, once Sweeney betrayed Hart, no matter under what duress, he would find it nearly impossible to feel loyalty toward him again.

He found a phone booth in Lyndhurst and dialed the number he'd been harboring for months.

It was one o'clock in the morning. Carmichael's wife answered. He could hear her nudging Carmichael awake. 'Get up, Jim, Some cop from Manhattan. Says it's urgent. Wake up . . .'

'Who the hell –?'

'Janek.'

'*Who?*'

'Frank Janek. Lunch at the Clam Broth House. We talked about the Wallace case.'

'I remember you. Why you calling now?'

'Oh, Carmichael,' Janek said, his voice lilting, high on what he'd done, 'I got a terrific gift for you, the Big Case you've been waiting for. So wake up and get your ass down fast to your station house and get a stenographer and be ready to read a man his rights. Meet you there in fifteen minutes. You're going to be famous, you luck lucky cop . . .'

Hours later, after he'd called Lou and told her what had happened, he stood on a Hoboken pier, facing Manhattan, a hundred million lights sparkling in the towers across the river, the city luminous against the cold black winter night.

She called his name. He turned. She was holding her camera to her eye. He faced her lens straight on. She pressed her shutter.
Click.

It would be a photograph he would study all the rest of his life, bringing it out whenever he questioned what he had done. Then he would look into his face, his eyes, searching for his passions, the costs he had paid, and, for all the brilliance of his end games, the melancholy that filled him when his two great cases were finally solved.

It was a great photograph, he thought, the city soft but present in the background, the face of the detective sharp, his features etched, filled with fatigue and triumph, sadness too. The face of a man who had made a dangerous journey into a lawless country that for years he'd been too frightened to explore. But with love and luck the man had made the crossing back. All that was in the picture. She had caught him cold, he thought.